FOR THE RECORD

A ROBERT DRAKE READER

Edited with Introductions by
Randy Hendricks *and* James A. Perkins

Preface by
James H. Justus

Bibliography by
Genevieve Nicholson-Butts

Mercer University Press
Macon, GA

ISBN 0-86554-682-7
MUP/H527

6316 Peake Road
Macon, Georgia 31210-3960

First Edition.

Book design by Mary Frances Burt

∞The paper used in this publication meets the minimum requirements
of American National Standard for Information Sciences—Permanence of Paper
for Printed Library Materials, ANSI Z39.48-1992.

Library of Congress Cataloging-in-Publication Data

Drake, Robert, 1930-
For the record : a Robert Drake reader / edited with introduction by Randy
Hendricks
and James A. Perkins ; preface by James H. Justus ; bibliography by Genevieve
Nicholson-Butts.
p. cm.
Includes bibliography references and index.
ISBN 0-86554-682-7
1. Tennessee--Social life and customs--Fiction. 2. Drake, Robert, 1930---Authorship.
I. Hendricks, Randy, 1956- II. Perkins, James A., 1941- III. Title.

PS3554.R237 A6 2001
813'.54--dc21 2001018054

A portion of the Introduction was previously published in another form in the Winter 1997 issue of *Christianity and Literature.*

Table of Contents

Acknowledgments

We would like to thank a number of people whose involvement in this project has been of great benefit to us. We owe much, first of all, to Marice Wolfe and her capable staff in Special Collections at the Jean and Alexander Heard Library of Vanderbilt for their cheerful and expert help with our work in the Drake papers. Genevieve Nicholson-Butts helped with research, working well beyond the academic term during which she was appointed to the task.

Carol Morrow and Kimily Willingham provided valuable service preparing the manuscript. We are grateful also to Westminster College Faculty Development Officer Frederick D. Horn, the Westminster College Faculty Development Fund, and members of the Learning Resources Committee of the State University of West Georgia for research grants that supported the project. Westminster College, the State University of West Georgia, and the Hodges Better English Fund of the English Department of the University of Tennessee all provided generous support for the publication of this volume in the form of subvention grants. Our gratitude also goes to Mr. and Mrs. John Ulmer. Ronald Blythe and Malcolm Jack kindly gave of their time to James Perkins to talk of their long friendships with Robert Drake. Thanks also to Edd Rowell and Marc Jolley, our editors at Mercer University Press, for their initial interest in the project and their aid as it evolved and to our friend and colleague James H. Justus for agreeing to write the preface.

Finally, a word of gratitude to Robert Drake himself is in order. He has made himself available to us as we have conducted this work and gone out of his way—in conducting the interview and a tour of Ripley, Tennessee—to make certain matters clearer for us. Before he was our subject, Professor Drake was our teacher, a fact that has had no small impact on our careers. This work is, in part at least, our attempt to thank him.

Randy Hendricks
James A. Perkins

Preface

Among the aficionados of southern writing, whose benchmark is a half-mythical thing called the Southern Renascence, Robert Drake falls into the group loosely known as Younger Writers, a shorthand designation for any post-Agrarian, post-Faulknerian author. But *Amazing Grace*, Drake's first collection, was first published more than a quarter-century ago; indeed it has been a full decade since its twenty-fifth anniversary edition appeared. As we see in his essays and interviews, Drake is not a shy writer, nor does he sit around waiting for just the right moment to listen to his muse. Since 1965, when *Amazing Grace* ratified his new-found calling to preserve in prose the feel of his hometown of a generation earlier, he has plunged into his project with increasing authority, honing in a half-dozen subsequent volumes, his distinctive meld of fiction, memoir, and social history.

Professors Hendricks and Perkins call their judicious selection of pieces over the past thirty-five years a "reader," but I like to think of this collection as a "sampler." For old Drake fans, we get to revisit some (but not all) of the family and neighbors that lend such heft to a time and place splendidly preserved. For the reader who meets Woodville citizens without benefit of earlier introductions, the occasion may be merely tantalizing. That of course is the purpose of sampling.

But it is appropriate, perhaps even gratifying, to regard this reader as a sampler in the other sense—as condensed handiwork, a coherent synopsis of its maker's view of life. This grand old concept is no longer fashionable—and hasn't been since Victorian times—but sampler in its long history has always made a virtue out of directness: truths to live by stitched into canvas for all the world to see. Even longer ago we gave up the original definition of the word (from Old French) as a model or pattern or symbol, which it enjoyed for nearly four centuries, but at least since the eighteenth century, when sampler became a material, made object—a piece of embroidery to show off a young lady's skill—its centerpiece, flanked by the alphabet and ornamental devices, was the proverb or a scrap of verse expressing something of the maker's take on life. The one that hangs on my study wall, the handiwork of one Martha Johnson, who finished her embroidery on June 3, 1833, celebrates this sentiment:

When we give up our youth to GOD
Tis pleasing in his eyes
A flower that's offered in the bud
Is no vain sacrifice

Rereading this selection of sayings and doings of Woodville folks, mostly from the 1930s and 1940s, I am reminded that though the sampler itself had about died out as a fashion by the turn of the century, the impulse that it represented lived on. We know from Drake's cast of characters—from his family, to his extended family of kin and near-kin, to the neighbors, and even to the "brought on" folks—that Martha Johnson never lived in Woodville. The townspeople there—the kind, the tactful, even the pious—are too tart-tongued to make that little verse applicable to anybody. But we have mottos, favorite taglines, heartfelt sentiments that serve just as well, and they too have to be expressed publicly. They might of course look strange memorialized in yarn and canvas: "Good Clothes Are Always in Style," "He's one of the Best Men That Ever Had on a Pair of Pants," "A Woman Who Won't Cook is No Woman," "People Don't Improve as They Get Older—They Just Get More the Way They Already Were," "You Can't Make a Cake out of Water and Margarine and Expect it to Stand Up," or "Now Didn't She Head Her Ducks to a Pretty Pond?"

Every one of these, and many more that punctuate the lives of the Woodville Tennesseans, might look out of kilter as an embroidered aperçu, but they all are precisely right on the pages that trace their characters. At whatever age, the narrator seems to think of these expressive people as naturally out of kilter, and not merely as the eccentrics who live on the Dogleg of Jackson Street (who are just "more Woodville" than the others). But even ordinary folks who are not "out of kilter or cut on the bias" have little inclination to trim their sails to community convention and even less to keep their opinions to themselves. Like Emma Moss, "who was a Methodist but didn't let it get her down," the Drakes and their neighbors know their own minds "and then some." If the narrator's mother is the soul of tact, she is also a good cook who resents a relative for claiming as her own a recipe for Spanish rice she had given her. In the bosom of her family she is the author of all kinds of words to live by: words of implicit warning, but mostly words of tolerant recognition that in the world of fallen humanity people were not so various after all—"you just couldn't ever really beat folks."

Like many of his other readers, I have always been struck by Robert Drake's remarkable knack for hearing the sounds of spoken English. Of course a lot of people—not all of them writers—have what we used to call "a good ear," but very few have the even more remarkable knack for inscribing in blunt type the rich timbre, lilt, pitch, and rhythm of oral expression. One of Drake's characters is widely known in Woodville for his "rough tongue," but orality itself (to appropriate the phrase for my own devices) is a rough tongue—a language, certainly, but also something both less and more. To seize and freeze those fleeting sounds is the task of the writer. It is not an easy craft, for the process involves what can only be called transliteration, a word we normally reserve for the work of transcribing between languages of different alphabets. Orality is instantaneous and evanescent; verbalism is, for better or worse, there, in cold black and white, permanent, a material object as physical as Martha Johnson's sampler. Most of us would agree that the best ears in southern writing belong to Eudora Welty and Flannery O'Connor, but Robert Drake deserves his place among them.

Drake's vivid country is not memorable for his good ear alone. There is sometimes, in the dredging of memory, the visual image of startling discovery, perfectly realized and singular, clamoring out of the welter of its surrounding details: funeral casserole dishes bearing their donors' name on adhesive tape affixed to the underside; testing a baked dish's consistency by inserting "a broom straw bent double into the batter"; a blind beggar accepting donated coins in a Mason jar on the console of his little reed organ; country people coming to the square on Saturdays sitting dignified in straight-backed chairs in the wagon beds; a chaperoning mother reading her book-club book beside the Heatrola; funeral home fans supplied to all church pews with Jesus in the Garden on one side and the donor's name on the other. An enterprising old lawyer solves the problem of gas rationing during World War II by making his own fuel out of coal oil and cleaning fluid; this inventiveness with his old Chevy calls attention to itself with "a good deal of smoke and a considerable smell." Like so many acts in Woodville, these are assertions in the public arena of folks making do with the good sense the Lord gave them.

Controlling and guiding all these acts is the Woodville narrator, sometimes a naïve boy observing and listening to the inhabitants of his world, which for his unblinking, fact-facing mother was always "a sort of superior zoo." The mother can't know that her inability to distinguish between celebrity and notoriety perfectly describes the kind of zoo of a later era, but the recording narrator does. Sometimes he is the adult exile working in Memphis, Chicago, or some other make-do place, wiser about the town and family he left and more relentless in nudging out the little mysteries he missed before. Early and late, he celebrates domestic rituals—singing conventions, funerals, piano lessons and recitals, Christmas gatherings, shopping in Memphis—which he invokes and recreates to anchor his reading of his world. Repetition and predictability are important aspects of the narrator's temperament; most of the time he finds the necessary stability, but throughout the Woodville stories he must deal with change. A Wal-Mart comes in, bringing with it the usual kind of economic hemorrhaging of local businesses; the combination furniture store and undertaker gives way to Taylor's Funeral Home because "you had to move with the times." Middle-aged wives start going to their pastors for "counseling," and women of all ages start wearing slacks because, they say, they are such a "protection." The young narrator in "Amazing Grace" complains that nothing ever happened "to any of the Drakes"—they just went on "year after year as slow as Christmas." But of course things do happen to them, along with the neighbors, as the maturing narrator comes to realize.

If a nostalgic (but rarely sentimental) narrator finally comes to cherish repetition and predictability—"you could count on it"—the capacious facers of facts, notably the mother and Auntee, become for him the personification of the reality principle. Among those facts is the inevitability of change. Drake gives to his mature narrator not only the gifts of a good ear and, on occasion, an excellent eye, but also a sensibility for accommodating change. The author's prose is studded with locutions that are neither precisely visual nor oral, but mini-images occupying an in-between state in which embedded metaphors attain a kind of material density. "It changed hands and went down" (said of hotels, restaurants, or stores); the old woman who in her salad days was "thought to have hoed a wide row"; spinsters who secretly mourn "the empty side of a double bed." The mysteries of the double standard are perhaps nowhere better suggested than in this quiet observation: "the sexes proceeded on their way with the business of life, looking straight ahead but not particularly at each other." Learning to face the facts of change as well as the dull stability of village routine requires not merely ears and eyes but imaginative reconstitution in the narrator himself, with something of the same tolerance for what people are and do that he so pertinently dramatizes in the fact-facers of his family. One kind of milestone is "Change of Life," a poignant sketch of how the son must come to terms with his mother's menopause.

But the old French proverb about change—the more things change, the more they stay the same—applies in Woodville as it does everywhere else. In the ruck of death, flight, renovation, new families, business consolidation, and other "improvements," the life of Drake's own postage stamp of a world goes on, even with let and hindrance, right up to the present. But making sense of change is one of the author's missions: trying to balance the ineradicable Old Adam (that's just the way people are) with the temporary tactics inspired by Activity and Zeal (the narrator's favorite section of the Methodist hymnal). If the heroes here are fact-facers, they are heroic not because they acknowledge the disfiguring gloom of realism, but because they understand that accepting the way things are does not exempt them from Activity and Zeal—or, for that matter, compassion, good manners, fidelity, and all the other sampler virtues. My Martha Johnson never lived in Woodville, but she might have led a more interesting life if she had.

James H. Justus

Reading Robert Drake: An Introduction

If one counts in volumes, it is relatively easy, and for the moment convenient, to see Robert Drake's career as a writer of fiction in two parts. The first may be defined by the publication within a single decade of his first three volumes of stories: *Amazing Grace* (1965), *The Single Heart* (1971), and *The Burning Bush* (1975). In these collections Drake worked out his central story: a personal (some might say peculiar) story of ontological exploration. In the first volume, particularly in the title story, the Drake narrator (something like a poetic persona, really) emerges and dominates all the subsequent volumes. Even in the dramatic monologues that make up a significant portion of *The Single Heart* one who has read Drake widely imagines this same narrator gone silent to function as auditor, present and recording, "for the record," as one of the revered Drake brothers was fond of saying before he took a photograph.

In 1980 Drake published the book he was "born to write": *The Home Place: A Memory and a Celebration.* Admitting that he fictionalized for the sake of unity, Drake explored the significance of his family history to his own consciousness. This was really, in one sense, his story, and perhaps it helps readers see that all his stories are ways to define or position himself, a kind of personal poetry. With portraits and anecdotes in *The Home Place* he frames segments from the family experience and arranges them much as one might arrange photographs on a wall for inspection or study, not simply to memorialize (though certainly to do so is part of the purpose) but to see what they have to reveal, what they have to say, what they have to teach. *The Home Place*, a deeply personal assessment of the meaning of the past, represents a sort of "middle" period, a bridge between the early work and the later. Unfortunately some misguided editing designed to "improve" the language made the publication of this book a very unsatisfying experience for Drake, until a restored edition was published in 1998.

In 1987 when Mercer University Press published Drake's fourth collection of stories, *Survivors and Others*, a twelve-year gap in the publication of his fiction in book form came to an end. The additional publication in 1990 of the twenty-fifth anniversary edition of *Amazing Grace* awakened a new interest in Drake's work. In 1991 a special session on his fiction was held in Atlanta at the annual meeting of the South Atlantic Modern Language Association, the proceedings of which were published in the Mississippi Quarterly the following year. *Amazing Grace*, a popular text in college classes, has sold out of stock. Meanwhile three more volumes of stories have appeared—*My Sweetheart's House* (1993), *What Will You Do for an Encore? and Other Stories* (1996), and *The Picture Frame* (2000).

With one or two exceptions, Drake returns in these more recent volumes to Woodville, the fictionalized version of his hometown of Ripley, Tennessee, where he was born in 1930 and where he lived until he went away to school at Vanderbilt. (Drake still owns land in the area and returns for regular visits.) A majority of the stories in these later volumes are again told by the familiar narrator, whose attempts to frame the reality of life in the small town during his childhood in the 1930s and '40s constitute the central drama of Drake's fiction. The body of Drake's work forms a tapestry of key scenes in the life of

Woodville, and readers of all the volumes are familiar with certain characters and types. Yet the life of Woodville is extended in the later volumes to include new areas of experience, and it was perhaps only with the accumulation of these books of the 1990s that readers could begin to recognize the full extent to which certain stories have unfolded over the course of the successive collections, among them the remarkable love story of the narrator's mother and father: the first a realist who buys her own diamond ring as a symbol of her independence and her vanity and who criticizes women who won't cook, the latter not really an idealist, simply more squeamish in matters of sex and human frailties, and yet capable of extraordinary devotion and loyalty both to individuals and institutions. Their influence is pervasive throughout the volumes, but "Amazing Grace," "Her Name on a Tombstone, Her Diamond Ring on Another Woman's Hand," "Change of Life," and "The Clothesline" are included here together as stories that concentrate on their part in the larger story.

Neat and useful as this brief survey might be, it does not tell the whole truth about Drake's career as a writer. Any sense of his development derived solely from a history of his volumes has to be checked by the fact that some stories were written early but published late. One important example is "The Time the Bank Failed." This story (included here) was pulled from *Amazing Grace* at the last minute because in 1965 the scandal on which the story is based was still too much a part of the consciousness of Ripley. It was later published in *What Will You Do for an Encore? and Other Stories.*

This incident, along with the obvious correspondence between "facts" recorded in *The Home Place* and other memory pieces and the "fiction" of the Drake narrator and his family, leads to some fairly obvious questions about Drake's work. How much of what Drake gives his readers is fiction? How much fact?

And how much does it matter? Certainly it mattered to those readers in Ripley who penned in what they thought were the "real" names of his characters in their copies of his early books, but if Drake were simply writing up Ripley there would be little appeal to readers outside the ostensibly small circle of people who have continued to feed his imagination over the years. It also matters to those interested in the process whereby experience is transformed into art, to readers who lean toward one or another of the schools of biographical criticism.

Drake's art does thrive on his personal experience and experiences "told" to him, or told over his head, really, while he was growing up. As Eudora Welty says of herself in *One Writer's Beginnings*, Drake learned early to listen for the story as well as to the story. Perhaps even more significant is the fact that he began to write stories only after leaving his home in the South. Heidegger wrote, "All the poems of the poet who has entered into his poethood are poems of homecoming"; perhaps this need to reconcile oneself with home accounts for Robert Drake's impulse to write (and perhaps the impulse of a good many other Southerners). We certainly are not denying the validity of interest in such biographical questions, for indeed the questions of the relation between then and now, here and there, self and family or self and community are often themes in the stories themselves. But we have preferred to let Drake speak for himself on this point, through the interview with James Perkins and through the inclusion of four of Drake's numerous essays on the craft of writing.

Here we can concentrate on another level of significance in the stories, achieved cumulatively, a level at which the relation between fiction and fact seems less significant and the relation of story to story more important for understanding Robert Drake. This is just shifting from a biographical to an intertextual reading, one might say, but Drake's stories provide special reasons for doing so. The stories we have included here are representative of his work in their subjects and themes, and they are examples of what we believe to be Drake's best work, but we have arranged them neither by a chronology of composition nor by a chronology of publication. They are arranged, on the one hand, by point of view or genre. The first fifteen stories are all first-person narratives told by the Drake persona. Then follow two stories that represent Drake's work in the dramatic monologue, the form in which he captures most directly what he once referred to as the "voices of women at the back of [his] mind." Finally we have chosen two stories from the Ann Louise series. These third-person narratives feature one of Drake's most dynamic protagonists.

Within this division, the stories further reflect an order of consciousness, a chronology derived from within the stories rather than from without. This chronology of imagination, rather than one of event, leads us to begin with the story "The Tower and the Pear Tree," which is the recorded testimony of the author's awakening to his art. The stories that follow are all in some sense, then, the result of that awakening. Our arrangement might seem another instance of misguided, or at least heavy-handed, editing, but as we hope this volume will seem a gift to Drake's long-time readers and serve as an introduction for new readers, we offer it also as an interpretation of his work.

Whatever the point of view and approach in a given story, the world in Drake's fiction can be defined with a few important generalizations. His characters, first of all, are known by their relation to the communal forces of their time and place, but they are neither the narrow-minded bigots of much Southern Realism nor the grotesque "victims" of the Southern documentary school, or this genre's Romantic sister, the Southern Gothic. Nor is there much sympathy in this literature for the stunned patriarchs and matriarchs of a crumbling world. One of Drake's achievements lies in making his characters distinct without making them caricatures or monsters. They are individuals struggling to make and maintain their own place both in and against what they take to be the world entire, a world, as Drake himself wrote in his foreword to *My Sweetheart's House,* "composed...of close family and community ties, all of course rooted in Protestant Christianity, which gave all human relationships validity and significance. It was a world that was coherent, a world that made sense." Any writer who inherits such a world is "blessed," he says, for he has something larger than himself to write about.

For all its coherence and surface narrowness, Drake's fictional world is not a world without mystery, and one senses that it is not despite the coherence of that world but because of it that his stories include such a rich variety of human experience. His art is of a type that critics and literary historians have tended to minimize (or marginalize). He writes, as he says in an earlier volume, "something like the tale" in which there is "a brief illumination but no cataclysm." Yet "a whole world may be implicit in that quiet moment of revelation." Still the range of subjects and variations on the genre are striking. There are fully realized short stories, anecdotes, extended jokes, and character sketches or meditations studded with narrative.

As tales Drake's stories would seem to hearken to an earlier time, but alert readers become conscious of an ulterior purpose in their anachronistic flavor. To understand their appeal and power we can examine certain tendencies in the stories in the light of both traditional and recent regionalist theory. One is the tendency to decenter modernist assumptions, sometimes subtly, sometimes overtly. In "The Living Room," for example, Drake critiques a modern understanding of what is natural and at the same time a modern tendency to misread regionalist literature by pointing out the similarity between an older Woodville and the central Massachusetts of Emily Dickinson's time: "In a small country town in Massachusetts in the middle of the nineteenth century death was all around you and thoroughly domesticated, not seen as something out of line. And thus her treatment of death often as a familiar friend, even a suitor is nothing 'peculiar' or even pathological. Nor is the attitude that he's a household inmate. He is perfectly 'natural' but not in the way modern usage would have us believe."[1] Here and elsewhere is a reflexive urge to teach contemporary readers how to read this fiction. The assumption is that readers need the aid. Readers are in the same position occupied by Ann Louise's husband in "1975 Has Come and Gone"; Woodville has to be explained to them.

Drake's regionalist sense is also reflected in his handling of place. Woodville is a compendium of the inner problem for the narrator, not simply the backdrop for quaint reminiscence of peculiar folk. Drake works with the tools of the realist: holding a mirror to the world he writes about. But the mirror metaphor functions at another level, becoming emblematic of the problem of vision. In "The Legacy," an uncle, the "corrector" or "reprover," seems a man about whom there could be no mystery until by accident the narrator happens to glimpse in a mirror his uncle bending to kiss the corpse of his wife and is astounded less into a new understanding of his uncle than into a confrontation with a profound mystery: "It was as though I had intruded on the most private moment in the world for my aunt and uncle, more private, much more so even than the act of making love."[2] The mirror image is the metaphor for the real story here, and perhaps for all Drake's stories, the story of the way of seeing, indirectly, so that the story can only be suggested, not told. Often the plotlessness seems not a failure of the narrative but the point, the point of the unendingness and of the intermingling of many of these stories in the narrator's consciousness. Drake seizes on minute details of life in Woodville in the very need for something concrete in the face of mystery, something on which to rely in the vital work of "reading" life.

A related and seemingly yet another dated trait of Drake's art is its oral nature. His readers are likely to feel less written at than talked to. Part of this achievement rests in the colloquial language and folk rhythm of speech that Drake works to capture in his writing, but when the stories are read consecutively, the illusion of talk is further sustained by repetition. Each time the grandfather, Pa Drake, figures in a story he must be defined, always in the same terms—his status as a Confederate veteran, his age, his mustache, his reluctance to bathe. Other characters have their like details, benchmarks, indices, a way for the teller to position the listener in relation to the characters in the tale at hand. The stories create their own private conventions that function somewhat like the conventional dawns and repeated metaphors of Homer or the verbatim repetitions of God's Old Testament commands. They mark the orality of the original without dialectal affectations.

But the repetitions also imitate the tale-telling of the previous generation of Drakes who figure as major subjects in the stories. As anyone who has ever been associated with such a close family of talkers knows, the repeated tales can get tiresome for children and outsiders (they certainly did for the young Robert), but their function as ritualistic reminders becomes quite obvious when considered on the whole. Like going out to Maple Grove every Sunday or out to Salem church for the Barlow County Singing Convention, telling the tales is what the Drakes do as part of knowing who they are. For the insiders there could be no more objection to hearing them told over and over again than there could be to hearing a liturgical service they had heard before or to singing an old hymn for the thousandth time. At some level the purpose of all three rituals is the same. Drake's stories, taken together, seem to perform a similar ritual. Drake seems to write the stories, in fact, as a way to stay inside the group. And their power, their joy, really, lies in his ability to bring readers inside, too. Collectively the stories have the effect of a series of visits, not unlike Joel Chandler Harris's use of visits in his Uncle Remus stories, or one thinks of Sarah Orne Jewett or perhaps the Charles Chesnutt of *The Conjure Woman.* What is most remarkable, perhaps, is that Drake is working now, and successfully, in his own version of an art form whose vogue seemed to be waning near the turn of the century.

In further evidence of the oral nature of this art, Drake himself has said that he hears his stories; he does not see them. Yet for a writer whose dominant sense works through his ear, he creates some fine and sometimes startling visual images. To mention only a few examples: Pa Drake's walrus mustache, Auntee's Medusa-like hair, Miss Effie's being chased by Father Time pushing a lawnmower. Related to this underrated visual sense is a rather acute sense of space. In the first three stories included here readers become keenly aware of the physical dimensions and shape of Woodville, a town built mostly on ridges and without much in the way of planning. There is a square, but it does not sit in the center of a grid; the streets shoot out from this hub like spokes in a wheel so that, as we learn from "Up on the Corner, on the Dogleg," one has to go back to the center of town in order to go anyplace else.

Such a feature distinguishes, in some ways even personalizes, Woodville, but the image also suggests a mental process being worked out in the stories themselves, for the narrator, or the speaker, or the protagonist, or, finally, Drake himself. Each is an instance of going back to the hub, to the center, Woodville (Ripley), the past, to find one's bearings again. The spatial imagery corresponds to a map of consciousness, or rather an attempt to map it, to discover the self in relation to place and past, family and community. A train runs through Woodville and, like the river and steamboat that ran through Twain's Hannibal, becomes the symbol of the journey out, but also of the journey back—the train "relates" Woodville with Chicago and New Orleans, and the North-South sense of geography dominates the consciousness, as the narrator learns in the first story here, "The Tower and the Pear Tree." From Woodville one goes "out" to Texas, or "out" to Salem Church or "out" to Maple Grove. A sense of where one is in space so permeates the thought and language of Woodville that in one comic instance one of the older women who are always talking in Drake's stories says, commenting on the dangers of the Cold War era, "before long we were all going to blow each other up, and the whole universe too. And then where would we be?"[3]

The most common presence in Woodville is, in fact, an elderly woman talking, telling, and reckoning the town's, some other individual's or her own experiences. These female Ancient Mariners figure prominently in any estimation of the "meaning" of the Woodville story. It does not diminish the variety of life and experiences they represent to say that they, like all Drake's characters, really, are valued for where they fit on a scale between the extremes of celebrant and deadener. These differences are readily demonstrable in a story like "Now, Baby, Do You Know One Thing?" which juxtaposes the celebrant Helen Campbell (Auntee) with the deadener Cousin Rebecca (a pairing that echoes Twain's Widow Douglas and Miss Watson). There is more here than a simple good witch/bad witch conflict, although one is reluctant to dispose of the term witch too readily because of its associations with feminine power, and certainly there is much more than a local-color exploitation of middle-aged, small-town gossips of pre-World War II West Tennessee. Drake locates a source of moral power in Auntee that is reminiscent of Jewett's Almira Todd and Mrs. Blackett in *The Country of the Pointed Firs.* Auntee is a dispenser of real knowledge and good sense, and she is a source of solace and comfort; she becomes a moral guide for the narrator, perhaps becoming more significant in that way finally than the mother and the father.

That Drake takes Auntee as a representative of a kind of feminine power is suggested by classical allusions early in "Now, Baby" as he describes both Cousin Rebecca and Auntee:

> [W]hereas Cousin Rebecca [again shades of Miss Watson, the "tolerable slim old maid"] was tall and thin ("poor as a snake," their cook, old fat Florence, used to say) and all sharp edges and angles, hair firmly swept back into a "club" behind her head, no excess baggage for her in either body or spirit, Auntee was short and stout, almost dumpy really, and everything about her was round and comfortable. Her hair was naturally curly and very difficult to control, but she took that in her stride, too. "I just can't worry about it," she would say. And so it usually looked as though it were in various stages of exploding, in a mass of pepper-and-salt ringlets, from her head. After I learned something of classical mythology, I even thought of comparing her to the serpent-haired Medusa—a benevolent Medusa, of course. Also, though she wasn't ugly, Auntee wasn't by any stretch of the imagination pretty or even attractive: she was plain. But then beauty wasn't high on her list of commendable attributes: "pretty, pretty," she would observe with disdain, of some highly touted beauty, implying of course that pretty was as pretty did and anyone could look good.[4]

Interestingly both women are likened to serpents; in Cousin Rebecca's case the "poor as a snake" image seems a complement to the imagery of weaponry derived from the rest of her physique (hair like a club and a body all over "sharp edges and angles"). It's hard to work her into an Eve figure. But the Medusa image is much more significant, for it aligns Auntee with a central figure of female power in classical mythology even as it reshapes that figure from one of terror to one of benevolence. The transformation is accomplished without diminishing Auntee's sexuality, part of the power she uses to scandalize Cousin Rebecca and her type—"whoever was too refined or genteel or, finally, dead." Her sexuality is a source of scandal and power, as we see within the same paragraph quoted from above when she comments on her full figure by saying that when her husband "reached out to hug a girl, he wanted a handful. And then she would nod, maybe even wink." All making Cousin Rebecca very uncomfortable. Auntee is puritan enough to distrust appearances, but she is no deadener.

The classical echoes continue as we learn in the very next paragraph that Auntee's given name is Helen. We learn this without fanfare, but it sends us nevertheless back to Auntee's comments on beauty and the ironic fact that she is the namesake of the woman who is the most beautiful in Western myth and along with Medusa another of the major figures of female power. The narrator rejects this potential source of power, symbolically at least, by immediately rejecting her given name and all its potential associations, even the irony (which he does not mention) for the name and qualities of "Auntee." If the mirror image in "The Legacy" is a sign of confusion or the difficulty of seeing and interpreting, the Medusa image sharpens our understanding of the main source of wisdom and soul wellness available to the narrator as he faces that confusion.

The truth that emerges from Drake's stories is that, in the balancing act that defines family and community, the tension between belonging and not belonging is constant. Neither condition exists purely, neither condition exists without the other. This is what the narrator, sometimes as a youngster, sometimes as an adult looking back, struggles so often to grasp: the complexity that the adults cannot or will not articulate, as illustrated in "The Time the Bank Failed" when the boy experiments with newly learned words to join in the talk about two prominent citizens arrested for malfeasance: "Why, if they ever came back here, they would be ostracized. They're nothing but hypocrites."[5] For his pains he receives a tolerant smile from an aunt but an unqualified "Hush, Robert" from his mother. We cannot discount the fact that this response is dictated by a culture that believes children should be seen and not heard, but it is more than that. It is the superior pose of the child—suggested by his abstract approach with his new words—that is not to be brooked. He will qualify for adult status and conversation only when he understands that the scandal is, however one feels about the men, a sign of their humanity, when he understands something of why their families, despite the scandal, decided to stay on in Woodville and why at least one of them plans to return when he gets out of prison. The story he is not ready to comprehend is as much a story of communal loss as it is of community scandal, and the story being told here lies in large part in its very construction within the narrator's consciousness.

But the adult world, not even as represented by the moral authorities in the boy narrator's world, is not always something he can move toward. In "The Summer of the Window Peeper," the only story, according to Drake, in which he wrote consciously of race issues, he reveals another permeation in the language of Woodville. When in the opening passage the mother says that "Aunt Estelle didn't have the instincts of a white woman,"[6] the tone is set for a revealing story of bigotry, and more. One's place is a matter of race as well as a matter of geography, and when the window peeper begins to annoy and then to terrify the women of Woodville, the immediate assumption is that he is a black man: "Of course, everybody knew, Mamma said, that it must have been a colored man because it just wasn't the kind of thing a white man would do. I said why not and, for that matter, what would anybody want to look at Miss Jo-Ellen for, as old and dried-up as she was? But Mamma just said 'little pitchers have big ears' and looked at Daddy, and I could tell she had a good deal more to say to him after I went to bed."[7] The passage reveals the reliance on socially constructed truths, trite language, and even gestures that have to be read and interpreted. A black man *is* the window peeper as it turns out. Drake, in the essential honesty of his vision, does not find it necessary to club Woodville with an "innocent Negro," though in another sense he might be clubbing his readers with a guilty one. No one in his world is immune to the hazards of Original Sin, and the "point" of the story would seem to lie in the mystery of experience to which the boy awakens, one the adults never seem to recognize. Here are the final lines:

> But, every now and then, I used to think about John Alfred all shut up there in the state penitentiary and wonder whether, in spite of all his college education, he was thinking about the white ladies in Woodville as much as they still thought about him. And I wondered whether he ever really thought, when he used to call them all those names and beg them to let him come in, that they ever really would let him. And I wondered, if they had, whether he would have been pleased or disappointed with what he found there.[8]

This problem of knowledge, of wondering, remains the theme in the dramatic monologues and third-person stories. In the two monologues included here—"The Single Heart" and "I Never Have Been a Well Woman"—older women reckon the meaning of certain lives, their own or another's. In the first the mystery of Eustace Cameron, who dies "out of pure plain loneliness," exemplifies the counter-side in Drake's world of love—the deep gulf that often stands between human beings, into which, it seems quite clear, anyone can fall. What can we ever know about another? And even with the comic situation of the 100-year-old narrator of "I Never Have Been a Well Woman" the recurring question is: what can we ever know? "Amazing Grace" and several other stories included here are stories of great warmth, but "The Single Heart," along with the first-person stories "Were You There?" and "Do You Know Ben Webster, Have You Seen Him? (whose very titles suggest the centrality of the vexing questions), lowers the temperature in the Drake canon by several degrees. Moreover, Drake achieves this chilling effect in all three of these stories without resorting to the absurd, the grotesque, or even the "naturalistic." All serve as an acknowledgement that even in the coherent world of Woodville some do lose their "position." Their stories have to be told, too, and what we know finally is that their stories are not really separate stories, but a part of the whole. Woodville is not Winesburg, but neither is it Walnut Grove or Mayberry. More of a Southern Dunnet Landing, it is a waiting place for some Captain Littlepages and Poor Joannas. Woodville is a distinct addition to America's literary small towns.

Ann Louise Parker, the main character in the last two stories included here, is in some ways a female replica of the Drake persona—Drake even loans her the ancient Confederate grandfather. Yet the world she moves through is decidedly the world of a small-town girl in the thirties and forties, and she is also a bolder and more adventurous spirit than the persona. Whether crawling under her mother's bridge table to verify the bareness of a woman's legs by pinching them or organizing a "masked strip tease" to benefit her candidate for football queen, she tests the boundaries of Woodville. The story of her contemplation of the meaning of "Ella Biggs" is a masterful handling of symbol on Drake's part, as the title character comes to represent both a great mystery and a binding tie—part of all that web of experience that Ann Louise plays over again in "1975 Has Come and Gone..." to frame for herself what Woodville means for her, to find, in the other words the coherent terms that would explain the mystery of Ann Louise to her husband Johnny, and to herself.

Drake, like Ann Louise in "1975," is a conscious regionalist, one who works with the knowledge that the folks he writes of and his approach to them differ significantly from the main stream of American life and literature, or the fictions of these. Robert Penn Warren, however, described Drake's art as a "small, but authentic, miracle" showing us "a small, simple segment of life clearly." It is an art of illumination, he went on, that moves us, "[a]nd because it is life, it may well become a permanent possession." Perhaps it is in this segmentation of life, this regionalism, that the theological significance of Drake's stories can best be located. And perhaps he himself has provided the clue to that significance as well as the best metaphor for his own stories by his use of the term celebration to describe them. As he writes in the brief note at the head of *What Will You Do for an Encore?* "[W]e begin to have some idea that what we really have been seeking is not a climax, which, like a drug, necessitates literally an infinite series of encores, but a celebration, ultimate and eternal. And who needs an encore then?"

Reading Robert Drake we eventually come to think of Woodville, of Barlow County, as eventually in reading Faulkner we come to think of Yoknapatawpha—existing whole and entire in space and time. Two very different places to be sure, but each real and true in the deepest poetic sense.

Randy Hendricks

[1] What Will You Do for an Encore? and Other Stories (Macon GA: Mercer University Press, 1996) 47.

[2] Ibid., 69.

[3] "If She Knowed What I Knowed, She Never Would Woke," Survivors and Others (Macon GA: Mercer University Press, 1987) 95.

[4] Survivors and Others (Macon GA: Mercer University Press, 1987) 104–105.

[5] What Will You Do for an Encore?, 55.

[6] Amazing Grace (Macon GA: Mercer University Press, 1990) 48.

[7] Ibid., 49.

[8] Ibid., 53.

Stories by Robert Drake

The Tower and the Pear Tree

A Story for Phil Reagan Phelps

WHEN I LIVED IN CHICAGO, I USED TO GO HOME TO Tennessee once a year in the spring, to see my parents and other family. They had tried to dissuade me from settling in the Middle West—perhaps the most alien of all regions to the Southerner. But at the time I was young and full of the self-confident wisdom of emancipated youth and thought that I alone knew what was best for myself.

And, to be truthful, I thought it would do me good to get outside the South, about which, at the time, I had feelings that were not unmixed—perhaps somewhat akin to Stephen Dedalus' about Ireland as an old sow that eats her farrow. And I suppose I felt also that living and working "up North" would give me some sort of glamour in Southern eyes, if only the glamour of the prodigal son. And I was tired, I thought, of Confederatism and those Southern qualities which used to exasperate me most—the good manners which, I thought, all too often concealed true feelings and the constant stream of small talk which, though extremely pleasant and comfortable, seemed to me often inconsequential and designed to obscure what I took to be the harsh realities of existence.

Southerners, I thought, talked and talked about nothing at all really—people, places, and things, past and present, and especially past. And the towered cities of the Northeast and Middle West seemed to me pulsating with life in the raw—no screens there, I thought, between yourself and reality. And they did have the "facilities"—universities, libraries, theaters, museums—and everything else which seemed to me then to make life bearable or even real. Surely one could come to grips with the verities there.

But when I went home in the spring, I immediately stepped back into that other world—almost from the moment I boarded the Illinois Central train in Chicago. This is the railroad above all others which has a distinctively Southern air, with its brown and yellow and orange streamliners streaking back and forth between the Great Lakes and the Gulf over what it calls the "Main Line of Mid-America." In my childhood, of course, there were no streamliners but magnificent steam engines pulling long trains of conventional gray cars in a great thundering surge through our town. And I used to stand at our little station and watch them sweep grandly and triumphantly by; few of them stopped *there.*

But even then they symbolized—as did the glistening rails over which they passed—what I thought was a life-giving link between my slow-paced small-town existence and what I took to be the exciting adventures of the bustling North and the languid allure of the coastal South and the tropical seas and lands which lay beyond. But it was to the Great Lakes rather than to the Gulf that I was drawn. Perhaps, instinctively, I knew already that it was "life" rather than "languor" that I craved. There has always been too strong a Puritan residuum in my blood to allow me to feel really *comfortable* in Latin lands—and this despite their obvious and compelling enchantments.

It did not take me long to learn, however, that perhaps the bustling North was just too bustling. And despite what one hears of the decay and death of our cities, I found Chicago stimulating—but again perhaps too much so. Energy and drive there were aplenty, but toward what, really? Toward what end, finally, did those gleaming towers, the skyscrapers, aspire? And healthy, my God, it was healthy, with those sleek suburbs on the north shore all growing the right amount of grass and the right number of safety-net idealists, with respectable façades of liberalism masking sound and impregnable interiors of money and minds closed to the dark sinister mutterings of defeat and frustration which course as second nature through the blood of all people from my region.

Sometimes, in exasperation, I longed to take my banker, lawyer, and public relations friends aside and whisper to them, like Thomas Hardy, "Yes, but if times be not fair—what then?" Or else I longed to say to the clean-scrubbed, harsh-voiced matrons who frequented Marshall Field's, "Yes, but suppose you didn't have all those nice safe investments but had to worry about the caprices of the weather and the resulting state of your cotton crop and the price it was bringing not in Memphis but in New York?"

But I was still too stubborn or too proud—and perhaps it all comes to the same thing in the end—to confess that I might have been wrong. So I continued to work at my not very inspiring job, year in and year out, with the icy blasts from Lake Michigan chilling my vitals and the superb self-assurance of my associates freezing the genial marrow of my soul. *They* didn't talk much about such particularities as people and places, only good solid abstractions like money or maybe power as manifested in business or politics. These were the realities—or, as they liked to say, the issues—for them. And as for history, that was just something in books, something that happened to other people. What had it to do with them?

So I found that more and more I looked forward to my trip southward every spring. And my spirits lifted perceptibly as the train rolled down through what I found myself ironically terming the Great American Heartland—virgin soil in every way—no bloodshed there, no conquerors either, whether military, political, or economic, and, of course, finally no history worthy of the name. No past and no piety—just corn and cows—and, for the most part, flat and uninteresting.

Only when the train reached Cairo, however, did my spirits really begin to soar, as we crept forward over the great Ohio River bridge toward the green willows of the Kentucky bottom lands beyond. And then for several miles we would run right beside the Mississippi, which you couldn't see from the Ohio bridge at Cairo. But you knew that that grandest of all American river unions *had* been effected just above. And now the proud, Pittsburgh-born Ohio, like it or not, had been absorbed into that dark and muddy river of all rivers moving slowly and imperturbably on its quiet but inevitable way toward the past and the piety embodied in those soft liquid voices murmuring, on porches and in parlors, of dead glories and lost causes, too chastened now by experience and heartbreak to venture more than modest hopes for men and things and taking all talk of grand enterprises and great endeavors with considerably more than one pinch of salt.

But it was at Fulton, Kentucky, where the train spent some time refueling, that spring and the South would burst most fully and forcibly upon me—in the form of an ancient pear tree which stood in the backyard of a modest house near the station. Year after year I would watch for it. And if the spring was "on time," there it would be—old, black, somewhat wizened, perhaps dying, but bravely, almost defiantly, lifting its silvery blossoms to the warm spring sun.

It was not a beautiful tree in any conventional sense. It was not symmetrical or graceful—anything but. Rather, it seemed to have put out a branch here and one there wherever it could, to catch the sun however and whenever it might, as though it sensed that the straightest way up was not always the best or most literally *fruitful* and that perhaps the sun and the other elements would not welcome such boldness and directness on its part. (There was nothing of the tower about this tree.) There were dead branches there too, but the surviving limbs seemed to take no notice of them. They simply went about their business in whatever way they could; what did they care how they or even the tree *looked*? Their business was to catch the sun, to produce first flowers, then fruit. And there they were, twisted, age-incrusted, but alive, rejoicing simply that they *were* and content with their lot.

Every year I watched for the pear tree, sorry when spring was late and there were no blooms, rejoicing when I caught it in flower and comparing its performance then with that of previous years. Usually, some more limbs had died; but miraculously there were always some new shoots sprouting from the old trunk, whose essential vitality never seemed to fail. And I would give thanks—I knew not why then—that it was still there, alternately blackening and silvering as the spring winds tossed it in the sun.

Fulton, just above the Tennessee line, was the last stop before home. And as we sped southward, my vitals would alternately chill and churn with the same excitement I had known years before when returning from school—half-longing for those soft voices and outstretched arms, half-fearful lest those voices ravish me with their sweetness, those arms embrace me too tightly for my own well-being. But then all was resolved as the train swept round that last long bend, slowed, and, with a sense of tremendous power held but momentarily in check, ground to a halt just long enough to set me down. And those familiar faces and scenes would burst upon me again with the loving warmth of their old welcome.

A few more years, and many of the familiar faces were gone, some of the scenes themselves changed. But, coming home, always I watched at Fulton for the pear tree, saluting it each time as an older and dearer friend and finding that it occupied more and more of my idle fancies as I sat at my Chicago desk. For a few years more those sun-drenched black and silver branches continued, sometimes at the oddest possible moments, to sway in my mind and sparkle in my heart until they gradually seemed to possess me, to become almost my only reality amid those gray grim hives, those great proud towers by the lake.

And then it was that I decided finally that I had had enough of the "facilities" and the "harsh realities" of the North and that I would do well to take myself back to what had been my father's house, no matter how painful its own memories or those of its region. I had discovered that they, like the pear tree, were in my blood, whether I liked it or not, and that it was only in some sort of harmony with them that I could most fully *be*. And this knowledge came finally in no blinding revelation or flash of insight but gradually, almost casually, like a gift, or else some precious cargo, once rashly jettisoned, now, in some blessed moment of grace, cast up at long last by the sea.

The Square

LAST YEAR WHEN I WAS HOME EVERYBODY WAS talking about the new Wal-Mart that had just been opened out on the bypass. It was supposed to be one of their "mega"-sized stores, with practically nothing you couldn't buy; and so one trip would do it all for you. And it would be more convenient and all the rest. Up till now Woodville had gotten along without a mall or anything else, even a McDonald's, but now it looked as though we were about to join the modern world—and with a vengeance. Because lo and behold, McDonald's was putting up one of their "stores," as they liked to call them, right next door to the Wal-Mart parking lot.

Unfortunately, I didn't have time to go out and inspect the premises right then, but I wondered whether Wal-Mart would be following the traditional format, of having a "greeter" at the front door, who was really nothing but a new version of the old-fashioned floor walker but more folksy, just to make you feel more comfortable and of course help to preserve their down-home image. As it turned out, they did indeed acquire a greeter after they got really going some weeks later, and on future visits she would always confuse me with one of my cousins; but after we got that straightened out, she was very helpful with information about what items were stocked where and also her memories of

"Mr. Sam" Walton and the time she had had her picture made with him. "He was my darling," she said, after he died.

Her husband had been the fire chief for a good many years, and she herself had once been a beauty operator, so she continued fixing women's hair on the side, even after they moved into the firehouse, which was downtown, just off the Square. And I supposed that lent something to the drama of your weekly shampoo and set: you never knew when the alarm might sound, with the whistle blowing the requisite number of times to indicate what street the fire was on so the volunteer firemen all over town could jump in their cars and get to the scene as quick as the fire engine itself. Unfortunately, however, the firehouse was somewhat on the modest side, with no brass pole coming down from the second floor for any resident firemen to slide down and create a dramatic scene for the beauty parlor, especially if a terrified customer was all connected up to the permanent wave machine and couldn't get out of there in a hurry. But then I decided you couldn't have it all, even in Woodville. And anyhow you could always call "Central" and ask her where the fire was, and she would do her best to provide all the details. And in many ways it was a very comfortable world.

But I had lived in cities for many years, and I knew that sooner or later the old time and place would have to go, even though I had more or less had to agree with one of my city friends who lamented that he had lived to see the "malling" of America. But what I hadn't yet gotten around to was that Wal-Mart and McDonald's and all that went with them sooner or later would spell the end for the Square and as such would doom much of what for me had always stood for Woodville or any other small town. And in due course there would be nobody left down there but bankers and lawyers and the folks that worked in the post office and the courthouse. And everything else would have turned into a ghost town: no ten-cent stores, no picture shows, no "famishing" stores, like my father and uncle's, where tenants got financed to make their next year's cotton crop.

Of course the through traffic on Highway 51 ("Great Lakes to Gulf") had long since quit going around the Square: that was what the bypass was for. Used to, the Square was the almost literal heart of the town. For one thing, Woodville was built mostly on ridges between ravines, and so all the streets, which followed the ridges, mostly had to go back to the Square to go anywhere else. And so the Square was sort of like a great heart pumping blood (all the traffic) to the town's various extremities. And sooner or later you could see most everybody you knew by just standing on the Square and watching the traffic go by.

And it wasn't just *life* that you could watch either: the presence of death was part of the scene too. Messrs. Waterfield and Hill owned a furniture store on the south side of the Square, but upstairs they had an undertaking establishment. (I think in the old days undertakers and furniture dealers had a natural affinity for each other because somebody had to make the coffins as well as the furniture, and so such dual establishments were quite common on the small-town scene.) And often as not, you would see Waterfield and Hill's hearse backed up to the front of the store, and you knew that some "body" was upstairs being worked on. And somehow it never seemed morbid or depressing—just life and death keeping company, side by side, in the most natural relationship of all.

But they were long gone now, and Woodville had a real funeral "home" just like everybody else—a rather grand old house that had formerly belonged to the town's leading banker before he passed on to his reward. But anyhow everybody said the house had been so easily converted from a private residence into a funeral establishment, it was all right spooky, just like a corpse looking "natural." But whatever the case, I think the Square for most people always stood for life and continuity, the essence of the place, the community itself. And most everything that happened down there was not only of public interest; it was somehow the substance of life itself.

Of course it was not without its own element of color. On Saturdays when I was a little boy, you could see the farmers' wagons (some of them with straight-backed chairs in them, to give the passengers more dignity and comfort) and their mules and horses too, hitched just off the Square in the forerunners of modern-day parking lots. And the Negroes naturally all congregating in their section of the downtown scene they called the Zoo, laughing, talking, visiting with each other. And there would be the throngs, both black and white, collecting in front of the picture show—the New Dixie, where I saw my first movies, seated in my nurse's lap in the Jim Crow gallery. And they would all be impatient for the first show to let out so they could go to the second one. (Most of us in my crowd thought you had to see the whole program—horse opera, Three Stooges comedy, and serial—at least twice to have any standing at all.) And everywhere there would be noise, laughter, life, so much so that later on I came to think of it all in terms of Dr. Johnson's description of the "high tide" of London life along the Strand as one of the great felicities. To see the Square during its finest hour you really needed to be there on Election Day, but of course such occasions were few and far apart. And any day would do when you came right down to it.

There were the drugstores too, all with their soda fountains of course—one of the fountains even christened the "Mattie Maud" for the respective wives of the two owners, another selling that best of all local ice creams, Fortune's "all cream ice cream"—and the ten-cent stores, one of them called the Ben Franklin, presumably to honor one of the Founding Fathers who had always had an eye out for a good bargain. And there were even a couple of "up market" men's and women's stores that catered to the carriage trade that didn't always choose to go to Memphis. And the slogan of the men's emporium was, grandly, "one man understands another," while the ladies' shop, even more ambitious, called itself a "salon." But one of my aunts told my mother, child, not to ever in this world let old Mrs. Harris, who was the boss and manager there, fit a corset on her because she would fit it so tight nobody in her right mind could even *breathe.* And of course my mother always had to have plenty of room because she kept her money inside her brassiere (in a little crocheted bag) when she went to Memphis or some other "big" place which might be dangerous. But it was bothersome when she needed to get some money out of there because she always had to retire to the Ladies' Room to carry out the transaction.

The courthouse was naturally the center of the whole thing—not a very "historic" one but a Roosevelt public works edifice erected in the mid-thirties. But I thought it was handsome, with its yellow brick exterior and, in the very center of the first floor—where the north-south and east-west corridors intersected—an inlaid map of the county, highways, country roads, railroad, and all. And in the yard outside there was an enormous cannon, brought up from Fort Pillow, down on the Mississippi, where Forrest's alleged "massacre" had taken place, and now serving as our Civil War monument. Not for us "the little bitty man with the great big gun," so often denigrated by the Yankees as an incarnation of Confederate vanity, but a reality which had once done yeoman service in the fray and as such demanded respect and veneration now from both Blue and Gray alike: no stage property at all.

The yard was also where the old men sat—on benches provided and appropriately so labeled by one of the local lumber companies—smoking, telling tales, playing checkers, even a few of them playing chess, a game I never could understand—and all of them irreverently dismissed by a friend of my mother's, who had dutifully nursed and buried a father and two uncles and all of them as mean and cranky as you could want, as the D. P.'s, which in her context meant not Displaced Persons but Dead Peters.

There was also an ornamental fountain which splashed nearly continuously into a pool around its base, surrounded by red and yellow cannas. And in and out of the whole scene played the squirrels, who lived in the big oak trees nearby and seemed to think it all belonged to them. When we were all quite small, our nurses would sometimes take us and our ice cream cones (brought across from one of the drugstores) to play in the yard; but on the whole, it all seemed too crowded, too busy for us and them too. And so we would usually adjourn to the Methodist Church steps, a couple of blocks away, where we could chase each other around the velvety lawn and play hide-and-seek in and out of the flying buttresses, while the nurses could sit in the late afternoon sun and gossip about both themselves and the white folks for whom they worked.

But back to the Square again. Yes, it was the center of the town's commerce, but other matters were transacted there too—and often matters that were concerned literally with life and death. In those days the doctors' offices were nearly always situated up over the drugstores on the Square—I assume for convenience in case prescriptions had to be prepared and purchased right on the scene. But anybody that had any sense, my mother always said, knew that sick folks didn't have any business climbing the stairs. And, as previously noted, the undertakers were there too; and of course they were the ones who would take you to the hospital in Memphis—in the hearse naturally—if your case required that. And obviously if you died en route or after you got there, they were even more useful still. (It was all quite conveniently arranged if you thought about it.) Then finally just off the Square and right behind my father and uncle's store was the county jail, and you could hear the "jail birds," as we called them, singing nearly any time, from the back door of Drake Brothers. And since they were mostly Negroes, it would be spirituals that we usually heard, full of both joy and grief. It was all of it right there around us too—life and death, Heaven and Hell, the drama of our lives, the drama of the Square.

Well, it took more than Wal-Mart, even coupled with McDonald's, to bring about the modern decline of the Square. We all should have expected it—and perhaps some of us did—when it became apparent that the big trade day (when the farmers came to town) was no longer Saturday but Friday (when the factories paid off). It was really a whole culture that began to go. Wal-Mart was perhaps just the final sign or symbol; it wasn't the cause but the result. And in its own way it too constituted something of a community, though one based not so much on custom as economic necessity, even survival. But where else, we may well ask, does custom, community itself come from? One way or another we must all hang together in this world: no amount of social or technological development can change that, whatever other innovations it brings about. The forms may differ, may undergo mutation in the fullness of time but never the substance, the essence, I believe. And yes, we need each other today as much as we ever did; and no, it is still not good for man to be alone.

Up on the Corner, on the Dogleg

JACKSON STREET, THE STREET WE LIVED ON, MADE a sort of dogleg before it got to our house, coming out from the square, and for almost a block ran sideways to itself before it righted its course, if I make myself clear. They never bothered to change its name either: it was still Jackson Street, no matter which way it ran. And it never occurred to me that that was in any way peculiar till we had a cousin come out from Memphis to visit one time, and she said it just didn't make sense and showed a lack of urban planning or something of the sort. But my mother just said everybody in Woodville knew what it was and where it was going, and that was good enough for *them*. (The cousin was not a close one anyway. And my mother didn't see any use in taking her *seriously*, especially when she had come from out at Fisher's Crossing in the first place, where hardly anybody had ever heard of a stoplight, much less urban planning. And anyway, she was my *father's* cousin.)

But I always thought it was interesting, in any case—that Jackson Street could still be itself even when it ran sideways. And I even wondered whether that sort of arrangement maybe did something to the people that lived on the dogleg and certainly the ones that lived up on the corner from us. Did it mean that they were just a little out of step with everybody else or that they sort of enjoyed being contrariwise to the prevailing opinions of the day and the ordinary ways of doing things, like material cut on the bias? Of course, they were still themselves, no matter what—just like Jackson Street, no matter which way it ran. Certainly, our town, Woodville, was peculiar in its layout—mostly existing on the ridges that lay between the ravines (people said it was a city set on a hill), and all radiating out from the square like spokes in a wheel with few conventional blocks to be seen, no "grid" at all. And you had to go back to the square—the hub—and start over to go almost anywhere, certainly to go from one side of town to another. But the dogleg on Jackson seemed rather extreme, even for Woodville.

But it might have been just the folks that lived up on the corner from us, as Jackson Street straightened itself out to run parallel to its first section leaving the square, that made me wonder about it all in the first place. Not that they were *peculiar* or all that different from anybody else: I've always said that if you knew Woodville, Tennessee, you could go round the world with few surprises. But maybe they were just more obvious. Of course, you could argue that a small town like that had more than its fair share of anomalies: some people would have you believe that right now, especially if the towns are down south. But again, I think not: everybody is just closer to everybody else and there are fewer secrets, fewer places to hide—that's all. In any case, I thought the people up on the corner, for good or for ill, might just possibly be more *Woodville* than anybody else I could think of. And I always more or less made a sort of private study of them, watched them, thought about them, to see whether they added up to anything special.

But what could be all that unusual about them? They weren't hiding any bodies in the basement or imprisoning lunatic members of the family in upstairs bedrooms or defiling the purity of family life by illicit affairs with their colored servants—or, for that matter, with each other. Nothing lurid at all—certainly nothing for the national "media," as it's come to be called, to get up a sweat about. But what they all were, first and foremost and very emphatically, was themselves—what my father would have called their own boss and manager. And they didn't mind being different, but they didn't make any big deal out of it either. That's just the way they were, and I suppose they thought everybody else in the world was the same—or ought to be. (Again, who cared which way Jackson Street ran?) Maybe I never would have thought there was anything unique about them either unless I had grown up and gone away to earn my living in Memphis and then could look back on Woodville as where I was *from.* But this is all forty years ago now, and maybe Woodville has "progressed" and gotten to be like every other place you can think of. I'm almost afraid to go back there now, for fear of finding out that it has.

I do know that some years ago the Board of Mayor and Aldermen hired a big-city firm of "consultants" (all the way from St. Louis, I think) to come in and take a look around and recommend whatever they thought fit to improve Woodville's "image" and its economy, or something of the sort; and one of the first things they lit on was the dogleg on Jackson, which they labeled a very back number indeed and a holdover from simpler times. They very strongly urged its elimination—or rather just its renaming, the sideways part, that is. But the people up on the corner weren't having any of that, and they all showed up in a group before the board to protest. Some of them were old and feeble too; some had hardly been downtown or even out of the house in a good while. But they thought it necessary to take a stand on such an important matter. And the board listened too—and granted their request to leave Jackson Street alone.

I was living in Memphis by then, but I saw the whole thing prominently written up in the *Commercial Appeal* and read it all with considerable interest—and amusement. And I thought, well, Woodville never changes, and there's no other place like it, and hurrah for all those stout-hearted old folks that wanted to live and die on Jackson Street, dogleg or no! We need more people like that in the modern world, I thought, and score another one for the American Resistance Movement! But I wondered whether it was just change of any sort they feared, or did it go deeper than that? And why would they really want to hold on to such a confusing anachronism or whatever you wanted to call it? Come now, tell the truth. Wouldn't it really make things simpler for all concerned if the Jackson Street dogleg got itself straightened out and into the modern world? The people up on the corner would still be themselves, still be the same. But then of course, I gathered, *they* didn't see it that way.

So I began to think about them, individually and collectively, and to wonder whether they were all that different or were they just trying to cash in on whatever nuisance value they had and get themselves a lot of notoriety thereby? (My mother never distinguished between *celebrity* and *notoriety*, and she may have been ahead of her time because there really doesn't seem to be any difference now.) God knows, there seems to be plenty of that sort of thing in the world today, with demonstrations and martyrdoms for all to see, on very short notice, on worldwide TV and everything else. (Of course people like me always wondered whether there would be so many martyrs if the witness-bearers weren't so sure of an audience.) Whatever the case, these people—up on the corner, on the dogleg—were not your everyday, garden-variety sort of folks; that much was certain.

Just to start off, the two old bachelor brothers Fitzpatrick—Dr. Will and Mr. Jim, one a doctor and the other a lawyer—who lived in the big brown house were not without some interest. I don't know why neither of them had ever married: some people just thought they never had gotten around to thinking about it, they had been so busy getting started in their respective careers and then making money when they did get established. And maybe there was no passion for that in them anyway; but there certainly was for other things—hunting, for instance. Wherever either of them went, he was usually accompanied by one or more dogs, and of course the house literally swarmed with them. I don't recall hearing that Dr. Will took them into a sickroom (and this was back in the days of house calls, remember); but wherever he went, day or night, one of the dogs was sure to ride along, in the backseat of his little car. (For some reason, doctors then seemed mostly to drive coupes, just as they always seemed to have their home and office phones on the same two-party line—so you could find the doctor instantly, I suppose—and the same way all their offices were down on the square up over one of the drugstores.) Mr. Jim was the same as Dr. Will. He never took a dog into the courtroom as far as I know, but there was always one sleeping in the doorway that you had to step over when you went into his office, which was up over the bank.

Dr. Will had a rough tongue, especially for people that wouldn't follow his advice; but he was considered to be very good always with children and old people—people who mostly couldn't or wouldn't talk back to him. And when he gave doctor's orders, they were just that. Once he laid my father out when he stopped taking some medicine Dr. Will had prescribed as soon as he began feeling better: "I said for you to take the whole bottle of medicine, and I meant the whole bottle too." And my father then meekly obeyed. When Dr. Will was finally able to persuade Cousin Serena Cobb, whom he had been treating for a chronic urinary infection for years, to let him take out her tonsils because he feared they were badly diseased, he took one look, after he had gotten her all laid out on the table in his office and deadened with some sort of local anesthetic (we didn't have a hospital in Woodville back then), and exploded: "Good God, woman, I've been working on the wrong end of you all this time! Your kidneys aren't even in the running: these tonsils are as big as a bear!" This sort of thing didn't endear him to some of his patients; but then my mother, who was always the most sensible of women, said you didn't go to him to be flattered: you went to be cured and whatever it took to do that was certainly all right with her. She had long ago lost any illusions she had ever had about the way things *looked*.

Dr. Will didn't miss much. When he was a very young doctor just out of medical school, he had been taking some special courses up in New York one summer; and he took in all the sights too, including the trial of Harry K. Thaw, who had killed Stanford White in a much-publicized "society murder" but was duly exonerated because he was supposed to have had a "brainstorm" at the time. There was naturally some skeptical opinion about that. Because of Thaw's wealth and position, it was suggested that the brainstorm theory was nothing but a kind of rich man's alibi. But not to Dr. Will: he said you could just take one look at that fellow and tell he was crazy. And anybody that would shoot his wife's lover in such a public place as the rooftop restaurant of Madison Square Garden had to be either crazy or stupid. And he didn't think Thaw was stupid, though he ought to have known better than to marry a chorus girl in the first place.

Mr. Jim didn't seem to be so colorful, but I do remember that during World War II he tried to run his old car on a mixture he concocted out of coal oil and cleaning fluid. That was his answer to gasoline rationing. So whenever you saw him coming, he was attended by a good deal of smoke and a considerable smell as the old Chevy lurched down the street. But it kept running all through the war, and that was what he wanted. Their married sister, Miss Olivia, who lived in Memphis, used to worry about them a lot: who would look after them in their old age, and were they eating properly, and why hadn't they ever married? But they seemed to do a good job of looking after each other, and you never would have known they felt the lack of family life. I remember my mother said that, if you ever called up there late at night for Dr. Will, Mr. Jim would always answer the phone; and you never knew whether Dr. Will was there either till Mr. Jim found out who you were. For that matter, the community itself did a pretty good job of looking after them. When Dr. Will had his first heart attack (the first time, I remember, I ever heard the word *coronary*), the town stationed a policeman down on Jackson Street, right in front of our house, to reroute traffic around by the primary school so the noise wouldn't bother Dr. Will when he was so sick. (He was sick at home because they hadn't been able to move him to the hospital in Memphis.) And I remember my mother kept the policeman supplied with all the coffee he wanted while he was on duty: she said she couldn't do anything for Dr. Will himself, but she could do that.

Old Mr. Conner, who lived across the street from Dr. Will and Mr. Jim, was another matter. He and his family had moved into town from out in the country years ago: he was supposed to have made a good deal of money somewhere along the line and sold his farm and was all ready to retire. But my mother said she never would believe he had done all that well just in farming—and certainly not on the kind of land he owned; and, to cap the climax, he was supposed to be some sort of jackleg preacher on the side, and that didn't help. Why, he might have spoken in tongues, for all she knew. When she talked like that, my father would always profess himself embarrassed: he never thought she respected the ministry as much as she should. But she just said, never mind, he would see; and he did. Because "Brother" Conner, as he had first insisted on calling him, seemed to be up to all sorts of tricks in the way of mortgages and lawsuits; and it looked as though anybody that had any sense ought to think twice before getting involved with him in a business transaction. They even told it on him that he once moved into a house he had bought and nailed down the rugs before they could be removed and thus was able to argue that the rugs had gone with the trade. But what really opened my father's eyes, apparently, was hearing the old boy preach, which he did once at a funeral of a tiny baby that was held somewhere out at a country church. "Brother" Conner held forth for nearly two hours on the subject of infant baptism! And my father was scandalized and never referred to him as "Brother" Conner again: usually it was just "that old devil" from that time on.

Since I've been grown and no longer live there, Mr. Conner's granddaughter has told me (and we grew up together) that he still continued to perform funerals into his very old age. Once she drove him out to a church somewhere in the tall and uncut; and just before they arrived, he told her he had forgotten whose funeral it was to be. She naturally asked him how he could officiate under such circumstances, but he merely replied that he would know whose funeral it was when he got there and saw the family. And anyway, he added, you always said the same thing. I was sorry then that my parents weren't still around to hear that one. I don't think either of them would have been surprised.

Mr. Conner was sometimes a trial to his neighbors, especially after his wife died—a silent little old woman that I never heard say a word. Old Mrs. Higgins, who lived on one side of the Conners, said she was sorry the old boy was so lonesome now but she couldn't take him on with all the rest she had to worry about: running a boardinghouse along with, in summer, fighting the weeds in the yard with only a bunch of no-good Negroes to help her and, in winter, keeping the pipes from freezing underneath that great big house that had no underpinning at all. Her hands were full, and she let him know that right away when she told him her hens wouldn't lay on coffee grounds. She said he was just that lonesome: he would come traipsing over to give her chickens his "table scraps," just so he could pass the time of day with her. But she said she didn't need anything *he* had to give her. Whether she was conscious of the innuendo I don't know: she certainly wouldn't have been embarrassed if she had been. My mother certainly wouldn't have been either. My father, though, like many men of his generation, was more prudish (and less realistic) than many of his female contemporaries. He was definitely outraged when another old man of his acquaintance once confided to him that a man his age didn't need sexual intercourse but about once a year and then went on to add, "But my wife—she don't mind."

On the other side of the Conners lived the Malones, with "more beautiful women in one house than you ever saw in your life," people used to say (they had five lovely daughters and their mother had been a beauty too). But everybody said it was just as well Mrs. Malone *had* been beautiful because she certainly couldn't have counted on her brains. One time, I know, after she got up in years, she broke her hip; and my mother went to see her when she got home from the hospital. She told my mother that the doctors had all assured her that, no indeed, that leg wasn't going to be one bit shorter than the other one after it got well: if anything, it was going to be a little bit longer!

Next to the Malones—and just before you came to our house—was old Mrs. Scott—"Miss Alma," as most of her friends called her. I've tried writing about her elsewhere, but I doubt that I'll ever be believed. Still, it won't hurt to add a little more here. Having outlived her husband by a good many years and raised assorted children and grandchildren, Miss Alma was naturally the one you *turned to* when you were in a tight place. One time, I remember, my mother was horrified to find that the country ham she had planned to serve the Tuesday Bridge Club was much too salty, and the "girls" were due in only an hour's time. But Miss Alma didn't turn a hair: she told her just to put it on again in cold water and bring it to a boil. And that was that. She was that way about everything else: when she had grandchildren running in and out of the kitchen all day long, she said she just turned the handles of whatever she had cooking on top of the stove to the inside so the children couldn't knock it off and went on her way rejoicing. By mistake, someone called Miss Alma on the telephone once, under the impression that she was the Mrs. Scott whose husband had a little machine shop, and asked whether he was still sharpening lawn mowers. To which Miss Alma quickly replied that he *could be*: he'd been dead five years and she didn't know what he was doing now! Oh, I could tell you a lot more, but Miss Alma needs a whole story to herself. *Down to earth* is putting it mildly.

The upshot of all this is that the folks up on the corner, on the Jackson Street dogleg, weren't any different mostly from anybody else. That's something I know now—as I look back on them after all these years. They were just highly visible, that's all. Their situation was somewhat different from that of the rest of us—out of kilter, as my mother used to say. And so you just noticed them more. But they did like who they were and where they were, and they knew where they were going too. And it didn't matter really which way Jackson Street ran. I'm sure there were probably a lot more people around town just like them too, but I don't think there are so many people like them in the world today. We don't seem to have as much room, as much time to spare for people a little out of kilter or cut on the bias, people who live on doglegs. And I think that's too bad. But the times have changed, the world has changed, and I'm sure Woodville has changed too. (I hear they've even got a shopping mall there now.) But then you can look at it another way. My mother always said that, give or take so much, people were always pretty much the same wherever you found them, and the human animal didn't really seem to vary much from time to time and place to place. Whatever the case, she said, you just couldn't ever really beat *folks*.

The Living Room

"WELL," MY FATHER WOULD SAY WHEN HE AND MY mother drove past the crowded parking lot of the local funeral home, "I see they've got somebody in the *living room*," which of course always irritated her because that meant they had a *body* out on display in the front part of the house, which was a converted "old colonial home," and yes, in what had been the living room. It had belonged to the Banks family for years till they finally all died off or moved away (the children weren't about to come back to Woodville). And so they sold it off to a new "concern" called a "funeral home," which was an institution gradually taking over the undertaking business.

Of course my mother held no particular brief for the olden time or the Banks family or anything to do with them. She said old Mrs. Banks, the Dowager Duchess of the tribe, you might say, was the bossiest old cat she ever saw in her life: she bossed her husband and her children and the Baptist Church and anything else she could get her hands on. And God only knew what she would say if she knew her former abode was now the funeral headquarters of the community. And indeed I think my mother took some wry pleasure in contemplating the fact. The Bankses were always more show than anything else, she said. Anyhow, Mrs. Banks was gone now, and you didn't have to worry about her anymore.

The form in those days (back in the thirties) was for some enterprising undertaker to find an old house—an imposing one of course—that had come on the market because none of the heirs wanted to live there, then buy it, and turn it into a funeral "home," which nomenclature always made my flesh creep. I just didn't see how you could domesticate death so easily: "home" was the last word I would have thought of, at least as the site for such a business. Of course before that there were "funeral parlors," usually down on the Square or elsewhere in the business district. And they were often owned and operated by furniture dealers. (I suppose it all started out with them making coffins as "furniture" and going on from there.)

Well, everybody said those days were going fast: now people wanted the whole business—at any rate the service itself—transacted away from home and preferably at the funeral home itself if not in the church. But that of course usually depended on how "big" a church member the deceased had been or perhaps whether there had been anything sudden or scandalous about his death—anything that might turn it all into a "big" funeral. In the old days the service had usually been held at the "residence," as the black-bordered funeral notices distributed to all the places of business around the Square would put it—along with who the pallbearers (both active and honorary) would be and where the "interment" would duly take place. And so the funeral "home" was the natural answer to that. And people said places like Waterfield and Hill, the furniture-store undertakers down on the Square, were on the way out: you had to move with the times in the funeral business, just like any other.

And so, like I said, some enterprising mortician would buy an old house—usually a very fine one—and remodel and redecorate it—and turn it into a funeral home. And the new one in Woodville—the first one most people around there had ever seen—was moving in on the territory and would, in due course, do a land office business as they put it. And it was quite uncanny, people said, how easily the old Banks house lent itself to the new dispensation: you would have thought it had all been planned as a funeral establishment from the word *go*. The former living room was indeed a long drawing room, where the congregation could sit during the services (always on those folding chairs you could ask to borrow, if they weren't in use, for family reunions and club meetings). And there was a connecting sun porch, which was easily turned into a "family" room so the immediate kin could be secluded in their grief. I think they even had the dining room, which opened out of the living room behind glass doors, all lined up as the back-up room in case they had more than one body at a time to deal with. The coffins and "preparation" all went on upstairs. And it was all an asset to the community, people said, and particularly at Christmas time when they had a replica of the "little brown church" displayed in the front yard, all lit up with Christmas lights and with Christmas carols all piped into the edifice from the public address system inside the house. And of course, they made their presence known in all the local churches with the fans they put in all the pews. They usually featured Jesus in the Garden on one side and the funeral home's advertisement on the other, where, among other things, they always made a point of telling you they had a "lady attendant" on their staff—to preserve the proprieties, I suppose.

Over the years the funeral home became more and more important in the community, and Waterfield and Hill finally retired from the business, just sold furniture these days. So when somebody looked knowing and nodded his head and said, "You know, they've got John Doe"—Or whoever—"up at the funeral home," you didn't have to ask what for. You knew *he* was the body and the star of the show. And everybody would say, "Well, I declare...," or even one time when Cousin Rosa Moss went over to see the undertaker's wife (they had an apartment in the back of the house), she was surprised to find that her old friend, Miss Carrie Bond, was the main attraction, only as she put it when she called my mother she said, "I came over to see Mrs. Taylor and I found Miss Carrie Bond here." Like she was still alive or something and just paying an afternoon call. Like I said, it was all very much a community affair: Taylor's establishment was the only one in town and simply in charge of that side of life—or death—in Woodville. And perhaps, little by little, people did begin to think of it as some sort of "home." And thus they were domesticating death there, though they wouldn't have him in their own homes these days. And that was perhaps a credit to the atmosphere the place created—and of course a very wise business stratagem.

I know my uncle Buford, who was very conservative in most of his views, thought the rise of the funeral home had, as he put it, been one of the biggest "improvements" in modern life. (I wonder now what he would have thought of Forest Lawn.) And I used to wonder why he felt that way until I recollected that when he and my father and their brothers had all been growing up out in the country, death had to be dealt with right there on the premises, and perhaps he thought it all too domesticated. You had to come into town and buy the coffin, then prepare the body right there at home and usually hold the services there as well. And it was all immediate and intimate and going on right there in your face and you couldn't get away from it. But the funeral home took all that away and made a professional thing out of it (no real domesticity there), and you didn't have to worry about it beyond selecting the coffin and maybe providing burial clothes for the body.

And I thought this somehow an improvement too—but altogether impersonal, like death was just another business (was it?). But I do know that many older people had a horror in those days of being taken away from home for such purposes: they still wanted the ministrations of family and close friends at such times. And right now I have a very vivid memory of seeing the body of the lady who lived across the street from us arriving from Memphis, where she had had surgery and in due course died. (And they always seemed to do that especially when they had been rushed to the hospital in the middle of the night," usually for some sort of abdominal operation, like a red-hot appendix or "locked bowels," as an intestinal obstruction was called in those days, which made it sound absolutely final and like the Unpardonable Sin or the Last Judgment.) But anyhow, I was only about five or six and didn't really know what I was seeing—just Waterfield and Hill's big ambulance/hearse (convertible either way) pulled up in front of the house and the driver and another man taking out a stretcher with something on it all covered up under a blue bedspread and carrying it into the house. And I wondered what on earth it was but didn't know until years later that the deceased had said she had a horror of being "prepared" by strangers away from home and they could just come to the house and do it all. And she wanted Waterfield and Hill too and not just some more "brought on" folks. So that's what she got. They said she was yellow as a pumpkin too, so I assume they had their work cut out for them.

Well, little by little Waterfield and Hill were phased out. And so Taylor's Funeral Home took over more and more of the business. But still people were reluctant to make a clean break with the past and still wanted the body brought back home after it had been prepared and their friends could pay their respects right there. They often continued the old custom of sitting up with the body the night before the funeral too.

But then gradually the funeral home became absolutely the center of the whole enterprise, and I don't know now when I've ever heard of anybody's "loved ones" being brought back home to "lie in state," a phrase which always fascinated me when I was little. (It wasn't as though they were royalty or anything like that, so why "in state"?) Now they're kept at the funeral home for the wake, with people socializing right there in the same room with death and not with any disrespect either: it was the time when you usually saw your kinfolks and friends you hadn't seen since the last funeral. But of course if you did go by the "residence" to pay your respects to the immediate family, you found that there had been enough food sent in to feed a regiment, the casserole dishes all bearing the name of the donor on a piece of adhesive tape affixed to the underside for easy identification. And so some things still hung on from the old days despite the attempts to professionalize it all. I had heard that the funeral business was a very lucrative one indeed. After all, they had you, if you were "making the arrangements," when your resistance was low and you weren't able to put up much of a fight against a hard sell.

But it was all still death no matter how you sliced it, whether you spoke of the "living room," where the honoree reposed, or called it "passing away" instead of "dying" and all the other euphemisms. And now we treat the whole business as some sort of anomaly. People don't die at home any more but usually in hospitals and nursing homes. And they don't say much in the way of famous last words either, what with all the drugs they've been given, merciful though that can be. If they do manage to die in their own homes, you usually hear of it thus: "They *found* old Mrs. Harrison this morning." And then usually there is speculation about how long she had been dead and what she had died of and it was all too bad, none of her family there but then that's what often happened when folks lived alone. And they buried her with her glasses on because hardly anybody had ever seen her without them: indeed she didn't really look "natural" otherwise. And of course that was what the death industry was all about now: conflicting views of *nature* and *natural.* And when you said the deceased looked "natural," it really meant anything but that—just prettified and all dressed up "like a country corpse," as they used to say. And when the old and dying *were* secluded in hospitals and nursing homes—away from all the young folks, their children and grandchildren, what sort of impression of life was that in aid of? Instead of having several generations living in one house or even just down the street from one another, you had separation, exile, segregation, all the rest. And death and dying were no longer seen as definers of life and at the center of the drama. A funeral "home" was no substitute for the real thing, just a makeshift in a changing world.

It was not thus in the world that, say, Emily Dickinson wrote about. In a small country town in Massachusetts in the middle of the nineteenth century death was all around you and thoroughly domesticated, not seen as something out of line. And thus her treatment of death often as a familiar friend, even a suitor is nothing "peculiar" or even pathological. Nor is the attitude that he's a household inmate. He is perfectly "natural" but not in the way modern usage would have us believe. And perhaps we do wrong to exclude young people particularly from his presence like some scandal they will be better off not knowing about. *That's* what I call really *unnatural.*

So it was some such conflict, said or understated, which I suppose led to the teasing which went on between my parents about who might be in the "living room." No, it wasn't a "living room" to either one of them now, and my father believed that just as did my mother. Both of them were absolutely down to earth and facers of facts when it came to what life and death were all about. God knows what they would have said about a marquee I recently saw outside a small-town funeral establishment, which blazoned forth for all to see the name of the deceased and the hours of "visitation," like you were going to a movie. Tacky as all get-out, you might say, and making it all sound like yet another roadside attraction. But again it was death as part of the community, part of life, and something your friends and neighbors would want to know about and would feel disappointed, even hurt to miss out on. They would have felt *left out*, just like they would if they didn't get to "view the remains." So perhaps there's something to be said for the rise of the "home" side of the establishment though sad to think it's perhaps due to the erosion of the traditional home and family in our world. And yes, it *is* almost a community center, you might say, though run as a business and a very professional one at that. But we can't have it both ways, really. The "living room" is anything but that now: deep down inside we all know that, despite all the showcasing and window dressing. And I can hear my father right now snorting and saying, "Just who do they think they're fooling?"

Amazing Grace

I DIDN'T MUCH WANT TO GO WITH DADDY AND Mamma out to Salem Church that Sunday. They were going to have dinner on the ground after preaching, and then after that the Barlow County Singing Convention was going to meet. I was twelve years old, and it looked like to me that I never was going to get away from the country. Every Sunday afternoon we had to go out to Uncle Jim and Aunt Mary's at Maple Grove, where Pa Drake used to live. Pa had been dead for several years, but it looked like Daddy and Mamma didn't know how to quit going. And every time we had to sit around and listen to all those old tales about when the Drake boys were growing up and all the fun they used to have with their neighbors like the Powells and the Sweats.

Pa Drake had come from Virginia after the War and married Grandma, who had been a Sanders, and I think his folks always thought he had married beneath himself. But Daddy used to tell Mamma and she told *me* that they would all have starved to death if it hadn't been for Grandma. Pa had been raised with slaves to wait on him and had gone off to school and learned to read Latin and Greek before he went off to the War, and I reckon he wasn't ever about to learn how to do anything else.

But, anyhow, it looked like everybody in my family was from the country and wasn't ever going to be anywhere else. None of them had ever been off to college because they didn't have any money for *anything*, much less education. They just all went to school out at Maple Grove a few months every year and went to church every Sunday, and that was about as far as any of them got, except Uncle Buford; and he finished high school because Daddy quit school to let him go.

But I was bound and determined that wasn't going to happen to me. I was going to get all the education in the world so I never would have to be ashamed of saying *seen* and *done* and *taken*, and I was going to go places and do things. They needn't to think they were going to keep me in Barlow County all my life. I had already had a big argument with Daddy, though, because I said I wanted to go to school at Harvard, which was supposed to be the best school in the whole country. But Daddy said no, sir, I wasn't going to get above my raising and go up there to school with a lot of Yankees that all loved the Negroes so much; I was going to school in the South and like it. It made me mad because I thought he just couldn't stand for me to go off and do things nobody in the whole Drake family had ever done before.

Well, anyhow, somebody in the Salem community had asked us out that Sunday, so about ten o'clock we got in the car and drove off. It was laying-by time, after all the weeds had been chopped out of the cotton, and the cotton was growing like wildfire all along road. But it was hot as a fox, and I wasn't looking forward to the prospect of eating off the ground with all those ants and worms crawling all over the food and you, too.

It didn't take us long to get out to Salem; it was only about five miles out from Woodville. The church, which was a Baptist church, sat back off the road under some great big oak trees, and people had parked all over the yard without any system at all. They just up and stopped wherever they got ready. Most of the cars were old and broken-down looking, and there were a lot of pickup trucks, too. Daddy was always talking about how poor farmers were and what a hard time they had, so I was used to them looking run-down. But what made me kind of tired was the way Daddy seemed to *enjoy* talking about how bad off they were, like there might be something good about having to work so hard and never having any money and never going anywhere and doing anything. For my part, I just couldn't wait to go to New York and see all the museums and theaters and famous people and everything that was going on. But nothing ever happened to any of the Drakes; they just went on year after year as slow as Christmas.

There were still a lot of people in the cars, like couples courting and women nursing babies and changing their diapers right there in your face. But then they began getting out to go in the church, and they were all laughing and hollering like they hadn't seen each other in a thousand years. I thought it was all pretty disgusting and common. It didn't look like any of them had any refinement, and I didn't see how Daddy could be so crazy about them. But he was. He was always talking about some old man out in the country who probably didn't know how to read and write and saying, "He's one of the best men that ever had on a pair of pants"; or he would mention some old woman that was ugly as homemade sin and say, "Yes, I know she's so cross-eyed, when she cries, the tears run down her back, but she's one of the best women you ever saw." That kind of thing worried me because it looked like you had to be ugly and ignorant in order to be good, just like if you really enjoyed something, like going to the picture show, it was probably a bad influence on you. Or at least that was the way a lot of people acted.

The sermon was a pretty regulation Baptist kind with lots of emphasis on whether you were a wise or a foolish virgin and whether you would be ready if Jesus should come tonight. It looked like to me I had more and more things to worry about all the time. It wasn't enough for you to worry about whether or not you were going to get all A's on your report card so you could go to the picture show on school nights and whether you had practiced your hour on the piano every day. Then, on top of all that, you had to worry about going to Heaven and all. It looked like some people just couldn't be satisfied.

So I was pretty glad when church was over and it was time to eat, even if we were going to eat off the ground. The women went on out in the yard and started unloading the food from the cars and spreading their white Sunday tablecloths out under the big oak trees. There was lots of fried chicken and country ham and sliced tomatoes and stuffed eggs and all kinds of cake and pie. And somebody had gone into Woodville right after church to get the ice for the iced tea. Then everybody got a paper plate and started going around and helping himself to everything. When we started around, Mamma whispered to me that we had to take some of everything so as not to hurt anybody's feelings. That was another thing you had to worry about—whether or not you were going to hurt somebody's feelings. But it didn't look like to me anybody was sitting up late at night worrying about whether or not he had hurt *my* feelings.

We went around helping ourselves to everything and trying to eat a little on the side. A cross-eyed woman with buckteeth and dyed hair came up to Mamma and said, "Have you had any of my *cormel* cake?" And Mamma said, "Why, it's Cousin Lucy Belle Sanders, isn't it? No, indeed, I must get some of your caramel cake right away." It seemed like it was always people like that that we had to be kin to, and you always had to be nice to them when you didn't really want to. I used to wonder sometimes whether it would hurt you as much to be nice to people with straight eyes and straight teeth; but then, of course, when they were like that, you didn't have to worry about being nice to them in the first place.

Brother Jernigan, the preacher, was stepping around, speaking to all the ladies and eating enough to kill a mule. It looked like I hadn't ever seen a preacher yet that wasn't a big eater and a big man with the ladies; it looked like that just sort of *went* with preaching. And *they* always acted like they had it coming to them just for getting up there once a week and making you wonder about whether or not you were worrying about all the things you should. But they didn't seem to worry much about anything themselves. I reckoned it was sort of like the ravens feeding Elijah or doctors never getting sick or something

About two o'clock when everybody was full as he could be and all the babies had gone to sleep, everybody began to get up off the ground and brush themselves off and put away the food and everything before the singing convention started. There was going to be a Bette Davis movie on that afternoon at the Dixie Theater in Woodville, and I begged Daddy to let us go on back home so I could see it. But he said, "Now, Robert, we're not going to eat and run like that. That would be just plain ordinary." I didn't like it, but I had to stop and think. It never had occurred to me before that *I* could be ordinary; it was uneducated people out in the country that were ordinary. I didn't exactly know what to make of it, so I followed Mamma and Daddy on into the church without saying anything.

The church was just like an oven, and you could tell that a lot of those people in there weren't any too familiar with soap and water. The place was jam-packed, and there didn't seem to be a breath of air stirring anywhere. The singing convention met only about four times a year, so they were always pretty sure to have a good crowd on hand. People came from all over the county to hear the different solos and quartets and things from every community. Daddy said, though, that they used to meet more often; it was just one more old thing that was dying out.

Everybody got real quiet, and then the Boyd's Landing Quartet got up to sing. They were supposed to be the best quartet in the county; and Daddy said that Mr. Tom Newman, who sang bass, had a voice like distant thunder. They started off with "Alas, and did my Savior bleed?" which was another one of those hymns where you had to low-rate yourself and say you were a worm. ("Would He devote that sacred head for such a worm as I?") It was just like everything else; you never could enjoy anything without thinking maybe you didn't have any right to and were probably going to have to pay for it some day.

I looked at Mamma to see how she was holding out, but she and Daddy were sitting there looking like they couldn't think of anywhere else in the world they would rather be than right there. So I decided I might as well make up my mind to sit there all afternoon, but I sure hoped God was taking notice of how good I was being and was putting it down by my name in the Lamb's Book of Life or wherever He kept all His records.

Finally, after they had sung "Near-o, my God to Thee" (they always pronounced "nearer" that way out in the country) and "On Jordan's stormy banks I stand," they got to "Amazing Grace." That was the first hymn I had ever learned; my nurse, Louella, had taught it to me when I was five years old. And it was written by John Newton, who was a converted slave trader. So I followed right along with the Quartet in my mind.

The first verse went:

Amazing grace! how sweet the sound,
That saved a wretch like me!
I once was lost, but now am found,
Was blind, but now I see.

There you were calling yourself a wretch again, and yet there was supposed to be something sweet about it. I looked around at all those people; and I could see, from the way they looked so far off from the world, so calm and peaceful, that they all thought there was something sweet about being a wretch, too. But why was it so sweet to be a wretch? If it was good to be a wretch, it might also be good to live out in the country and have nothing but lamps for light and have dinner on the ground. Did it mean that maybe God didn't really care whether you said *taken* or got all A's on your report card or lived at Salem or in New York, and that maybe He sort of enjoyed some people saying *taken* and living out in the country, and that maybe He didn't really care whether or not you were worrying about Jesus coming tonight? Was grace maybe something like rain that just fell anyhow and didn't care where it was falling and that was why it was so amazing?

I looked around at Daddy, and his eyes were full—just like they always got whenever he talked about Grandma and Pa or whenever he told me he loved Mamma even more now that he did when they were married or whenever he said he wanted me to have all the opportunities he had never had. Then the Quartet went on to another verse and sang:

> 'Twas grace that taught my heart to fear,
> And grace my fears relieved;
> How precious did that grace appear
> The hour I first believed!

I was sitting there thinking that grace must be about the most wonderful thing going if it could do all that and that that must have been the way John Newton felt when he wrote that hymn, when, all of a sudden, Daddy put his arm around me and whispered, "Son, you just don't know how much Daddy loves you." And then, right there, in front of all those people, I just reached up and hugged him around the neck.

Her Name on a Tombstone, Her Diamond Ring on Another Woman's Hand

MY MOTHER WAS THE MOST REALISTIC PERSON I have ever known: she always told it like it was and didn't pull any punches either. Like, for instance, when she was sounding off one time about women who were having marital or other problems (and I think my mother thought the only kind of problem a respectable woman could have would be marital) and she was inveighing against the women who went to their pastors about such things—for "counseling," a word she heartily despised. And she went on to say that a woman who would do that didn't have much sense anyway: if it had been her, she said, she would just have gotten herself a good lawyer—which might have told you a good deal about the way her mind worked. "Practical" was her watchword and "businesslike" was another, and the highest compliment she could pay anybody was to say that he was thoroughly down to earth or, as I've heard her put it, "When time comes to cut the head off, he's ready to do that too."

When a lady down the street whose husband had been carrying on an affair of long standing with her best friend, a maiden lady who lived next door to them, suddenly died, I waxed somewhat dramatic about the whole affair and exclaimed, "I wonder how Miss Eugenia [for that was the lady's name] feels now. Here she thought she and Mr. Caldwell were doomed to a life of illicit passion—or at any rate, a life of thinking about it—and now all their problems have been solved. And Miss Eugenia may be well on her way now to having 'a husband and a home of her own'—like people are always calling the fringe benefits of marital felicity." And I paused for effect. And then, "Mamma," I said, "what do you imagine Miss Eugenia is thinking now? Just look how the events of one day may have changed the course of her life forever! How do you suppose she feels right this minute?" To which, without looking up from her darning, she replied succinctly, "Better." And that was the end of that. Like I said, she simply called things by their right names and didn't waste any time doing so. Not that she went out of her way to be plainspoken, and she was never rude. Her social graces were many and her tact was famous. But she thought the world was, at best, a sort of superior zoo; and she seemed to think you ought simply to face that fact without blinking.

My father was, as strange as it may seem, somewhat more squeamish, even prudish about such matters. Yes, he knew there was wickedness in the world, but why dwell on it? And anyway, like a lot of men of his generation, he thought there ought to be some sort of double standard because of course the innocence of women had to be protected though naturally they knew about all such matters but maybe men weren't supposed to let them know that they knew that they knew. It all sounds now somewhat perverse and like Henry James, but it was all such open secrets as this that may have underlain the whole concept of the double standard and of course made it work. Anyhow, when you come right down to it, of course nobody was fooled. And the sexes proceeded on their way with the business of life, looking straight ahead but not particularly at each other. Some things you might know separately, but you couldn't let on to the opposite sex just how much. And that seemed to make everybody feel better and make the social machinery run more smoothly. Which of course was the idea behind the whole business. I'm sure that if I had asked my father how Miss Eugenia was feeling that night, he might have emerged from behind his newspaper just long enough to snort, take a big puff on his cigar, spit in the nearby coal scuttle, and never utter a word. But you could tell what he thought of the whole business and no mistake. His very silence spoke volumes.

My father was more long-suffering than my mother. And of course in that world it was the women who had the long memories, never forgiving or forgetting; and I used to wonder whether that was all left over from the Civil War. The men had taken their animus out in fighting, but it was the women who tended the memorial flames and remembered. And my mother had a very long memory. She also had a very strong sense of obligation and duty. The world should *work*, you should do your duty in that state to which it had pleased God to call you, you should pay your bills—on time, indeed fulfill your obligations whatever they were. And your word should be yea, yea or nay, nay.

I remember one time one of my aunts (by marriage) who was considered the poorest cook in the family, which prided itself on its food and the preparation thereof, was asked to submit one of her own recipes to a local cookbook being sold for some worthy cause in the nearby town where she lived and she didn't do a thing but take one of my mother's recipes—for Spanish rice, I believe—and submit it with her own name signed to it as author. And to put it mildly, my mother was furious. And when I expressed some surprise at her anger, she said, "You don't know how hard women work at such things, how proud they are of something really good and new that they have created themselves. Why, I'd just as soon she'd taken my diamond ring!" And I knew then she was as angry as she could be because her diamond ring was something very special indeed, almost some sort of icon in her life. It was the only really good piece of jewelry she had ever owned, and she had bought it with her own money before she ever married. So, although it was a handsome solitaire in a Tiffany mounting with platinum prongs, it wasn't really an engagement ring; my father hadn't given it to her. Perhaps we would say now that it was a kind of symbol of her independence as a woman: she didn't in any way owe it to a man. Whatever the case my father took a somewhat cavalier attitude toward it as but one more instance of the vanity of women and the vain pomp of the world, and he enjoyed teasing her about it just as he did when her own hair began to turn gray but that of one of his old flames who was the same age stayed henna-red till she breathed her last. But when he mentioned her name, it was then my mother's turn to snort, not really on moral grounds (though she had been brought up to believe that nice women didn't dye their hair) but just because she thought it was simply another form of deception and not unlike her own attitude toward women's wearing slacks: when another woman said they were such a "protection" to you, she replied calmly that she'd never yet seen anything she couldn't do in a skirt as long as she behaved herself. But the diamond solitaire was one of the fixed and unchanging measures of value in her life: it stood for worth, reality, truth, beauty, and God knows what else, as few other things did. (She never took it off either, not even when she was washing dishes, because she said soap and water never hurt a good diamond. And at other times she would look at it fondly and say, "There are bigger diamonds in the world but none finer.") And of course she had bought it with her own money too: it was none of my father's doing or anybody else's, just as that recipe was hers alone also. She didn't owe it to anybody else in the world. (The secret, she once confided to me, was in the chicken giblets.) And she would have been glad to *give* it to anybody: she said she always felt complimented when anybody asked her for a recipe. But she did want the credit for it, somewhat, I suppose, like the diamond ring: it identified and defined her self and her strength of character and nobody could ever take it away from her.

But I think I never realized this so clearly until I was in my late teens, really just about ready to go off to college. And it all came about because we had been to a funeral down at the Mount Zion Methodist Church out from Barfield. We had a lot of kinfolks buried down there and a lot of cousins still alive too, but Daddy always said Barfield was the sort of place he could spend a whole week in on just one Sunday afternoon and Mamma said every time we drove through there on the way to Memphis that it was just one more thing we had to be thankful for—that we didn't live down there. Because, you see, it was mostly widows and old maids, all living in big old houses that they had been born in—most of them well to do too. But healthy, able-bodied men seemed to be in short supply down there, and I had even wondered whether it might be safe for men, at least the young ones. Or maybe they just all left town as soon as they were grown and went to work in Memphis; Barfield didn't seem the kind of place where there would be much future for them. Maybe it was all too genteel and there were too many grieving widows or something. And the most excitement that ever took place was when the night train from Memphis that ordinarily didn't stop there would do so because they had a body on board being sent back home for burial. And of course the news would be all over town the next morning (along with whether old Mrs. Sexton that was always having relapses with her lumbago had had a "good night") because Miss Sadie and Miss Carrie Hargrove that ran the telephone office up over the bank would be looking out the window no matter the time of day or night and would naturally spread the word far and wide, just like they would tell you it was no use calling the folks across the street: they had just seen them leave for Memphis to go shopping.

But anyhow this Sunday afternoon we had driven down there to the funeral of Mamma's first cousin Maybelle Evans, whose husband Cousin Abner, Mamma said, had been dead so long it just proved he had probably given up the ghost years ago in self-defense. Because Cousin Maybelle not only had most of the money; she also had what you might call a whim of iron. Nevertheless, she always talked about him as *a man among men* and said she expected to follow him into the grave most any time now, which Mamma said was all a lot of foolishness because anybody that knew Cousin Maybelle would know that she intended to bury everybody in her whole family—and cheerfully too. And she said it was all just like Daddy: if she died before he did, he would be so grief-stricken he would probably try to jump in the grave at the cemetery but then end up going home with another woman.

Anyhow, there we all were at the graveside and, yes, there were lots of family buried all around so I thought maybe the Evanses were all getting sort of moribund. But at that point what should I see but a big, double-size tombstone where they were about to bury Cousin Maybelle and there was her own name chiseled on the tombstone too, right beside her husband's and with the date of her birth (she was older than I had thought) and a quotation from Tennyson about Cousin Abner ("the white flower of a blameless life") and everything else waiting for her, just like the empty side of a double bed. And I was just about to point it out to Mamma when I heard her let out something like "hmph" and I knew she had already spotted it all. But on the way back to the car she had a good deal to say about any woman's doing such a thing as that, let alone a woman like Cousin Maybelle, whom they would probably have had to knock in the head on Judgment Day if she hadn't fallen and broken her hip. If she knew what was good for her, she would know that you had better leave all such matters to Providence anyhow. And no man knew the day or the hour either. Why, she even had the first two digits ("19") of the date of her death written in since probably not even she expected to make it to the twenty-first century. And so there was that empty space just yawning for the last two figures to be filled in. But then Mamma said that was probably just like all those old women down there—they didn't see how their husbands could possibly get along without them whether in this world or the next. So those unfilled-in dates were some sort of reassurance for the dear departed and notice to the community that they were planning to honor their marriage commitments even after death. But she herself certainly had better things to worry about than that. And besides there wasn't supposed to be any marrying or giving in marriage in the case, and sometimes she thought that might be all right too, which I don't think was intended as a slap at the married state or Daddy either one: she was just plain worn out and needed a good long rest, she said.

But what summed it all up—Mamma's characteristic views on the world and folks and most everything else, herself included, surfaced some weeks later when I was packing to go off to school for the first time. And I knew it was a stressful time for her and Daddy, just as it was for me: I was their only child, and they were no longer young, indeed had been middle-aged when I was born. But Daddy always loved to tease her about getting older and letting her hair get gray and saying that if she got too old for him, he was going to trade her in for a newer model and such like. But at last I suppose he went too far because he said that now that I was about to go off to school and in due course would be getting married, certainly she would want to pass on to my wife her beautiful diamond solitaire because she was getting too old now to be concerned about such things. But that's where he had reckoned without *her* sharpness and her wit, indeed had simply reckoned without her. Because no sooner were the words out of his mouth than she turned on him suddenly and said, with some vehemence, "Well, young man, don't make your plans too soon because let me tell you right now there are two things I never expect to see in my lifetime. And don't you ever forget it. And one of them is my name on a tombstone and the other one is my diamond ring on another woman's hand!" Daddy was tickled of course, but he knew when enough was enough. So he hushed up; and as far as I know, that was the last word that ever passed between them on that particular subject. And really I don't suppose there was anything else to be said in the matter.

Change of Life

WHEN I WAS TWELVE YEARS OLD, MY MOTHER began to go through her menopause, which my father and other people of his generation usually referred to as the change of life. And of course, like most of my contemporaries, I had had no sexual instruction from either of my parents—mostly just a lot of misinformation from my schoolmates. And as is usual in such cases, I got the idea that it was all dirty and something to giggle about, while naturally being horrified by the whole thing—something I hardly dared communicate to my buddies, who were probably just as ignorant as I was. Anyhow, when my father began, awkwardly and with obvious embarrassment to try to communicate to me what it was all about, he said merely it was a time when "ladies" quit being "mammas" and began being "women." But not a word about the gynecological facts involved in what it all *meant*.

But then after I was grown, one of my aunts (the wife of one of my uncles) told me that when she began having her periods early in her teens, she had no idea on earth what was happening. And when I asked her if she wasn't absolutely terrified, she said well, no, her girlfriends told her what it was all about. Apparently, it had never occurred to her to ask her mother. But what I found even more horrifying was that it had apparently never occurred to her mother to tell her what to expect when she got to "that age." This was the same mother, by the way, who, when my aunt told her their neighbors across the street, who were Jewish, were going to have their brand new baby boy circumcised, and then asked her what that meant, simply told her to look it up in the dictionary. I don't know whether the South in the forties, the time I'm writing about, was any more prudish than the rest of the country. Certainly, it had always considered such subjects matters of great delicacy, to be handled with great tact and as many ellipses as possible. And I remembered, in reading *Gone with the Wind*, that Margaret Mitchell had observed, in speaking of the antebellum South, that at no time, before or since, had so low a premium been placed on feminine naturalness. But all such anecdotes as I've just related often seemed to me to smack of ostriches with their heads in the sand, indeed pure, almost criminal negligence.

Whatever the case, when my father told me about my mother's condition, I had no idea, really, what it was all about except that she seemed depressed in spirits and extremely anxious most of the time. I do remember waking up in the night once and hearing her crying and my father trying to comfort her. And she told him she wished she was dead and she feared he might "go" before her, and then what on earth would she do? And my father told her to hush or she would wake me. And I remember it was the first time I had ever realized that my parents might have lives that were secret, separate from mine; and I could feel some sort of wall going up between them and me.

But perhaps most frightening of all was the Sunday afternoon, when we were driving out to my uncle's in the country, where my grandfather used to live—a place that had always seemed the most safe and secure of all—where more than one generation of my family had lived, where my uncle and aunt were always at home on Sunday afternoon because all the family expected them to be; they were all so used to going out to see Pa at that time, they continued doing so after his death. *And you could count on it.* And such knowledge of course is the main source of security for any child. Anyhow, not long ago I was driving out on that same road, to my uncle's house: he's long been gone of course, but his daughter still lives there in her widowhood. And suddenly I looked about me and in a flash recalled this was where it had happened—my mother's suddenly bursting into tears—wild, hysterical, incomprehensible—on that Sunday afternoon so many years ago. I even remembered what my parents had been talking about moments before: my father's reminiscence of the time some years ago when a young man from down in Mississippi had come acourting a local girl who duly married him but continued to live with her parents because her husband was a traveling salesman and was so often away from home, which nobody in town thought was a good thing.

My father suddenly stopped the car and leaned over and put his arm around her and whispered, "Now hush, Mamma, you don't want to get Sonny all upset. Think of him and remember your duty to the family and all the rest of us. You just can't lose control of yourself this way, and so far you've handled it all so well." But she wailed, "I just can't seem to do it any more, and now what *will* I do? I'm nothing but a millstone around your neck, and I wish I was dead." But my father said, "You'll just have to try harder. You know, all of us are pulling for you, and you have a duty to all of us too. You can do it; I know you can." And then we drove on to my uncle's as though nothing whatever had happened; and by the time we got there, my mother had more or less managed to compose herself and nobody would have known there had been the outburst of a short time before.

But of course I never forgot it, and I suppose it was one of the rites of passage in my young life—my mother, so charming, so bright, all of a sudden seeming to go haywire right in the middle of a fine Sunday afternoon, when she seemed in good health, and looking forward with pleasure to visiting family whom she was very fond of. None of it seemed to make sense, and I couldn't imagine what could be wrong with her. She hadn't seemed to be ill, and she *looked* all right. I was of course terrified and wondered if she might be going to die, like the lady across the street from us had done several years before, leaving two children one of whom was my playmate. Could any loss be more terrible?

So it was that night when my father came into my room when I was getting ready for bed that he told me about "the change" and what it was doing to my mother. And he said I mustn't worry: all ladies went through it and I must be patient with her and it would come out all right. Our family doctor, Dr. Tom Baynes, had said so; and he was in touch with high-powered doctors in Memphis who could tell him what the latest developments in treating this trouble were. And nothing bad was going to happen, but I should keep it all quiet from my schoolmates because they might think it was all a subject for snickering and joking. It was the first time I had ever heard that illness and suffering could be a subject for levity, and I found that knowledge puzzling, not to say appalling. But again, my father never told me why; and I still perhaps hold that against him all these years later. In general, I knew that he was more prudish than my mother, as was the case with many Southern men and their wives; and in my own adulthood I have known a celebrated football coach who, in listing the "bad language" he wouldn't let his team use, called only the initials of the words, all of them familiar obscenities too. But then later on I met his mother, a good stout Methodist; and I got the feeling that there was little you could tell *her* about football or the men who played it either and she had probably washed out a good many mouths with soap in her day.

So the months went on, and on the whole there were few more dramatic outbursts like the one on that dreadful Sunday.

But my mother couldn't sleep at night, and more and more she began withdrawing from the friends and family with whom she was—and always had been—so popular. She had always been so amusing, such good company, everybody said—and such a delightful hostess who was a wonderful cook; and now it was as though she wanted to give it all up and stay at home. And at the least sign of any trouble, she would call my father and he would have to come home from the store and try to reason her back into good spirits. And of course she seemed to have less and less time for me, seemed less and less interested in my lessons at school, my progress in studying the piano; and I felt that somehow she was being changed into another person and one I didn't really know or understand.

The one thing that my father was firm about, though, was her bridge club, which had met every other Tuesday since before World War I! And he wouldn't let her quit going to every meeting: he said it was good for her to be forced to put her best foot forward, even if it was only an act. She couldn't just retire from life: that way madness would surely lie. But it got to be more and more of a struggle to persuade her to go every time the club met. She would manage to get through the meetings with no apparent trouble; but when she came home afterwards, she was exhausted from all the effort it had cost her. Different friends tried to cheer her up, telling her about their own experiences in similar circumstances; but her misery didn't want that sort of company. But what did it want? I doubt that she or anybody else ever knew. More and more she became simply withdrawn into herself and seemingly uninterested in so much that had been her life and her loves before. And it was obvious that she was continuing to go downhill.

Finally, Dr. Tom said she would have to be taken to Memphis, where she could be treated by people who specialized in the sort of illness from which she was suffering. There were also hospitals where such people could be treated to the exclusion of all others too. That was the place for her, Dr. Tom said. So that's where she was taken, and she stayed for six weeks with only my father being allowed to see her. It was decided that I shouldn't go: it might upset her too much and might not be very good for me either. And secretly I was glad: I didn't want to see her any more in the state she had been in when she left home—not her old self, not the mother I knew. And I was learning, I now know, what illness could do to people besides afflict them with pain and suffering—how it could isolate them from all those they loved, wrap them entirely in themselves, cut them off from the world about them so they became immured in a kind of living death. Who could want anyone he loved forced to suffer such horrors, such indecencies?

So I stayed with various ones of the aunts and uncles on the weekends when my father went down to Memphis to see her. And to tell the truth, I began to enjoy those weekends, where there was no sickness, no sorrow, no suffering—where everything seemed "normal" and I was back safely in childhood and not forced to take on so much of the world that I felt was way too big for me. But I felt guilty for what seemed like my deserting my mother. Did I want her to stay in the hospital forever if she wasn't going to come back her old self? Would even death itself be preferable to the shadowy existence she had endured as her illness deepened? And such thoughts were terrifying: how could I feel that way about my own mother?

I remember when my father came home on Christmas Eve (I had had to write all our Christmas cards that year) so he could call my mother's Memphis doctor in some privacy, which he did, then burst into tears ("of joy," he said) at the good news the doctor gave him, that my mother would soon be well enough to come home. But I had mixed feelings myself. Did they *know* she would really recover or would she have a relapse? Would we have to be with her all the time, watching for the first signs of such impending trouble? It was a disturbing thought and one I didn't want to dwell on.

I had been making my own adjustment to her being gone very well, I thought. I was getting used to doing my lessons and practicing my piano pieces diligently, with no urging from her or anybody else. And there was no one around to ask questions about whatever I wanted to do, perhaps no one to say "no." And did I, without saying so or facing up to it, really enjoy my new freedom so much that I didn't ever want to return to the old ways? That was a disturbing thought also. And doubly so because it was tinged with guilt. If I really and truly loved my mother, would I be feeling that way? And of course it was something you couldn't ask anybody about. And how much would she be changed when she returned? I had been told that some of the treatments she was being given affected the memory, even caused some temporary loss of it; but would it be only that—temporary? Suppose she didn't remember me or her other family and her friends? Would it all be something you would have to make allowances for, for the rest of her life? That was a dreadful possibility. Did something inside me *fear* seeing her again? I was afraid even to think about it.

Finally, a few weeks after Christmas the Memphis doctor told my father that my mother could leave when he came down to see her the next Sunday. And of course he was overjoyed and couldn't wait for the next weekend to come. I was to go spend the weekend with my uncle and aunt out in the country, and he and my mother would stop by there on the way back from Memphis and take me on back to town. Needless to say, it was a day of considerable stress and strain for me—wondering what my mother would be like when she returned, wondering whether we could go on with our lives as we had been, whether she would realize that some things couldn't now be the same as they had been and that I had become something of a "big boy" in her absence, mainly because, I suppose, I had been forced to. And would she accept that? It was all such matters that preyed on my mind that weekend—eager to see my mother again, hoping that she would indeed be restored to her old self, the person I knew and loved, yet somehow fearful that it might not be that way.

So it was with some diffidence that when they drove up into my uncle's driveway I ran out to greet them. But I saw at once that everything was going to be all right. Because my mother spoke up strong and well, in her old voice, like her old self and called out to me, "I'm back—I hope for keeps—and you've turned into a regular *man* while I was away. I certainly can't call you 'Sonny' any more." And then much to my surprise, I found myself bursting into laughter. But then after that I went up and hugged her good and hard.

The Clothesline

WHEN MY MOTHER AND FATHER WERE MARRIED, they went to live in her parents' house on Jackson Street in Woodville. Her parents had been dead for some years, and her only close relative was her brother; and he wanted the family farm. So it was all very amicably arranged, and my mother took the house, and he took the farm. My father was already established in his hardware business—a partnership with his younger brother, and he said he couldn't take on a farm as well. So that was the way it was all settled. The house, which had been rented out since my grandparents' deaths (they died almost one right after the other in the great flu epidemic of 1918) needed a lot of repairs and refurbishment, so that was what they did before they moved in.

Meanwhile they had rooms down the street at Mrs. Stewart's and took their meals at Mrs. Higgins's boarding house. Of course it all sounds somewhat antediluvian now and something like living from hand to mouth, but in those days (back in the early twenties) there wasn't much choice. And of course newlyweds didn't expect to have a complete house and home right after they married then: you worked, you saved, and you waited. And when you could afford it, then you made your move. And I think my parents must have been very cautious in the fixing-up they did do, mainly painting and papering. But they made few structural changes. O, they put a built-in bookcase on one side of the living room fireplace and a window seat on the other, one of their few gestures toward grandeur. But they didn't take out the old cistern that dominated the back porch, and they didn't move the bathroom, which opened out of a tiny hallway, where the telephone was, between the living room and their bedroom. Only years later, after I was in college, did they extend the hallway all the way to the back of the house and do away with the long back porch that had been partially filling in the "L," which constituted something of a "shotgun" design for that part of the house all those years, and thereby give it something of order and symmetry, which it had never had before.

They made a few other efforts at modernizing but nothing too pretentious. One thing was that they cut a door between the dining room and the kitchen. Before that, whatever the weather, hot or cold, you went from one to the other via the back porch (they both opened onto that), which ran the length of the house. And I remember as long as she lived, my mother always spoke of going "up in the house" when she was ready to leave the kitchen for any other room. And I've wondered since then whether that might not have been a holdover from the days when kitchens were often placed in the backyard—completely separate from the house, mainly to avoid the danger of fire. The only other bedroom besides their own was what we always called the guest room, even after I adopted it as my own in childhood, another holdover perhaps from the old days when everybody made a point of having a "spare" room for company even if they weren't expecting a great deal. Years later, after I was grown and they decided to fill in the back-porch "L," they added another bedroom and bath which duly became mine and the "guest room" reverted to its original status. After all, this was still the South, and hospitality wasn't just a word. (I still can't imagine anybody on earth coming to our house any time of the day or night without being given *something* to eat or drink. He might decline the offer, but it was always made. To overlook it would have been considered barbarous.)

But really that was about all they did at first except for buying some new furniture. My father, who was one of seven children, five boys and two girls, had little if any household goods to contribute: there were simply too many others who had a claim on it, furniture and all the rest. And my mother and her brother had had a sale shortly after they lost their parents (or as my mother used to put it, "after our home was broken up," which in my childhood became the most terribly final phrase imaginable). So there was very little of their furniture left. And neither my father nor my mother was inclined to look backward to the old days, at least not at that point. They wanted a new day and a new life, I think, after the sorrows they had recently experienced. (My father's home had also recently been "broken up," with the death of his mother and his younger sister.) And anyway nobody thought anything about old stuff then; in fact, they most of them wouldn't have given *antiques* the time of day. It was just "old furniture," and many of them thought they had entirely too many things left over from the past, too much dead wood, you might say, right that minute. O, there were a few old things that were around, mainly just because they were needed, like the old oak dinner table from my father's family he said they had all grown up fighting around. But there was nothing particularly "fine" about any of it.

But when I was in high school, my mother did decide to start getting together and having refinished as many of the old family pieces as she could—the old secretary that had been her grandfather's and an old linen chest, put together with wooden pegs instead of nails, that had "come over the mountains from North Carolina in an ox cart." But again, they were just things you *had*, things that were "in the family" and not something to go off and *buy* just to show off with and have folks "ooh" and "aah" over. You certainly ought not to abuse them, certainly ought to respect them, the old family things; but finally they were nothing to *your* credit, any more than your ancestors. The real question perhaps was not their distinction, which might rub off on you, but simply whether *you* could be worthy of *them*. And my mother had no more contemptuous dismissal of both folks and furniture which were venerated simply because they had outlived their time than to call them "broken down aristocracy." And as for the D. A. R. and the U. D. C. and all such, well, you could join if you wanted to; but she certainly didn't need any organization to tell her who she was, she said: that was something anybody who was "folks" was born knowing. And it had nothing to do with money and appearances but what was on the inside of you. My father went even further. He said all this foolishness about working on your family tree might reveal some things you'd just as soon not have known: you might find some of your ancestors swinging from branch to branch thereon!

So they moved into the old house, which, I should say, did have a distinguished if somewhat shabby looking exterior—white columns, green shutters and all—and built shortly after the Civil War; but again, they weren't going to spend money they didn't have right then fixing it up. The cosmetics could wait. And then of course after I came along, they always said, well, every extra penny they now had must go towards what I called my "keduation." And in some way even then I think I knew it was just one more restatement of the old adage "Pretty is as pretty does." And more than once I thought, one way or another, I had been hearing that all my life. Why couldn't things be both beautiful *and* real? And why did you always have to have veneered furniture or silver-plated dinner ware instead of *the real thing* that was genuine all the way through? Even then I wanted the real thing, and I recall my increasing respect for such words as "genuine" and "sterling," sayings like "all wool and a yard wide." And I didn't even like to play simplified "arrangements" of the classics when I began taking piano lessons.

My mother did have her mother's Haviland china (dead white with the scalloped gold band around the borders and so delicate you could almost see your hand through it), and after she and my father were married he did "finish out" the place settings for her: she finally had twelve of everything. And in due course she even bought some fine crystal, but she never had much "real" silver. But that didn't seem to bother her at all. It was what went with the dining utensils that counted with her; and she knew she was a first-rate cook—and a real artist too: she was not one to paint by numbers, and yes, the genius was in the details. But I never knew her to use a recipe for anything except some difficult kind of cake or other dessert, some complicated casserole or pudding, some "made" dish. The rest was all tasting and smelling and judging the consistency by inserting a broom straw bent double into the batter, to see whether it was firming up in the right way. And it was a pinch of this and a "season to taste" of that, and any real cook needed no instruction in that.

Of course the worst thing she could say about another woman was that she *wouldn't* cook, and somehow she always managed to make such a failing seem the unforgivable female sin, worse even than adultery. After all, a woman who *wouldn't* cook was repudiating the entire female function. And whatever adultery was, it wasn't that. Once years later in a conversation with the barman at the Ritz Hotel in Paris I found him thoroughly sympathetic to such views: a woman who *wouldn't* cook was "no woman," he said. And I wished my mother had been alive to hear him. Yes, Woodville, Tennessee, and Paris, France, weren't so different after all. And maybe it was the French themselves who put it best: the more things changed, the more they stayed the same.

So I was used to doing without things that were more for "show" than substance and concentrating on the things that had something of value on the "inside." Yes, I wore good clothes, but always they had to be good ones that would last. And since I had no younger brothers to pass them on to, that somehow seemed a waste. But quality always showed, my mother said, and she had rather have a "few good things" than a lot of junk, no matter how elegant it *looked.* And always you had to look neat and clean, but you couldn't spend a lot of time worrying about your looks. If the Lord hadn't intended you to be pretty, well, you just had to live with that and let Him take care of the rest. And anybody that took too much thought about it or placed too much importance on looks wasn't worth worrying about anyhow.

So early on I began to feel somehow that my parents weren't helping me much with my social standing. For one thing, they were older than the parents of all my friends: they didn't marry until "late in life," and by the time I came along they were both middle-aged and, I thought, old and dowdy. And they didn't smoke or drink or dance, like the parents of my friends; and they always kept talking about the future (the last thing a young person ever wants to hear—his favorite word is *now*) and the things that really mattered, the things that would last; but all such things had somehow to be validated by the past too. And somehow with them it was all one: past, present, and future.

Often the old ways, the old times were best but not necessarily so: neither of my parents seemed to have any illusions about that. And my father would sometimes snort, "People are always talking about 'the good old days.' But I can tell you they were often bad old days." But he never said anything more after that, so I could only imagine what he meant. *Fashion* obviously didn't mean anything to him nor did *style.* And keeping up with the Joneses would have been impossible for him to contemplate. In fact, he didn't even seem to think much of that great American word *new.* So what did he go by then? Well, like I said, things that were inherently of value, that would last, and depended neither on the social context nor the world's approval for their worth. I even thought at times it was like my mother's saying "Good clothes are always in style." Like the Bible said, he certainly wasn't carried about by every wind of doctrine.

Of course every year my mother bought one good black dress at Levy's "Ladies Toggery," as it was called, in Memphis, where the sales ladies up on the third floor were always to be found calmly seated beneath the crystal chandeliers in elegant Louis Quinze chairs that might have come from Versailles. (Certainly, the idea of them standing behind a counter would have been unthinkable.) And when a customer did appear, they would graciously rise, pince-nez and "foundation garments" firmly in place, and with the condescension of a Queen Dowager ask whether they could "help." My mother deliberated long and hard before she bought the annual black dress too, but I never knew her to be dissatisfied with it afterwards, certainly not to the point of wanting to return it. Both she and my father knew their own minds, and they did their deliberating beforehand and after that never looked back. I did venture to ask her one time why she always chose black for her "good" dress, and predictably she replied that black was always in good taste, always in style, and of course it would go with *anything.* Also, she added that since she was not a small woman, she didn't want anything that made her look even more of a blot on the landscape than she already was. And black was good for that. As I've already suggested, she was a woman of little vanity and few illusions.

So I thought I knew them, their thoughts and views on manners and morals and most everything else. And I thought they would continue in their appointed ways as long as they lived, and their lives would hold no surprises. But that's where I was wrong, as we so often are when we think we know it all, especially about the past. And more and more the Bible tells it like it is when it says we are fearfully and wonderfully made. But ironically the revelation didn't come until after they were both dead and gone, and then it came from one of the aunts—the one I always called Auntee, who was as much of a realist as my mother ever was, indeed perhaps even more so because she didn't call a spade a spade but more likely, as she said herself, a dirty old shovel. And furthermore she had been married to a widower who had been married twice before and was *old enough to be her father.* So she knew about things. And it was she who told me what happened one morning at the breakfast table shortly after my parents were married and, I suppose, hadn't yet finished the work they were doing on the house and weren't really settled in yet. And it was this.

All of a sudden my father seemed to freeze in mid-air with his coffee cup halfway between the table and his mouth as he looked out the kitchen window into the backyard—seeing something out there that was apparently new to him, something he hadn't noticed before. And without saying a word to my mother, he deliberately rose from his chair and just as deliberately walked to the back door, opened it, and stepped down from the porch into the yard and made straight for the clothesline, almost as though he had never seen one before. And very carefully, and again very deliberately, he took it down from the posts to which it was fixed, rolled it up, and brought it into the house and, according to what my mother told my aunt, seemed to stand there with it in his hands as though he were confronting her with some heinous offense (she couldn't imagine what) and said to her, as calmly as if he were making his final pronouncement on human behavior and particularly on the married state itself, "If it hadn't been for the washtub and the clothesline, my mother would be alive this day; and I'm not going to have you killing yourself with nothing but drudgery while you're still a young woman. And the first thing I'm going to do tomorrow is get you a wash-woman so you won't ever have to do that. My mother wasn't but sixty-two when she died, and we all thought she was an old woman. Just worked to death was what it was, really. But by God, people don't have to do that now, anymore than they have to die of typhoid fever at twenty-seven, like my younger sister." And he walked over and threw the clothesline in the garbage can, then stalked out the back door to the garage and his pickup truck.

I gather my mother wasn't unduly perturbed by this display of temper: she had seen that before. But she told Auntee she *was* surprised to hear him take the Lord's name in vain, and indeed I never heard him use profanity or a four-letter word in my life. And I wondered what his mother, my grandmother, whom he and all the others adored, would have said. But I thought his reckless language might have been some indication of his affection for her and his fear that something of the same fate might overtake my mother. And she would have understood. Suffice it to say that it was only shortly thereafter that Aunt Georgia Simpson began to do our washing: my father took it by her house down on the railroad cut every Wednesday morning on the way to the store, then picked it up on his way home to supper on Saturday night. And that arrangement went on till well after I left to go off to school.

But I never forgot Auntee's story of how it all came about, how I learned something then about my father and, to some extent, my mother too that I had never known before and how I came to know them in a somewhat different way and thought about them differently even now that they were dead. And I would recollect that, unlike many people, my father never got the giggles when he saw a washing machine almost defiantly sitting on the front porch of some sharecropper's house down in the Mississippi Bottom after TVA came to our county the summer I was twelve. And he would never complain that nobody could cook a ham or bake a coconut cake now as good as my grandmother back in the old days, beloved though she was by them all. And though his father, my grandfather, had been a real live Confederate veteran, he didn't spend much time lamenting the fate of the Lost Cause either. For him I think it was just one more thing you had to put behind you and go on ahead from the present—and the past—into the future, no matter how sad it might be sometimes. And he could even laugh at a photograph of my grandfather and two other old veterans down at our depot all dressed up in their Sunday best, waiting for the train that would take them to the annual Confederate reunion and say he knew those three old men still had stout soldiers' hearts whatever their age because there they were going off to the big city (Birmingham, I think) and all ready to kick up their heels and cut the pigeon's wing and he would bet they didn't have as much as $50 between the three of them right that minute!

Well, in due course I went off to school and fell in with a group of Southerners, both students and faculty, that spent a lot of time discussing the ways of history and the imminent decline and fall of Western Civilization and always more or less refusing to let the dead bury the dead, Southern or otherwise. And of course enjoying every minute of it too.

For a time I found it all somewhat romantic and glamorous, all their talk of the War and Reconstruction, to say nothing of the antebellum days; but I noticed that their version of it was inclined to be much more deodorized than what I had been brought up on. It was all high constitutional issues too and Technicolor, with little dysentery and no pneumonia. And I thought I might finally have to beg to differ with them, like a real revisionist historian. They didn't have any monopoly on the script and certainly nothing that entitled them to imply that they owned the show and your testimony was but naught—just like saying "you should have seen the garden last year."

After all, there had been my own grandfather, whom I remembered very well; and he had been at Appomattox and had seen General Lee riding down on Traveler to bid his men farewell. And he hadn't particularly distinguished himself in combat either: he ran away from school, to join his older brother, who had already enlisted, and remained a private in the artillery until the very end, when he was "paroled" at Appomattox. And after the war he had emigrated from Virginia to West Tennessee hoping to recoup his failed fortunes, which of course he never did; but he did have the great good fortune to meet and marry my grandmother, whose people, unlike his own, had not been slave owners but did have a small farm, from which they managed to eke out a living, with little help, I gather, from my grandfather, who mostly liked to sit on the front porch and talk about the old days. And more than once I heard my father imply that if it hadn't been for their mother, they would have all starved to death. It was something like this that I longed to tell my new friends, though I wasn't altogether sure what they would make of it. Indeed I wasn't always sure what I thought about it myself.

But I knew this much. History wasn't just something I had "taken up"—another enthusiasm, another sport, like genealogy. I had often had it, the ocular proof, right there in the house with me, in the person of my grandfather, who ate peas with his knife and didn't like to bathe any more often than he could help. And it was all quite literally in my blood. But most of all I wanted to tell them about my father and the clothesline. It seemed to me somehow that they needed to hear about that more than anything else I could tell them, and I always wondered what they would say.

Now, Baby, Do You Know One Thing?

"NOW, BABY, DO YOU KNOW ONE THING?" THAT WAS the way Auntee always began her most startling revelations, her signal that something extraordinary was coming. Never did the dramatic *slide* into her conversation: she heralded it from afar. She knew what it looked like too, the color of its eyes and the smell of its breath; and she called a spade a spade, though there might occasionally be euphemisms for the sake of her younger, more innocent auditors. ("Oh, he's just got his 'pizzum' sprung," she would remark about someone who was suffering from the "old man's complaint," prostate trouble. Again, "men are *weak*; and if it weren't for women upholding the morals of the community, there just wouldn't be any! And that's why people expect a woman to keep her skirts down." That was her watered-down explanation of the double standard.) But she would immediately nod her head perfunctorily as if to indicate that she had observed the proprieties and knew she had; and now that she had gotten *that* out of the way, she would proceed with the conversation, "go ahead on," as she would put it, to the scandal of her old-maid sister, Cousin Rebecca, who thought that was a tacky expression. "Common" was what *she* called it.

And in some ways that was the story of Auntee's life: scandalizing Cousin Rebecca or someone like her, whoever was too refined or genteel or, finally, dead. Because that was what Auntee stood for—*life* and lots of it. You could even tell it from the way they looked, those two: whereas Cousin Rebecca was tall and thin ("poor as a snake," their cook, old fat Florence, used to say) and all sharp edges and angles, hair firmly swept back into a "club" behind her head, no excess baggage for her in either body or spirit, Auntee was short and stout, almost dumpy really, and everything about her was round and comfortable. Her hair was naturally curly and very difficult to control, but she took that in her stride, too. "I just can't worry about it," she would say. And so it usually looked as though it were in various stages of exploding, in a mass of pepper-and-salt ringlets, from her head. After I learned something of classical mythology, I even thought of comparing her to the serpent-haired Medusa—a benevolent Medusa, of course. Also, though she wasn't ugly, Auntee wasn't by any stretch of the imagination pretty or even attractive: she was *plain.* But then *beauty* wasn't high on her list of commendable attributes: "pretty, pretty," she would observe with disdain, of some highly touted beauty, implying of course that pretty was as pretty did and anyone could look good. As for her fully developed figure, she would say that that had never held her back: why, her husband used to say when he reached out to hug a girl, he wanted a *handful.* And then she would nod, maybe even wink; and Cousin Rebecca, if she were present, would purse her lips and look stern and reproving. But then she would sigh and set her eyes on the ceiling as if to say there was just no controlling Auntee.

And of course there wasn't, and I don't suppose there ever had been. Auntee was really a cousin of my mother; but I had never known her well till her husband, Mr. Campbell—who had been a well-to-do farmer over in the next county but then "lost everything he had"—died and she moved back to live with Cousin Rebecca. Auntee's given name was Helen, but I never thought about that because "Auntee" seemed to suit her so much better: she *looked* like an Auntee ought to look—comfortable and indulgent but by no means undiscriminating—so I must have given her the name very early in the day. I certainly can't remember ever calling her anything else. She accepted it quite naturally too; and one of my earliest memories of her is of snuggling my head into her very ample but firm bosom (she thought women who didn't wear brassieres were no better than they should be). I was full of some childhood grief that I can't even recollect now, and she hugged me very close and said—as if it were all a great wonder, some sort of miracle—"Baby, Auntee *loves* you." And that was the only thing that mattered. Truly it was indeed such a wonder and such a miracle—and still is. And I'm not too old either to enjoy thinking that there was once somebody for whom I would always be a child, always be a "Baby. " Perhaps it's significant that I now have no memory of my sorrow, only Auntee's assurance of her love, which was complete, unconditional, and forever.

Because that was what it was in her nature to do—to love. Unfortunately, she and Mr. Campbell had had no children; so she had been denied that outlet. But she had been devoted to him, and now she was devoted to Cousin Rebecca. And in both cases that might have taken some doing. Mr. Campbell was a good deal older than she was and had been married before; and, I gather, in addition to suffering the bad luck of hard times, he had also been something of a profligate. ("He just ran through everything he had in no time at all," I once heard my mother say.) Cousin Rebecca was also a difficult object of the affections. An old-maid school teacher for most of her life, she was now retired on her savings and her very modest pension, with nothing to do but boss the whole world as though it were just the fifth grade all over again. She would have been more than willing to boss Auntee too, but of course Auntee wasn't having any of that. That might have been difficult too at first because I suspect now that Auntee was financially dependent on Cousin Rebecca—at least until a couple of years after she came to live there when she just went out and got herself a job as manager of the high school lunchroom, a job that she loved and performed very well. (Florence the cook, had no such graceful deliverance from Cousin Rebecca's bossing: she finally had to die in self-defense, my mother always said.)

For one thing, Auntee's job kept her out in public with people; and, as she put it, she *loved* people though—she said—she still knew a knave or a fool when she saw one. And she got to be around young people and perhaps adopt them, in her mind, as children of her own. Certainly, the feelings were reciprocated; and "Miss Helen" became a fixture at the school: listener to teenage sorrows and complaints, dispenser of advice, healer of wounds incurred in the line of duty (the football team always adored her), fine cook and comfort-giver—ultimately, everybody's aunt. And so she found further objects for her affections. She kept on loving Cousin Rebecca too—when Cousin Rebecca would let her. Cousin Rebecca had led a life really swept and garnished, with few human entanglements along the way; and I think she secretly—perhaps not always so secretly—harbored some resentment against Auntee, who had *gotten away* and been married ("had had a husband and a home of her own and nice things," as someone always put it) but then had had to return home as something of a prodigal daughter, whose husband at least had wasted his substance. And so Cousin Rebecca may have behaved to Auntee as something of the elder brother in the parable: after all, she had been a good girl and stayed home and *behaved*, so why should there be such a fuss about the bereaved Auntee? Perhaps she even thought there ought not to be any more cakes or ale for *anybody*. But once again Auntee had gotten away—this time only as far as the high school lunchroom—but that was far enough.

I'm sure now that she knew, in the normal course of things, that she would have to care for Cousin Rebecca in her last years. But there was no point in taking on that burden, certainly in withdrawing into old age along with Cousin Rebecca, until she had to. And even then, Auntee wasn't promising anything. She certainly wasn't going to let Cousin Rebecca turn *her* into an old woman before her time. As matters turned out, she didn't have to make any difficult choices. Cousin Rebecca went into a long physical decline, fortunately never becoming senile; but in those days (back before World War II) you were still able to get enough domestic help with such affairs on your own. And let's face it: it was a case of *necessity*. There were few nursing homes or such like then. You simply kept your sick folks at home and *managed*. So Cousin Rebecca died and left Auntee her modest estate, and Auntee could have quit the lunchroom right then. But, of course, she didn't want to: it would have meant withdrawing from a good part of her life. And she wasn't about to just sit at home and hold her hands.

She was always on the side of life, indeed, soon after her death, years later, one of her friends (not the most alive one, as you may imagine) said to me, in some sort of wonder, almost amazement really, "Helen got so much out of life." To this comment I replied with, I fear, ill-concealed exasperation, "She put so much *in*!" And I don't know what my rejoinder did for Auntee's old friend, Miss Susie Larrimore, who I always thought was too lazy—and too stingy—to do much *for* anybody, good or bad: in any case, she certainly wasn't *giving* anything away. But it did me a lot of good to say that to her: I thought she had it coming, for one thing, after a lifetime of leeching off her friends, both in substance and in spirit. Further, it did me good in another way to begin putting Auntee together in my mind. What had she meant to me, what did she still mean to me—and why?

What she meant, for one thing, was absolute realism in facing what had to be faced: no whining, no complaining, and no Pollyanna smiling through it either. She could suffer fools gladly but only just so long, and she didn't always have the soft answer that turneth away wrath either. Once when I interrupted her in the middle of one of her best stories, she snapped, "Now, who was telling this anyhow?" And she didn't call me "Baby" that time either. Then once when I was "taking dinner" with her and was so thoughtless as to ask *what kind* of pickle that was on the table, she replied, with some heat, "The best pickle in the world! I made it myself." And I knew that I stood corrected. (She always said it was the worst manners in the world to be so persnickety about what you ate: anybody like that, well, you could just put it down every time, he'd been raised on branch water.) But temper rarely colored her judgments about matters of faith and morals. Concerning the possibility that she herself might be an invalid in her last days, she told me, "For goodness' sake, Baby, if I have to be 'put somewhere' "—her contemptuous reference to the modern distaste and consequent euphemisms for ultimate necessities—"see that I'm at least kept *clean* because I've certainly washed many a butt in my day." Another time, when a couple of our town's leading citizens had to serve time for embezzlement, she said, "Now it's all very well to say they are *hypocrites* who ought to be *ostracized* (two words that fascinated me when I was little) if they ever come back here. But that's beside the point. They just got in over their heads and tried unsuccessfully to get out, and anybody else might do the same. And if you think different, you just don't know human nature." When the Presbyterians had to get rid of their preacher because he was too openly affectionate toward the young boys in the church, she said to me, "There's no use getting on a high horse about all that. Now, Baby, do you know one thing? That sort of thing is just like anything else: it's a *disease*." And when the doctor-husband of one of our cousins left her for a nurse he had met during his tour of duty in World War II, Auntee silenced comment with, "There's nothing to it but that they were far away from home and thrown together in very terrible circumstances. Why, Baby, do you know they were working right over there behind the front lines night and day, cutting off arms and legs and heads and everything else? And you just don't know what you'd do in a situation like that."

Another time, when one of the cousins lost her husband (who had been some sort of off-brand Baptist or whatever), Auntee brought back the following report from the funeral: "Well, after she moved to Memphis, Irene always did have the most peculiar-looking friends. I don't reckon they ever *stole* anything, but it certainly wasn't because they didn't look as if they could or would. But anyhow, when we got down there for the funeral, do you know that Irene had a woman to preach his funeral? Named 'Sister' something or other. Anyhow, I looked over at Irene's niece, Mary Elizabeth, who's right civilized, and raised my eyebrows; but she just nodded and went right on. So I gathered there wasn't anything earthshaking about such doings among that set of folks. And, Baby, do you know one thing? Sister Do-funny or whoever she was made a real good talk too. On the text 'Thou preparest a table before me in the presence of mine enemies,' which I did think rather strange in view of the fact that Irene was always the world's worst cook and lazy into the bargain. But then, you know, there's just no accounting for tastes."

Another time, when one of her sourpuss friends (that same Miss Susie Larrimore probably) remonstrated with her for not attending church more regularly, she snapped out, "Well, I just don't want to be struck by lightning! Because the last time I set foot up there in the Methodist Church (where I was born and raised) I looked around at who *was* there, and I never saw such a bunch of sots and backbiters and whoremongers in my life. And that's the God's truth. But do you know one thing? God Almighty's not going to stand for all that carrying on forever, and someday He's going to take a hand up there, and I don't particularly care to be there when it happens! I know I'm a sinner too, just like everybody else; but I'm not a fool. And I resent all that crowd sitting up there on Sunday looking as pious and sanctified as a herd of white-faced cattle. I don't know what the Lord thinks about it all, but they sure haven't fooled *me*!" Then there was the Sunday when one of her contemporaries asked the *whole Sunday school class* what they would think if she carried her senile older sister to a matinee at the picture show *on Sunday* and some of the class members expressed reservations. When Auntee got home, she exploded, "Thunderation! The poor deluded old thing don't know who or where she is or one day from another; but if it will help her sister, who's been nursing her night and day and who's really the one to be considered now, I say go ahead on and *go*. The Lord has certainly got more things on His mind than to worry about some old women desecrating the Sabbath. But then most people don't really like to credit the Lord with having more sense than they do."

No prude, no hypocrite, Auntee always faced the truth, told the truth, and finally, I think, *did* the truth—but always with joy, almost zeal, you might say. (When I was growing up there was a section in the Methodist hymnal that fascinated me: "Activity and Zeal." What it all meant was beyond me, but the hymns therein were some of my favorites: bold and militant, even sanguinary, but full of fervor and a joyful noise.) Life might not have seemed to deal Auntee a very good hand, but what cards she had, she played wholeheartedly and well. She had nursed and buried an old husband and then nursed and buried an old sister. But neither of them was able to bury her. She had no children of her own, so she became an aunt to all other people's children. In more ways than one, she was a life-giver, not a death-dealer; in more ways than one, she never stayed home and held her hands. And always there was joy, even when she began her pronouncements with "Now, Baby, do you know one thing?" The world was good; the world was bad, usually a mixture of the two. The wonder of it all never ceased to amaze her and ultimately to give her joy—that she had been privileged to be part of such a spectacle, such a drama.

Once when we were driving home from a day in Memphis, she looked out at the lush West Tennessee countryside in the summer twilight and observed, "How beautiful it all is, and it's only *lent* to us for such a little while! How can people go through life just making money, 'getting ahead,' as they call it, accumulating *stuff* really, and just working and sleeping and eating and not having any *joy*? I never have understood that." Some years later and after I had moved away, she went to bed one night and just never woke up. But I understood that she had told the next-door neighbor the night before that she had had a sudden yearning for some catfish that afternoon and had just gone downtown and bought some to fry for her supper. And she had said, "I know it seems like a fool thing to do, but I wanted the fish and I had the money. And if I can't please myself in my old age, I might just as well not have lived at all. And do you know one thing?" And I could imagine her adding "Baby" if she had been talking to me. "If I die before morning, you can just tell everybody that here's one old woman who died with a belly full of catfish. And died happy too!"

The Legacy

THAT MORNING WHEN WE GOT TO MY UNCLE'S, the backyard was full of cars, some I didn't even recognize because they were from out of state. His wife, my aunt, had died after a very short illness two days before; and I hadn't been able to bring myself to enter the house since then. But I had heard all about everything that was going on over there because my father had hardly left my uncle's side the whole time: my uncle was seven years younger than he and thus his baby brother. And in many ways, my father still regarded him as a little boy; indeed, he called me by my uncle's name half the time, something I hadn't always appreciated until my mother had explained that it didn't mean that my father loved me any the less: my uncle and I were both his children, to his way of thinking, and thus equally precious. You couldn't imagine anybody having a favorite *child* now, could you, she wanted to know. But since I had no brothers and sisters myself, I wasn't sure about that either.

What my uncle ever thought of this confusion of names on my father's part, I never knew because he never said. Indeed, he never really *said* much of anything; my father did most of the talking in their business (they owned a hardware store) and in their personal relationship, I believe. (They had never had a cross word either, my mother always said.) When my uncle did speak, it was usually simply as a footnote or an emendation to something my father had said. And for the most part, this was true in his dealings with me, at least until I was an adolescent.

I remember once hearing him speak—and I thought with some approval—of old Dr. Steele, who had healed the sick and raised the dead—or at any rate presided over the births and deaths—of several generations all over our county years ago and in the process amassed a considerable fortune in money and land. But he never *said* much. And my mother said that was true: Dr. Steele would come and look at you and watch the progress of your ailment and you could die or get well or be resurrected but Dr. Steele hadn't said yet what was the matter with you or whether you would recover or anything else. But my uncle said Dr. Steele has gotten rich by not talking.

I suspect now, of course, that my uncle was jealous of me; and why shouldn't he have been? My father didn't marry until late in the day, and he was already middle-aged when I was born. And there was my uncle, who, all these years, in a big family (five boys and two girls) had been my father's favorite, his own little boy, you might say, now abandoned for a child of my father's own. So I suppose it was natural for him to resent me. But then I couldn't *help* being there either.

Of course my uncle wasn't abandoned: the mere thought would have horrified my father. But I knew that he never seemed to mind taking me down a peg or two, never seemed to mind deflating me when I was flying too high, or he thought, getting above myself. (He viewed my childhood enthusiasm for the movies and my later delight in opera with wry amusement: he said if I didn't watch out, I would begin to sound like a "Hollywood product" when I talked and look like a "Dago singer" when I gestured with my hands.) And when I was still older, especially after I went off to school, he would always begin with, "Now here's something you ought to know that your

Daddy probably hasn't told you...." And it would all suggest that my father was somehow mistakenly shielding me from the harsh facts of life, especially where money was concerned: perhaps he thought I was going to be something of a prodigal. But he, my uncle—the corrector, the reprover—was going to set both me and the record straight. (He never ceased to remind me that such limited success as he and my father had achieved in their business was all their own doing: "We had to start from scratch, with nobody to help us," he would say, "and what we've got, well, it's just what we've made ourselves.") Finally, there would be, "Of course, I never had all the opportunities you've had. Do you know that I always wanted to be a doctor, but where was a poor country boy like me going to get the money for that back then?" Of course it was all my own fault anyhow, he implied to have had so much *done* for me. (I don't remember his ever using the word "spoiled" at such times, but I always felt it somewhere near, hovering unstated in the air.) But then I remember that Daddy was supposed to have quit school to let him go, and I wondered whether he had forgotten that. And I sometimes wondered just how badly he had wanted to be a doctor anyway.

There was a time, after I got to be grown, when it all really used to get me down. When somebody lends you some money, you can repay the loan with interest, and the debt is cancelled. But a *moral* obligation, well, that's almost impossible to pay back. Sometimes, even after my uncle's death (and many years after my father and all the rest were gone) and after I had gained some small recognition in the world, I wondered even then what he would say if I could call him back from the grave and ask him, "Are you satisfied *now*?" But of course there's no profit in such speculation: indeed, that's one reason you write, to try to lay such ghosts.

Of course I would have given anything in the world for some sort of outward sign of affection from my uncle, but it never came. I even heard him speak once—I thought perhaps with some pride too—of not being a naturally "demonstrative" man; some things just didn't need to be said, he added. And indeed, the only time I ever saw him "lose control of himself," which is to say break down and cry, was the day my father died, and then it was all over in a minute. But always I looked up to him as a kind of second father (that's what he really was, Daddy always said) and wished we could be closer. As a little boy, I know it was all I could do—prompted by my father of course—to work myself up to asking my uncle for a nickel. You just didn't *ask* him for things; somehow I already knew that even then. And when I was much older, my mother told me that, where business was concerned, my uncle was a much "harder" man than my father, much more likely to say "no." Of course, my father never saw the distance between my uncle and me: in his eyes, my uncle could do no wrong. (Once when a customer ventured to doubt my uncle's word about his account—he kept the store's books—my father reached for one of the axes on display nearby and told him to get out of there and never come back!) But the distance was there, and of course it would only widen with time.

My aunt, of course, made all the difference. Warm, outgoing, really loving, one of a family of great charmers, she was easily the most popular woman in town, my father always said; and I simply adored her. She had taught school for many years and also directed the Methodist choir, and she knew everybody in the county. But the main thing for us was her affection for my uncle: "she's absolutely wild about him" my mother always said. (But even then I remember thinking she never said how he felt about her.) They had no children, which I always thought too bad; my aunt would have made a wonderful mother, I imagined, and perhaps my uncle would have been warmed and liberalized by parenthood.

But now my aunt was dead, after only a short illness too. She had never been very strong, I gather; and she couldn't ever say no to anybody who asked her to sing at a wedding or a funeral or take on yet another volunteer job. (She always got called on to arrange the music for all the home talent shows—the blackface minstrels, the beauty revues, and such like.) And I remember hearing my mother say that really, she "just lived on excitement." One time I even saw her dance a jig on the front porch for sheer joy when an old friend she hadn't seen in a long time arrived from Memphis for a visit. Finally, I suppose, it must all have caught up with her; but she had always said she had rather wear out than rust out, according to my mother. And now I was simply devastated. I was only thirteen, and it was my first real grief. My grandfather had died several years before; but he was a very old man, and I was afraid of him because of his great age and his big walrus mustache, and so he didn't count. But my aunt was only middle-aged: she had no business to go and die like that. But she had, and my uncle was left all alone now, a widower.

And I think that was probably the reason I didn't go over to their house after my aunt had died, not until the morning of the funeral: I didn't want to face him. He was such a restrained, quiet man—except for his sardonic wit, what everybody called his "dry" humor, which had sometimes been aimed, uncomfortably, at me—and so different in that way from my father, that I dreaded seeing him in the throes of raw grief. Surely he would be "demonstrative" now. On the other hand, I may have been fearful that he wouldn't appear grieved enough. My father, of course, could not mention my aunt now without tears. But perhaps my uncle was being his usual undemonstrative self. How could anybody know *what* he was feeling? And I remembered he said Dr. Steele had gotten rich by not talking.

So I had stayed away until then, but of course I had to go to the funeral. My mother was unwell, so I went all alone with my father. And shortly before we were to leave for the church, my uncle's small house was bursting with people, our family and my aunt's (some from out of town, even out of state) and a few close friends. We had come in through the kitchen: and of course there was enough food for an army there—sent in by friends, as is the case in small towns in a time of sorrow. But there was little time to say more than a few words to anybody now because it was almost time to start for the church.

However, I did notice one thing. There was a line of people all waiting to go into my aunt and uncle's bedroom, looking very solemn and speaking only in whispers. And I wondered what it was all about. Then suddenly I knew: they were going in to have "the last look" at my aunt before the coffin was closed. And then for the first time the finality of her death—maybe all deaths—laid hold of me: she was gone, and I would never see her again except as a corpse, *something to be looked at*, on display. And people would say—or not say—how "natural" she looked. And I couldn't take that, so I signaled to my father that I would wait for him in the kitchen. The line continued to move into the bedroom, but my tears were coming too fast now for me to notice anything else until I heard a woman's soft voice in the distance. And then I raised my eyes; and by some curious freak I was looking right up into the mirror on the dresser in the bedroom where my aunt's body was lying, and I could see reflected there the people passing by her coffin but not the coffin itself, only its raised lid. And then I saw what I had heard. My aunt's sister had her arm around my uncle's shoulder, and she was supporting him as he bent over to kiss my aunt goodbye. She talked very quietly to him, and of course I couldn't hear what she was saying but I could imagine. She didn't let him linger, though, and she raised him back up to an upright position. And that was all: the little scene was over.

But I was shattered. It was as though I had intruded on the most private moment in the world for my aunt and uncle, more private, much more so even than the act of making love. I wasn't even sure I had ever seen him kiss her before; and now this was the end of the affair for them, the most intimate relationship possible between two humans, and the finishing off of what I could only assume had been their great happiness. And I felt that neither I nor anybody else had any right to be present at so sacred a moment: I was shocked and embarrassed both for them, my aunt and uncle, and for us, who had been the unintentional spectators of the scene. And indeed, so strong was its effect on me that I've never spoken or written of it to a living soul until now. I had intended to walk with my father in the procession into the church, but I saw now that he was going to walk beside my uncle (with my aunt's sister on the other side). And I couldn't bear to be so near the remnant of the intimacy I had seen so recently exposed; so I faded into the background, to walk with one of my cousins. And in that order we went on to the funeral.

That's been over forty years ago, but that scene has stayed with me ever since—indelibly etched in my memory. What had my uncle shown there, in that last kiss? Warmth, affection I had never known he possessed? Or had he merely been forced into the act by my aunt's sister, a sentimental gesture and that only? Was there some sort of key to the puzzle of his character there if only I had known how to read it? Even today I don't know; and it's been such a private matter I've carried in my heart all these years (between my uncle and my aunt and me, really), I've never been able to tell anybody about it. Of course, there were other spectators to the kiss (and I had seen it only second-hand, as it were, in the mirror); but I didn't think any of them knew what I knew about my uncle's seeming coldness, my aunt's great love for him, and my own sense of bafflement about what their relationship must have been.

And today I still don't know what to make of that tableau, which flares up before me from time to time, sometimes almost in a white heat, to pose the same questions, not only about the three of us, my aunt and uncle and myself, but maybe even about human relationships in general. Had my uncle been as "wild" about my aunt as she had been about him? And if he could love, why couldn't he show it while you were alive? Couldn't he say "I love you" to *somebody*? (Were some people simply that way? And whom were they getting back at anyhow?)

He loved my father: I felt certain about that. I remembered once seeing him dash out of the store, my father's raincoat in his hand, and, without saying a word, place it around my father's shoulders as, oblivious of a sudden shower, he wrestled with a refrigerator he and one of the clerks were preparing to deliver to a customer in the store's pickup truck. Then, just as quickly, my uncle returned to the store; and my father went right on with his work, both of them still silent. And of course no words were needed: action said it all. But did my uncle also somehow resent that warmth which so characterized my father in his relationships, perhaps resent my father's still treating him like a little boy? Was that one of the reasons for his coldness toward me? My uncle had known a great love once and generosity: I knew that with every shovelful of earth that went into my aunt's grave. He couldn't tell me or anybody else he hadn't had *that* opportunity. But I knew this also: *my father loved me, and my uncle had never really forgiven me for that.*

I remember the scene of the kiss came back to me once years later, long after my uncle had remarried, when he cautioned me, now alone in the world, unmarried and with both my parents dead, against possibly getting too intimate with my many friends, both in this country and abroad: friends could let you down, he said. (Did he imply that your family never would?) I remembered it again and again when I saw him seeming to lavish on his stepchildren and their children the affection he had never shown me. (Had he changed or was it something else?) Finally, I remembered it when I got word of his death—once when I was out of the country—and learned that his second wife, who was also "undemonstrative," had had his funeral not in the Methodist church, where he had been a steward for fifty years, but in the local funeral home; and she had buried him not beside his first wife, as I learned he had apparently intended, but in her own family's lot, beside her own parents. And they were not any of them people I could imagine ever dancing a jig on the front porch or anywhere else. One of the cousins wrote me the details, and she said she was glad I hadn't been there.

He didn't remember me in his will either, but I hadn't expected him to. My mother had told me years ago, not long after he had married again, that that would be the case. And as in most judgements concerning individual people and human nature in general, she had been right. But there were many memories left and especially that memory of the kiss that I could never forget. (Was that a kind of legacy?) Had I tried to read too much into it and thus deceived myself about a lot of things then? I've wondered about it ever since, maybe wondered even more as the years have gone on and I've seen more of life. And I still don't know. But I didn't make it up; it really did happen, just like I've said. And I did see it. And nobody can ever take it away from me now.

Miss Effie, the Peabody, and Father Time

"WHY, WHEN SHE FIRST CAME HERE AS A YOUNG married woman, she was wild as a buck!" That was what my father said to me about Miss Effie Herrin, who was the grandmother of my closest friend, John Howard Herrin, back when we were growing up in Woodville in the 1930s. John Howard had all his grandparents still alive then, as did Mary Sue Green, who was a good buddy of ours; and I was jealous because all I had to show for any of it was just one ancient grandfather whom we all called Pa. And he was cranky as the Devil and ate peas with his knife, and all his children (my father included) were still afraid of him, lo, these many years later. Every time they all talked about Pa as the sole survivor of the Good Old Days—my father and his brothers, that is—I would think, well, History was OK, but you didn't want to let It get you down or hold you back either, especially when History had a mind you couldn't change with a sledgehammer and didn't want to bathe any oftener than It could help.

On the other hand, there was Miss Effie Herrin, who looked and (I thought) acted just like a grandmother ought to. She had put on some weight as she got older, they said; but she had a warm smile and a twinkle in her eye and was always very comfortable to be around. And she obviously adored John Howard, who of course returned the compliment. Her hair was snow white, and she wore it in a very dignified "updo" like the ladies—or the older ones, at any rate—were all messing around with in those days: swept up on top of her head, which my mother said gave older women especially a distinguished look. The only thing was, she said, it was hard to arrange yourself: you might just have to break down and go to the beauty parlor. And she didn't think much of that: you ought to be neat and clean always, she said; but as for trying to look any prettier than the Lord had made you, well, she had better things to do with her time. It was mostly just women who didn't really have enough to do around the house—the ones that were too lazy to really *keep* house, the ones who *wouldn't* cook (always the worst thing she could say about another woman—who resorted to beauty parlors and such like). Her own hair was naturally curly; and every time somebody would ask her who gave her that lovely permanent, she would observe, "God Almighty gave me this permanent the day I was born." And that would settle that. But then she took a dim view of anything that tended toward the voluptuous, to say nothing of the sybaritic. The idea of even a tame little bubble bath was abhorrent to her. "Now as far as I'm concerned, a bath is strictly a business proposition, and I just get in and get out and don't waste any more time in the tub than I possibly can," she would say, "and besides, with skin like mine, you don't need any more soap and water than you can help anyhow."

Her skin was not her "long suit," as she would have told you herself. Once when she was afflicted with two different kinds of "breaking out" at once, our family doctor sent her to Memphis, to see the great Dr. McCall, who was the *leadingest skinologist* in those parts back then and, according to my mother, the ugliest white man she'd ever seen in her life. However, she wasn't going to him for his *looks* but because he knew skin backwards and forwards, she said: first things first. And after he completed his diagnosis, he told her that however many times a week she bathed was just that many times too many and she could just keep clean with cleansing cream for a while until her trouble cleared up; besides, God Almighty hadn't given her very pretty skin to start with. When one of her friends asked if that hadn't made her mad, she said no indeed, she knew it was the truth and she hadn't needed *him* to tell her that. There was nobody like my mother for facing facts.

But to get back to Miss Effie Herrin. I can't remember now what provoked my father's remark about her "wildness," probably some observation of mine that she always looked stylish and well dressed, even if she was John Howard's grandmother. Maybe I even said her outlook on life was still young or something of the sort. In any case, he was very quick to put both me and Miss Effie in our places. And when I ventured to demur, saying something to the effect that I could hardly believe in her past "wildness," she was such a sweet and loving grandmother, he snorted and said, "Why, son, Father Time has caught up with her!" Then he clammed up right away: he wasn't about to get into any kind of discussion with me about sex or anything connected therewith. God knows, neither of my parents ever told me even the rudiments of the "facts of life." And what I finally learned, not always strictly accurate, I should say, I learned from my contemporaries. Of course, the secrecy in which much of the information (or misinformation) was communicated, the whispers and the bated breath only emphasized the shame and the distaste. Why, Mary Sue had even told John Howard and me (you always have to have at least one good girlfriend who is not a romantic attachment to *tell* you things) that her mother hadn't told her a thing about what to expect when she got to be a teenager, and the only reason she hadn't been scared out of her wits when she began having her periods was that some of her older girlfriends told her what it was all about.

So my father didn't say any more than that: I was just supposed to *know* something about Miss Effie's lurid past in spite of her domesticated present—at any rate, know enough. My mother did observe, when I asked her, that it was common knowledge that Miss Effie and two other young matrons (they were young *then*) of very correct background had once been asked to leave the Peabody Hotel in Memphis. And that did open up exciting prospects for speculation, but I couldn't imagine *what*. The Peabody was unquestionably the great hotel in everybody's life in those days—everybody in the Mid-South, as they used to call it. And most of us thought if we'd been very good, we should get to go there when we died! My mother had even told me, when I was very little, that since my name was Drake, the celebrated ducks in the lobby fountain were some of my kinfolks! As for anyone's misbehaving amid all that elegance, it was inconceivable to me. Why, all the bridal luncheons, all the debutante parties in that part of the world were held in the Peabody's Skyway, up on the roof, and you weren't legally married if you didn't spend at least your wedding night there. So what could Miss Effie and her friends have *done*?

Auntee, who believed in the Old Adam more strongly than even my mother did and was always the one I could *ask* things, said, "Oh, Baby, you know it must all have had something to do with *men*." But that was all she would say, not from any reticence or squeamishness, I felt, but just because she wasn't really very much interested. Neither the Peabody nor Miss Effie's alleged misbehavior was any news to her. There wasn't really anything glamorous about either one, certainly not anything worth making a production out of. And as for getting all dressed up and going down to have lunch in the Skyway or the Venetian Dining Room on some festive occasion or even listening to the music of Jan Garber ("the Idol of the Airlanes") or Clyde McCoy, who had composed "Sugar Blues" and played the trumpet part himself when they broadcast from "the breeze-swept Plantation Roof," well, she couldn't be bothered. She could eat better in her own house anyway, she said, and she certainly didn't need some black former field hand right out of the Mississippi Bottom to explain a French menu to her. Miss Effie herself had originally come from over in Jackson County, where there were Campbellites and Republicans just as thick as ticks on a hound dog, she went on to say. So what else could you expect? And pretty was as pretty did, for both Miss Effie and the Peabody. If truth were told, they were all of them probably just as loose as a bucket of juice! And then she cleared her throat and pulled her corset down, to indicate there was no more to be said on *that* subject.

So I grew up and passed on into adolescence, never *knowing* about Miss Effie and always *wondering* about the Peabody. It looked, to say the least, as though you couldn't count on appearances: more often than not they would deceive you. And yet, of course, you wanted things to took nice, to look good. Even in my speculations about Miss Effie, she never took on any other guise than the sedate, eminently respectable white-haired grandmother of John Howard Herrin, even if she did have a twinkle in her eye. I simply couldn't imagine her acting otherwise. Even when, prompted by my father's assertion that Father Time had caught up with her, I began to conjure up visions of that encounter, Miss Effie always looked and acted as she should. In the back of my mind, every time I thought about her, I could see her, clad in a long white nightgown (with bare shoulders, though), her hair neatly swept up on top of her head; and she was running long and well across the green lawn in front of some stately home. Father Time, dressed for some reason as a clown (Death as the ultimate joker?), was pursuing her closely but not with a scythe; instead, he was fiercely gaining on her with a lawn mower! Now what Dr. Freud might have made out of all this I can't imagine, but I think I now read it as some sort of fable about life and death. Life *would* go on, even in the immediate proximity of the end, with death gaining on it every moment. And death *was* funny, to think he could compromise you in any way, cramp your style. Who did he think he was anyhow, to come cut you down in your prime, as you'd always been told he might—before you'd had time to do all you wanted? Better to think of him as somebody straight out of a Marx Brothers movie, a joker like Harpo, chasing the girl in the grass skirt with a lawn mower, something fairly lunatic and making no more sense: that would put him in his place. And in my fantasy he didn't faze Miss Effie either. She ran smoothly and serenely on before him, not batting an eye or in any way compromising her dignity. You had to admire her imperturbability: she had *style*!

Oh, it was titillating to think that that dignified old lady might have kicked up her heels in the old days; and you could rejoice to think she hadn't yet been made to feel her age, to grow old, to lose her "rhythm," as a friend of ours lamented about her only daughter (whom they all called Sister) when she changed music teachers: Mrs. Johnston had taken every bit of the rhythm out of Sister, she said. Miss Effie was like a very stately old gal I encountered many years later in a very proper hotel lobby in Texas—the St. Anthony in San Antonio, to be exact. I was sitting there, comfortably ensconced in a deep sofa, reading a detective story, conscious that there was a sound of revelry by night coming from the ballroom that opened off the lobby—a wedding reception, probably. And here came an old lady slowly wending her way down the length of that long, elegant lobby, where a string quartet played every day during the luncheon hour. She looked like a queen dowager at a state reception—and was dressed very much like one too, in evening gown and jewels. I looked up, impressed by the spectacle, to follow her progress. But when our eyes met, she simply nodded and said, "There're lots of drunk little girls back there." And that was all. At first it seemed almost indecent, to have heard such a thing from her lips. Then it seemed funny, to think of the incongruity. Finally, it seemed rather sweet, to understand that age need never stop you from living, from participating in life. Something like this was what I felt in the years ahead, whenever I thought of Miss Effie. Well, good for you, old girl, I thought; they haven't gotten you yet, they haven't taken the rhythm out of *you*! And you keep right on outrunning that clown-driven lawn mower, as long as you can. And long may you wave!

Something of the same thing I also felt about the Peabody all those later years, as the times changed and the world that the Peabody had served changed too. I saw it begin to go downhill, going through several different ownerships and managements. (As my mother and her generation would have said, of a restaurant, a department store, or anything else, "It changed hands and went down." But then, as one friend pointed out, did you ever hear of anything that changed hands and went up?) And I saw the downtown district of Memphis declining, almost by the day, the familiar stores fled to the suburbs, the movie theaters now dark and deserted. Hardly anybody would be left there before long but bankers and lawyers, one of my cousins remarked. And finally, I read in the Woodville paper (I was long gone from those parts but, of course, continued to take the weekly newspaper) of Miss Effie's death. I had heard, too, that the Peabody had been closed by order of the bankruptcy court. Now it just sat there, in the middle of downtown Memphis, all locked up.

But do you know this all has a happy ending all these many years later? Because I've only recently returned from a visit back home, to Woodville; and while I was there, somebody asked me to lunch in the newly reopened Peabody. And I found it marvelously restored to its former elegance in decor though not up to par yet in the catering. And the whole lobby, which had been modeled on the courtyard of a Venetian palazzo, I believe, has now been turned into a gigantic bar, to the scandal of the abstemious. You can sit anywhere in the place and order a drink! Mercy! But the ducks are still there in the fountain, and now the management makes a big thing of bringing them down from the roof (where they sleep) every morning and returning them there every night—a real ceremony. And I suppose before very long, they'll start having bridal luncheons in the Skyway again. Already they're having Sunday brunch there—unheard of in the old days—complete with champagne too! And so I was cheered up, to think that grand hostelry was back in business again—and winning new fans among the next generations.

Nonetheless, the best news of all was something I learned on the same visit. Calling on an old friend, who had known who was who and what was what back in the old days before I came along (she was a generation older than I), I idly remarked that I had just been to see the resurrected Peabody and loved it, that it had always been *the* great hotel in my life, and it was still so beautiful, perhaps even the unseemly might be glamorized if connected with its name. But all my life, I added, I had wanted to know just what Miss Effie and her friends had actually *done* to cause their ejection all those years ago. To which my friend said, "Good Lord, I can tell you all about that. Nothing to it, really. Old Effie and her buddies were going off to Memphis on Saturday and meeting the traveling men at the Peabody, having a few wild parties, and only getting back home just in time to sing in the choir on Sunday morning!" And we both exploded into laughter. So that was all it amounted to—what an anticlimax! No grand passions, no torrid romances, no gilded halls of sin, really, but just the good healthy vulgarity of the jokes that used to be told in the smoking car about traveling salesmen and farmers' daughters. All very tame and somehow very engaging, I thought. But at the same time it all gave me a good feeling, about both Miss Effie and the hotel. The Peabody had managed to escape death and destruction; it had held the wrecker's ball at bay, to be restored to life and looks. And in a way, I thought, Miss Effie had survived too, as comfortable as ever, the twinkle in her eye still intact. In the back of my mind I could hear that lawn mower still whirring away, but somehow I could also see her, in the long white nightgown and swept-up coiffure, sailing serenely on ahead.

The Summer of the Window-Peeper

THAT SUMMER WHEN THERE WAS SO MUCH CARRYing-on about the window-peeper in Woodville, I was eight years old; and everybody was saying it was the hottest summer they could ever remember. It looked like, day after day, the sun blazed away at you until by night you were ready to fall into bed from pure exhaustion; but it really didn't get cool enough to go to bed until about midnight. (Aunt Estelle said she just put on her nightgown straight after she got out of the tub without drying off and that was how she stayed cool all night. But Mamma just raised her eyebrows and pursed her lips, and I heard her tell Daddy afterwards that sometimes she positively thought Aunt Estelle didn't have the instincts of a white woman.) Everybody said how badly we needed rain and worried about what would happen to the cotton crop if it didn't come soon.

The first I heard about any window-peeping, though, was one Wednesday when Mamma came home from the Bridge Club (she had belonged to the Wednesday Bridge Club since before the World War; Daddy said sometimes he thought she must have been born with cards in her hand) and told Daddy at the supper table what all the ladies had been talking about.

It seemed that Miss Jo-Ellen Bates that lived out on the edge of town all by herself and said she wasn't afraid of the Devil because he wouldn't have her had been undressing one night to go to bed and, since there weren't any neighbors close around, wasn't too particular about putting her shades all the way down. All of a sudden, Miss Jo-Ellen heard a man's voice talking to her through the window, asking her to let him come in and calling her "honey" and telling her how much he loved her and "all that kind of rot," Mamma said. Miss Jo-Ellen had been so surprised at first that she said she didn't have her wits about her; but, when she thought about it, it all made her so mad that any man would be bothering her at her time of life (she was sixty and had waited on her old devil of a father for years until he finally died and then had to put up with two no-good brothers all the time trying to borrow money from her) that she forgot to be scared. Instead, she ran over to the window and started beating on it and hollering, "Get away from here, you low-down son of a bitch." And then of course the shade flew up with a terrible rattle and flapped around the roller, and Miss Jo-Ellen screamed, and whoever it was outside the window took to his heels and left.

Miss Jo-Ellen had tried to pass the whole thing off as a joke, Mamma said, but the Bridge Club "girls," as she always called them, didn't think it was so funny. Of course, everybody knew, Mamma said, that it must have been a colored man because it just wasn't the kind of thing a white man would do. I said why not and, for that matter, what would anybody want to look at Miss Jo-Ellen for, as old and dried-up as she was? But Mamma just said "little pitchers have big ears" and looked at Daddy, and I could tell she had a good deal more to say to him after I went to bed.

Well, the summer dragged on without much relief from the heat, and it didn't help matters much when, from time to time, there would be some woman living by herself who would be scared at night by the window-peeper, as everybody began to call him. And it was always the same: he would call them "honey" and all sorts of pet names and beg them to let him come in. He never did try to force his way in, and he never made any threats; so maybe that's why people got more bothered than really worried about it all. But still it made a lot of women uneasy, though the men didn't say much of anything. (Miss Jo-Ellen, though, said she wasn't the least bit "uneasy," if the nasty, stinking thing ever bothered her again, she'd just fill his backside full of buckshot.)

As the summer went on, the window-peeper got bolder and started coming into the middle of town and scaring ladies that weren't living alone, and people began to get really worried about it all. Most of the women took it for granted that the window-peeper was a Negro. (Most of the ladies he had scared had said he sounded like one.) And most of them said that it was just one more sign of modern times, how back in the old days when their fathers were alive, no colored man would have dared do such a thing. Their husbands never said much to that, but they began to talk about seeing that the old pistols and shotguns they kept around the house were loaded, and the city police put a couple of extra men on the force until things got "straightened out."

Then one night the window-peeper turned up next door to us and started talking through the screen to Miss Lavonne Matthews that taught the third grade and was going to marry Mr. Billy Hancock that had the Buick agency. It like to have scared her to death, and she said she'd never heard such language in her life, some of the words she didn't even know but she could just guess what they meant; it made her blush to the roots of her hair just to think about it. Of course, she ran across the hall right away to her mother and father's room; old Mrs. Matthews immediately rose up, with a whoop, and got out their shotgun and went out the front door in her long white nightgown to find the man. Of course, she never even bothered to wake up Mr. Matthews. She told Mamma she knew she couldn't expect anything from him at that hour of the night; it would have taken her fifteen minutes just to get him waked up good, and then before he got out of bed he would have to tell her about his right big toe that was sore, just like he had for every day of the forty-two years they had been married. So she just marched on out the front door in her nightgown with the shotgun under one arm and proceeded on around the house. By that time the man had realized somebody was after him and had gotten away. None of it fazed Mrs. Matthews, though; when she was telling Mamma about it, she said, "And it's a good thing I didn't meet him because I'd-a shot him as sure as anything in the world." And Mamma said yes, she knew Mrs. Matthews would have, but the thing for them to do now was to put their heads together and lay a trap for the window-peeper because obviously (and here Mamma looked at Mrs. Matthews over my head), he was coming back to peep at Miss Lavonne again.

But before they got their plans laid good, something happened that got things even more mixed up. One stifling hot afternoon, Mrs. Virgil Hays that lived across the street came running in our front door with her tongue hanging out and said, like it was something she was really proud of having done, "Well, I've just seen our window-peeper! I know that Negro must be the one because I've seen him hanging around here out under the streetlight in the late afternoons, not doing anything much but looking around, and now I've just this minute seen him go in Miss Eva Kendrick's back door!"

Of course, Mamma didn't do a thing but step to the telephone and call Miss Eva down the street. Miss Eva was always as thick as thieves with the Negroes; she lent them money at ten per cent and was always having business dealings with them, even seeing them in her kitchen late at night until everybody said she was going to get knocked in the head by one of them if she didn't watch out. Well, when Mamma got her on the telephone, Miss Eva said the only colored man to come to her house that afternoon was John Alfred Washburn and he was her cook's son and going to the state college for Negroes and she could vouch for him. And then she proceeded to turn around and tell John Alfred, who was standing right there, that Mamma thought he was the window-peeper and wasn't that funny, with him being a "college boy"? And it scared Mamma and made her so mad that she just hung up in Miss Eva's face.

Well, Mamma and old Mrs. Matthews got their trap set for the window-peeper as soon as they could. One of the night watchmen on the city force was to be hiding behind the big hydrangea bushes by Miss Lavonne's window, and there was to be a dummy fixed up to look like Miss Lavonne in her bed. Everything was ready, and then of course old Mr. Alec Sides, the watchman, went to sleep sitting in his split-bottom chair behind the hydrangea bushes and didn't wake up until he heard the window-peeper talking through Miss Lavonne's window, calling her "honey" and "darling" and begging her to let him come in. Mr. Sides hollered and ordered the man to stay where he was, but he ran; and, when Mr. Sides, who weighed two hundred and fifty pounds, started after him, he tripped and fell over a tree root. The shotgun went off and sprayed the window-peeper across the back, but he got away.

Mamma had already told Mrs. Matthews her suspicions about John Alfred Washburn, so the next day, the officers didn't do a thing but call on him at home. They found him washing a bloody shirt (he said he had cut himself), so they just made him take off the shirt he had on; and, sure enough, there was Mr. Sides' buckshot streaked across his back.

Well, that was all the evidence the officers said they needed for a conviction, and so John Alfred was sentenced to two years in the state penitentiary and ordered not to ever set foot in Woodville again when he got out. And so most people began to breathe easy again—that is, all of them except Miss Eva

Kendrick, who went to the judge and told him John Alfred was her cook's son and in college and wouldn't have dreamed of doing anything like that and they must have made a mistake. Of course, the judge and officers didn't pay any attention to her and, besides, they all knew what a nigger-lover she was. But it made Mamma perfectly furious when she heard about it; that was twice, she said, when Miss Eva had betrayed her own people. And, as for herself, Mamma said she would always live in fear that John Alfred would come back to Woodville someday.

And so the summer finally came to an end, and it rained, and the cotton crop turned out all right after all. But Miss Lavonne Matthews broke off her engagement to Mr. Billy Hancock and got sick and finally had a nervous breakdown. They said she would cry and wring her hands and say she couldn't bear to give herself in marriage to Mr. Billy now that she had been "defiled" by all those words John Alfred had called her through the window. But Mamma said thunderation, that was all a young girl's foolishness and any God-fearing white woman ought to be nothing but glad that John Alfred was shut up now where he couldn't ever look at or talk to one of them like that again and she was sorry only that he hadn't been put there for life.

But finally all the to-do about the window-peeper died down; after a while, people began to talk less and less about him and turn their attention to something else. There always was plenty to talk about in Woodville anyway. But, every now and then, I used to think about John Alfred all shut up there in the state penitentiary and wonder whether, in spite of all his college education, he was thinking about the white ladies in Woodville as much as they still thought about him. And I wondered whether he ever really thought, when he used to call them all those names and beg them to let him come in, that they ever really would let him. And I wondered, if they had, whether he would have been pleased or disappointed with what he found there.

The Time the Bank Failed

I DON'T KNOW VERY MUCH ABOUT WHAT HAPPENed downtown the day the bank failed because I was in school all day long, but that night at the supper table Mamma and Daddy were talking about it. I got the idea that times might be harder; but then they always were hard in a town like Woodville, what with cotton bringing only sixteen cents a pound. It seemed like as long as I could remember people were always talking about how scarce money was. This didn't seem to have anything to do with the Depression that everybody in the newspapers was always talking about; it seemed like farmers always were poor, anyhow.

When Mamma and Daddy started talking about the bank, it took me a little time to figure out what was going on. They kept talking about the bank being closed; and, when I asked what that meant, they said it meant that the bank didn't have as much money inside as it was supposed to. Of course, I knew the bank perfectly well. It was across the Square from Drake Brothers' store with a big sign up over the front door that said "Farmers and Merchants Bank." Mr. Bartlett Evans was the president, and I was a little afraid of him because he reminded me of a bulldog. He was real stout, and I thought he always looked mad about something.

Mr. Evans had a daughter named Miss Alice that had been to school at Vassar, and she had even studied awhile at the Sorbonne over in Paris. She was real artistic, and every Christmas at the Presbyterian church she put on the Christmas pageant. The part I liked best was when they had "living pictures." Miss Alice had people posed in a little house with cheese-cloth over the front, and they were supposed to represent a famous picture. Finally, after everybody got posed just right, they would pull back the velvet curtain; and there would be people all dressed up like shepherds and angels and things, and sometimes Mary and the Baby Jesus in the manger. What bothered me was how they could stand still that long. Mamma always said, "Robert, you can't stand still even for one minute," and I wondered how they could stand that still while the choir sang a whole Christmas carol. But last year Miss Alice had married Mr. Harold Beasley, the high school principal, and I wondered if she would keep putting on the Christmas pageants. The day she got married Mr. Evans didn't come back to the bank after dinner, and Daddy said he hadn't ever done that before. Daddy said, "He just hated to think about his little girl getting married, I guess."

The cashier of the Farmers and Merchants Bank was Mr. Sam Chism, and he was the Superintendent of the Baptist Sunday School. Every time we went down to the Baptist church for a wedding or a program of any kind, he would say, "Just think of all those Drakes from out there at Maple Grove that used to be Baptists, and now they're all Methodists. I sure hate to think about all them being lost to the Baptist church." Of course, Pa Drake was the only one that had ever been a Baptist; but he joined the Methodist church because there wasn't any Baptist church out at Maple Grove when he settled there after the Civil War. Mr. Sam never said anything about this when Daddy was with us, but Mamma always smiled and shook her head every time he said it.

Mr. Sam's wife was Miss Mary. And they had six children that I had a hard time keeping straight, and they lived in a big old white house out on the edge of town where the children could all run and holler as much as they wanted to. They were always entertaining official visitors to Woodville—Rotarians and Baptist missionaries and people like that; and it got to be a standing joke that every time they had company it would always be written up in the society notes of the *Barlow County Appeal* that the table was draped with an "imported lace cloth."

But Mr. Sam was always on hand at every function in town; he usually crowned the queen at the beauty revue and gave away the turkey at the Thanksgiving football game. And he did a lot of real kind things, too. He was always getting people into the Baptist Hospital in Memphis when they didn't have any money to pay for it; and he would go to see them while they were there, too. And if they weren't going to get well and maybe had some property, he would help them make out a will. And when anybody died, he was right on hand and always offered to help you get the insurance straightened out. One time he went to see old Mrs. Latham when she was in the hospital. She had just had an operation for hemorrhoids, but he didn't know what she had been operated on for. So he just said, "Well, Mrs. Latham, I know you're glad your operation is behind you." People used to tell that on him and laugh, but they all thought he was a mighty fine man, and they would trust him to do anything. One time Miss Agnes Hall, a friend of Cousin Rosa's that taught school in Woodville, took him $5,000 that she had saved up and just laid it in his hands and said, "Here, Mr. Chism, invest this money for me like you want to." But when she told Cousin Rosa what she had done, Cousin Rosa was horrified and said, "Agnes, how could you?" And Miss Agnes said, "Why, Rosa, I trust him completely. After all, he's Mr. Chism." Cousin Rosa said, "Hmph! I don't want anybody to trust me that much." But that was the way most everybody felt about Mr. Sam. Another time he sent over to Miss Mattie Russell's and asked her to send him her lock-box key because he needed to attend to some of her affairs, and she sent it right over.

But I don't think Mamma was ever so fond of Mr. Sam. She used to say, "Sam Chism always comes slipping around when anybody is in trouble and talks so sweet and strokes your arm and asks if he can do anything for you. I always feel like telling him that if they wanted him, they'd send for him." But then Daddy would say, "Now, Mamma, don't be so hard on folks. Not everybody's perfect like you are." And then she would say, "Thunderation! Everybody knows I mean what I say. And I don't pretend to be anything but what I am." And Daddy always said yes, that was so.

The third man in the bank was Mr. Roger Thurmond, who was younger than either Mr. Evans or Mr. Chism. People said they had trained him in the banking business ever since he got out of high school, and everybody knew he looked up to Mr. Evans just like a father. I didn't know him very well because he never had much to say to folks. He talked like it was costing him money every time he opened his mouth, but I liked Mrs. Thurmond and Betty Ann and Roger Jr. a lot because they played games together just like they were all the same age.

But now, wherever you went, everybody was talking about the bank. All the merchants on the Square and all the people around town were worried because they didn't know whether they had lost any money or not. What they were more upset about, though, was that the bank examiners had let it out that maybe Mr. Evans and Mr. Chism and Mr. Thurmond hadn't just *lost* the money; maybe they had *taken* it. People didn't know what to think, and they didn't know whether to go sit up with Miss Mary and Mr. Sam and the others or to call up and sympathize or what to do. But a few people didn't take any longer than a minute to make up their minds.

The morning when the bank didn't open and the news began to get around town, Mrs. Edgar Rice came stepping across the yard to Cousin Rosa's house next door like putting out fire. Cousin Rosa was fixing to have the house redecorated, and she and Malcolm Watson from the Watson Construction Company were standing up in the living room floor trying to come to terms. Mrs. Rice was a big Baptist, but for some reason she never had liked Mr. Chism; so she prissed in where Cousin Rosa and Malcolm were talking and said, "Well, Rosa, Mr. Rice just phoned from downtown and said the Farmers and Merchants Bank has been closed by the bank examiners, and I'm really not surprised. I've said all along that there was something wrong with Sam Chism."

Cousin Rosa sort of gulped and then said, "O, Maggie, it can't be as bad as all that. You know Sam Chism wouldn't be mixed up in anything crooked. Malcolm, I expect we'd better wait on this business a little while I find out exactly what's going on and what state our finances are in." She sounded just like she did when one of her first-grade children misbehaved and it made her sad, but after a while she went and called Daddy down at the store.

For the most part, people were so shocked they didn't know *what* to think. Mr. Parker Reynolds next door to us, who had moved to Woodville from over in Arkansas a couple of years before, was terribly hurt over it all. He taught the Men's Bible Class at the Methodist church every now and then, and people said he could make the floweriest speeches you ever heard. He was always going on about things like the golden sunrise in Heaven where there wasn't any night and a mother's tears for her children that were as precious to the Lord as diamonds. One night about a week after the bank failed we were sitting out in the yard with the Reynoldses, and nobody talked about anything else but the bank. Mr. Reynolds said, "I don't see how those Christian men could have done such a thing—taking the money of all those widows and orphans in cold blood. I know I couldn't ever have done anything like that." And then he brought his fist down on his other hand, just like he did with the quarterly lesson magazine when he was making a point in Sunday School.

When we went back in the house, Daddy said, "Parker Reynolds doesn't know anything about all this. There's no use getting up on a high horse about it. Those men just made some mistakes that other people have made and are making right now, only they got caught." Mamma didn't say anything; she just raised her eyebrows and pursed her lips, and I could see she was going to talk to Daddy more about it after I had gone to bed.

But a lot of folks were real upset about it all—like Miss Eva Kendrick. Miss Eva was a friend of Cousin Rosa's and a real big Baptist, but she made a lot of money off of lending money to Negroes at ten percent. Cousin Rosa said, "Every time Eva Kendrick gets around me, she starts talking about how awful it was for Mary Chism to take such a prominent part in the Baptist church and do all that expensive entertaining, knowing perfectly well that her husband was little better than a thief. I just told her that maybe Sam didn't really mean to do anything wrong but just got caught where he couldn't help himself and that maybe the way he got his money wasn't much worse than the way some other folks got theirs." And then I could see that she was crying, and I didn't understand why. It seemed to me like she had gotten the best of Miss Eva.

A lot of people were sort of glad about Mr. Evans, I think. He had the reputation of being mighty hard in a business way, and I guess people thought maybe this would pay him back for being so important and sending his daughter away to school up north and having all those trips to Europe and everything. I think some people even tried to go up and sympathize with him, but it seemed like that was the one thing he didn't want. I don't think any of the men around town had ever been very close with him; he was too standoffish, and I think now they were real glad they could feel sorry for him, even if he didn't seem to want them to. But what really surprised everybody was what happened a few days before the trial. Mr. Evans was at home eating his dinner, and all of a sudden he jumped up from the table and ran out and got in his car. He started up the motor and roared down the street like he was going to a fire and lit out down the highway toward the river. Nobody could stop him, and I guess maybe nobody tried to. But when he was going down the bluff into the Mississippi Bottom, he seemed to lose control of the car; and it went right over the bluff and smashed into a big sycamore tree. The car was completely torn up, and he was critically injured, but he didn't die. A lot of people said, "It would have been a blessing if he could have gone on that way. I guess he just couldn't stand to think of all those people he had swindled."

But Mr. Sam didn't seem to be bothered a bit. He stepped around town like there wasn't a thing in the world bothering him, and the next Sunday after the bank failed he was planning to go down to the Baptist church just like he always did. But Brother Yancey, the Baptist preacher, got word that he was coming and called him up and told him maybe he better not come, feeling was so high. Mr. Sam said, "Well, all right if you think it's best, but I'm not afraid to come. And I'm not afraid to meet my Maker face to face right this minute. I haven't done anything wrong." When Cousin Emma heard about that, she said, "Well, I'd be afraid to tempt Providence that way myself, but that sounds just like Sam Chism." Even when they had the trial over at the courthouse and nearly everybody went (nobody could have stayed home that day except a few people like Mamma, who said she wouldn't be seen at such a revolting experience), Mr.

Sam didn't seem to be the least bit worried. He even tried to go up and take Miss Mattie Russell by the hand, the way he always did all the old ladies; but she just turned her back on him and marched off.

Everybody felt sorriest of all for Mr. Roger Thurmond. They all said he was a victim of circumstances, and it was too bad about his wife and children. But his own brother, Mr. Stanley Thurmond, had quit speaking to him.

When the trial was finally over, all three of the men were sentenced to several years in a federal penitentiary because some of the money they had taken had been government money. Miss Mary Chism went to live with her married daughter out in Texas, and we heard that she even worked in a department store out there; but everybody else in the men's families stayed right on in Woodville. I used to wonder why they didn't all move away; but, when I asked Mamma, she said, "Well, maybe they can face things better right here in Woodville than they can anywhere else. And wherever they went, this thing would follow them." And Daddy said, "One thing's sure, they can't ever live it down; they'll just have to live it out."

Several months after the bank failed we were all sitting up on Cousin Rosa and Cousin Emma's porch one night, and somebody began talking about the bank. A new bank had been started by this time, but a lot of people were saying that they didn't want to put their money in it; after all, it was in the same building as the other one, and some of the same people were running it. But, for the most part, you didn't hear as much about the old bank as you used to, except for things like that Miss Mattie Russell had had to rent out part of her house because she lost some of her money in the bank. And several boys and girls in high school weren't going to be able to go to college.

Daddy was talking and he said, "You know, Frank Patterson was in the store today and started talking about Bartlett Evans again. You know, he had lent him $10,000; and, of course, he never got any of it back. And it's just about to kill him, he loves money so well. He can hardly talk about anything else. But I told him he could afford to lose it as easily as anybody in town. I just told him he ought to be thankful he hadn't lost any more than he had and that he hadn't done anything for his family to be ashamed of. But you can't reason with a fellow like that. I reckon he thinks they're making shrouds with pockets in them now so he can really take it with him when he goes."

Everybody laughed, and then nobody said anything for awhile. Finally Cousin Emma said, "You know, Mr. Rice next door said the worst thing about a thing like this is that it makes you lose faith in human nature." Somebody said yes, that was so; but Mamma just shook her head and said, "Edgar Rice ought to know more about human nature than that."

Then everybody was quiet for a long time, and I could tell that they were thinking about the bank and all those men mixed up with it and how they felt toward them. Then Cousin Rosa said, "You know, they say that Sam Chism is really coming back to Woodville after he gets out." And then I remembered some new words I had learned and thought this might be a good opportunity to use them, so I spoke up and said, "Why if they ever came back here, they would be *ostracized.* They're nothing but *hypocrites.*" Cousin Emma smiled at me; but Mamma looked at me right straight and said, "Hush, Robert."

Were You There?

IN THOSE YEARS, WHEN ANYBODY FROM HOME WAS taken "over to Bolivar," that was more or less the end of him. The mental hospital for our part of the state was there, and the name of the town became pretty much synonymous with the institution. (Did anybody actually *live* in Bolivar? I never knew.) And "mental hospital" was a big step forward, I guess: they had only recently stopped calling it the lunatic asylum. At least now they were supposed to *treat* people over there, not just perform some sort of custodial function. But I hardly remember anybody ever coming home from Bolivar—coming home *well*, that is.

Our county was said to be represented adequately there. Indeed, people even made jokes about its having filled its quota and then some: it was said that somebody from home got "sent" over there one time, but the authorities said they were full up with our folks and wouldn't keep him. That was the way it was then, when I was growing up in Woodville in the 1930s: you got "sent" over there, maybe even by court order or something. And it was halfway a shame and a disgrace and maybe halfway a joke but hardly an illness. So when anybody was "in Bolivar," you didn't say too much about it.

I suspect that many of the patients there were merely senile, and there wasn't anything else to do with them: it was always hard to handle such things at home. And who knew much about psychosis or neurosis back then? But from time to time, you would hear of somebody who had gone over to see some relative and found him "belted to the bed" or something of the sort. That conjured up all sorts of visions of the Dark Ages and the sins of the fathers and insanity as a divine visitation for wrongdoing—an *affliction* in every way. And in those days plenty of people didn't hesitate to use that word, whether for a birth defect, a retarded child, or anything else like that. (Had such things been *sent*?) *Insanity* is what it still was for most people, not "mental illness." When the gates of Bolivar were shut on you, it was as though you had been sent to prison—and for life. Perhaps that was why people were inclined to joke about it; it was too terrible to think about otherwise. And unlike crime, it all seemed such a mystery; often there was no rhyme or reason as to who and what were so afflicted and why.

This seemed particularly true of the young—not the old and the senile, but those who hadn't even reached adulthood when they were "put" there. I remember several such cases in my youth—young people somewhat older than I whom I had only heard of, never remembered as active and well. I remember that my father once told me that Mr. So-and-so had a boy only a few years older than I who had been "over at Bolivar" for some years. And I hadn't even known of his existence: he was dead as far as Woodville was concerned, I suppose. When my father was telling me about it, I remember that he hugged me and held me to him, as though thanking God that, at any rate, I was all right. And now I find that memory very moving—though at the time I think I was very much embarrassed, as I always was when older people showed emotion.

But I never saw the young man my father spoke of, and he became something of a myth to me—perhaps an *exemplum*, even a *momento mori*; in any case, he was a sobering representation of what could happen in a world where order and reason did not always prevail. And perhaps all the more present for not being seen: he followed you everywhere in your mind.

What I did see, though, was a young woman from Woodville who was a patient at Bolivar, whom her family used to bring home to visit from time to time—always with a nurse. And that was something very disturbing indeed. Because there was nothing mythical about her: she was herself the very ocular proof of madness. I had heard that when she first began to "go crazy," she had pulled out her eyebrows with tweezers, then threatened to cut her mother's head off with a butcher knife. She was *violent*, they said. And I wondered if they ever had to belt her to the bed. But she belonged to a prominent family in town—and if they wanted to bring her home for a visit, not many people would have been bold enough to object.

My principal memory of her concerns seeing her at the Baptist revival one summer when I was about seven or eight and she would have been about ten years older, in her late teens. My family were Methodists, but we always attended big meetings in other churches—at least for one or two nights, to show our community spirit, I suppose (though I always tried to avoid the last night of Baptist revivals, since some of their more fire-eating evangelists would always feel called on then to preach on the Second Coming—and that usually scared me to death). There was some sort of special soloist that night who had been brought out from Memphis; supposed to be the star turn of the evening, he rendered "selections" during the collection and just before the sermon. And the one I remember was the spiritual, "Were You There?"

I had heard it before, of course—sung by my nurse, Louella, or maybe when I had gone to church with her and her family out at Morning Star. But never before had it gotten hold of me as it did then, the Baptist soloist (a soulful tenor, as I recall) giving it all he had in the way of pathos and "expression." The words I knew already, and they always depressed me. It began, "Were you there when they crucified my Lord?" Then, in the next verse, "Were you there when they nailed him to the tree?" and finally on to "Were you there when they laid him in the tomb?" And those were dark horrors enough—the sacrifice of the Savior, the Lamb of God, perfect God and perfect Man, for the sins of the whole world.

But what made me shiver, even *tremble*, as the song went on to mourn ("Sometimes it causes me to tremble, tremble, tremble") was the suggestion that I too had had a hand in it all; I too had been guilty of this greatest of all crimes. I too, like Peter, had denied my Lord, maybe even gone to sleep on him when he needed me. I too had watched idly as they crucified my Savior and was perhaps no better than the soldiers dicing for his garments beneath the cross. I too, afraid and ashamed, had hung back when they buried him, and it had finally been nothing to me. But even then I knew that it was more than just me that the song was indicting. Every one of us had stood aside; we had all been traitors, all mankind, because to be such was in our very nature. It was simply the way people were, and there wasn't a thing in the world you could do about it.

It was at that point that I remember looking up at the "crazy" young woman, sitting there with her nurse (a stout-looking matronly type who could handle her in case she got violent, I supposed) in the midst of her family. Tears were streaming down her cheeks, and there was such misery on her face that it seemed to me I had never seen such sorrow before—the oldest, deepest grief in the world. And I was both shocked and incredulous. Could she really know what was going on, both in the world around her and in the song? Could she really grieve for this greatest of all sorrows that humanity could endure, the sorrow of the self? Did she know what had really happened on Calvary, and did it really speak to her and her condition? I wondered. Did she have some glimmering of what was her own miserable lot as part and parcel of it all—the fallen world, the madness that lay in every human heart, sane or insane, the ultimate sorrow of the world? And would she have liked to talk about that, would she have liked to ask other people, myself included, where they were when she had suffered her own affliction?

I remember seeing several older people shake their heads when they saw the young woman's tears, as if to say that it was all too much for them—madness, grief, the universe itself—some terrible puzzle that they simply couldn't figure out and would really prefer to ignore. And I wondered whether any of them there would understand the feelings I was groping my way toward articulating. But it would be a very long time before I could do that, I somehow knew even then. Who could reach the young woman now, behind her tears, lost as she was in what they sometimes called mental darkness? Who could do anything for her, who could help her now? Finally, as her sobbing became more violent, her nurse had to take her outside, no doubt fearful that she would disturb the congregation or even interfere with the service itself. I suppose many people wondered why her family had brought her there in the first place.

And that's all. I don't know that I ever saw the young woman again; I just knew that, as the years went along, she was still the same and still "in Bolivar." But then about the time I went off to school, I heard that they had performed a new—and, it was said, very daring operation on her, a lobotomy. And it had turned her into a different person altogether. Now she was calm and quiet, never inclined to be violent, and sometimes even talked about things that had happened before she got sick. She never worried about anything now, they said, never seemed disturbed by anything that happened.

And her family, who had insisted on the operation when they first heard of its possibilities (not without some reservations on the part of the doctors, I understood, because of its "radical" nature), were all delighted and even spoke of sending her out to California to live with an older married sister and perhaps get some sort of job. They said she never cried at all now, didn't seem to let anything bother her one way or the other and, as my mother would have joked about anybody who didn't sweat *anything*, was just as happy as if she had good sense. In any case, everybody in town said it was simply a miracle, and nobody was afraid to be around her at all anymore.

Do You Know Ben Webster? Have You Seen Him?

I SUPPOSE NOW WE'D CALL HER A BAG LADY—YOU know, the kind you see in derelict waiting rooms in old train and bus stations, everything they own carried in a large shopping bag and with a good warm coat with lots of pockets to carry their toilet necessities in. Sometimes they even suggest elements of former grandeur: the coat is fur—moth-eaten perhaps or maybe just a leftover from a rummage sale. But on the whole these ladies are dowdy if not worse. Sometimes in New York when I go to see an old friend on the upper West Side, I see them out on Broadway feeding the pigeons, sometimes even talking to them. The old friend I go to see, now in her eighties, lives alone with two cats—Martha and Evelyn—and she says that if it weren't for those two other living creatures to share her space, somebody to talk to, she'd have gone mad long ago. And perhaps the pigeons perform the same service for the bag ladies—give them somebody to talk to, even somebody to patronize.

Well, we're more or less used to such waifs and strays now. We think of them sometimes as the homeless, the forgotten, but usually just as other human beings fallen on hard times or just about to drop through the cracks of a civilization that has little time for losers and would prefer to be like the Levite and just pass by on the other side, content that we have done our duty by them by contributing to the United Fund—these people who haven't been able to run as hard and fast as they can just to stay in the same place. And today we see them everywhere.

But that wasn't so in my own childhood in a small town in West Tennessee. Of course those were Depression years, and there were plenty of tramps coming to the back door to ask for handouts, often in exchange for doing some work around the house or in the yard. But they were always young or middle-aged men in rags and tatters and badly needing a shave. And there seemed no female wanderers among them. Indeed, the very idea seemed somehow shocking, unnatural: in that world women were supposed to stay put. I remember how uncomfortable I was at seeing an old blind woman—well, perhaps only middle-aged but then I thought all adults were old—playing and singing gospel hymns on a small reed organ on the street right outside my father and uncle's hardware store down on the Square. And I wished she would go away. Why? I'm not sure. But I remember feeling *embarrassed* by her presence, some sort of reminder that there was a darker, nether side to human experience that lay beyond my ken. And I didn't want to think about it.

Whether she was collecting for some sort of fundamentalist church or operating altogether on her own, I have no knowledge. But as she raised her sightless eyes to "look" at the passersby (some of them even contributing a few coins to those already in a Mason jar on top of the console), I wondered what she was trying to do—what her thing was, as we would say now. Was it just alms she was asking for or was it something that went deeper? Was she trying to convert anybody, bring the Good News to those who heeded it not, the real blind who would not see? Or maybe she was just silently asking a question of her own: is it nothing to you, all ye that pass by, her own affliction and all mankind's? In any case, she was just *there*, a sort of version of Melville's Bartleby, who seemed simply sent into the world to stand still, to be some sort of question mark (again, is it nothing to you?) continually put to the narrator of the story and all others (the *world* really). What did he stand for, what did he symbolize? Perhaps nothing, really: he just *was*, a joker, a wild card to upset all balances. But before it's all over he has enormously widened the sympathies of the narrator and many of us as well: "Ah Bartleby! Ah humanity!" the story concludes.

Well, of course the blind woman at the organ couldn't have possibly meant anything of the sort to me then—young boy that I was. But she worried me, as I said, made me stop and think. And she was so altogether *public* and right outside Drake Brothers' store too. Would people think it all had something to do with *us*? And you couldn't ignore her, run away from her: she was just there, like Bartleby. And I remember I was happy when she moved on to fresh woods and pastures new. Every now and then I would *think* about her though; I knew she had been there, that she was real, and that she was destitute and blind. And she wouldn't go away. Again, she was just there, like the man with the hammer banging away in the minds of the prosperous in Chekhov's story "Gooseberries." (At any rate Ivan Ivanych thinks there should be one such, just to remind the successful that there are other possibilities here.) And I can still hear her nasal voice rising above the sad, whiny sounds of the organ as she pumped away, broadcasting her own message (her own Gospel?) to all those who passed by, all the world. And yes, the memory embarrasses me still: what should I have done, what could I have done for her? Could I have mortified my own flesh just by dropping my picture show money in the Mason jar and thought well, I had done it unto the least of these and let it go at that? Should I have tried to engage her in conversation? (All she ever *said* was "thank you" when she heard the clink of new coins in the jar.) Should I have tried to find out more about her situation and told my father and uncle and maybe they could have "done something" about her or for her? Well, I must have been only eleven or twelve; and that was much too big an order for me then.

And there was a flip side to all this, as we might say now. Who knew just how much—or how little—good faith and truthtelling there might be behind all such witnesses? Were they altogether honest, were they somehow faking it all? (And this long before anybody dreamed of "televangelists" and their scams.) I know I heard my uncle say one time, he was so worn out with the continual solicitation of merchants around the Square for worthy causes, the only fellow he would be ready to give a cent to finally would have to be a one-legged man with a harelip. But he spoke too soon. Because one cold winter day he heard the front door open and close but saw nobody come in until my father, who was well aware of my uncle's sentiments, hollered out, "All right, here's the man you've been looking for." And there, so near the ground my uncle hadn't been able to see him before (he was always back in the store's tiny "office") was a man with no legs at all, propelling himself around on a platform with wheels, providing the motive power of course with the only thing he had left—his two hands. And he was selling pencils around town that dreary day. And of course my father and my uncle, both being Drakes and blessed—or cursed?—with the peculiar family sense of humor, almost had to run out the back door to keep the man—and their customers—from seeing them explode into laughter. And of course most people (including some of the women who married into the family) would never in the world have understood that they weren't laughing at the poor man's plight but rather, something like the sheer absurdity if not downright outrageousness of the universe's playing such a joke—and it was all of that somehow—on anybody in the world. And yes, they laughed at wooden legs and glass eyes too.

Perhaps it's all very Southern and rooted in some sort of orthodoxy of the imperfectability of man, perhaps a twisted

Calvinism or something of the sort. But I don't see now—never have really—anything like this sensibility displayed in our modem industrial society where many passersby wouldn't know a freak if they saw one. (Flannery O'Connor observed that was the reason Southerners often wrote about such things: they were the only people left now who still did.) People who believe that one really can, by taking thought, add a cubit to his stature are more prone to be saddened, disappointed, or something like that. If they believed in Original Sin (an absolute must for anybody who pretends to a sense of humor), they would know that yes, you often do have to laugh to keep from crying. And yes, Dante called his great work not a tragedy but a comedy. None of all this is laughter in derision but perhaps in commiseration, as when Hemingway remarked to Fitzgerald, "We're all bitched from the start." Or again it's like the Rev. J. C. Goodyhay in Faulkner's *The Mansion*, the former Marine sergeant who finds his life in shambles when he returns from World War II, gets religion in a powerful big way, practically builds his own church and almost literally goes out into the highways and byways and compels his congregation to come in. And his characteristic prayer is "Save us, Christ, the poor sons of bitches." And that says it all.

But again, perhaps it all comes to the same thing: the poor, the outcasts, the Bartlebys we have with us always. And we're all of us S. O. B.'s and have come short of the glory of God. And yes, the world is really all one. (As the late Professor Randall Stewart suggested many years ago, Original Sin is the greatest democracy there is.) I don't know exactly when I began to come round to that view, certainly a more mature perception than formerly of what it was all about. Obviously, I look back on much of this now with wisdom acquired after the fact. But I do recall when I was somewhat older, perhaps almost ready to go off to school an old woman who left a lasting impression on me—I wasn't altogether sure why then. Her name was Inez Webster, and she and her husband had once owned a few acres out in the county but lost their place during one of the ups and downs of the cotton economy. But for years they had continued living on what was now their creditor's place and worked it for him on the shares, no longer landholders now but sharecroppers. But they jogged along asking no favors from anybody and held their heads high: after all they had once owned the land they now farmed for somebody else.

But then the husband, Ben Webster, sickened and died. They had no children or close relatives: there had been just the two of them against all comers, you might say. So what was Inez to do now? She was obviously up in her seventies, and there was no social security or much on the order of "welfare" back then. For a time people tried to get her domestic work to do, despite the prejudice in those days against "white" help. But that was finally no go: her mind was failing, and she easily got confused, broke china, didn't clean properly, all the sort of things we think we mustn't have in a well run world. And so she took to roaming the streets, and she was already a Saturday fixture on the Square. That was the big trade day back then, when the farmers came in from the country, sometimes in a Model T or else in wagons, sometimes even sitting in straight-backed chairs therein. (Was that some sort of assertion of dignity and pride? They might not have the wherewithal for a car, but they weren't just dumb driven cattle either.) And all day long old Inez would roam the crowd, her rheumy old eyes seeking, seeking like the blind woman's at the organ in my childhood, asking again and again, "Have you seen Ben Webster? He's my husband, you know, but he went off somewhere not long ago and he hasn't come back. Where do you reckon he is?" And then sometimes she would burst into tears, and the kinder folks would give her some money and pat her on the back and move on. But always they left her with that look of puzzlement on her face: it wasn't money she wanted, it was Ben Webster.

Nobody knew exactly where she lived or how she managed, and again she was something of an embarrassment. Somebody even suggested she might be living with one of the Negro families who were sharecropping their old place now. But many found that hard to believe. Finally, something had to be done about her: you couldn't have her just wandering around town at all hours of the day and might. She was becoming something of a nuisance too, perhaps even a scandal: it was said she performed all her ablutions in the White Women's Rest Room at the Court House, and none too often either. It just wasn't a good thing for the town: everybody felt that. So the "authorities," as they were always called—perhaps to give them the dignity yet anonymity they always craved, arranged for her to go to the Poor House—or the County Farm, as it was then called. And there she lived out her days. She was no longer on the Square; she was no longer "public." But I always knew she was out there: I never forgot. And it's hard to say why. (Was she but another version of the old blind woman at the organ?) And I wondered what she was doing out there all that time. Did she have a room of her own, or did she have to share with several other women? What did they eat out there? Did she have to do any sort of work to help "pay her way"? It wasn't quite as bad as being in the asylum over at Bolivar: those people were *sick*, whereas Inez and people like her were just more or less *unfortunate*. Of course both places bore a stigma: they were supported by public funds, and you had to be *sent* there, "committed," almost like going to jail. But everybody said you had to have such places; and yes, one of my cousins said she had always thought they were fine for other people's folks.

Inez lived on for several years out there, and sometimes I would think about her—I was off at school by then—and what kind of life she had. Did anybody ever go out to see her? I didn't know whether she had any friends who cared about her, and of course her husband had been dead so long many people couldn't even remember him. And then I used to ask why I myself had not gone out to see her, ask her about her life, what it was she had cared for besides her husband. And I don't think it was because I was developing what we've come to think of now as a social conscience. Perhaps I just felt that she was part of my town's structure, one of its own peculiar institutions that I needed to understand. And again she was always there, perhaps not so "public" but some sort of witness nevertheless. And it still mattered that the community took some notice of her even if it was only in the way of a delegation of good ladies from the missionary societies of each church going out to visit every month or so. She was still one of us. I felt that strongly somehow, maybe because I had come to know some of the less attractive features of city life now. And I hated to think she had no "connections" to see that she was well looked after. You had to *do* something about such people but what?

Maybe before I went off to college I should have gone out and played hymns for her and the other old folks to sing: I took piano lessons and was pretty good as an accompanist. I could have at least done that. But I hadn't. And now I was about to graduate from college and one day just happened to notice a little item in my home town paper to the effect that Inez Webster had died—the oldest resident of the County Farm though no one knew her exact age. And I wondered where she was buried (a potter's field?) and what sort of funeral they had given her and who went. It all made me sad, but I was older now and perhaps a little wiser. And I thought I knew the answer now to several things that used to puzzle me. I never had been able to let Inez alone, all those years, any more than I had the blind organist. She was still there, at the back of my mind, like Bartleby, motionless and still but always in place, like the man with the hammer in the Chekhov story. But I thought I knew now why I had been content just to think about her, never do anything about her or for her really. I suppose I must have been afraid of her, not so much as I was of the old blind organist, who with her dead eyes I always felt could *see* more than others and might then suddenly turn on them and ask them whether her situation was anything to them or not. With Inez I think I simply feared she would ask me the question that sooner or later she always put to everybody: "Do you know Ben Webster, have you seen him?" And I never did know what I would say to that.

The Single Heart

WHEN EUSTACE CAMERON DIED LAST WEEK, YOU know, I couldn't really be sorry. Because, to tell you the truth, I think that man died out of pure plain loneliness. Which I suppose sounds almost as silly in these days as saying he died of a broken heart. But really I think it's the truth.

We were about the same age. In fact, I even went with him before he went off to college. But by the time he'd finished college and then medical school, most of the girls around here his age were married and bringing up their own families. So there really wasn't anybody around here for him *to* marry, assuming of course that he wanted to marry anybody, which I don't think he ever did.

But then I think that was all part of his trouble or whatever it was that always made him seem a sad person to me. For one thing, his mother almost spoiled him rotten. He was an only child; and old Mr. Cameron, his father, who was almost old enough to be his grandfather, died just after Eustace was born. And when Eustace was growing up, everybody around town said he probably wasn't going to be worth killing because his mother never seemed to find any fault in him whatsoever and let him do just about anything he wanted to. The neighbors, in fact, said they all expected him to end up in the penitentiary before he was twenty-one—into and out of devilment *all* the time.

By the time Eustace came along, the Cameron money was almost all gone; old Mr. Cameron had managed to see to that—drank up most of it, I think. But his mother was determined that Eustace was going to have all the so-called advantages. And somehow or other, she managed to provide him with them—mortgaging this and borrowing on that. And so she got him through college and medical school. And after he'd interned a year in St. Louis, he came back here to practice.

I remember how surprised we all were at that. I'd have thought Eustace couldn't wait to put this place behind him and maybe go off after the bright lights of New York or somewhere. But he didn't. Came right back here to Woodville and settled down with his mother in that big old house and went to practicing night and day as hard as he could.

Of course, everybody said it wouldn't be long before he up and married some high-stepping gal he must have known when he was in medical school in Memphis or maybe even up in St. Louis, and then he'd more or less fit right into things around here. But, you know, he never did. And, for what it's worth, I don't think it had anything to do with his mother either. She never seemed to me like one of these possessive mothers you hear so much about these days, though I don't doubt there must have been something of the iron-hand-in-the-velvet-glove about her. Otherwise, how else could she have spoiled Eustace without seeming to ruin him, much less gotten him through school? But I believe, whatever he really thought about her, Eustace must have always had great respect for her. After all, she had more or less made him what he was, for good or for ill. I remember, after he was grown, he never referred to her in public as "Mamma;" it was always "my mother." On the other hand, he certainly never gave the impression of being under her thumb in any way. Eustace was independent all right—always had been, as far as I know.

But, like I was saying, he plunged into his practice around here almost with a vengeance. Of course, there wasn't any hospital here in those days; you practically had to go to Memphis to even die unless you did it in your own bed. And that was all before we had the good roads all around the county like we have now. Three months out of the year Woodville was what you might have called just mud-locked. But Eustace had himself an old Ford that he laughed and said he could almost lift out of a quagmire by its own steering wheel; and he never slowed down one bit, come rain, hail, mud, or snow. Mrs. Cameron was always right there by the telephone to take whatever messages came in and knew where to catch him along the way so he would know where to go on to next. Really, she and Eustace were almost a team. And there never was weather bad enough or somebody sick far off enough that he didn't manage to get there *somehow.* Sometimes, when the roads were literally impassable, he'd just leave the Ford alongside the road and borrow somebody's horse or mule and slog right on through.

But, anyhow, he never really seemed to fit into things around here. Not being married of course had something to do with that. In a place like this there's just not much room for single folks, man *or* woman. But I think really there was more to it than that. Now don't ask me what it was. I haven't the least idea of what his "story" really was, like they're always saying on television when they purport to be giving you the real lowdown dirt on some long dead and gone politician or historical figure. When you come right down to it, *every* man has such a "story," only some of them just get made more public than others, that's all. And every man and woman in this world has got secrets he don't want made public and which the public, furthermore, ain't the least bit entitled to know, despite everything you can say about the claims of history or posterity or whatever other name you're using just to hide your own devilish curiosity. And everybody sooner or later has to look in the mirror and see a number of things leering out at him from behind his own eyeballs that don't look too pretty, to say nothing of having to sit down across the table from his own personal devil every time he eats his dinner alone. So I don't have any idea of what Eustace's "case" or "trouble" or whatever else you want to call it was. And it ain't any of my business whatsoever except that I always liked him and was sorry he was unhappy. Because I really think he was—all his life.

I know he worked his head off with his practice, and I know he made lots of money. And furthermore, he did lots of free-gratis-and-for-nothing medical work on the side that he never got one penny for, only he'd have been the last person in the world to ever tell you about it. And I know he was a mighty good doctor too. In fact, everybody used to say that whatever Eustace said you had, you always *did* have by the time you got to Memphis and some big high monk-de-monk specialist had the looking over of you.

They always said Eustace was better with children and old people than anybody else. Maybe he wanted somebody that wouldn't talk back to him, I don't know. But he sure didn't have time for folks about his own age that ought to have sense but thought they knew more about what was wrong with them than he did and wouldn't do what he said. And he didn't have any patience with them at all—like one woman he told she'd better take a tetanus shot after her husband had gotten on a blind-drunk and stuck the pruning shears in her backside. But she said, no, it was all part of her cross, and she would just "rise above" the whole thing with faith, love, and forgiveness. I don't know what Eustace said to *that*; he had a right rough tongue when he was crossed about a professional matter. But I do know that, after days of pleading with her to go on and take the shot, he finally just washed his hands of her and told her she'd better get to Memphis as fast as she could and take her false teeth out before she got there because she wouldn't be able to open her mouth by then. And it was the truth because she died of lockjaw in three days' time. I reckon she really did "rise above" it all right!

But Eustace was the best thing in the world with all my children and with Mamma and Papa too when they got old. And he wasn't ever gruff or forbidding with them—really as gentle as he could be. And he would spend hours talking to old Dr. Mitchell, who had retired, and was always asking his opinion about cases of his own and then taking Dr. Mitchell around the county with him on all his calls. Dr. Mitchell's old-maid daughters, whom he'd nearly bullied into untimely graves before himself, were delighted to have him out of the house, I know. But, to hear them tell it, Eustace made the old man's last days much more pleasant simply by making him think his opinion was valued and that he was wanted and needed by somebody, which, God knows, I doubt if the daughters ever made him feel—or wanted to.

And then when Mrs. Cameron got old and feeble, Eustace devoted all his hours outside work to doing things for her. He would take her round to see all her friends or just for a long drive—wherever she wanted to go. You could see them riding up and down the streets around here every night in the hot summertime, trying to cool off before it was time to go to bed, I suppose. And in the winter Eustace would never go out at night unless it was an emergency. He would just sit at home by the fire reading medical journals until his mother had gone to bed. And after all, if he had wanted to go out, where was there for him to go—around here? O, you'd sometimes see him down at the drugstore talking to one of the men on duty. I know one time he even proceeded to up and diagnose me for the mumps when I went in there to get some medicine for one of my children he'd been to see that afternoon. And I ended up about as sick as anybody in the house!

But if he wasn't at the drugstore, he was usually at home every night, just sitting there with his mother and, as far as most people would know, perfectly content. But though I suppose he *was* content, I don't really think he was happy, which of course is not the same thing at all.

Because when you come right down to it, Eustace didn't really have anybody to love. He was a dutiful son, a fine doctor, and an upright citizen. But he *didn't* have anybody to love. And, to tell the truth, I've often wondered whether he *could* have loved somebody or other. Now, like I said before, don't ask me why; but I think it was the real truth about him. I believe Eustace tried to fill up the emptiness in his life with his work and with his duty, and there's a great deal to be said for those things as substitutes, I know. But that's all they are finally—just substitutes. And I don't think either one of them can finally give you what almost any other human being can, if he wants to and—here's the hard part—*you* are willing to just take it for the great gift it is and let it go at that, which of course is really the only sensible response you can make. And so Eustace was condemned—yes, that *is* the word I want—to a lifetime of work and duty—all good, all worthwhile, all, at least on the surface, unselfish. And yet I always thought he was unhappy and somehow incomplete in his life.

And I think one of the reasons for all this was that somehow Eustace was afraid of love, which does involve a big risk always. I think that was one of the reasons he preferred children and old people as patients; they were more apt to do what he said and not talk back. But love, of course, inevitably involves a certain amount of talking back or even fighting back. And somehow or other I don't think Eustace was prepared to take that—or risk it.

Had all his medical training literally sterilized him as a flesh and blood person capable of such things as love; or had he had the wrong kind of love from his parents—none from his father and too much from his mother? I leave all that for the head doctors and busybodies and such like to figure out. Personally, I don't think it's anybody's business but Eustace's and the Lord's. He *did* live a useful life, and he *was* a workman that needed not be ashamed. And that's more than you can say for most folks, by and large. But, from where I sit, I should think he'd have missed a lot. And I happen to think he was unhappy because he realized he *had* missed a lot, whether by his own choice or otherwise. But then you never can be sure about that either. My husband used to say that you never knew what was going on in the other fellow's mind, no matter how well you really thought you did. And the longer I live, the more I'm convinced that he was dead right.

But what I do know is the way Eustace acted the last few years of his life and what happened at the very end. After his mother died, he lived all alone in that big house, with just their old faithful black Ruby to come in and clean up and cook his meals for him. And Ruby told me she didn't know what he did with his time at night, except sit there playing one game of solitaire after another when he wasn't reading "them doctor books," as she called them. He never had drunk, doubtless because of his father's example, about which I suppose he'd heard a great deal. And, to my knowledge, he hadn't ever run after women, respectable or otherwise. But every night or so he would drive downtown after supper and just sit there in his car on the square, watching people go by, never saying anything to any of them, but just looking. And, really, I think that's what he'd been doing all his life—just looking, both as a doctor and as a human being.

By that time, most of the crowd he'd grown up with were parents and even grandparents. A few of them had even begun to die off. But Eustace was still there, looking, watching, observing, maybe even waiting—like he'd been doing all his life. And don't ask me what he was looking or waiting for; I can't tell you any more than I suspect he could have. Maybe it was somebody he knew in his heart he'd never really find; maybe it was just his own life itself, which you certainly can't find between the covers of a textbook or around another man's hearth. O, child, *I* don't know.

But then one night last week, when Eustace was sitting there on the square, he began to feel pretty bad; and soon he must have realized that he was desperately ill. But by that time almost everybody downtown had gone home. There wasn't even anybody for him to call to. And so he started up his car and somehow managed to drive out to the new hospital, right up to the front door, and staggered in and collapsed in the lobby. Dr. Graham, one of the brand new doctors that came here after the hospital opened, happened to be there. So he and a couple of nurses rushed up and bent over Eustace and started to working on him right there—didn't even try to get him to a room and put him to bed.

But Eustace just looked up at them and smiled in that rather ironic way he always had and said, "Don't bother. I've known for some time my heart wasn't what it ought to be, and I think it's finally caught up with me." And then, to their amazement, they saw there were tears streaming down his face. I don't reckon many people in this world had ever seen Eustace Cameron cry, come heaven, hell, or high water. And then he did the strangest thing of all. He opened out his arms as wide as could be, like he was trying to embrace Dr. Graham and the nurses all at the same time, and gasped out: "It's so dark out there, and I'm so tired and cold. And my heart, O God, I think it's turned to ice! Can't anybody do anything for me at all?" And then he just fell back and died right there. The nurses, who had always held Eustace in considerable awe, were terribly shaken up by the whole thing. And even young Dr. Graham, who hadn't known Eustace but a short time, said it would be a long time before he forgot that scene. He told somebody later that Eustace was the healthiest looking dead man he'd ever seen; he could hardly believe he was gone. Dr. Graham said it was a funny thing but Eustace somehow gave him the impression of a man who had frozen to death in front of a roaring fire.

I Never Have Been a Well Woman

YOU KNOW, I NEVER IN THE WORLD THOUGHT I'D live to be this old—a hundred! And that's exactly what I told that young man that came round to interview me, as they call it, for the television the other day. As I told him, I really never have been a well woman. Oh, nothing ever really bad wrong that I couldn't get over, but—especially since I've gotten so old—just aches and pains and that old arthritis and what that new young doctor called an allergy when he examined me about ten years ago. In my time, there weren't any such things as *allergies*; you just had a breaking out and called it nettle rash and went right on. And to tell you the truth, I don't know that they can do much more than that now.

Of course, I never married; so I never had any children of my own (just taught other people's)—even if I'd wanted any, which I'm not too sure I would, considering what the world seems to be coming to these days. On the other hand, folks have been saying that about the younger generation from time immemorial, I suppose; and the world keeps right on going. So I don't suppose now will make any difference. Anyhow, I don't know that people really improve or not as they get older; mostly, I think they just get more the way they already were. So you can look at it either way.

But anyhow, after I fell and broke my hip about five years ago, my nieces and nephews got together and decided this nursing home would be better for me. (All of them think I'm going to leave them something when I die, but I may live it all up myself first!) So I gave up my house and moved in and here I am, and I reckon here I'll be till they carry me out feet first. I'm more or less used to it now, which I suppose is a good thing if you look at it one way but a bad thing if you look at it another. Maybe I'm really getting "institutionalized," like you hear about in those "public-health scandals" they're always revealing in whatever you read or listen to now. On the other hand, I'm certainly not going to lie here in this bed or roll around in that good-for-nothing wheelchair and give up the ghost either. You have to stay up and get around and be up and about and be *interested* in folks and in the world if you want to live a long time. And God knows, I have; and I guess I still do. Why, I fight old age every day of my life!

That young man the other day wanted me to say what all I had *learned* in my "first century," as he put it. And goodness knows, I wasn't sure of anything I *had* learned, which sounded, I suppose, as though my whole life had been nothing but a water haul. But when you come right down to it, I don't suppose many of us can ever say just exactly what it is we have learned. Like I said, I don't think people improve with age—not like a wine. Of course, the silly ones just get sillier, and the fools just get more foolish: time don't do a thing for them, I can tell you. Like that silly Mildred Perkins down the hall from me—won't even look at the dance numbers when they show them on the television—thinks they're godless or something. But what else can you expect, with her such a *big* Baptist and with maybe grandparents that weren't but just a jump away from being Holy Rollers or Pentecostal Nazarene or God knows what? Anyhow, she sits beside me at nights when we watch; and every time somebody prances out in an abbreviated costume and begins any kind of gyration, Mildred automatically ducks her head and won't look up until it's over, except occasionally to ask me, "What are they doing now, Myrtle?" And I tell her, for God's sake, use the eyes she was born with and look for herself. We're all more than twenty-one out here. But I don't think Mildred has ever gotten away from Mamma's apron strings, and she's only a couple of years younger than I am right this minute. If I weren't right here beside her, I suspect she'd put the clock back more years than that, but she can't fool me. I've known her ever since she grew up right next to us out in the country (we didn't move into town until long after I was grown) and ran after my brother Ben until he positively had to get himself married to somebody—anybody—else, just to get away from her.

He married Ona Mae Stanley from over on the other side of the county, who didn't have the sense God gave a billy goat, but she made him a good wife all the same—raised some fine children, too: that's the nieces and nephews I was telling you about. And Ben and Ona Mae are both gone now, so it's just me and the nieces and nephews; but I see as little of them as possible because there's no point in having them come out here and get all upset because I'm ailing: at a hundred years old, what else do you expect? All things considered, I think I'm doing pretty well.

And that's what I told that young man when he interviewed me the other day. Wanted to know what were the main changes I had seen in my lifetime and what all. And I said, well, folks out in the country had electricity and indoor plumbing now, and people didn't die of typhoid and pneumonia anymore; and, of course, there's always the automobile, which to my way of thinking is an infernal machine in almost every sense. But as to whether there were better or happier people these days as a result, the quality of their lives improved, I really wouldn't know. And I think he was sort of surprised. Probably thought—most folks do—that just because things were different—changed—they were bound to be better. But I've lived too long to believe in any of that. Like I said, people—*folks*—don't change; and you're a fool if you believe they do.

Of course, there's not as much sheer drudgery as there used to be. I don't think people are as much worked to death, literally, as they used to be—on the farms and, I suppose, in the factories. But then, so what? So they don't have to earn their bread by the sweat of their brow as much as they used to, so they do have more free time; what do they know to do with it all? That's always been the question as far as I could see. And more and more folks, it seems to me, are afraid of good, honest work. And the way the government's going, you might think Washington was conniving at that too. Like one of the Negro maids out here told me the other day: her sister didn't have to work, she said, because she was "drawing," which meant she was on welfare or social security or God knows what other form of "relief." But nowadays it's not just restricted to *them*; white folks are just as lazy and ornery, as far as I'm concerned. And Jews are just as bad as Gentiles and Catholics like Protestants. I am certainly *not* prejudiced. I just believe in Original Sin, which covers a lot of things I can't understand any other way. Just like it used to say in the Episcopal Prayer Book (but that's one more thing they've gone and changed): "We have left undone those things we ought to have done and we have done those things we ought not to have done and *there is no health in us*," And the longer I live, the more I want to shout "amen" to that.

You know, I was a school teacher for nearly fifty years—yes, a real old-maid school teacher, just like you hear and read about. And if I learned anything in all that time (I just taught the first grade, but it's all the same: nobody, young or old, much wants to learn *anything*), it was that human beings have an amazing capacity to resist enlightenment. And considering the homes that many of my pupils came out of, I thought it might be a merciful dispensation if they didn't learn too much because then they'd wake up and see what a really terrible mess their lives were in (father a drunk and mother a slut and God knows what for brothers and sisters), and then they really would be miserable! Quite often, you know, ignorance really *is* bliss. When I was younger, I would have thought that shocking for anyone to admit, especially a school teacher. But I guess that's one of the things that you notice as you get older: fewer and fewer things have the power to shock you. After a while, you just feel like relaxing and saying, "Well, yes I have seen the nature of the beast; so tell me something else I didn't know."

Does this mean that age hardens you? I hope not, really; but you just don't make a big hurrah about a lot of things anymore: eventually, you just feel there won't be any more surprises. But that's a dangerous way to look at it, too: the Old Adam is still up to his old tricks, and there still ain't nothing like *folks* anywhere. So that's why I don't get much excited one way or the other about who's president (and this one sent me a birthday telegram—did I tell you?) or congressman or what not: they're all pretty much cut out of the same bolt of cloth—and the people who vote for them are no better. I tell you, it's a pretty widespread ailment—Original Sin. But we Americans particularly, I think, put our trust in princes and in machines more than we ought. We go wild over personalities and pretty faces and whatever other gadgets get thrown at us all the time on the "media," as they call it—whoever makes the most noise is what it amounts to, really. And to tell the truth, it's all just like we were deciding on which new car to buy—a *product.* Or so it seems to me. And most of it leaves me quite cold, I can tell you. If I've got *convictions* about anything, I don't change them to suit the season, like they were clothes or something. They're *there* and they *stick,* if there's anything to you at all.

And that's what I guess I've learned in my life, if I have indeed learned anything. And that was what I tried to tell that young man when he asked me all those questions in that interview the other day. God knows what he must have thought of it all—and of me. But one thing he did say, before he left, was that I ought to be declared some sort of national monument. And I haven't yet decided whether that was a compliment or not. But I'm going to take it as such anyhow; I'm sure he meant well.

Well, I'm sorry you have to go now; but be sure you watch the six o'clock news tonight: that's when my interview is supposed to be shown. That young man promised.

Ella Biggs

YEARS LATER, LONG AFTER ANN LOUISE PARKER and her best friend Martha Alice Craig were grown and married, you could send them into a fit of the giggles any time you wanted, just by mentioning the name Ella Biggs. Actually, she had come into the world as Ella Biggs Scott and then gone on to marry Tom Banks the lawyer; but everybody in town still naturally referred to her as Ella Biggs. For one thing, it wasn't the sort of name that could be confused with any other. And then there wasn't any danger that Ella Biggs herself might be taken for somebody else.

Because, when they made her, they threw the pattern away: everybody always said that. In the first place, she was a very pretty girl who grew up into a very handsome woman, for all that old Mrs. Scott, the grandmother for whom she was named, had been a Biggs and therefore one of the homeliest women you ever saw. In her teens, Ella Biggs was considered quite delicate, though, and at one point had even been put to bed, to take the rest cure—weak lungs, they said, a phrase which in those days could strike terror into the stoutest heart as a harbinger of consumption. But she had apparently recovered and ultimately gone off to school at the state university in Knoxville where she had then been supposed to cut quite a swath—or, as some less reverent spirits put it, was thought to have hoed a wide row.

Men, of course, they said—and a good many of them. And there was a time, apparently, when her reputation wasn't any too good, either in Knoxville or Woodville. Or so Ann Louise had gleaned from her mother's guarded remarks. There was even some kind of dim allusion occasionally to the quarter Ella Biggs had spent out of school, nobody knew where. Had she "gotten into trouble," Ann Louise wondered, maybe even gone away somewhere for what was then called an "illegal operation"? Nobody ever knew. But it wasn't long after that that Ella Biggs married Tom Banks and came back home to Woodville to live in that big old house with him and his widowed mother; and everybody thought whatever the case, she would now settle down and "start a family," and that would cure whatever was wrong with her.

But all this was background for Ann Louise: it was all "before her time," as people said. And she had mainly pieced it all together from her mother's elliptical comments and even from some things her mother *didn't* say. Because her mother and Ella Biggs had grown up together, even gone off to school together. And even at age eleven—right that minute in 1941—Ann Louise knew that this was one of those ties that *bind*. And she would have to be careful whatever she said or asked about Ella Biggs. Because even then Ella Biggs was a subject of fascination for her. For one thing, Ella Biggs was the first nice woman Ann Louise had ever seen who didn't wear stockings. No matter how dressed up she was, even when she was wearing her fur coat in the winter time, she still didn't wear hose. And once when she was even younger, Ann Louise had crawled under one of the tables when her mother had the bridge club and pinched Ella Biggs's leg, to make assurance double sure. And no, Ella Biggs wasn't wearing hose; and yes, Ann Louise had gotten a spanking for her pains.

But anyhow, Ann Louise always thought that was very peculiar of Ella Biggs—but somehow exotic and glamorous, maybe even a little wicked—not tacky like dyeing your hair (which no nice woman then would admit to doing) but rather what you might call *dashing*. And she wondered whether it might have anything to do with Ella Biggs's having taken the rest cure or maybe even having an illegal operation, if indeed she had had it. But of course she couldn't say anything to her mother about it, just mainly talk it over with Martha Alice and *wonder*.

As it turned out, Ella Biggs never had started a family, just gone on working downtown in her husband's law office and living in the house with old Mrs. Banks. And Ann Louise thought that might be a trial. For one thing, Mrs. Banks couldn't let there be a crack in the Baptist church door without her being there to see what it was all about; and she couldn't meet you on the street or even in the checkout line at Kroger's without asking you were you saved. Ella Biggs's own family, the Scotts, were all Methodists, though Ann Louise didn't think any of them had ever worked at it very hard; so she couldn't imagine living with old Mrs. Banks was any kind of jollification for Ella Biggs.

But then Ella Biggs was different, and maybe none of it ever really bothered her. The more Ann Louise thought about it, the less Ella Biggs seemed to fit into any of the Woodville molds anyhow. And more and more, she began to fascinate Ann Louise as a figure of romance, even drama—maybe something like those characters Bette Davis often played—women either doomed or damned, sometimes even both. And the mystery was further enhanced when Ann Louise stopped to reflect that she had hardly ever spoken to Ella Biggs in her life; she wasn't even sure what Ella Biggs's voice sounded like. It was almost as though she was one of those people (a symbol?) you talked about rather than talked to. But you couldn't ever ignore her; that much was certain. Whatever the case, she was a very attractive woman with an aura of mystery about her, and she might even have had a past. And her present life was probably none too pleasant.

Every time Ann Louise saw her coming down the stairs from her husband's law office up over the bank in the late afternoon, especially when it was cold weather, and Ella Biggs had her fur coat just lightly draped over her shoulders instead of securely and snugly worn and of course not a sign of a stocking anywhere in sight, she wondered whether Ella Biggs might not be preparing to rush off to meet her fate in the form of a dramatic car wreck (in a convertible of course) or else as the result of double pneumonia. (And when people went *into* pneumonia, as they were often said to do in those days, they rarely ever came *out.*) That's what would have happened to Bette Davis, Ann Louise knew; but of course she could tell right that minute that Ella Biggs was simply on her way to the post office with the day's outgoing mail and not about to wake up and find herself the heroine of a melodrama. Ann Louise had sense enough to know that. Real life was funny that way: it often seemed awfully shapeless and things didn't always add up—not like they would have in the picture show. But whom could you tell that sort of thing to? Most people would have thought you were crazy.

As it turned out, what actually happened was wilder than anything Ann Louise could ever have dreamed up; and she wondered, was it really true what people always said about truth being stranger than fiction. Because not long before Thanksgiving that year, Ella Biggs set out in her car late one afternoon, with a light snow failing, and headed down the Memphis highway. She was seen by all manner of people, of course, and was even said to have waved at a couple of them. But apparently she got no farther than the bridge over the Obion River. Because that was where they found her car about an hour later—parked right beside the railing, the lights still on and her fur coat right where she had left it on the front seat. (They found out later she had taken the day's outgoing mail by the post office on her way out of town.) There was the footprint of a woman's shoe in the snow on the bridge railing, so of course they started dragging the river right away. But they never found Ella Biggs then or later; and for all anybody in Woodville knew, she had indeed vanished into thin air.

Well, of course, it was decidedly the most dramatic—and the most talked about—thing that had ever happened around Woodville in Ann Louise's memory; and her imagination had a field day. Some people who saw Ella Biggs driving down the highway that day said they had just assumed she was on her way to the early picture show over at Monroeville, but Ann Louise thought anybody ought to have better sense than that. Who on God's earth, she wondered, would want to leave home late in the afternoon of a snowy day and drive through the cold of the early dark just to see a picture show that would be playing right there in Woodville the very next week—and Jeannette MacDonald and Nelson Eddy at that, teeth and all? Later on, other people said they knew Ella Biggs must be in the river (and by this time Woodville was almost divided into two camps—those who did and those who did not believe Ella Biggs had committed suicide) because, they said, no woman, in her right mind or out of it, would ever have jumped in the water with a perfectly good fur coat on. But then Ann Louise thought you could have argued that either way: what woman anywhere would want to go off, to the grave or anywhere else, and leave a perfectly good fur coat behind? But then why did they never find Ella Biggs's body after days and days of dragging for it? And then why did nobody ever find a note or anything? There never was a funeral or anything like that either, so nobody even knew what to say to the family. And *they* certainly weren't talking.

A week later, Tom Banks did put an "acknowledgment" in the weekly paper, to thank all those friends who had sent food and flowers and kind messages to him in what he called his "bereavement," but he never said a word of thanks to all the ones that had dragged the river. And some people thought that was strange, but then so was everything else about the whole business. And if Ella Biggs wasn't in the river, where on earth had she gone? It was the biggest mystery Ann Louise and Martha Alice and all their friends could ever have imagined; and they spent hours trying to "solve" it all, looking for clues, conjecturing motives, even acting out "The Disappearance of Ella Biggs," as they called it, like it was a picture show, with Ann Louise sometimes playing the lead and sometimes Martha Alice (depending on whose mother's fur coat they could get hold of).

But of course, they always had to steer clear of Ann Louise's mother, whatever they were doing. Because she *was* nothing if not *loyal*, and she always maintained that Ella Biggs was in the river. She told Ann Louise she thought maybe "poor Miss Ella Biggs" was afraid she might have to take the rest cure again and just couldn't face the prospect and that was why she had "done it." But Ann Louise noticed her mother was always looking out the window—or somewhere else—whenever she said that. And anyway, Ann Louise thought Ella Biggs must have had more sense—more *to* her—than that. There were other theories around town, of course: some people said Ella Biggs just couldn't stand living in the house with her Big Baptist mother-in-law any longer and it was her way of getting back at Tom Banks, who had always been something of a mamma's boy anyway, and whom she never had really loved anyhow. But they didn't know where she was either. The wildest speculation of all had Ella Biggs's disappearance connected with the fairly sudden departure from Woodville a few weeks later of a very personable young man named Johnny Gitchell who worked up at the funeral home, a fairly new institution in Woodville back then. (The old families still patronized Waterfield and Hill, who operated their undertaking business on the second floor of their furniture store down on the Square; but everybody said they were on their way out because they weren't keeping up with the times.)

Ann Louise didn't remember that she had ever heard anything about Ella Biggs and Johnny Gitchell before all this happened; but then it just might be natural for two such people to be drawn to each other, she thought. There was Ella Biggs, who came of nice folks and had maybe had a past but, in any case, certainly didn't wear stockings, and Johnny Gitchell, whose history nobody knew except that the folks up at the funeral home said he could lay out the prettiest corpses you ever saw in your life—why shouldn't they be somehow connected? (It was the way Hollywood would have written it.) And why weren't Tom Banks and Ella Biggs's own family more grieved than they apparently were? And what all did they know anyhow?

It was all the great mystery of Ann Louise's young life; there was simply no doubt about that. And even better than the picture show, in some ways. After all, it had really happened, right there in Woodville; and she herself had actually known Ella Biggs, even one time pinched her naked leg under the bridge table, to see for herself whether she was wearing hose. That was about as real as you could get. But why did they never find Ella Biggs, dead or alive, and nobody ever know for sure what had happened to her? The movies wouldn't have done it that way: they wouldn't have left you dangling like that. So the mystery went on and on and, in some ways, became more alluring still. After all, when you found out about Santa Claus and where babies came from and all that sort of thing—or even who had "done it" in a murder mystery—that was the end of it. But the mystery of Ella Biggs only deepened with time.

Over the years, while Ann Louise was growing up, there would be reports of people seeing Ella Biggs—usually "out" in Texas or somewhere west. (Places like that were always "out.") And every summer for years after that, Ella Biggs's mother, Mrs.

Scott, would take a long trip somewhere by herself, and a lot of people assumed she was going to visit Ella Biggs, wherever she was—or perhaps they were just meeting somewhere, on "neutral ground." Ann Louise even heard of one man from Woodville who claimed to have spotted Ella Biggs and Johnny Gitchell operating a sideshow at an amusement park "out" in California; but she thought that was a little far-fetched even for California. But even wilder was the report that came back from Texas that Ella Biggs—this time alone—had been seen on the streets of San Antonio dressed in a nun's habit! Tom Banks finally remarried but had to get a divorce from Ella Biggs, *in absentia* as it were, because she hadn't been gone the seven years or whatever it took to be declared legally dead. And this time he built his wife a house of her own and didn't take her home to live with mamma. And this one was a real homebody—hardly ever even went downtown, Ann Louise heard; and she wore stockings too. Ann Louise, who was off at school now, had asked about that right off.

But the riddle of Ella Biggs abided—for Ann Louise and, she suspected, for everybody else in town. The whole thing, of course, had long since made Ella Biggs community property; everybody could always put in his two cents worth about what he thought had really happened—and why. And from then on, nobody ever had to ask *who* when you were driving over the Obion River bridge, usually on the way to Memphis, and somebody in the car would speak up and say, "Well, did she or didn't she?" Ann Louise herself could wake up in the night, all those years later, and think about the exciting time when Ella Biggs disappeared and ponder the mystery all over again and the revelation it had all become for her and Martha Alice in due course—what they had learned about folks and maybe even about themselves from it all. It had certainly been a kind of watershed in their lives, she knew. And she would think how funny, finally, it all was and wish Ella Biggs well, wherever she was, in this world or the next. And somehow it didn't seem to matter one way or the other.

So that was probably why when she and Martha Alice got together for the first time in a couple of years (Martha Alice lived in Memphis now, and they hardly ever saw each other), they both practically had the hysterics when Martha Alice was telling her about her oldest daughter, who had just married and moved to Washington, being royally entertained up there by an elderly cousin who had left Woodville many years ago. And when the daughter had told her mother what a great time she had had, Martha Alice had been a little puzzled. "Really, I can't imagine what you two had in common," she had said. "She's been gone from Woodville so long, and she's so much older than you are anyway. What on earth did you have to talk about?"

"Why, Mother," the daughter had replied, "we talked about Ella Biggs."

1975 Has Come and Gone

"THE YEAR 1975 HAS COME AND GONE, AND WE'RE still not wearing hoopskirts!" was what Ann Louise Parker—who had married Johnny Emerson—hollered to her old friend, Martha Alice Craig—whom she hadn't seen for a long time and whose husband, Don Phillips, was a big cardiologist in Memphis—when they happened to be seated near each other at a Kenny Rogers concert. Martha Alice had promptly snorted with pleasure, but there was no time to pursue the matter right then because the music—or rather, the sound—was getting under way. And afterwards the two couples had time for only the briefest of greetings, since the crowd was so large and the next day was Monday. Larry Gatlin and his brothers actually introduced the program, which was just great as far as Ann Louise was concerned, though, if she'd been consulted, she would have had the program the other way round, with Kenny Rogers doing the introducing and the Gatlins the main attraction. But she wasn't going to worry about that, only about getting prematurely deaf from the sheer noise of all the music, which most people seemed to be used to: she reckoned they'd been to so many such affairs they'd lost a lot of their hearing. In any case, while it was all so loud that Ann Louise couldn't have understood the lyrics if she hadn't already known the songs, most people just sat there taking it all in, as happy and unconcerned as if they had good sense.

What the "1975" and "hoopskirts" was about, as Ann Louise explained to her husband when they were driving home, was all to do with when she and Martha Alice were growing up in Woodville and playing with their *Gone with the Wind* paper dolls, shortly after the movie had just come out and everybody was going to Memphis on Saturdays and taking their children to see it. Martha Alice had seen fit to hold forth then on fashion and style: how things came and went and were the height of fashion today but out of date tomorrow; and she had proclaimed that it was all perfectly clear to her that hoopskirts, which they both just adored, would certainly be back in by 1975. She would brook no argument, either, not that Ann Louise was disposed to give her much of one. For one thing, as Ann Louise afterwards told Johnny, who hadn't grown up in Woodville—where they still lived and he was the high school principal—when you disagreed strongly with Martha Alice in those days, she might bite you. And she could still see those teeth marks on her hand yet, too. She said she wasn't sure that biting you ever convinced anybody that you were wrong and Martha Alice was right. But anyhow it somehow proved something and, if you'd ever been bitten by Martha Alice, you'd be more or less inclined just to let matters stand as they were. Martha Alice was always more or less *positive* about everything, and hoopskirts were no exception. It all came from her mother being a Russell, Ann Louise said: too much temper all the way round. And their men all drank too.

But they were the dearest of friends growing up and always would be. It was just too bad that Martha Alice lived in Memphis now and she still lived in Woodville, which was fifty miles away; it all might as well have been on the moon for all they got to see each other anymore. They had grown up just down the street from each other and were the same age, and every afternoon of the world their colored nurses would take them up to play on the steps of the Methodist church, where all the other children in town who had nurses would be also. The nurses could all have a good visit and talk about their boyfriends while all the children told secrets and giggled and played hide and seek, in and out of the flying buttresses, as their mammas and daddies called those supports on the sides of the building.

Later they started to school together, in the class of Miss Rosa Moss, who had taught the first grade in Woodville so long that she had had three generations in some families. They went on to take piano lessons from Miss Caroline Miller, who had a thin gray mustache and who Ann Louise's father said could have been the Kaiser of Germany. (Miss Rosa Moss said she'd never seen a child yet she couldn't control, but in her case it was all done mostly with love and affection, unlike Miss Caroline and the Reign of Terror.) In fact, the first evening dresses she and Martha Alice had ever had were made for them to be in Miss Caroline's recitals, which were somewhat like stage productions on the one hand and military drills on the other—as Ann Louise had tried many times explaining to Johnny, who hadn't grown up in a small town and didn't understand things like that. He thought it all mildly amusing but more from the standpoint of a missionary learning tribal rites in darkest Africa, Ann Louise suspected. She was always having to remind him that, however funny you might think it was now, it had all been perfectly serious back then—and maybe to some people it still was today.

Like cheerleaders and drum majorettes in high school, she used to tell him. Nothing in your life could ever be quite so grand as being one of those (she'd been a cheerleader but missed out on the other). But all the little Bertha Jeans and Betty Sues had had their day right then and there and never would get over it. Think of them in later life, she reminded Johnny: they all got married right after high school, mostly to boys named Junior and Bubba, who drove trucks and drank Pabst Blue Ribbon. And almost immediately they all had four children with dishwater blond hair and snotty noses. They themselves weighed two hundred pounds in five years' time. Furthermore, Ann Louise said, their idea of being dressed up was to have their hair all teased and colored up like a new kind of cotton candy to wear with yet one more polyester pantsuit with jacket and trousers in complementary designs and preferably in what you might call *wedding reception green.* This got its name from a Baptist wedding where you had the reception in the church basement and so you couldn't have anything to drink but Kool-Aid punch that usually had lime sherbet melting in the middle of it. It had all been downhill after their high-kicking days, she told him. And as for the subsequent lives of beauty queens, Ann Louise said they simply didn't bear contemplation. As one of her great-aunts used to remark contemptuously of such like: "Pretty, pretty...." But pretty was as pretty did; and none of it would get you anywhere at all, she implied. Yet to Ann Louise and Martha Alice in high school, it had all been deadly serious, even heartbreaking. (Martha Alice lost out because her mouth was too big, they said; but maybe somebody also remembered her sharp teeth.) Ann Louise supposed they could have tap-danced, which even then she knew was the tackiest thing of all; but their mammas had thought they'd be better off with Miss Caroline and the Girl Scouts: that was quite discipline enough.

And it was about that time, anyway, that they began to go to dances and discover boys—just as they entered high school; and that Christmas Mary Lou Sanford—who always did everything before everybody else and her mother before her too—as Ann Louise had overheard her mother tell her father one night, invited the whole class to their first real dance. And the girls all wore their mothers' fur coats and their last year's recital dresses and felt terribly grown up. But Billy Joe Martin (whom Ann Louise had had a crush on all fall, but he wouldn't look at her except to scowl when she trapped him in Latin class and got a headmark before he did) danced cheek to cheek with Martha Alice before he even danced the first dance with her. (Somebody had turned all the lights down low in the Sanfords' basement recreation room.) Ann Louise's evening was spoiled. There was one bright moment, however, when Harry Johnston got carried away and got up on the Ping-Pong table and invited everybody to a dance at his house on New Year's Eve; and his mother, who Ann Louise always thought looked like an anteater because her lips were almost always pursed in continual disapproval of *something*, didn't know a bit more about it than a spook. And she had to make the best of it, and the dance took place too. But Ann Louise would always remember that Harry's mother, after having been dragooned into letting Harry give a dance that way, sat there all evening right back in the hall, apparently absorbed in her book-club book and rocking away by the Heatrola, never once looking up into the living room but with her ears bristling like antennae for the first sounds of rape or riot. That night Billy Joe Martin did dance cheek to cheek with her while the record player played "Moonlight Becomes You," but by then Ann Louise had decided his cowlick wasn't going to be nearly as cute in a couple of years as it was right then and Martha Alice could have him.

And so they proceeded, more or less neck and neck—she and Martha Alice—neither of them ever really *leading* the other but both mostly holding their own, which was probably why they stayed good friends. Martha Alice had stopped biting by now; but she had other ways of making her displeasure known—raising her eyebrows and shrugging her shoulders about anything she felt superior to, making sounds of nausea when it was anything she violently disapproved of. (Ann Louise had to content herself mostly with her ability to belch on cue; but she had discovered there was a limited audience for that sort of thing, to say nothing of what her mother would say if she caught her at it.) Martha Alice was still inclined, though, to get on a high horse from time to time and lay down the law like she had done that time about them wearing hoopskirts by 1975. There was just no question, she once told Ann Louise, but that it was really better the North had won the Civil War; and that way they would always be one country. And Mrs. Roosevelt certainly did look a lot better since she was in that car wreck and got her buck teeth knocked out and replaced with some false ones. Ann Louise, who remembered her Confederate-veteran grandfather (of whom she was always afraid) only too well, said, well, maybe it was but she sure hoped hoopskirts were coming back in 1975 anyway. And whoever said Mrs. Roosevelt was supposed to make her living by her looks anyhow? When you heard the president give one of his "Fireside Chats" on the radio, you just knew that there was somebody up there in Washington who was going to *take care of you* and you didn't have a thing to worry about. Besides, they couldn't help the way their children had turned out.

Martha Alice *was* probably the only one of Miss Caroline's piano students in captivity who ever ventured to stand up to her. And she did it in style. When Miss Caroline blessed her out for not having memorized all of her recital piece, which that year was going to be Brahms's "Hungarian Dance No. 5," Martha Alice just jumped up and called her an old Gestapo agent and snatched up her music and ran out the door and never had gone back either. It made you right weak to think about it; but, Ann Louise decided, you had to admire it. The only thing Ann Louise had ever done even remotely comparable to that was when she was ten and she had stuck an old-fashioned hat pin she had found in her mother's dresser drawer in Miss Evelyn Hartman's behind at Vacation Bible School. Miss Evelyn had been wearing them all out with stories about all the poor people starving to death in India and China; but since she herself weighed close to three hundred pounds, Ann Louise decided that none of it would ever come nigh her, and anyway, what were they all supposed to do about it—stop eating? So she stuck the hat pin in Miss Evelyn; and Miss Evelyn promptly turned on her, with tears in her eyes, and said, by way of rebuke, "It just hurts me to think that you don't have any more Christian love in your heart than to do me that way." And Ann Louise smirked and said, "It hurt something else too, didn't it, Miss Evelyn?" But Miss Evelyn just looked at her sadly and shook her head and didn't say anything else; but that night Ann Louise got a first-class spanking at home as a result.

So she and Martha Alice were never rivals but perhaps copartners in crime, colleagues, you might say—as she had tried to explain to Johnny. When they were sophomores in high school, Martha Alice had even produced the *Sophomore Scandals*, complete with a masked striptease (just half a dozen girls stripping down to their bathing suits while Doris Arwood played "Malaguena" on the baby grand piano back behind the stage) in an abortive attempt to help Ann Louise get elected Football Queen. And when they were Juniors, they had sneaked off all by themselves one Saturday, when their mothers thought they were at a big music-club district meeting in Memphis, and had lunch at the Peabody Hotel up in the Skyway. Later they cried all the way through a rerun of *Wuthering Heights*, which they had missed the first time around and was then playing at the Malco where, between showings of the movie, Milton Slosser groaned up out of the dark mounted on a snow-white Wurlitzer, and they would all gallop off into community singing. She didn't know whether Martha Alice had ever tried explaining it all to Don, the cardiologist. But then he came from Woodville too, so perhaps he would naturally understand. And it didn't matter, really, that they hardly ever saw each other. Martha Alice had always worked part-time after her children had got big, and Ann Louise always seemed to be involved in so many local good works (to say nothing of substitute teaching) that she seldom got to Memphis. But what they had been through together, what they had both lived to tell was, after all those years, still a bond as strong as death. One time, as she had tried telling Johnny about it some years after they were married, she had exclaimed, "Why, sometimes, when I'm doing the dishes at night—or the laundry, after you and the children have gone to bed, I could just cry about the things Martha Alice and I did when we were growing up, the things we *shared.* I don't think you ever get over that."

She never was sure Johnny understood; and, she supposed, it was maybe because he had grown up in the suburbs of St. Louis, where everybody's father mostly worked for a big corporation and automatically got transferred every few years to another suburb just like the first, whether it was in Detroit or Cleveland or somewhere else. And no, she didn't have to *see* Martha Alice now to keep their "relationship" going because it all went far beyond seeing. Further, it wasn't a "relationship" either: they had simply grown up together. They didn't even have to *talk* periodically either; they simply had each other on the mind and *knew* what the other must be up to—almost like telepathy. That was even the way it had been when they had gone off to college and Ann Louise had pledged Theta at Vanderbilt and Martha Alice had gone Chi O at Ole Miss—both the same but different, if you knew the two schools. And Ann Louise had met Johnny, who was also in school there; but even then Martha Alice had always known she would come back home and marry Don, who was already in medical school in Memphis. In those days, when they were going together and Ann Louise would try to explain to Johnny about her closest friend, he would say, "Well, then, you're sort of like sisters." But she would reply, "Yes and no. We grew up together in a small town, just down the street from each other. And we had everything in common—likes and dislikes, not just families, the way it can be with sisters, who may not really *like* each other. And all around us, twenty-four hours a day, was Woodville and everybody in it. We knew everybody there, and everybody knew us and our families back to the Year One. And you didn't have to *explain* anything to anybody because all of you there had it all in common. You never get away from it either. I've already found that out. When Martha Alice and I are together right now, we don't even have to talk if we don't want to: we seem to follow each other's thoughts anyhow. The main thing is, no matter where each of us is in the world, she knows the other one is somewhere else in the world too. She just *is*, and that's enough."

So by the time it got to be after 1975 and Ann Louise and Martha Alice, who hadn't seen each other for some time, were both old enough to start having grandchildren, Johnny should probably have understood something of their long association, their rooted connection, which all came out, all over again, in Ann Louise's greeting to her old friend at the Kenny Rogers concert. Maybe he never would understand it altogether because he hadn't grown up in Woodville; maybe, as one of his friends there used to tease him, you not only had to be born there, you had to have been conceived there as well! But he knew enough by now to understand that they were, in this barest of gestures, somehow touching base with each other, saying little but implying the whole world: "1975 has come and gone...."

Introduction to the Interview and Essays

I interviewed Robert Drake in his apartment in Knoxville for about nine hours on January 18, 19, and 20 in 1998. The result was eight audio tapes that were transcribed into more than 135 typed double-spaced pages. I then sent the transcription to Drake for clarification. His editing produced a 72 page single-spaced manuscript. (These tapes and the original transcription as well as Drake's revision are in the Robert Drake Collection in the Jean and Alexander Heard Library at Vanderbilt University.) The interview was too long. I was forced to edit.

While in England doing background research for this project, I asked two of Drake's friends, the writer Ronald Blythe and Malcolm Jack who works with the House of Commons if they ever got to say anything when they were talking to Drake. They both laughed for a good while. Each claimed the other was able to get a word in from time to time. Drake is a great talker. As he has said on a number of occasions, his narrative skill in fiction is closely associated with the oral storytelling tradition in which he grew up. When I looked at the transcript of the interview, I saw that my brief and halting comments added very little. I decided to take myself completely out of the interview except for brief parenthetical insertions to create context. Then I decided to group Drake's verbal tapestries by subject and let the discerning reader discover that Drake is as entertaining as a raconteur as he is as a writer.

The notion that Robert Drake was a storyteller was certainly supported by my interviews in England. Malcolm Jack said he overheard Drake telling a story when they were both swimming at the YMCA and decided there and then that he had to meet him. Ronald Blythe, on the other hand, was introduced to Drake by a mutual friend and has known Drake for thirty years. Blythe believes that London represents a sort of freedom to Drake. Jack observed that London is for Drake a place where he is "at home" and yet "away." The continent, on the other hand, is "foreign."

Each summer like clockwork, Drake visits Bottomgom's Farm, Blythe's Tudor-era home that was formerly owned by John and Christine Nash and full of art by Nash and his contemporaries. He rushes in for an afternoon lunch and a tea in the garden and then rushes to London for an evening at the theatre. He loves the theatre and sees more than a dozen shows on each of his trips. Blythe observed that Drake knows nothing of farming or gardening and that he is oblivious to the art on the walls or what is on his plate. One exception to that obliviousness occurred when Blythe picked fresh wild mushrooms and fixed a wonderful mushroom soup. When Drake realized what it was he exclaimed "I haven't come all this way just to be poisoned," and he would not touch it.

Drake seems to do many things "like clockwork." Both Blythe and Jack noted Drake's love of ritual. Jack said Drake loved the ceremony of the House of Commons, and Blythe noted that Drake looked forward to English tea in his Tudor flower garden. Drake explained to me in an excised part of our interview that he loves weddings and especially graduations. "We order our lives through ceremonies," he said. Jack explained that Drake's swimming is a ritual, a disciplined escape, a form of religion. "As a swimmer you put everything aside. It is a lone activity. You don't have to arrange anything. You do it for yourself." Jack's observations about Drake's swimming could well be made, in the same words, about the process of writing.

In the interview and in the four essays by Drake: "The Writer as Hunger Artist," "The Writer as Observer, the Writer as Outsider," "All This Material and Other Such Things," and "What I Write About: Death and Old Women," I have chosen to focus on Drake as a writer and on the process of writing. The careful reader will see a pattern of consistency in Drake's statements and a pattern of complete candor. As he says in the interview, "Again I keep saying I have no beauty secrets, I have no shortcuts, I have no quick tricks to offer anybody. Now, if you want to talk about work, if you want to talk about what we hope we can do, what we aim to do, then maybe we can do some business."

James A. Perkins

Interview with Robert Drake

On Reading and the Movies

My parents, they were not literary but that's a poor way of putting it, but they weren't. They thought you should be always "uplifting" or "elevating," you know, and I remember I told one of my Vanderbilt professors about it. It was Monroe Spears. And I told him once that I was ashamed that I had read so much junk when I was growing up. I said my mother took all these women's magazines and you know, and I just read all that stuff and I said I could have been reading Dickens' novels or whatever. And he said, no, don't worry about that; what matters is that you were forming the habit of reading. And later on, of course, that sorted itself out. I think basically it's true and that's what I tell parents now. They say, "My child is reading junk." And I say, "O don't worry. Because the main thing is that he reads." And I told my class just the other day, as a matter of fact, this was a writing class I think, that our teachers in school read to us. Usually after lunch, when we were still digesting things, I guess. Obviously there were things like Bunny Brown and Sister Sue, that series by a woman who obviously was many women and may have been many a man for that matter, whose official name was Laura Lee Hope. But then, the Bobbsey Twins and all that. But in the sixth grade, Miss Mary Majors, who was the first young, attractive teacher we ever had (the rest of them were old women, old maids and so on, and some were kind of dried-up looking, but the spirit of God was in them and they were some of the best teachers I ever had in my life). Miss Mary Majors I know at one point decided that she was going to read us *Huckleberry Finn.* So I heard *Huckleberry Finn* at the age of twelve. It never was any great revelation to me. Now I wonder if she, you know, along the way, censored passages. I never was aware that she did. But I remember particularly one thing, and it still tickles. Of course with my satirist's sense of humor, which some people think is sick, but is almost endemic in the Drake family.... When Huck is staying with the family, you know, where the King and the Duke are passing themselves off as the heirs. And one of the girls, you know there were three nieces of the dead Peter Wilks, and Joanna, I think, is the one who has a harelip. And when Huck starts to speak to her, he starts to call her "Harelip" and we all laughed, including Miss Mary. We knew that was funny. And so you could say that the colorful, so called sadistic, southern sense of humor was to be found right there at age twelve. I still think it's funny. And I come from a family that always thought deformities were funny. Harelips, you know, glass eyes, wooden legs, you name it. But we can talk about that some other time. Well anyhow, so I was encouraged to read but not by direct command. My mother belonged to one of those great institutions of all time, a women's book club. There were about five, eventually, in town. The oldest one was just called *The* Book Club, like my relatives in Virginia referred to *The* University, which is the place up at Charlottesville. My mother, though, belonged to one that was a step down from that in age and a lot of its members, I think, had jobs in the daytime, maybe downtown in offices or whatever, so they had to have an evening meeting. They just called it The Review Club and they passed the books around each time. And those women could get into the biggest...they couldn't remember who was supposed to get which book, and to see grown women actually go bonkers over trying to remember whose time it was to have which book was pretty silly. Well anyhow, it was always good because the refreshments were good and I got to lick the dasher, which was usually apricot ice cream. And why Howard Johnson and Baskin-Robbins have never discovered that exquisite flavor, I do not know. OK. So I was encouraged but, I mean, my people were not bookish at all. The closest thing they had to that would be my Uncle Lewis, the Methodist preacher, the oldest one of my father's brothers, who went to

Vanderbilt Divinity School. He ended up as a circuit-rider. He was, well, preachers are supposed to be bookish, you know. And I remember a wonderful rotating bookcase he had in his study. Well it was, you know, square and all that, but I mean, you just kept moving it around. And all the interesting theological and historical books were there. But anyhow, *that* was bookish, you see. But no, I did not come from people who were in any way like that. And I did not come from highly educated people. No money, for one thing.

I know I said what I've said to you, more or less, to a friend I was visiting years ago in Los Angeles. He had grown up in Minnesota and had gone to Harvard and done all those right things. And he had been a very successful author, and I haven't heard from him in a long time, but he lived right off Hollywood Boulevard and so he gave me the real guided tour. And he said, "What do you want to see?" I'll tell you, of course, the first thing I wanted to see, you'll understand this, was the Forest Lawn Cemetery. Some people of course don't even know why that is funny or bad or awful; they've never heard of it. Well, you and I are old enough to know what it means. And I must say it was worth it all. [Laughter] But whatever the case, he was disturbed when I told him what I just told you, that I grew up not reading a lot of books...I referred to the picture show, as we called it, as being my whole artistic and literary life maybe and I went every time the program changed as long as I got my lessons and practiced my piano lesson and all that. And if you were less than twelve it was ten cents. And every Christmas Santa Claus would put a roll of picture show tickets down in the toe of my stocking, see. So I said something about I just lived for the movies and I read all the movie magazines and all that. And then I wrote fan letters to movie stars requesting autographs, photographs and all that kind of stuff. But anyhow, I was telling him all this and he said, "Oh my goodness!" Well, he didn't know it but he was a great prig. Politically, he was very liberal, and I think he was naturally suspicious of me, knowing where I was from and all that. We were brought together, by the way, by our common interest in Saki, the writer whom I wrote my M.A. thesis on and he was writing a biography of. (So damned hard to write because so few people that knew him survived.) But he was horrified because he said I should have been *reading* all that time. And I said, "Well, I hate to tell you but the picture show was my literary life." Things like that always set my teeth on edge. There are always people interested in telling you what you should have written instead of what you did write. I've been told, as you know, until I'm sick of it, that I should write novels and I even had somebody once tell me I should write a play. And they were people with very good literary credentials, I might say. But you're not writing to please them. So anyhow, that's how the book thing comes up. Now of course later on when I went off to college, that was a whole new day....

On Saturday Serials and More Reading

Oh yes. Of course! Oh, I was at the picture show every Saturday afternoon. And in fact, you kind of lost status if you didn't see the whole program at least twice. And with careful arrangements you could see it three times. My father would come home for dinner, which of course for us was the noon meal, on Saturday from the store; and I would go back with him, and he would put me out at the picture show, in those days called the Dixie Theater, and later on the Strand. It was a converted store building on the square and had an entrance on the square and an entrance in the alley behind. A sure fire trap if ever there was one, but I didn't burn up as you see. And I would stay all afternoon, and he would stop by there on the way home for supper and pick me up. O, I saw every chapter of *Jungle Girl* and then I think for some strange reason I missed the last chapter of the *Lone Ranger*, where it was going to be revealed who he was, you see, but I think somebody was kind enough to fill me in. I used to be scared of all the shooting in the westerns, but I can tell you right now almost the day and the hour my serious movie going began. Serious, maybe in a rather elementary way but it was 1939, which, of course, was the best possible year. Because there have been books, articles written on 1939 as the great movie year, when it came into its own. I was in the fourth grade. The best part on the program, of course, aside from anything else, came if there was a Three Stooges comedy. Of course I adored it. I still do! As you know, I still think comedy is a very serious art form and indeed I'm prepared to say it's as serious as tragedy and sometimes you really can't tell them apart. I don't have any hang-ups about that at all. So when people say something is "mere comedy" or "mere entertainment," you know, I get angry. So, that's the way it all happened. But anyhow I certainly did get in the habit of reading and in many ways I didn't really get educated until I was out of my formal schooling and began to teach. And there were so many people I hadn't read that sometimes I would go out of my way to assign an author to a class. We had an option about certain things you had to have in a sophomore literature section, and you could choose amongst this and that. And I would deliberately choose an author I had not read enough of. I remember how I read Henry James because I hadn't read very much Henry James. It got on my nerves; so much of it still can. But he was one of the options in the sophomore survey. No, it wasn't the survey; it was a more or less genre course. So I assigned a whole spate of Henry James novels to make myself read them. And I've done that again and again in various other courses, too. And I systematically just sat down some years ago, and I wasn't teaching Dickens at the time. I never have taught much Dickens, but I decided that I simply had not read nearly enough of him, so I started out with the big ones. I had read up to that time...I suppose I had read *David Copperfield*, but anyhow, I had read some of the canonized ones—you might say that's a play on words, you see, but not the ones, the kind of minor ones, you know. I was even reading, before it was all over, I got down to the ones most people haven't read, I mean, like *Barnaby Rudge* and, well, the one about the man who comes to America, I can't even remember, O, and then *Little Dorrit*.... Dickens is so great. You don't care what he does because these people just jump off the page at you. And I know good people that have always kind of looked down at him in certain ways, but it doesn't bother me. Then some years after that, well about the same time, I got interested in Trollope. Trollope of course is one that people never have been able to make up their minds about. And so, you know, they get disturbed if you get too serious about him. And I got into him in a strange way. One of my friends said that she enjoyed reading (very much) the novels of Angela Thirkell. Did you ever hear of Angela Thirkell? Well, she's interesting. People always say no and then when I tell them who she was, they perk up their ears. Angela Thirkell had a very interesting family history. She was the granddaughter of Edward Burne-Jones, one of the pre-Raphaelites. And she was the daughter of gosh, I can't remember, but he had a "Mc" name, and he was a professor of classics at Oxbridge, I think. She was also a cousin of Rudyard Kipling and, I think, Stanley Baldwin and naturally moved in literary circles. She was married twice and she lived in Australia for a while and so on and so on. But anyhow, she knew all kinds of people in the world of the arts, including Henry James. Or rather, she was *talked to* by Henry James. And she said he talked just the way he wrote: you thought he would never come to the end of a sentence. So, I thought, my God, here I am talking to somebody...you know...it was like "Did you see Shelley plain?" Well, what she did, she wrote a whole series of novels and I don't know whether I've ever converted anybody to these; it's a very, very special taste, a whole series of novels using the Trollop geography and genealogy and machinery. She takes the Trollopian families from the Barchester novels and Parliamentary novels and so on and brings them all into modern times. Of course, hers is much more...well, it's not like she was *imitating* Trollope, but it's like somebody who can maybe tell you what such people would be like in the world of the 30s, 40s, and 50s. She died...she was the same age as my mother, born in 1890, and died about 19—in the early 60s. And I went to see her twice when I was in London—the first two times I was there—and she was graciousness itself, of course, as you would expect. Anyhow, the novels are tremendous fun. If you know some Trollope ahead of time, that helps, but it doesn't depend on that. And it has all the English, as I say, all the prejudices. I mean, you know, the county families and the upper middle class and maybe even some of the peerage and so on. Although she's not comfortable, it's been suggested, with anybody higher up than earls! She does have a duke or two but she's not comfortable with that—that's what people say. All right. But anyhow she takes on all that machinery. Well see, I'd always believed in England and one of the biggest things that griped me when I first started going to England, you always met people who told you nobody believed in the monarchy anymore. Nobody...believed in Lord Nelson, nobody believed in Elizabeth I, nobody believed in Winston Churchill. You know, there are people like that that you hope will be prepared for in Hell in some especially unpleasant arrangements. So it was wonderful to see there were more people still alive and at large that do believe in these things.

On Parliament

I'm not a keen observer of the way things *look.* And anybody in a small town, if they have any sense, is forced to be [a keen observer of the social status of that small town]. As you know also, I think I'm a pretty good observer about talk. Most southerners are. I used to say southerners must be afraid of silence because there never was much of it around. Yes, I find that fascinating. Because the average American, people in other parts of the country...you know the whole class system and all...they are the most class conscious people in the world but they try to cover it up. I've known people on the faculty of the University whose prime achievement in life, I thought privately, was to belong to the Cherokee Country Club. And one or two of them did, and I know they used it and they talked about using it. [Of] course they used it just for golf, you understand. [Laughter] So there you are. So anyhow, Trollope...then of course the Parliamentary novels, that gets you into the structure of Parliament and the government situation, which I know more about than I used to. I've known some members of Parliament. And I have a very good friend there who's a permanent fixture there I don't know if he's a civil servant or what, but he runs all kinds of...he's chairman of so many committees. Whatever the Government, he's still there. I've learned a few things from him. And I've been there for a couple of sessions of the House, and all, and I've been entertained to drinks on the terrace overlooking the Thames. The first time I went, I thought they might ask for a blood sample, because I mean, I had to go through so many people to more or less vet me and so on. And I was told, and I hope it's true (I don't know whether it'd be like that in Washington—probably would, though, in these security-conscious days) but I was told that was kind of a holdover from the seventeenth century when Charles I went down to arrest the five members. Because they're determined that *nobody* is going to come in and disturb them from their business. And when I got up in the gallery I was amazed. Now I would have thought this would have been the absolute pinnacle of propriety with everybody just being on their P's and Q's and thus and so. But you would have thought you were in the lounge of a bar or something. People sat there with their feet up on the seats in front of them and lolling about and just getting up and walking about and so forth. Of course the people on the front bench—you know the Government's on one side and the Opposition's on the other (I've forgotten how that goes) and of course the Speaker on this sort of quasi-throne in the middle. But on the front bench is who is really in control, and it's called the Treasury Bench, I think. Well, I did that [visited Parliament] twice. But I was amazed at the informality. And so anyhow, but I learned a lot from my visits, but Trollope's very good with all that too.

On an Early Memory

Well, you know, I simply have no idea what my first memory is because I didn't know it *was* the first thing. But I do know this. I think I remember, and God knows why, a friend of my mother's who, it turns out, was the first woman ever to be employed as a teller in a bank in our town. That was a bold thing in those days. And I remember her behind the teller's cage. Incidentally, she was also the first teacher of home economics, which used to be called domestic science, in the high school. And she had her degree from this place right here, which program, you see, was created under the Smith-Hughes Act...you know about that? Well, this was one of the first places really to do much with that and I'm happy to say it's one of the things that is best known about this place even today—that and the Agriculture school. But she was kind of ahead of her time...and went on in due course to become the first florist to set up a business in Ripley. But I first remember her behind the teller's cage in the bank and I found out that she quit working there when she married again (she was a widow). And I learned later that all took place when I was about two years old! [Laughter] There was no doubt about it. She was a very talented lady. No, I don't think I have [written about her]. I don't know.... No, I don't think I ever have. I suspect she's just too big for me right now, and perhaps I'm scared to get hold of her.

On Diction

I talk on more than one level. I'm talking to you. You are a friend and a former student. I probably am not talking the way I would if I were talking to some high-up official in some line of work, maybe academic or otherwise. I'm certainly not talking the language I would talk to customers in Drake Brothers store. I'm not talking to you in the language I probably use to some of my friends. I think everybody makes a certain number of concessions, adjustments. All my life...I remember hearing one of my professors at Vanderbilt reading from one of his stories or something to a class and he had somebody using language that I just knew was inappropriate for that level of society and the dramatic context. And I remember thinking "All right, I know what's going on."

On a Sense of Audience

I have that [an audience in mind]...as I told you the other day...I have that voice somewhere deep in my brain, or what passes for my brain, that is a constant monitor—"this person would—or would not—say this." Eudora Welty, I know, said something like the same thing—I didn't ever learn this from her though I learned an enormous amount about what your own language could do for you. But I mean, people just read her, and you see the different levels people talk on and it's the same thing. But she said somewhere that she had learned to listen to that voice, and...it was in those lectures at Harvard. And she said, "I learned to listen to that voice...I learned then to listen to that voice." And she added, almost parenthetically, "I still do." I think I know exactly what she means. And I think I told you one time people are always trying to catch you out. Somebody said, "I just can't imagine the way your characters would look." But I said, "Listen to them talk and you'll know how they look." And that wasn't frivolity. I'm not sure how I can explain that to anybody but I think you know what I mean. You know something about the social level probably implied. And you know something about where they live. Well, it—you're not going to think they look like Jack Kennedy, are you? On the other hand, as I told my students just the other day, if a girl is named Annie Maud and a boy is named Billy Bob, I think you'll have a pretty good idea.

On Teaching

You know when I hear some of the old boys who...some of them are gone now...when I hear them talk about the good old days, I think "Yeah, and I can see you right now. If you could have gotten away with it, you would have assigned everybody to teach umpteen sections every term." When I came here, for that matter, we were still on the quarter system, and the standard load was four, four, four. And I can hardly think about that now without getting angry. Because some of them just thought that's exactly the way it should be. And if *they* had had a hard time back then, well, none of us should have any cakes and ale now.

It's hard to say [which courses I have enjoyed the most], again. I know I have several times...well not just several, a good many times...taught a course in the British and American Ballad and Folktale. And that I enjoy, but I have to work awfully hard, because I have to keep working it up. Because you can forget a lot of that special stuff from year to year. But it's always exciting when something comes out of it, you know. I met a boy one time who, alas, I'd have given anything if he'd been taking the course but I had no way of knowing until it was too late. I heard him in the men's locker room down at the gym one day singing what was, it turned out—I kept listening and I thought this *cannot* be right—he was singing a Child Ballad. And it was the one about the death of Queen Jane, Jane Seymour, Henry VIII's third wife, who died in childbirth. And I went down to him and I said, "Where did you learn that? And he said, "Oh, my grandfather taught it to me." And I almost swooned. And I said, "Do you know what you're singing?" He said, "No, it's just a song he taught me." So I told him and then asked, "Do you know any other songs like that?" which he said he did. And I finally prevailed on him to come and sing for us in class one day. But he was very shy, he really didn't want to do it. And I felt just real mean, I almost dragged him in there. But I said, "You don't realize how valuable this is." And I tried to explain what it was all about. And then on the same...not the same day but another time we had another student, the one I told you about doing the dictionary of slang. He, of course, is from New York—New York City. It was a different ethnic background and everything else. And he sang ones that he had simply learned after he got interested in folklore. And maybe before he came down here to school. He's been here for years now. But the students were more impressed by him than they were the young man from down the road. I said, "I'm not surprised," but I said, "what you should know is one reason you feel, maybe, the way you do: the student from New York City was singing for an audience. But our local one was singing for *himself*." And I said, "Now that's the difference." And I think that's as good a way to put it as any I know. But whatever the case, that course always put a kind of drudgery on me; there was so much to explain to students who didn't have much of a foundation for understanding what it was all about. But I always enjoyed it. I was privileged, too, in repeating for my students what I'd learned from Mr. Davison. Then I always enjoyed teaching the short story. But I never particularly enjoyed teaching the graduate seminar on the Vanderbilt Fugitive-Agrarians. I had heard too much about them. I always enjoyed the novel. The novel, of course, is hard to teach. Right now, see, I'm just jumping into the beginning of Jane Austen. And that's hard to teach though because you see, you would like for all of them to have read every word of the novel before you ever begin to talk about it but you know that's not realistic. And so that always presents some difficulties. The same way that in my writing course, which I of course continue to enjoy a great deal and keep learning from all the time, I say, "Now this is described in the catalog as a course in fiction writing and it is. But it doesn't say *what* fiction." And I said, "Now legally, if you want to, I have to allow you to write a novel, but, I said, I just hope you won't because, again, it's hard to do that in a class like this.

On Writing

I tell students of writing the first day, I say, "Before we begin and go any further, I *cannot* teach you to write fiction. What I will try to teach you is something about how to *read* fiction. And I cannot say too often that this is a course in the reading *and* the writing of fiction. Most of our distinguished and expert writers have been also wonderfully expert readers. And it seems to me that I can maybe teach you something about that. But if I can teach you anything about writing it would be something like...I would like maybe to, if I could, to teach you to help you find what your real subjects to write about are. And then, if possible, to help you learn to write those stories as well as *you* can. But I'm not trying to get you to write like anybody else on God's earth. And it seems to me that that is all you can do for them. Anything else would be absolute madness. And I get very provoked when...oh, all the writers' conference people and all the workshops (workshop is just a dreadful word and it ought never to be used). All those people, when they tell you *that*, want "Five Easy Pieces" or "Six Quick Tricks," or...I feel sometimes like just lying down and kicking and screaming or something. Well, it has been suggested [that what undergraduates need to do is go out and live a good deal longer before they tried to write anything] and it's also been suggested that they just stay home and write. So who can say? But I would just say that there is finally no road except the one you figure out that works for you. It's just like whether you work in the morning or work at night or write standing on your head. And if it works for you, then I say, do it. But I'm not going to tell you. I'm not going to suggest it. That's for *you*. I'm reminded of something Eudora Welty said once. "Nobody can teach you the things you can teach yourself." And in general, I think it's true. And the next thing, it unsettles you too much, you know. You end up trying to please everybody. And that can be fatal.

And that's finally...all of the arts come back to the individual. And again, in a James essay, he says—I can't quote him exactly—"All the arts depend on an enormous presumption." And I want to say "Yea" and Amen." Because it's an enormous presumption to undertake, to illuminate, and dramatize a problem or a situation that anybody might have anytime, anywhere and assume that you can make people believe you. That's an enormous presumption. And in fact the act of writing by itself is an enormous presumption. I may have already said this, but that's one reason why I get a little disgusted with some of our writers who are supposedly very shy. "They are just so shy." They can't talk to people and don't like to have any controversial views, and they don't want to do this, that, or the other. Well, the hell with it. I think you've got to have an enormous amount of unshyness, which is to say, presumption, to even put pen to paper. That's what I think. And frankly, I don't want to hear anybody...it seems to me it's a very perverse form of bragging. "I'm too delicate, too ethical or too...something." That's a lot of hooey. But I think that's a very good word—presumption. It is a presumption to think you can make people accept your vision as the right one, or a viable one. After all, that's what every writer is working for and living and dying by; in the end of it all is belief. The worst thing you can say to a writer who has failed miserably in his job is "I don't believe a word of it." On the other hand, the best thing you can say is "I believed *every* word of it." And there's nothing, it seems to me, that a writer is saying...there's nothing he wants to hear more. I guess I'm saying that how you *achieve* credibility is something nobody can do for you. And I think that's just as true as it can be.

I don't find it curious [that there are numerous writing programs around the country]. I think it's—you might even say—it's original sin. I mean, you know, there are some people that just are deluded into thinking they can get by with different things. Maybe it's like this...maybe what Flannery O'Connor said, "You can do anything in fiction you can get away with. But nobody's ever gotten away with much." Well, in some ways I think that's true. But it's up to you. You have to find it out. And I mean her correspondence, which I've read, is full of giving advice to people on how to write the grotesque and all. But I think if you don't already know how to write the grotesque, you don't have any business thinking about it. I mean you know, to ask the question is to answer it in the negative, almost. And it just gives me the willies.

I would say that the hardest job I have, if you assume that I can do a job in a course like that, is to get students to write about what they know something about. Which is not to say their autobiography, thinly veiled. But it's what can they write about with authority? And that again is the fundamental problem. You see, this is not a science. I'm not even certain what it is. We say it is an art...I don't know. All the arts present it, you know—writing, music, sculpting, painting, maybe whatever. They aim at presenting one way of looking at the truth and making some sense out of this strange and curious thing that we call life. And I don't know that anybody can ever really define it better than that. I mean, you know, people say, "What are the arts all about?" Well, you know, that's a mighty big order. And I don't think some things are *meant* to be answered. See, I guess parts of the things that upset me are people wanting specific answers to all these problems. I'll tell you the thing that used to just drive me out of my mind was...I had a friend that was especially guilty of this. And she would always say...after I'd told her about, you know, some book I'd been reading or some novel or some play...she'd say, "Of course, what the author is *really* saying is...That drives me crazy. Because I said, "No! The author is not really saying anything. It's like saying, 'What Shakespeare is really saying in *King Lear* is blankety-blank.'" I said, "Shakespeare is not saying really anything in *King Lear* except *King Lear.* He's saying the whole she-bang." And it's kind of like what Cleanth Brooks said to the question, "Which of Faulkner's characters speaks for him?" And his reply, right on target, was, "All and none of Faulkner's characters speak for him." It's the total thing, it's the way it all works together. What does it mean considered as an entity? And I'm sure that there's a lot of this that goes back to Aristotle or goes back to whoever. Who gives a damn anyhow? But I don't think there's anything more you can say about it. But that particularly, that really drives me around the bend. What they're "really saying." I've been exposed to all this over the years. I used to tell my students when they asked about poetry, "Well, poetry is all a lie. You have to know that from the start. It's a lie that tells the truth. Now you go home and figure out what I'm talking about." Well, it is. It's a lie that tells the truth. And I'd say, "All right, Wordsworth says, 'She was a phantom of delight, when first she gleamed upon my sight.' In one sentence he is saying she is a very attractive young girl. But that's not all he's saying. And the total thing is the whole business. But you couldn't say it any other way."

> Tell all the truth,
> but tell it slant,
> Success in circuit lies,
> Too bright for our infirm delight,
> The truth's superb surprise.
> As lightning to the children eased
> By explanation kind
> The truth must dazzle gradually,
> Or every man be blind.

And that's from a world authority in Amherst, Massachusetts. And it's just as true as it can be. I think again, what is, oh when you try to explain...What's the secret of this? What is the code for this? I...for instance, get asked just something as mundane as "How did you lose all that weight? Tell me what your secret is." That's a very American thing to ask. You see, what they really want to know is a question that is always implied which is, "How can you be rich, famous, and beautiful without doing any work?" Now what you have to say to those people when they ask, "What's your secret?" Well, you have to find out what rules good health depends on. Then you have to adopt those rules and obey them every day for the rest of your life. And that just scares them to death. Americans just love… "I went to the Mayo Clinic in Rochester, Minnesota, and they cut me open and took out all my internal organs and it was just…you may not survive." They love that, you see. But you see, if you say that, well it's too scary. It's at once too difficult and it's too easy. Because you say you have to do this every day for the rest of your life. Oh, think about all that discipline. Although, on the other hand, if you have your insides all taken out, you don't have a damn thing to do about it anymore. And so it's the same kind of thing—how to be rich, famous, and beautiful without doing the work. What is the saying? "You pay or you don't play." You know it's like…it's not a chicken and egg controversy, but it's something kind of like that. I don't know what's…I just know there're a certain amount of things you have to learn in this world here to come near understanding some of the great mysteries that surround us. And it doesn't really matter how you learn, but you've got to learn. And I don't think anybody can say much more than that.

Remember how many freshman meetings I've sat through in my time, and I've heard every jackass in this country talk about how to teach freshman English. And I've always known how to teach it, and I'm not prepared to listen to any of that. I've heard everybody in the world sound off about it, and it always comes back to the same thing. There's more than one way of teaching, and you have to learn certain things. You can call them this, you can call them that, but it's the same thing. Well, *nobody* is willing to take the time [to do the writing], not just students. Nobody's going to take the time; nobody's going to take responsibility. You see, the surest thing you hear if you register a complaint at any organization on the face of the earth, "Well, I didn't have a thing to do with that—that's not my job." And that's not only lazy, it's irresponsible, and it's just generally bad.

And finally maybe it's all a lie, and I'm tired of hearing it. Well again, sometimes I think those lively neighbors the Gauls are still right when they say, you know, "The more things change, the more they stay the same." In that way, I don't know that things really change. Again I keep saying I have no beauty secrets, I have no shortcuts, I have no quick tricks to offer anybody. Now, if you want to talk about work, if you want to talk about what we hope we can do, what we aim to do, then maybe we can do some business. But I have no glad tidings for anybody, and that will damn me forever with some people. And I finally have to say, "So be it."

On His Education

There were two high schools in the county, one in Ripley and another one in Halls. And it's still that way now except that *all* the schools in the county have been consolidated in those two towns. So the country schoolhouses are gone. Ah, and in those days and now, of course, they bus students from around the county. We're talking about white children, of course. Nobody dreamed about busing the black folks back then, but of course that's all changed. And I know now—I was just thinking about it this morning—I know now what a good education I had. (Some people wouldn't think it was so good, but I did in the liberal arts and in the things that go beyond just your numbers and reading.) Of course, in those days we were not forbidden to pray, we were not forbidden to study the Bible, and I think by the second grade we had memorized the Ten Commandments and learned the 100th Psalm, the 23rd Psalm, and I don't know what all. And then on up the line, we still believed in reading, writing and arithmetic. I get just provoked at my students not knowing any geography; it's just almost a vacancy in the head. Well, I love geography. I had teachers that would tell you about the trips that they had been off on in the summertime and so on. I loved to hear about it. I went to what some people would call a backwoods high school that had no audio-visual aids to speak of, with only the bare essentials in the way of textbooks and a library and very few frills of any kind. But you may be surprised to know that I've always liked mathematics. And you know why? Because you can't argue about it. And I really don't like to argue because I'm not very good at it and I get too emotional about it. And I didn't think there was anything like that in the study of mathematics, but later on I got disabused of that misapprehension. It didn't give a damn about your *opinion*, but it wasn't the open-and-shut discipline I had imagined. And it still didn't care whether you were young or old or rich or poor; it was just the way it was and there wasn't a thing you could do about it.

And I felt the same way about Bach's music. I thought it was then—and remains now—just *inarguable*. And so I began to take piano lessons from my cousin Margaret, and my first piano lessons were paid for by Grandpa Drake out of his meager, meager Confederate pension, which, of course, was paid by the state of Tennessee. I loved Bach because I thought he was like mathematics. I was proud to be able to master all those little "ins" and "outs" and all those little voices and so on. I never got up to *The Well-Tempered Clavichord*, but I did pretty well by the inventions and some of his other stuff. And that was one of the glories of music: I wanted order; I wanted everything to match; I didn't want always to have to argue; and I loved the beauty of form and meaning.

And that was also one reason I liked Latin. Of course I didn't know until I was at Yale and reading medieval Latin, under a very distinguished professor, that all those years in high school and at Vanderbilt when I had been reading Caesar and Cicero and Virgil and Horace and on into Plautus and Terence and finally Lucretius, I had really been studying literature! I think by then I had decided that our professor just assumed that we were all first-rate Latinists and didn't need any more study of the grammar and its iron discipline. But I did begin now to sense something of the beauty of the language, to learn how a language other than your own can make you stronger in command of them both—just one of the gifts of what we term education. And finally, I even learned to read medieval calligraphy of the simpler kinds; I learned something about the so-called Dark Ages, and finally even the inevitable collision of East and West, the dawn of the Renaissance. Of course I can hardly read a word of it now, but certain aspects of its inherent order and perception still seem to abide in my blood, and I don't think I've lost anything.

I wanted to go to school up north. I had learned at that time that's where the best schools were, but my daddy didn't want me to do that. I think he wanted me to stay at home. My daddy financed my whole education, too, from the first grade on through Yale, and I never had a scholarship; well, the last year at Yale I did have a remission of the tuition of $500. And nearly all the work I have done professionally has been on my own time and my own money. And that's one reason that it means something, because I *worked* for it...I mean that quite seriously. Also, I worked on things that were not in the mainstream. I wrote my M.A. thesis on Saki. Most people now wouldn't even know who he was.

If you've looked at, as I suppose you will, my complete bibliography, you'll find it's about two hundred items long and a lot of it concerned with writers and subjects most people haven't even heard of now. For instance, I wrote, I thought, a pretty good essay on Frances Newman. I don't know if you've ever heard of her, but she was an Atlanta woman, to the manner born and a friend of Margaret Mitchell's family and a librarian at the public library downtown. She had a brief, but rather intense celebrity back in the twenties. She wrote two novels, one of them called

The Hardboiled Virgin, the other, *Dead Lovers Are Faithful Lovers.* Then she wrote a book of criticism called *The Short Story's Mutations*, and the last thing she did was a translation from Jules Laforgue, the French poet. Well, now I find she's beginning to be resurrected because, God help us, she is a woman. (Nobody seems concerned with her *talent.*) And many people think, of course, she's probably anti-male and all that kind of stuff. But back in the '20s, when she thrived, she was taken up by people like Mencken and his group, then James Branch Cabell and people like that. And then somebody else published an edition of her letters. Well, I mean, how far do you think Frances Newman will take you today? In a very limited way it might get you a little attention. But I mean, that's the kind of thing I've done. And I did my Ph.D. thesis under Frederick Pottle, which has always interested some people. Of course he's not one they expected. You know who he was? The Boswell man, the Director of the Yale "Boswell Factory," as it was sometimes called, and an international scholar of great distinction. It was a very gimmicky, yes gimmicky reading of the various poems of Keats, and of course it's never seen the light of day. But I look at it every now and then and think it's still worth having around the house. But I haven't got into the right things...but what I'm working up to is an anecdote about Austin Warren, who was the most—and best—anecdotal person I ever knew. He said once when I was looking for another job, which is what I was doing most of the time. (You realize this is my fourth job, but I wasn't exactly fired from the others but it was clear that there was no future for me in those places.) Michigan, and then Northwestern, and then Texas at Austin, then here.

Well anyhow, I was looking for a job or something and I worked on my bibliography, such as it was then—up to maybe just a couple of pages. And I showed it to Austin and I said, "How does this look, if it's submitted by a prospective job candidate?" And he said, "Robert, you must realize that to most administrators" (these are his exact words now) "this is horrifyingly eclectic." Well, it's true. It's true. And I could say, "Well, I got what I wanted because I always wanted to be a general practitioner.'" All right.

Who were my role models? Of course Donald Davidson, always, and then of course after I got to know him, Cleanth Brooks, and then always Austin Warren. And they were all people that had done a great deal of this and Donald Davidson, of course, was a published poet, and so on. And in those days I never dreamed of writing creatively. I mean, nobody believes that probably, but it's true. I didn't want to write. The only thing I could think about writing was a long novel like *Gone with the Wind* or something like that. I never dreamed of it. And I meet people all the time, mostly without talent, at least so it seems to me, who want desperately all their lives to write creatively. And I can truly say that never crossed my mind. But those are the people I always wanted to emulate. I didn't want to be a "Keats man," much as I liked him. I haven't thought about Keats in years. I mean every now and then I, you know, have to look up a quotation or something and a lot of it comes back. And I heard a lecture a couple years ago over at the National Portrait Gallery in London on Keats by a man who does a lot of stuff on Keats' letters. I went up to him afterwards and I said, "You don't know what you brought back to me." It's not like I put it behind me. You know, but my interests just went on to other things. I've always been the kind to go off on a tangent about things. Of course, I've always been the kind to go off on a tangent about things.

Some people say I'm incapable of having sustained devotion to one subject. I suspect I am. I don't know whether that's so bad either. Too many people spend too much time on one subject. See, I could never write a biography—or perhaps a novel. I don't have the patience. I guess maybe I don't care enough. I don't know. But well, we can't all be the same thing. Well, what does St. Paul say? "There are many gifts but the same spirit," you know. It never has worried me. But I could never see myself...I think that Joseph Blotner...dull, dull, dull...that book on Faulkner and the one on Warren too." You know, I'm sure he knew every time Red Warren sneezed, but so what? On the other hand, you look at Mark Winchell's guide to Cleanth, I think it's great! I mean...maybe I'm using "great" a little too liberally, but you know what I mean. He makes Cleanth Brooks come alive! But I've always gone off on tangents. I went through a Trollope phase; I went through a Dickens phase and all this sort of stuff. And why shouldn't I? That's the way you get educated. And you see one of the things, if I may say so, I've always envied the English for. And of course they work hard sometimes to maintain the posture and the appearance of, you know, amateurishness. They think professionalism is a bad word. Of course we don't. But the ordinary Englishman who's, I mean not ordinary, but an Englishman who has been to a good public school, has been to Oxbridge, and has had what they can give you at their best, it doesn't matter...I have friends over there who are ...well one of my friends is a member of the Clark family that makes these shoes I've got on (you know, Wallabees and Desert Boots and all), and he can talk to you about anything you want. Well, he's dead now, but he talked about anything he wanted to—you know, the arts, architectural design or the problems of the sewer system of Bath or whatever! Well, you see that always appealed to me. And I'm very limited of course, but I've tried to do something about it. Perhaps I wanted to be like an old friend of mine, who is a cardiologist and has had a very interesting career. He did his residency in cardiology at the Mayo Clinic and he said the whole *raison d'être* of the Mayo Clinic was to make all the people who studied there a jack of all trades but master of one. And I think that's…I kind of like that. And so I've had a lot of interests. Then I've had people who feel that…you know, say, "Well, Robert, you carry your learning very lightly." And I say, "Well, that's what you're supposed to do." You don't have to walk around like your ass weighs a ton. And I think, I'm pretty sure a lot of people have in some way underestimated me. I seem to have interests that are not everybody else's. Well, one of our former Deans liked to talk to me about celebrities I had known. (I never told him about Noel Coward in the steam room, though.) But you know, that kind of stuff. Duller than death. And I don't think it ever occurred to him that I had any sense; I tried in vain more than once to get him to give me a raise. I mean Flannery was so right about the people she met in New York at cocktail parties. She went to a party with her friend Robert Lowell, and it was held at Mary McCarthy's house, back when she was Mrs. Broadwater. And she had what was apparently a rotten time. She said, "You know what's the matter with them kind of folks?" I said, "I have some ideas. What do you think?" She said, "They ain't *frum* anywhere." And yes, the worst thing I can say or think about one of my colleagues or anyone else in this profession is, "I can't imagine him outside his work."

I did grow up in a small town. I did have an extremely wise mother. And I was surrounded by other wise mothers. And I was also surrounded by women who didn't have the sense to come in out of the rain. And some of them are the ones I write about. But they did think that life was not just, you know, earning your bread. It's so much more than that. They were not people who had much education as we think of it now, but then look at the kind of education we have now. But I was not among the chosen. And that's another thing. I think if people don't know that from reading my work…I've gotten so I feel, you know, it's almost…this is very, in a way very inappropriate but comparisons are invidious. People used to ask Eudora Welty about the racial problem in the south. She'd say, "Well, I'm a fiction writer. Go read my books." Well, I should think anybody would know this that's read anything I've written, but the two great things in my life have been rejection and exclusion. And if people don't have sense enough to know that, all I can say is, they don't read very well. And I don't write because I think my stories are topical or fashionable or anything else. It's that I'm *compelled* to write them. And I spoke about this thing at Vanderbilt last spring. One of my classes, see, it coincided with class reunions and it was my class' year to have a reunion, 45th I think it was, and one girl that was in my Latin class was there and came up to me and she'd read some of my stuff and she said...well, I knew this because I knew it. She was from East Nashville, and I could tell that she didn't belong to a sorority and I could tell she hadn't "had" things, and so there's no mystery. But she said how proud her family was that she could go to Vanderbilt and that she graduated and so on, and obviously she worked hard to save money so she could. But she said, "When I got here, I found out I was from the wrong side of the river. I had to change buses twice to get from my home to the university." And she said, "That's one reason I never could spend more time on campus." And I wrote to her later and among other things, just in passing, said, "I too, know what it's like to be on the wrong side of the river." And in some ways I wasn't shaped very much by Vanderbilt at all. All right, I *still* sometimes want very desperately to deal with people who have "had" things. And I want to have a civilized conversation. I don't know when I've had ...I have very few friends left...I mean, now that sounds ugly, but I see Austin, Texas, as the only place I ever felt I *lived* in. The other places were where I *worked.* Now you realize this is a generalization, but I have very few people that I can really feel close to.

On Race

The only time I ever *consciously* wrote about it [race] was that day (in 1960 in the British Museum). And that story is in *Amazing Grace.* It's called "The Summer of the Window Peeper." And some people have confessed, God forbid, that the title reminds them of Tennessee Williams! And it hasn't had much attention. If you remember it, it doesn't really take any party line about it. And I think in a way it was like almost saying a plague on both your houses. But that's the only time I ever knowingly wrote about it. And then as you notice, it was not in an ideological sense at all, it was seen in the context of a small town, and it really wasn't about school integration or even the concept of civil rights (it was way before then). It was just more or less the relations between the two races, more social than political. But it wasn't "selling" anything. And of course, told through the voice and eyes of a little boy, who was probably telling you more than he knew. Perhaps I felt it was even more effective. I don't know how many people tell me that one of the best stories I ever wrote was "The Time the Bank Failed." In fact when the little boy says, "They'll never come back here or else they'd just be *hypocrites* and they would be *ostracized.*" He wants to use those big words. And his mama immediately says "Hush, Robert," My colleague said, "I don't know if you know how good that is." And of course, I wanted to say, "Well, I'm not altogether unaware of some of the things I work for." But of course I didn't. I just said, "Well, it seemed right to me." O, God, I've certainly eaten a lot of it in my time, but we all do! [Laughter]

I would say for the record, and I sometimes say this in public to students—as you know, in our profession, year after year we teach people who are the same age but we ourselves keep getting older—and I say, "Now look, you misunderstand that the idea of having animus toward a group is absolutely foreign to me.

Nobody *ever* told me that I should dislike or that I should even hate these people." I said, "I came to know that there were groups of people who *did* but they were not"...all right, to use the forbidden word, "they were not the class of white people *I* came from." And I'll never forget the first time I ever heard and used the phrase "poor white trash." My mother immediately said, "Where did you hear that?" And I said "Well, ah well..." My nurse's real name was Dute, it was a nickname in her family, and her name was Johnny, but the family called her Dute, always. I said, "Dute." And she said, "Well, it's just not very nice." And then she said, "Just don't say that again." And remember, I belong to the generation that had its mouth washed out, you know, when you "talked ugly." But that was always part of me. Now I knew that Negroes were not treated equally. I knew that they were certainly discriminated against. And of course "enlightened" people like William Lloyd Garrison and all the Adams family that were so in the news because of John Quincy Adams coming from his deathbed to argue that case and it all came out. You know what Jefferson said about the Adamses? He said, "They could say a gracious thing ungraciously." I never liked any of them. And Henry Adams was the biggest pill in the whole batch. I think *The Education of Henry Adams* is one of the prissiest books in American literature. And its southern counterpart, for the record, is *Lanterns on the Levee* by "Uncle" Will Percy. All right...now that I've got that out of my system...But anyhow, I knew they were discriminated against, but it...I can't tell you what my feeling was...it's difficult to explain. I knew all that and I certainly didn't have the idiocy to say that the Lord made it that way. I just knew that they had been slaves, that they were set apart from white people, that they had different ways of looking at things, and that was that. And yet I knew in some ways they were kinder and more affectionate than white people. Now for instance my nurse, whom I adored, and of course, she left when

I started school, but that was a sort of pattern too. I have never felt safer in my life than when I was with her. Anytime we went to Memphis, of course, we took her with us because, you know, she could look after me while Mama was buying clothes and all that kind of stuff. And I remember the store that my mother liked very much was called Gerber's, which is gone now, but it was very "genteel." That's why Mama liked it. And it had a nice dining room up on the fifth floor, like most department stores used to have. And we'd go up there when it was time to have dinner—we'd stay in that store all day. And, of course, Dute was not allowed to eat out with white folks, she had to eat in the kitchen. Well, of course I ate with her. It was much more fun, much more interesting. She was, in some ways, a child at heart but she was no fool at all. And as my mother would say—and some people would not like to hear this—as my mother would say, "Well we, you know, can take her anywhere because she's city broke." She was used to being in cities. And just before she came to us, she was a witness in one of the most, well, most lurid divorce trials ever held in Ripley. And she had been a nurse for the couple's children. And so...both sides were wooing her, you know, in hope she would speak for their side. It was so celebrated and notorious in the correct, in the original sense of that word, people even went and took their lunches so they wouldn't have to get up and leave at lunchtime. And I've heard about it all my life and I know some of the choice things. But she...I know one of the famous things that Dute said...and every night each side would go down to her house and sit up with her, you know, which does not mean sitting up with a dead body, it means, you know, cuddling up to people to get their sympathy. And so anyhow, they had her on the stand...incidentally there were two lawyers involved, the two most distinguished lawyers in town. I mean it was...everything about it makes me wish I'd been older. Anyhow, when they got Dute on the stand, they were both...suing and counter-suing. And in due course they brought *all* the dirt out. And, you see, it was very exciting because it was the, well the older families that were involved. And it was, you know, like a society trial. All right, so anyhow they got her on the stand and it turned out that she had been the nurse to the two boys. And so naturally she was with the mother most of the time. And she had been down to the Gulf when their mother took them there. One of the lawyers had asked their mother, "What did you do when you took them down to Biloxi? For, you know, the Gulf air and God knows what, I suppose. But anyhow, she was supposed to have had an affair, or a liaison, or a rapprochement with some big rich man that owned a yacht. And so that had to all come out, you see. And so then the cross examination put Dute on the stand. "Well now, you know you were right there, you saw all this. What time did the lady of the house get in at night?" And without batting an eye she said she didn't know, "Two reasons: 1) I didn't look at the clock and 2) I didn't figure it was any of my business what time she got home." I mean she *was* city broke. And she was quite bright. And she related beautifully to me, and I became part of her family. I mean, you see no one ever heard of a babysitter in those days, but when Mama and Daddy were out for the evening or whatever, I would go home with her. And then when the party was over, well, they'd come by and pick me up. And I called the family by the family nicknames. Which were absolutely illogical; I never did know how they got started. Anyhow, they were my family, too. Now all right, the counter-argument, of course, is well, yes, we've had this false relationship, and it was all patronage and condescension. Well, it was. On the other hand it was a personal relationship. And it was a relationship of great affection. And well, so much...I guess I have no more to say. But *I* never took a strong line...*I* would never walk across the Selma bridge, *I* would never...I mean, it wasn't cowardice! I just thought every fool in the United States was trying to get into the act so he could talk about it. And I think a lot of it didn't do anybody, least of all black people, any good. On the other hand, there was no question: *something* had to happen. And it was going to happen whether to Martin Luther King, or anybody else. And I guess I was, unforgivably to some people, a disinterested observer more than anything else. Except that the more I was thrown in with the people that I told you I didn't particularly like in my travels, the more I thought, "*You* don't know a damn thing about it. Not really." And of course they didn't. And they were all so arrogant about it. And it was the same mentality to me as the abolitionists, really. The same thing—"God is on our side"—as Robert Penn Warren observed—"the treasury of virtue."

On Travel

Oddly enough, I was one of those people that loved to hear about people's travels. Now today, I think the most frightening words you can hear are "Come over and look at my slides!" But with slides you're sort of a captive audience or something. You know, I adored trains. And so I had a large collection of railroad time tables and I used to spread them out across the bed, especially at breakfast. I'd get up and fix my breakfast, which was two heavily buttered slices of toast with lots of crunchy peanut butter and Welch's Grapelade on top of that and a Coca-Cola. And I would spread out the time tables and start planning these elaborate journeys from coast to coast, with hairbreadth connections in places like St. Louis or Chicago. Ah, yes, and I must tell you this, it's important. From as long as I can remember, I always wanted to travel. My mother's cousin, who was an old maid school teacher I've written about her "A Ticket As Long As Your Arm"—that's what she wanted. And I loved everything about getting on and going to bed in a Pullman, you see, and sleeping on the train, and going to the diner (probably the last place in captivity to use finger bowls). O, it just sounded so romantic and, who can say, I don't know, it was just like an adventure in a far off world, you see. But I always wanted to travel and I think part of that was because my parents just weren't interested at all. My father sometimes did go to St. Louis on business. I can tell you, too, in passing, he was a great Cardinals fan. That was the closest big league team, which he listened to faithfully on the radio. But when he went to St. Louis he never made any effort to go see them play. And I tell that to my writing students and say "Now what do you think of that?" and we have some interesting discussions. And anyhow, neither one of my parents really *wanted* to travel. Before he had his own business [my father went to Connecticut]. He used to work for Mr. William Tucker, who owned a big hardware store. I'll have to tell you exactly what kind of store it was some time because it wasn't what you'd think—not a "general" store but hardware and staple groceries, a "furnishing" store to provide farmers with whatever they needed to make a cotton crop. But he was sent once to a Winchester Arms convention in New Haven, Connecticut, on the campus of Yale. And I have the photograph in my office right now, among the stuff I keep, of Daddy with the Tennessee delegation, all folks that happened to be there from Tennessee, and they're out in front of Woolsey Hall, which is still there, which is where most of the big concerts and speeches, take place. So I have a photograph of him in that venue. And he'd been to New York twice, once for that convention, which was in New Haven, then once for something else, I think both when he was working for Mr. Tucker. So I mean he had seen some sights, but my mother well, she once when I was about seven years old took me on a motor trip to the Smoky Mountains, in Cousin Cornelia Woods' little blue Ford. She and Cousin Sadie went all over the county, but now my mother's brother, Uncle Charlie, did all the driving because he had worked for the state highway department and knew all the roads. I think about it now and marvel at how much territory we covered. We left Ripley at about 4:30 a.m.—this was in June, July, summer of 1937. And we drove and stopped in Nashville, saw the Capitol, saw the Governor's Mansion, had lunch, went out to the Hermitage, and got on to Knoxville in the late afternoon. And I remember coming down what was obviously Cumberland Avenue and somebody saying to me, "Now Robert, over there is the University of Tennessee; some day you may go to school there." Well, little did I know....

We got on up here, and I remember that we turned right and went across a big bridge. Well that's the Henley Street Bridge, and we finally ended up spending the night; now think about all this. Fifty years ago, and we spent the night at a tourist home. Now that was back when people used to take in tourists, you know. And we also were in the depth of the Depression too. We spent the night in a tourist home in Sevierville and next morning we were up and drove, I think, to Gatlinburg for breakfast. I remember the water wheel at Pigeon Forge; I had always heard about them but never seen them. And Gatlinburg was, I must tell you, almost charming in those days. It was still a mountain village. And I think there were two hotels. And the arts and crafts stuff was probably genuine. There were six of us in that five-passenger car (of course I was little and didn't take up so much room). But after Sevierville we spent the next night in Brevard—beautiful scenery—as part of the great circle we were making around the national park. For some reason my uncle didn't want to go to the Vanderbilt mansion, Biltmore, so we didn't do that. We heard it was very expensive, but I think we could have managed it. The third and final night we swung back around to Chattanooga and the next day we drove all the way back to West Tennessee and home, all adding up to 3 nights and 4 days. And even today I still wonder at our courage and endurance. And my mother would always say that that's when she found out she could not ride on the back seat of a car for any length of time. As she'd always say, "O, I was most gloriously car sick!" And for several days after we returned she still said every time she went back to the kitchen to start a meal, her head just swam all over the place! And I don't think her memory of those signs that warned "Prepare to meet thy God!" every time you went around one of those hairpin turns helped very much either. Whatever the case, my parents were never really brought up to travel: really, there was nowhere for them to go, and they had very little extra money. And in those times extensive travel was only for the well-to-do. My Grandmother Drake, my father's mother, never rode on a train in her life! But then I thought about it one time and concluded well, there was nowhere for her to go either; and since my grandfather's people had been Virginia slaveholders, I gather that he mostly just took life as it came and was happy for whoever wanted to do most of the work. (More than once I heard one or more of his children speculate that if it hadn't been for their mother, they would all have starved to death!) Anyhow, maybe I was just reacting against my parents' feelings but I always, always wanted to travel. And then I always wanted, when I got a little bigger (not too much bigger) to find out about Europe and history and so I wanted to go to Europe, but especially England. Those were my dreams, always. I never particularly wanted to go to the Orient, and I never wanted to go to Mexico or South America. Well, it always made me think of two things—snakes and diarrhea, you know, that kind of thing. That was always what I feared. (One of my friends once said my trouble was that I had seen too many Maria Montez movies when I was growing up—things like *Cobra Woman*, where she was supposed to have inherited a curse which, from time to time, would turn her into an enormous snake! And I replied that I certainly had and, furthermore, I had believed every one of them!) You know, I've traveled a fair amount, certainly in Europe and a fair amount in this country, but I'm not a great world traveler, in that sense. Well, anyhow we had wonderful teachers that instructed you in geography. And then we learned things. I think Miss Kathleen Given in the fifth grade made us learn all the state capitals. And then in the seventh grade, Miss Carolea Nunn made us all learn to outline the U.S. Constitution. My students would drop dead if you asked them to do a thing like that now.

On Friends

[Off the tape, Drake said that Austin, Texas was the only place other than Ripley that he ever felt at home.]

I had so many very kind friends who…it wasn't in a little group but they were people who liked a lot of things that I liked and who were quite literary and a lot of fun. I don't think many of my colleagues are very much fun really. I mean I don't see any sign of real humor. Now of course at Yale that was so different up until I visited at Oxford and Cambridge because, you know, you were asked to have dinner with maybe some undergraduate in his college or asked to go to the graduate school for dinner and all that—martinis on the terrace, you know. Well, all right. That would ruin you if you let it.

I used to go back [to Austin] to visit every year or two, but I haven't been back in three or four years now. But I've been going to visit anybody that I knew there. I went to visit my former student, Michael O'Brien, the fine photographer who made so many of these pictures [gestures toward the photos on the walls], and his wife, Elizabeth, who also is a former student. (But it was here that I taught them.) They live out in a section that didn't even exist when I was there. And they love it.… So what do we find out now? That as long as you've got access to a good airport and you've got all the technology, you can live almost anywhere. Which I suspect is about the truth.

Well, now I had met, just by accident, some very prominent people from Austin once going to Europe. And we got to be friends and then when I found out a year or so later I was going there I wrote them. So they couldn't have been nicer to me.... Through them I met a lot of their friends who were prominent and had lived there a long time. But then that wasn't all of it. My friends at the university, some of them, were great friends. And when I began to have trouble and it became apparent that there wasn't going to be a future there for me, they of course...I spent a great deal of my life...you won't believe this probably...I spent a great deal of my life not talking about certain subjects. And there wasn't anybody there but one or two people I could talk to about this...well I was so private when I was young—well younger—I didn't know who it was safe to talk to. And tell me about departmental politics—I mean...there is very little you can bring out of the woodwork that I haven't experienced personally. When I could get around the one or two people I could talk to, I would explode and probably drove them batty.

These three librarians, we had lunch every day and we talked about everything in the world. It was just wonderful to be with them and not even *think* about the English Department. That's what I wanted—not to think about it. And they were so jolly, and they all had Southern ties of course. And I know, I'm sure, they may all be dead now. One of them was a sister of somebody I still go to see in New York, her name was...my memory...Mary, Mary Stone and her sister Alma Stone is, was a very good writer. She's going through the senile stage now—the last times I've seen her. It's sad, but I try to go see her. She's up on the fringe of Columbia. And she's written some very good books, novels. One called *The Bible Salesman*, which is about an old black woman who comes to New York to stay with her grandson who is the janitor of a building, one of those big apartment houses and so on, and also sells Bibles on street corners. And her ear is the best I've ever heard. But anyhow, I had lunch with them every day at Texas and we...and until it was all settled and I had accepted Tennessee's offer...now this went on you understand for two or three years...I never said a word to them about any of the troubles. But the day I had officially accepted Tennessee's offer, that day or the next day, well anyhow the first lunch we had after that I said, "Now I've got something to tell you." And I told them what I had been going through. And I said, "I want to thank you because you have kept me sane." I don't deserve any credit for doing that. I've spent a lot of my life not talking.

[Drake was then asked if he ever felt at home in Knoxville] I don't think so. Part of it , I'm sure, is my age. Because after all everybody else was married, probably. That has something to do with it. But I think part of it is East Tennessee.... You realize that about sixty percent of our undergraduates come from Knox County or the adjoining counties. It's not a state university at all. It ought to be called, if anything, the University of East Tennessee. I don't know when I've talked to anybody much from West Tennessee. Now some people tell me they're getting a lot of students from Memphis. Well, I wish God would send me a few of them. And everything contrives, or I might even say conspires, to make it provincial and local, with very few students coming from out of state, see. At Michigan, we had two Michigan students for one out-of-state. And I think they would have liked to have had more out-of-state, but the Regents objected. I taught kids there from all over the country—New York City, Jewish students from New York City, all of them so bright. Well, they weren't all Jews either, but you know what I mean. And then from New England, and I had a girl there from Palo Alto, California. I said, "Why aren't you at Stanford?" And she replied,

"Well, I just wanted to come here." Michigan is very, very strict about out-of-state admissions...they were in my time. I mean, you had to prove that you had actually lived in the state for I've forgotten how long. I mean it wasn't just say-so.

I have indeed [lived in all three of the grand divisions]. And I'll tell you something else. The University has never seen fit to take advantage of this in any way. I used to know an enormous number of people in the state. In each of the three grand divisions. They have almost systematically and consistently failed to make use of much that I could have done. Well, I know about "a prophet's not without honor." But I mean it was almost...I don't know whether anybody in the administration has ever thought about it but I have. If there is the weakest single link in the whole chain here, it's the lack of any real concerted effort at public relations. Now this, to me, is a mystery—how any institution that depends for its very existence on public funding can ignore that. And that there are some things on the seamy side I can tell you that I have found out here that are not known to my friends in the legislature in Nashville. And I just marvel at some of it. And well you know, I really do. And it makes me sad.

And you see...my arithmetic is all skewed up about because I was born late in my parents' lives. See otherwise how could I have a grandfather who was a Confederate veteran? Everybody always said, "I'll bet he was your *great*-grandfather; you weren't old enough for that." And I would say, "No, he was my grandfather, and I've got his discharge papers from the Army of Northern Virginia and signed at Appomattox framed and hanging on the wall in my living room. Don't tell me about that. I remember it all "very well."

Well, they're not used to that. So that's part of it. See, all my life...see, writing...trying to write has many advantages about self-knowledge. One of the things you learn, more and more, you learn about the world when you try to put it down on paper. You also learn about yourself. One way or another, I've come to realize that I've been out of step all my life. And that's not said to garner sympathy, it's just said as a matter of fact. Because I didn't *belong* anywhere. My parents were older, and my playmates...well, they weren't boys, they were mostly girls, mostly because of the demographics of our neighborhood. And also their mothers and fathers were the age they should have been. But my parents, I thought they were old fogies, and then a lot of other things, which I won't go into.

And so, I mean I went off to Vanderbilt, and I didn't really seem to fit into many things there, but then I went to school up North, and I loved it. And they wanted friends too and I've never forgotten the excitement of being in a place where they had it all together. But I still, in some ways, didn't fit in for obvious reasons, part of them resulting from my own ignorance. Then I taught in the Middle West in my first two jobs. And I can't think of any place on earth where I was more "outside" than the Midwest. And then Texas, which I did come to love in due course: it was more like the culture I came from than any of the others. And then back here in East Tennessee, where, after over thirty years, I still don't feel at home: it's certainly not my part of Tennessee. And so you will say, "Don't be a fool, everybody's out of joint, in one way or another." Well, yes, but I have never...I think part of it is I've never been comfortable. I never was able to feel at ease in Zion. Maybe that's my way of excusing myself for the way I am, I don't know. But I mean I never have felt I belonged in many ways, anywhere.

I know how I felt. You see, I've never felt that I've actually lived anywhere. All my life...it's very difficult...Okay, I'll tell you this. When I was a little boy and we used to play games and we would play like, you know, one child would be over here and this is my house and another would say this is my house and so on and so on, I remember thinking after we had made arrangements to have a tea party together or we—or we'd made up some sort of silly game—and then it was time for everybody to go back to his respective home—and I've never forgotten what it felt like to go back to my respective house because the same old question came up again and again. "What will you do when you get there?" Which is not unlike "What will you do for an encore?" I mean, that's the truest title I ever gave anything. And I still can't answer that question, maybe nobody ever can. I don't know. But that's just the way my mind works.

On Shyness

I was interested in what the man said who came to evaluate my papers last year for Vanderbilt, you know, from over close to Chapel Hill—Mr. Turlington. But he, in his official report.... Well, he evaluated them, you know, for what I thought was a fair price. But most of that went for tax deductions. In the official reports (he sent me a copy of what he had sent Vanderbilt) he said, "Most of Mr. Drake's letters are concerned with seeking outlets for his work and also trying to find another position." And I thought well, that's about right. But I don't know what else he *could* have said. Summing up my life to that point, and in some ways it's still true, that's what I've done with my life.

Remember I told you about the mercantile background I have. You see, I didn't think that was so important when I was growing up. I realize now how enormously important it was and what an effect it had on me. I didn't realize what it was doing to me.

I ain't never been shy. I get so tired [when] I hear [that] the Queen of England is really a shy woman. I just don't believe that! She couldn't do what she does if she was shy! And somebody is going to tell you before long that that was really Hitler's trouble, see, the reason that he was such a demon was that he was shy! No, I've never been shy. And yes, I've always been ready to put my best foot forward. And yes, I've always known instinctively—nobody ever had to tell me this—that you have to take care of yourself. And all right now...this conversation I think I've told you about. If I haven't, it's time you heard it. Is that thing [in reference to tape recorder] still going? Well, all right. Be sure to get this one down. Because this exact same conversation has taken place twice—once with an editor at Eerdmans Publishing Company in Grand Rapids, whom I was trying to persuade to bring out a paperback edition of *Amazing Grace*, which he finally did do—that was in 1979. And I had arranged to meet with him in San Francisco at MLA—that's where this conversation took place. And that's the first time. And the second time was over in the office of a high official here [the University of Tennessee] several years ago. I went to see him just to kind of mention some things I was concerned about—one of which was that I didn't think I was getting enough money. And in general people don't think the less of you for asking for more money either. So anyhow, it was the same conversation. The man from Eerdmans said exactly what the man here did. After I had more or less made my case, I was told, with what I thought was exasperation, "You are so persistent about your work." And I said, in both cases, "Certainly I am. I have a quality product. And if I'm not persistent in my own behalf, who will be for me?" And neither one of them could say "boo."

I know that my parents had respect for people who worked hard and people who did not expect the world to owe them a living. They didn't think anything about it at all. And I have never had any time for laziness. And the thing that I think is just almost unforgivable is waste. Now that doesn't necessarily mean the waste of money though it certainly can. But the waste of talent, the waste of human resources. I don't want to speak too much out of tune, or out of turn. I'm feeling better about my work in the writing business. I have two careers. But yet I'm fortunate they helped each other. I feel better about that now because I've more or less accepted what I do and what I try to do. I would like for my work to get some wider recognition. I would like maybe to see one of my books reviewed in the *New York Times.* I think I told you what Cleanth Brooks said when I complained about that. "O Robert, you've appeared in more important places than that." Now why did he say that? I thought that was really unkind, but of course I never remonstrated with him. You can say what you want, everybody in this country who writes wants to be noticed by the *Times* and to pretend otherwise is just folly. I feel better about it because, well, of course, I've been given a little more attention lately and that's helped. But I also know now that, at least I feel that, I am doing the work that it was put in me to do. Right or wrong. And that's all I can do. And I don't [think] that you ought to be sanctimonious about that. I don't think the Lord intended me to write a novel. I never felt any interest in writing a novel. I mustn't become obsessed by that. And I certainly don't feel that He intended me to write a play. I've become more enthusiastic or partial to people that would take that attitude—that make the best of what they have. Like they say now, you know, you've got to play the hand you've been dealt. I always believed it intuitively, but now I know it. I can put it into words. And more and more I want...that's what I want. That's all I can do. And I am proud of the stuff I've done. And if it doesn't suit this one or that one, well then, tell them to go fuck themselves—I mean, I can't worry about it. And I am not very nice about it anymore either.

On Teaching Writing

Well, I don't think I ever thought about [myself as a social historian] until more recent years. I'll tell you this about Jane Austen. I read *Pride and Prejudice* when I was in high school, I guess, but I don't know that I read any others. And I thought she was funny. Much later, after I was out teaching, maybe at Northwestern, I read a lot of Jane Austen. I read *Emma*, and I began to see what a great novelist she is. And again, I never worked these things out in so many words. But it was not lost on me how really limited she was. But I didn't put it in those words. But then I thought, you know, in some ways, her villages were not unlike Ripley. I didn't make any theoretical deductions from that. And so I just thought, well, what does that say? What does that add up to? And of course, more and more I realized one way or another, and I tell students, I'm not saying you have to experience something to write about it. Always there is the example of *The Red Badge of Courage*. But I always say you have to know something about it. And how you know about it may come in entirely different ways. But also I think I told a woman at Kroger, in the check-out line. She ran the cash register, she's very nice, and I always speak to her, and she speaks to me and so forth. And I didn't know she knew who I was or anything about me. Lo and behold, one night she said, "How do you write a book?" And I said, "I wish you would tell me." And I don't know, but I didn't want her to think I was making fun of her, because I really wasn't. And I said, "To tell you the truth, I don't know. But I'll tell you this. I think that it has to do with having something eating on you." And so I went on my way and as I left I heard her say, more to herself, "Something eating on you." And I think that's true. And I don't...the longer I fool with it I don't want to...I don't want to hear anything or talk about...it's not like it's too sacred to talk about. But you know I don't...when Kenneth

Knickerbocker hired me for this job he said, "Now we don't envision having any writing program around here. We figure that all those people can go up to Paul Engle at Iowa." I said, "Well, I'm pretty much of that opinion." And I was and maybe I still am! Well, as you see, it hasn't quite turned out that way. At Vanderbilt there was one course, Mr. Davidson's course, very modestly entitled "Problems in Advanced Writing." And you could write anything you wanted to. I was the only one in the class who was *not* writing stories. I was trying to write poems. And he got rid of that pretty quickly. But he really began taking an interest in my work when I started writing criticism. That's that. And I don't like writers' conferences. Of course, my vanity is flattered when asked to read in public because...it should be obvious to anybody that my work is the kind that thrives on oral performance. I love to do that. I love to make people laugh. I don't think there is anything shameful about that. Yes, all these things are part of it

On Storytelling

All right. The week just before I came back to Knoxville after Christmas I went to stay with some very dear friends in Pine Bluff, Arkansas. She, the wife, is my age and believe it or not, she is still a beautiful woman. And I don't mean attractive; I mean beautiful. And her husband is a wonderful, good old boy of the best sort. He's an ophthalmologist, and he grew up in that part of the world (she was from Memphis, originally). But she used to come out and spend a lot of time in the summer with her aunt and uncle in Henning, which is just six miles below Ripley, you know, home of Alex Haley. And her aunt and uncle lived right next door to my Uncle Walter and my cousin Frances, the one that I go to see out in California. It gets a little more complicated, but anyhow, I hadn't seen her in years until I was asked to teach as a visiting professor over at Hendrix College, back in 1982. And incidentally, it paid me more money than I'd ever earned up to that time. All right. But she, now living in Pine Bluff all these years, made strong efforts and I certainly wanted to make an effort too, to bring us back together. Well anyhow, through them I met their friends in Pine Bluff. And we had other friends down in what's called the Delta of Arkansas, which means exactly what it says—cotton and all that. So anyhow every couple of years I go over to see Jane and Robert Nixon. I hadn't been for several years, so we had a lot to catch up on. Well, anyhow the talk just goes on and on, and I had told her before, I said, remembering when I was over at Hendrix and all, "Jane, some of the best tales I've ever heard are at your dinner table." And she said. "O Robert, you bring that out in people." And I said, "Well, I don't know if that's a compliment or not." But anyhow, she had folks in the first night I was there. There's a wonderful restaurant out on the edge of town. The drive too is dramatic. All of a sudden you realize that you've gone downhill, and you get out in the Delta before you know it. Maybe you know about this restaurant called "Mrs. Jones'." Well, the next time proceed with haste to go there. Mrs. Jones is now 95 or 96, and I think she's gotten senile, but I did meet her back when she was all there. And I could see this woman knew what she was doing. The family was all working there. Now it's the son's business, more or less. She still comes in, but it's the son's. They've got these black people there that have been there since before Christ, you might say. And the matriarch of the black family there, her name is Mutt. [Laughter]. So anyhow, what I'm trying to say is here were some more people...I knew all these people...I didn't know one couple till the night before, but they were new friends now (the man had even played football here years ago under Bowden Wyatt), but they of course became new friends now. These other people

I'd gotten to know over the years from visiting over there. And it was just marvelous.

All right, Robert Nixon, who is a wonderful tale-teller and then all these other people. And of course you see, they have all the same things in common. They laugh at the same things. They laugh at human folly. And they laugh at anybody that doesn't have sense. Now if that's cruel, so be it. And peace to Edmund Wilson who said that Sut Lovingood was cruel. And so I was right in the middle of that. One tale after another and I said to my host, "Robert, I want to hear the tale again about the naked burglar, and he obliged." It's about back in World War II, and some people in Pine Bluff were renting rooms to people connected with the services and factories and so on. And somebody had as a roomer a man that was alone and not married. He was so nice, they said. But they couldn't figure out why there was always such a greasy streak around the bathtub after he had bathed. Well, come to find out, he had been going out in the town and assaulting all these women and he always oiled himself up real good and so at the end, when the police got after him, he would literally *slip through their hands*! [Laughter]

On Types of Humor

I've heard Tinkum Brooks, Cleanth's wife, say that one of the biggest indicators of where people are from is in what they laugh at. And she was drawing examples from moving from Baton Rouge to New Haven. I told a very disturbing story from The *New Yorker* at a dinner party in Evanston, Illinois, one time. It had to do with the murder rate in Texas. It was about the woman in Houston who called up the police and said she had just shot her own child, and she was distraught because she had really meant to shoot her husband! And all the people there thought it was so sad. I went almost the next month to assume my duties in

Austin, Texas. There I told the same story to the three librarians, whom I mentioned to you earlier, and they laughed themselves sick. And the male (two of them were women, one was a man) of the three followed me out of the cafeteria and said, "I want to tell you something about that." His eyes were glimmering in amazement or amusement. He said, "I've got a sister in Houston who had a cleaning lady who got upset with another woman on her party line who was always using the line when she wanted to use it. So one day she just lay in wait for her at the bus stop where she usually got off the bus, and she put five bullets in her and said, "I thought I was going to have to reload." And I had silent merriment wondering what those people in Evanston would have to say to that. And that's the difference.

I was told once by a very, very pretty girl, of Greek extraction... Now I remember that about her, see? I believe her last name was Nikopolous or something. She was an undergraduate at Northwestern, and she was dating one of my younger colleagues in the English Department. Delphi Nikopolous, I think. Her family apparently was an old one, and I gather were [a] prosperous Greek banking family in Chicago. And one day in the soda fountain place that we congregated in quite often over coffee, I don't know what I said, but anyhow she thought it was amusing and she said... "You have good comedic timing." And I said, "My dear, why do you think I became a school teacher?" And I think I know it [comedy] when I hear it. And again, it's something I think you're either born with or you aren't. And I think Southerners...well, it's all part of why people laugh. I don't know and you don't know, but I mean people know...I think it's just something that you're born with. Now if I may tell tales out of school, I had an old friend in my hometown who was the mother of one of my contemporaries. And in her last days she was still in pretty good health, but she was losing her vision and all, and she didn't live so very much longer. But anyhow, she was talking, asking me what I was doing, what kind of work—if I was teaching, what I was writing. I don't think I had then really written much of anything. Well anyhow, she knew that I was a great admirer of Eudora Welty. And so I...I've forgotten how it came up in conversation but she got off on the time she was visiting in Jackson, Mississippi. And I don't know what the circumstances were but they're not material either. But she was just saying...there's no way to prepare you for this except to just tell you. Sarah Bernhardt herself, risen from the dead, could not have gotten the timing better than she did. And she said, "O, I'll never forget, I went to a party and there was your friend, Eudora Welty. [Pause] Not a pretty woman."

All right. Well now, see some people wouldn't think that was funny at all. But I stand by "Sarah Bernhardt couldn't have done it better." Superb! [Laughter] And don't you realize also how Southern that is? See, Southerners...my family, now none of us were beauty queens or kings, but that always came up, about somebody's looks. You know, they'd say, "Oh, he's the ugliest thing that ever came down the pike" or the one that used to really get me was, "She's the ugliest white woman you ever saw in your life." And that was just an ordinary comment on somebody else. And I don't know other cultures that have made so much of that, but it was just part of the way they judge character. Certainly the way they judge a woman. And I asked, oh you know, William Humphrey right out in Texas...he died recently, did you know that? Well, he did. And he was a guest at Hendrix when I taught there. And we were talking about this very thing. See, he's an East Texan, and they're very Southern down there. And I said, "Do you know what I'm talking about?" And he said, "Yes." And I said, "Why do you reckon Southerners go on so about a woman's looks? They don't seem to worry about any of her other qualities." He said, "I don't know, but I suspect they think that's the only thing a woman's good for." [Laughter]

And of course I never thought *anybody* up North had a sense of humor. But, I've always felt at home in England, from the first time I set foot in London. And even as much or more in Scotland. You see, you're getting very serious up there, you know. And well, it's hairy. Jokes are, well...just be careful what you say, no telling what will come out of the woodwork. Yes, I've felt this very much. And of course, anytime you have a community you're going to get "in" jokes. Because that's part of their community. I hardly know what to say except that the British also are kind of strong on, shall we say, "the darker side of things." Yes [they have a sense of what evil is]. I guess maybe that's what we need to say. Now for instance there's a friend of mine here in one of the other colleges who will be nameless, and it doesn't matter anyhow. He's from Michigan originally. Well what else do you expect? Anyhow, he was telling me about a man I knew in his own department who was, I think, a distinguished professor and long ago was tenured so they couldn't just readily dismiss him. But he was apparently getting too thick with the young girls and the co-eds and the secretaries and what not. And so, how to get rid of him without causing a scandal of a most disturbing sort? I think some easy way was finally found when he was given another position somewhere out on the West Coast. Now this is what I was told. I can't vouch for the veracity of any of this. And I suppose I was very much interested. I knew the man. I used to swim with him, as a matter of fact. So anyhow, after my friend had finished his tale, I said, "O, I hadn't heard this at all, and it is most distressing." Everything you're supposed to say, I guess. And he said, looking off into the distance as though he were just pondering on this very bad situation, "You know, he just must have a glandular problem." I said, "When you were a little boy, did you go to Sunday School?" He said, "Well, yes, but what does that have to do with anything?" I said, "Well, if you'd listened very hard, you'd have found out that what is wrong with that man is not a glandular problem. But something called the 'old Adam' "; and I said, "Everybody was born with it and there's not a damn thing you can do about it." I still don't know that he knew what I meant. But I mean, you see that was just the ultimate...well, he's a fool. That's all. People like that. If you don't have any more sense than that, you deserve everything you get. And again it comes back to that thing I raised earlier. Those people really thought that you could raise the dead if you just had the right equipment.

Well, all right. I've lived long enough to believe in it [evil]. I look in the mirror and I believe in it even more. And I would listen to the TV and read the paper and by God if you don't believe in it you just haven't got any sense. Well, anyhow, those are some instances of...and I think about the Southwestern frontier, you know, and all that. Well, look at Mark Twain and Huck...that wonderful passage when he finds the "Walter Scott" sinking...you know a boat and all. And then he comes back later on and it is now sunk. And he said, "I kind of felt sorry for all those folks on there that drowned, but I reckon if they could stand it, I could." [Laughter] Well, what about that, see?

On Beginning as a Writer and on Publishing

Out in the hall where the mailboxes were kept, I went by to check the afternoon mail. Those were golden days. We had two mail deliveries a day in the English department and one on Saturday. They'd also do that here. But we also had Saturday classes. Well anyhow, school was almost out. I can see it right now. He [Professor Warner G. Rice, Chairman of the Department of English at the University of Michigan] said, "Mr. Drake, what are you going to do with your summer? And of course, I knew him all those years, but he never called me anything but Mr. Drake, and I never called him anything but Mr.

Rice. He just died—98 years old. I'm surprised he didn't live forever. And despite the fact that he was, he was...nobody wants to call it...but he was Carlyle's "Everlasting No." And that really says it all. And yet in a curious, and I suppose a perverse, way many of us were fond of him. He was thoroughly professional, there was not an ounce of animus or malice in him.

Well, he said, "Mr. Drake, what are you going to do this summer?" And I said, "Well, I think I'm going back to Yale and maybe do a little work in the Yale library." I seemed to work rather well there, and I got to see my friends. He said, just apropos of nothing, not "You should change what you're planning," but simply "Have you at all thought of writing stories about things down South? You always tell funny stories about your family and your friends." And I said, "Well, you know, I never have." And he said, "Why don't you think about it?" And that is almost the total conversation. I did go back to New Haven, and I did do some reading, but I didn't work on any of the projects I had thought of, but I began to think seriously about what he said. And so that summer and I think while I was still at Yale (I stayed for about three or four weeks before I went back down home), I began to try writing down memories. And obviously they were a far, far cry from fiction. In those days I didn't even change the names. There is, and you better not tell this, but I can show you in my office right now, what must be the primal copy of *Amazing Grace* with all the real names used and then crossed out with the names that finally appeared. Obviously there were liberties taken with the action too. But anyhow, I started just writing down remembered things, and then little by little, and this is what is impossible to understand— Was this God? Was this my glands? What was it? Did it really matter? I began to think, "No, this is not right. These memories are not right. It's not just what you remember; it's what you did with them." And I realize now I was beginning to learn what fiction is. But then see, I went on to Northwestern, and that's where *very* interesting things happened. If I don't talk about Northwestern much it's just that, well, it was like Vanderbilt—you know, moved north—and I got an enormous amount of work done in those years but I also made two friendships there, got to know two men, whom I liked very much but who are now no longer with us. One I had met, just before I left Ann Arbor, Russell Kirk, the conservative philosopher. And then when I moved to Northwestern, I met the people who—Kirk was still the official editor of *Modern Age*—but then I met all the other folks who were in the organization and I began to go to their meetings—and I met Richard Weaver at the University of Chicago and I got to know him. And then my close friend there in Chicago was David Collier, who had a Northwestern Ph.D. and oh my, he was so conservative. I don't know whether he still believed in slavery, but he was out-Heroding Herod to some extent. Anyhow...he became a close friend. He had spent a great deal of time in the Orient and he, I think, had fallen under the Japanese influence. Well now, that wasn't necessarily the way to my heart, but whatever the case, I think that was probably when he was in the service. But we had lunch together from time to time and he obviously had real money at his disposal. He'd take me to lunch...at his favorite place, which was the Victorian Room at the Palmer House. It's not called "Victorian" anymore, they jazzed it all up and of course ruined it. The big, big room just off the lobby—the Empire Room—was where there was dining and dancing in the evenings, and it was very grand. But then the Victorian Room was very genteel and obviously very class and quality oriented. And that's where we ate lunch. But David was the sort who knew the head waiter, and was all very much a part of the establishment. And of course I loved every minute of it. And I must say that...and this maybe is important for you to know...every time I would get on the "el" and go down to the Loop, my feeling about it was the same as when I was a little boy and we went to Memphis for the day.

That [reference to the time Austin Warren was asking Drake to bring him a new story every Monday] was after I started writing and what I should tell you, you see, the breakthrough for me though was...and here's the Northwestern element in my life, or the Chicago element, after I moved there because you see David Collier and Russell Kirk saw some of my work, and Kirk said some...he was a very, very kind man...maybe too kind...he's dead now. And he solicited things for *Modern Age*. And then David was very kind also but...now this is off the record...if he had stayed on as editor much longer I think the magazine wouldn't be here today because it was becoming more and more doctrinaire and ideological and well, there's no way...and George Panichas, who is editor now, is just what the doctor ordered. Of course he's been very sympathetic to my work and naturally that influences what I say. But he has turned it into a sort of mainline journal in humanities. Which is what it started out as. But anyhow that was one side of the Chicago experience. And the other side was *The Christian Century*. And that all, again, came in a roundabout way because Dean Peerman, who was a Northwestern graduate, was also a friend of some of my colleagues and I met him socially, and so he said, "I wonder if you'd mind...would you like to do a review for us sometime?" And I said, "Well, I guess." And he said, "Now we don't pay for reviews." Of course, they didn't pay much for anything—it was all for the greater glory of God. But anyhow I said, "Well, we'll work that out." Because that was a time in my life I needed to appear in print, you see. And so I did. And then there were book reviews. And I remember the first one I did, somebody ventured to just make a mess out of it, of course. And I told Dean, either personally or by mail, I said, "I can't work for you if I don't have a say in it." And he said, "Well I think I can promise you that

that will never happen again." And then gradually my first stories began to appear...the first story I ever published was in the *Michigan Alumnus Quarterly Review.* I think Mr. Rice asked me if I was interested in sending it...and I did. And it's a story that's never been published again. It's not very good. And then I think I had published one or two in the *Arizona Quarterly.* But that comes after...Well, it's all...you'll have to check the dates.

I would hate for this to be widely known. You know, I don't like it when the magazine starts thinking they know more than I do. But once or twice I have had to concede in my private mind that they really made some changes for the better. Now as a rule, incidentally you have to watch this, some magazines, you know...boy they just...if you don't mention getting to read proofs they won't do anything about it. And that was particularly the case with the *Christian Century* for years. But once or twice they did cut some things that, I think now, needed cutting. For instance, you may remember that story called "I'm Counting with You All the Way" about Ann Louise's recital? Well, I just can't remember whether I got to read the proof on that or not...anyhow when I saw their doctoring, I thought, you know, this really is better. They really cut out some things that were extraneous, and not purposefully extraneous. And so I let it stand. Now I've had trouble with them now and then particularly because, as you know, they are based on an ideology. And I never will forget one of the first stories I ever published in there, years ago, called "Easy Steps for Little Feet" about the Bible stories. Well, their managerial people, whoever they were then, were just adamant about de-Africanizing the featured black people. In that story I had quoted my nurse—who appears in several things, she's called Louella, as you may remember. Well, I quoted her as saying, "Well, he's just gwine where he's gwine." Of course that meant he had a mind you couldn't change with a brickbat. Well, they just were adamant that it must be changed. And I said

"Well, what to?" "Well, he was going where he was going," they suggested. Which is...if you don't know why the other's better then you have no business doing anything like that.

You must remember when you start out...and you know, you give way because you want it in print, you need it in print, and other worldly reasons. And so I gave way. But as soon as *Amazing Grace* was on the way—that story was going to be included there—I just corrected it right back...I "discorrected" it back to the way I had written it. And I have done that on several occasions. Now there's another story that they published not so many years ago and incidentally the dramatic situation had been in the back of my mind for years. And I remember it was the summer of 1986 because I was just back from Europe and I had had my first trip to Russia—I can't imagine that that had anything to do with it. Of course I ended up in London, like I always do. But all of a sudden one day I thought, "I've got to write that story!" Of course the recurring motif, you know, was, "Were you there?" And the poor deluded woman, of course, was brought to tears, in the middle of the church meeting. And I can't tell you now, but they made a number of changes that I thought were for the better and I think I let some of them stand. But it's very difficult, and of course you know, when you're dealing with ignorant people.... I just recently learned that ignorance and arrogance are almost bedfellows—they go together. But anyhow, I let it stand. What really upsets me is when they get the rhythm out of place. Or they get the rhythm skewed up or they take the rhythm out. And like that wonderful anecdote that I think was in one of my stories, about the woman that had a daughter that was taking piano lessons, and because she was the only daughter, they called her Sister (her real name was something else, of course). And her mother said, "Sister used to play real well but since she changed teachers and started taking from that new woman, Miss So-and-So, she has just taken every bit of the rhythm out of Sister." Well of course, if you don't like that, you're beyond redemption. But anyhow, that's what they've done from time to time and it drives me wild. I hope I don't sound too much like I'm pontificating. But the fundamental rule that I go by is, if I can't hear it deep down somewhere in the inner ear or wherever it is…if I can't hear it, then it's no good.

On Tom Wolfe, Jr.

I think, you know, he's an old friend of mine. Haven't seen him in years, haven't heard from him in years. But he hasn't changed. He's not intimate. I don't think he ever had any intimate friends at Yale. But then I've had very few intimate friends myself. I've had lots of friends, but they've not been intimate. Two things you should always remember about him. One, he's a big tease, though sometimes it's hard to tell. And two, I don't know that anybody but God, if He, knows what he thinks about anything. He plays extremely close to his chest. He's terribly bright and terribly amusing, and sometimes you don't realize how amusing until afterwards. But he was working on a Ph.D. in American Studies, while I was doing a Ph.D. in English, and he's a graduate of Washington and Lee. And he was one of the founding editors of that magazine up there called *Shenandoah.* And he has written wonderful blurbs for some of my books. And very, very kind, and we've gone to dinner in New York from time to time. I don't know of anything he has ever said or expressed thoughts about that I would be very much opposed to.

I don't know how he votes, I don't know anything about that, but I mean he's got sense. John Fisher, our former English Chairman and Hodges Professor, by the way, said that he was the foremost moralist of our time. Now you go home and think about that. He certainly, as you know, is not afraid to say what he thinks. But it's always with great tact, all with great tact...he's a tease. He likes to pull legs. And so on.

One of the last times we were together, he came and had lunch with me. O, this was ten years ago or more, and I was staying at the Algonquin Hotel, where I've been staying for thirty years. They keep on trying to, well, they try to glamorize it, I think, and I probably won't be able to afford it. And I tell them that too. I said, "People that made this place were literary, theatrical, artistic people. People from *The New Yorker* magazine staff. And you know those people don't have any money. Now if you're just trying to get ready to entertain conventions of traveling salesmen from Grand Rapids, then maybe this is what you want." But I said, "The original clientele will leave." But they're having seminars on Sunday night about the old Round Table group and I'd be curious to see how long that lasts. Because when all is said and done, you know, that whole group was a very limited outfit. They weren't really all that bright or that educated. They were all smart alecks. They didn't know anything. And well, we don't have to get into that. We were having lunch there and what...O, this is awful because I'm not going to be able to deliver on this story...I can't remember what the punch line is. But anyhow...we were talking about...okay. People, for good or for ill, *are* still capable of being shocked. Now they wouldn't be shocked by...

He said, "O yes, that's perfectly true. People are still capable of being shocked." He said, "I'll tell you a story." He said, "...now I don't know what the context was...I don't know, wherefore...one night for some reason, I was riding around in a big limousine in Manhattan with, among others, Tiny Tim (this must have been over ten years ago; he's gone on to his reward some several years as it stands, as you know)." And I myself thought, whatever people thought, he *was* in the mode and he was making money and that's the way our culture is, you know, whatever people do you've got to take notice of that, you see. There are two things people still take seriously—their money and their bodies. Maybe that's all people take seriously. But you jeopardize or compromise or threaten those, and you get some action. Well anyhow, he was getting a lot of attention. And these were all, I think, big, theatrical tycoons or maybe Hollywood...they were all, I think, *media* people. That's an awful word, I'm so tired of it. So this bunch in the limousine were saying...they were talking about drugs. And see, this is just typical, I wonder if T. K. even opened his mouth. I don't know but I bet he sat there through the whole thing in this big limousine without saying a word. And so anyhow they were suggesting to Tiny Tim, as I recall, that he could improve his act or improve his expertise or whatever if he would turn on with this and shoot up with that and the whole drug culture, you see. That was really what they were talking about. And finally, I don't know that it was any one thing that brought Tiny Tim out of his lair; but he said, "O Mr. So-and-so, I would never do that; I don't want to defile my body in that way." And T. K. said he could tell that maybe for the first time in his life that man was shocked. And...it's a wonderful story.

O, I'm sorry. You didn't know that [Wolfe was always called T. K.]. O, we never called him anything else. I'll tell you who was a good friend of his at Yale—John Muldowny. Do you know John—in the History Department? You might want to, sometime, get in touch with him. He's a lot of fun. Actually, I haven't seen him much lately. See, he's now mostly in our "opposition"—the administration. Well, we have lunch together maybe about twice a year. But John and some of the rest of us, we always called him T. K.. I don't think anybody in the world called him Tom in those days. His name is Thomas Kennerly Wolfe, Jr. And I never met his father. His father, you know, was the editor of *Progressive Farmer* or one of those farming magazines. He comes from a very correct Richmond background. People should also remember that. He went to St. Christopher's School, the, you know, right private school, naturally Episcopal. And right across the street from what is wonderfully called The Country Club of Virginia. Of course it's not quite as outrageous as the one in Brookline, Massachusetts, which is supposed to be the first country club in this country. It's called simply, *The* Country Club. Like *The* University in Charlottesville. But anyhow, he went to school at St. Christopher's, and then went to Washington and Lee. And then he came on to Yale. All of us...oh, he was...I just can't tell you...oh, he was wonderful. He decided we should, before school was out one year, we should have a garden party. He'd been reading a lot of Evelyn Waugh. Naturally, he liked Evelyn Waugh, and I'm sure you can figure that out. And remember, this is a strong thing in one of Waugh's books about...well, of course, *society*...and it had a list of guests in the hostess' little book—which of them qualified and for what. And some of them had G. P. O. beside them and I said what does that mean? And he said, "O, garden party only." So he decided to have a garden party and he got permission from the Yale authorities to use the Yale Botanical Gardens. And of course, it rained, but that didn't bother us. And everybody was dressed *à la*, well, not exactly Edwardian, but everybody had an umbrella of a very floozy kind, and the girls had on a lot of organdy and were wearing picture hats, you know, the summertime stuff.

I think I did see him in a white suit one time some years later when we dined at a Middle Eastern restaurant in New York. He was always taking me places like that, you know. And of course he knew all the waiters and everybody. And we ate things that I'd never known about before, but it was all good. You never knew where you might end up, see. And the last time we were together I think we had Sunday lunch. And we went to his apartment afterwards, and he opened the closet door to hang up his coat—

it was cold...wintertime...just before Christmas, and there was a woman's fur coat in there. I said, "T. K., it's none of my business, but whose fur coat is that?" And he said, "O, that's So-and-so's" and that turned out later to be the lady he married. Who was an editor of *Harper's Magazine* then. And I've been told she was crazy about him, which I hope she is. They have two children, and T. K. was a father at age 50. A boy and a girl.

On the Ear and the Eye

Sometimes a story gets started by something I hear. You see, I'm much more liable to be turned on as they say, by a recollected memory of speech...rather than a recollected memory of sight. See, I'm just no good at that. And I think about that a lot, and it may be important. For instance, as I told you, one of my friends characterizes the decor of my apartment as "institutional," which is perhaps even then too kind. I love beautiful things. I love beautiful houses. I had a friend in Fulton, Kentucky; in fact I mentioned to you yesterday, he no longer lives there, he lives in California. But he had, he bought an old house that we thought was ready to fall in, and I'm sure he spent a lot of money just making it habitable. And immediately then, being quite well-to-do, he started buying a lot of eighteenth-century furniture—I mean the real thing. And including a lot of, you know, eighteenth and nineteenth century, even some Chinoiserie. And every time I would go there, I would think, "O, this house is so beautiful, I couldn't have imagined that it would be in Fulton, Kentucky. Which was really snotty of me to think that. I finally told him one day, I said, "You know, I love this house. It's beautiful, and it must mean a great deal to you." I knew that it did because he's oriented that way. And I said, "I think it's wonderful for you to have it, and I love coming to visit here but I wouldn't want it myself." And he understood that was not being rude, it was just…I'm not programmed that way. For instance in England I won't go out of my way just for the hell of it to see stately homes. Now I've seen some of the great ones—Chatsworth, Blenheim, Longleat, and some others; but it was because somebody made it possible for me to. Some of those places, incidentally, are very hard to get to. And if you don't have some kind of private transportation the only thing to do is take a tour in which the house will be included. So maybe on the Continent it's different because it's more exotic and you know, all that. I know the first time I saw the Arc de Triumph in Paris, I think everybody's first reaction is it's so much bigger than you thought it was. Well, things like that. I am in general—I know it has worried me sometimes. Does it mean I'm not susceptible to beauty? I love to go and look at paintings. I once went to spend a weekend in Paris just because of the show they were having of the paintings of Georges de la Tour, who's a seventeenth-century painter that I admire very much, and I knew I would get to see more of them all in one place than ever before—maybe before or after. And I went twice. And I was just entranced. You know, he paints those people with light coming through their hands and things.

Now on the other hand, I remember once hearing a performance in New York, one of the great memorable experiences of my entire life, hearing a performance of *Tristan and Islolde* at the Met with Birgit Nilsson, and it was a new production conducted by Erich Leinsdorf. Of course it was long sold-out when I got there. But when you tell me something's impossible to get, that just brings out the other side of me. I got in a taxi; it was Thanksgiving Day. Everything was just a ghost town. I went to the box office and there was somebody on duty. It was the next night that *Tristan* was being done. And I said, "Is anything at all open tomorrow night?" And he said, "Sure." And I said, "Oh really? What?" And he said, "Well, in the first row of box seats."

Now that is the most elite place in the house. And I said, "Oh, no, how much are they?" He said, "Twenty dollars." Of course, now you wouldn't think you could get in the back door for twenty dollars, but that was 1971. So I said, "Quick, give me one." And it was the best seat, it was right in the center box. And I went and called a friend whom I was later meeting for dinner. He, by the way, is now retired from the practice of dermatology...no, he's an allergist. And he lives in Charleston. And I had a call from him not long ago, first time in years, and he wondered if I was going to be here during Christmas. And I said, "No, but I'm coming to Charleston, I hope, in the spring." He said, "Well, you've got to come see me, and all that." So we hope to have a nice reunion. Anyhow, so I went and called him and told him what had happened and he said, "See if you can get me a ticket, too." So I went back, and they said, "Yeah, you can get one for him too." And so, you know, from then on I was just walking on air, to think about the experience that lay before me. And I'm happy to say that it lived up to that every bit. The best part, though, was yet to come. Well, I don't know what you'd call it in artistic terms. It wouldn't be the coda or the climax, perhaps just the ultimate denouement. Anyhow, the real snapper, to use a vulgar term, was that just before the curtain went up, or just before the overture began, who should come in and take the two seats in front (there were two seats in front and two seats behind) but Leonard Bernstein and a young man. And I thought, "Oh, I can't believe this. I just can't believe it." So throughout the evening we had two conductors...Erich Leinsdorf down in the pit and Leonard Bernstein conducting in the box. And I went back to the hotel, I went back to the Algonquin that night, and I don't know whether I slept much, but it didn't matter because you know what...all night long I replayed the music of *Tristan* in my head. I don't apologize for that. Yes, and I make an effort. And I like to go to museums. I've found, incidentally, if you have time, the best way in a foreign country or some place far off where your time is limited, go to the museum that you want to go to and run around real quick, and see the main things there are to see, and don't stay longer than an hour, and then leave. Then the next day, go back and see what it really was that caught your attention and spend a lot of time. But I can't discuss art, I can't discuss music, really. I learned to play the piano, but I can't talk about the structure of music. And I can't talk about a lot of things that people presume to see in art that I don't see. And there are some things that I'm certainly immune to. Now I went to, when I was in New York last Christmas, to the Museum of Modern Art; they had an exposition of the paintings of Egon Shiele. He was one of that Viennese group of the secessionists (along with Gustav Klimt, who was the best known and Oscar Kokoschka) who flourished right before World War I and the collapse of their world. I've seen most of their works. A lot of these were on loan. I have seen most of their things in Vienna. Klimt has got weird things going on. And Vienna, of course you know, beneath all the *Angst* or *Schadenfruede* is also. It's no accident Dr. Freud was from Vienna. And then again and again in art galleries in that part of the country you will see some disturbing paintings by the old masters. They're very fond of showing decapitations and all kinds of mutilations: Salome with the head of John the Baptist and Judith cutting off Holofernes' head or whatever. You have to look beneath the surface, but there are strange things going on there. Of course I always get tickled. But in the magnificent museums of Vienna—like the Kunsthistorisches Museum, there's a whole room of this great master. A whole room, you know, just like that. I love to go to places like that. But anyhow, back to the thing in New York. I just thought—you know, let's just tell the truth. Shiele just does not speak to my condition. Now there's lots of nudity but it's always out of joint. I had an idea what he was doing, but I just thought "Oh, ho-hum, I've heard—or seen—all this," you know. And yet there're some things I go to see again and again. And my favorite museum maybe in the whole world is the Frick Collection in New York. You know where that is? It's down from the Metropolitan Museum. And that's about the first real museum I ever went to. The first Thanksgiving I was at Yale, one of my classmates asked me to spend Thanksgiving with her and her family, which was a wonderful, lovely, sweet thing to do. And so we went. They lived out in the suburbs of Westchester County, and of course we had to take the train back into New York the day after Thanksgiving, when things would be open and see the sights. She said, "Now, the first thing we're going to go see is the Frick Collection." Well, I'd never even heard of it. And I was converted instantly. And I haven't been there in the last year or two, but I can tell you right now where every picture in that place is hung. But hardly a time passes that I don't go to the Frick. I go to galleries every chance.

On Agents

I always tell people, if you want statistics, it took seven years to write that book [*Amazing Grace*]. It really began, if you can count that Yale summer, that was '56, and I finally finished it, as it is now, about '63 after I was in Texas. And then you see, along about that time I met Flannery O'Connor and she said "Why don't you send your work to my agent, Elizabeth McKee?" And it was Elizabeth who placed the book with Chilton. And then that Christmas when I was at the Modern Language Association meeting looking for a job because I was having to leave Texas, fortunately finding this one here, my first editor, John Marion, from Chilton came up from Philadelphia to meet me and told me how much he liked my work. And I have been to see the Chilton people once or twice over the years, and John was always so kind. I fear he's dead now. I haven't heard from him for ages.

I didn't stay with him or with Chilton. That same winter I was also being considered for a job, which goodness knows what it would have been like, at Muhlenberg College, out from Philadelphia. Is that Allentown? I remember that they were surprised that I wanted to come up by train, rather than fly—well, that was when I was still afraid to fly. Well anyhow, I like trains so I came up on the "Texas Eagle" and changed to the "Spirit of St. Louis." But anyhow, I stayed over the weekend, and John arranged an interview for me; he was so kind to me. He wasn't a "pusher" either; he was just a nice man. And so anyhow, he did everything that he could for me and so on. And Elizabeth managed my affairs for the first couple of years, and then she let me go, which did not surprise me or make me angry because I knew I wasn't making any money for her and she couldn't deal with that. Until a few years ago, I still sent her copies of almost everything that I published, and she always wrote me a very nice letter. And I even asked if she would recommend some other agents I might try and she did. And I gave it a try. Now, of course, it's almost as hard to get a really reputable agent as it is to get a book published. And I talked to various other people about it and Allen Tate said, "Well, I never had one. Just do it yourself." And then I met William Humphrey, you know I told you about him. And he said, "Well, I don't think you need an agent except when contract time comes or something like that." And well, I haven't had one since. Don't you see what is a recurring motif in my life? It's all just me, just me. And I say...and I hope not with vainglory...almost everything I've ever done has been on my own time and my own money.

On Yaddo

I've been there [Yaddo] three times. Summer of '78, I was there for just two weeks. Summer of '81, I was there for three weeks. And then the last time, '83, I was there six weeks, and that was the time I fell and broke my wrist and all that. Austin Warren was the one that kept after me to apply. He'd been there and all. And of course they had very nice euphemistic nomenclature. They refer to the chosen ones as "guests," you see. Their roll of guests reads like the Academy Awards. Except of course, I think more and more they have leaned—and that's certainly all right and maybe a good thing—they have leaned toward the young people who are just beginning to show promise. And maybe that's good. But the idea originally was to give people quietude, room and board and no expenses except laundry, but the last time I was there, they had even installed a Laundromat. But you know, it's this baronial old house that would be a wonderful place to have a murder take place, that was left the Yaddo Corporation by this couple, Mr. and Mrs. Spencer Trask. She was a literary lady, and I think it was to honor her. He was a broker, and it's the old New York crowd, maybe right out of Edith Wharton. It's on the edge of Saratoga Springs. In fact, you just get off the Saratoga Springs exit on the interstate and you run into Yaddo immediately. (And the race track is right next door.) It's so called, I understand, because they had a very tragic life (their children, I think, all died in childhood, I think that's right). And I was told that one of the little girls, though, had always referred to Yaddo as a place where there were lots of "yaddos," by which she apparently meant "shadows," all the trees and shrubs.

Well, now that has been disputed by some people who, of course, have never been there. But I've said, "Well, now that's what they told me and I was a guest there." And Austin said, "O, you've got to go there. And I went there. He said, "And maybe the main thing about going there is the people you will meet. Well, of course I thought, "Well, I hope that it will be a place to work in." But anyhow that's what he said. Then I came across a letter of Mr. Davidson's—he must have been one of the first guests they ever had. Because I think it was opened as an artist's colony in the late Twenties, and this letter's from the late twenties. And he wrote, "My time here has been productive," or something like that "but I think it is probably a better place to finish up things than it is to really write something new." And in a way I can see why he said that. Now I can tell you what I did when I was there. I did the same thing every time. Immediately after breakfast I'd go back to my room and they'd tell you to pick up your lunch. They gave you your lunch in those old-fashioned pails like you used to take to primary school, so you didn't go back in the dining room until dinner. But anyhow, I'd go back to my room, and I would start working on something new or something that I had begun. In other words, whatever I was writing was new, even if it was started two or three days before. And then I would take off about twelve o'clock and go outside and eat. They had a swimming pool, which I sat beside as I ate; but I didn't swim then. (I didn't learn how until 1980, when I was 50!) And then I'd usually go up and lie down, something I've never done in my life, on my jobs. And sometimes doze off. But then I would get up and from then on until suppertime I was revising. And then after supper, which was a more leisurely meal, of course, you could talk to people if they wanted to talk. Then I would go back to my room, and there were just books, books, books, all over the place. Everybody was tacitly expected to give them whatever books of his had been published, especially if they'd been written at Yaddo. And of course it's nice if you can say in the preface "I am grateful to the Yaddo Corporation" and all that. And so, after supper I would have picked up a book or two from the corridor, they were all over the place—book cases everywhere you turned around. And I would read, and then I'd go to bed. And I did that every day. Now Austin said that business about meeting people. I would say I think I did some valuable work there.... I don't think it inspired me. I don't think I've ever been inspired by any one phenomenon! It made me feel like...it was a sort of a catalyst and gave me a sense that we were all engaged in a communal enterprise. That everybody there was pursuing the same kind of thing. And nobody was putting pressure on me to do that, but I felt it would be awfully nice if I could return their hospitality by doing something up there.

It was a conference place, I guess. It was an artist's colony. I don't know what else to call it. The first one I ever heard about, of course, was many years ago—the McDowell colony in Peterboro, New Hampshire, named for the composer, you know. But this was of a more literary slant, I believe. And of course, the town was interesting. It was an old town. But of course the famous hotel was gone. The Grand Union, I think, was where Diamond Jim Brady and Lillian Russell stayed and, of course, the racetrack. And, as I said, Yaddo is right next door to the racetrack. But I blush to say that all those years I was there, I never went to the racetrack. And that's awful.

Before I began to swim, I got my exercise by walking into town every afternoon—that's when I went in for the mail. And the station wagon would take off and go to the post office and all, but you would walk into town ahead of that. Which was about two or three miles down the main street—Union Avenue. And then I would turn off on the main business street, and of course Skidmore College is there. You could use that library if you wanted to, I think, but you know it was not a research library. Then I would meet the station wagon in front of the post office at the appointed time and get my ride back. And you did get to know some very nice people and then some that I didn't think I needed to bother with. And well, there were sometimes more celebrities than there were at other times. The last time Elizabeth Spencer was there, but I already knew her. And once there was a woman who taught at one of the big East Coast universities, and she was always very serious and took everything you said that way too and seemed to weigh and consider it for all it was worth. She caressed all her words too, as though she was trying to savor them as they left her mouth, to taste them as though she had great affection for them. And one thing in her life had led to another, and she was now writing novels. She's published several very successful ones now, I believe. And I remember she was the one that put a sign on the table where she ordinarily ate her breakfast in this big Gothic dining room. And it said: "This table is reserved for those who do not want to talk during breakfast." Well, that's all you need to know about *that*.

Hayden Carruth, the poet, was there. And I saw the room, of course, that Katherine Anne Porter had done her great work in, *Ship of Fools*, I think. And Carson McCullers, I believe, had stayed in a room that was supposed to be haunted—on the other hand, it was one of the other "guests," I believe, who told me it was Carson herself who did the haunting—very enormous and spacious, with what looked like medieval window panes. Richard Selzer [was there] too, a surgeon from Yale, who also had a literary career—a very, very kind man and ultimately friend to whom I'm indebted for much encouragement and generosity. And then some kind of minor people that I had heard of and I still…one girl, I know, who was very sweet to me. She's married to a doctor in New York City, Jewish. And I think her work appears under her maiden name, which is Patricia Volk. And now and then I see a piece of hers in the *Times* on Sunday or somewhere else. She thought I did good work. And she said "I am a Jewish girl from New York and your world is unknown to me. But I like it." Another one of my friends, Barbara Harrison Grizzard, whose name you see now from time to time—she was Italian, but somebody had yanked her away from the Pope and everything and made her into a Seventh Day Adventist or Jehovah's Witness or something. I believe she's written a lot about how she came back home, her roots, you might say. Her daughter, at that time naturally, like all good artistic people in New York City, had gone off to fight for or against the Sandinistas in Colombia or wherever, you see. And there were always plenty of people to tell you about the old days, and especially Mrs. Ames, the first Director, who apparently ran the place with an iron hand and didn't suffer fools gladly. Well, the whole place was full of people, some of whom had talent, maybe a lot of talent. But it was also full of people that I thought...well, they weren't imposters, but they should have been working at Walgreen's or something. And the last time, there were lots of young girls—I guess maybe they'd graduated from college and all, but they complained incessantly about the food, which I thought very good. Finally one day I said, "Well, it's better than most of you get at home." And then there was a girl who came in one morning and literally *screamed* at the breakfast table. I don't mean just a stage scream, I mean a real scream like you [were] being killed by Alfred Hitchcock. And nobody batted an eye, except me, of course. And I said, "Was that your primal scream for the day? And she said, "I think you might say that." And I said, "Well, next time why don't you do it outside?" And I could see that with just a little more...I think she would have hit me. I mean literally. Well, I could tell she had never been talked back to. The place was often right full of people that had never been talked back to. And every night the phone outside this wintertime dining room, which was much smaller and grand than the main one, would ring, and that's when their lovers would call them up and so forth and so on. O I don't know, I just...after a while I just...I thought..."Well, I'm just tired of spoiled people, you know." But I suppose I was none too easy to be around myself then: I was wearing a cast on my wrist (which often hurt like the devil) and having to send my work back to the University in Knoxville to be typed up because I couldn't use my own machine then.

Essays by Robert Drake

All This Material and Other Such Things

"NOW WHY DON'T YOU TAKE ALL THIS MATERIAL and just turn it into a novel?" asked my old friend, one of the most distinguished of twentieth-century American literary critics, as he looked over a batch of what blue-haired dowagers have often called my "little stories." And all I could think of for a moment was my mother's going up to the second floor of Goldsmith's department store in Memphis every spring to consult her old friend, Miss Mag Bowling, who worked in piece goods, about what sort of "material" she ought to buy for the coming summer's "nicest" dress—what she could wear to both church and the Tuesday Bridge Club. Then after she had made her purchase, even with Miss Mag's advice and counsel a difficult decision, she would take it back home to have her dressmaker, Miss Susie Lankford, make it up—and usually according to a *Vogue* pattern, because, she said, they were considered the best: they never went out of style.

Well, the analogy may not be perfect, but that's the way I always felt about my friend's query. Because I didn't think the "material" and the pattern, the form, and the substance of my stories were two different things but instead somehow complements, which constituted a unified whole. (Hadn't Aristotle said something to that effect?) Anyway, it was what, in teaching my students in literary criticism, I referred to as the heresy of the *beautiful envelope*, the belief that form was just a beautiful envelope to encase the substance and the theme and as such was a somewhat immaterial consideration as far as the arts went. And I've never understood why my friend took the line he did in this instance: nobody I've ever known had more respect than he did for what Conrad called the "perfect blending of form and substance." And from anybody else such a question would have seemed the depth of ignorance, and I've puzzled about it for a good many years now.

In any case, I wonder whether it doesn't conceal some sort of prejudice on his part—a speculation extremely hard to entertain—against the short story as a form and perhaps an unstated conviction that it's only the start toward a novel the author can't finish, some sort of literary abortion, because of defective ambition or even, God help me, timidity or sloth. Americans, especially, like big things—big and bold, I may say. And I've seen—and heard—critics go into agonies of contortion, trying to come to some real hard and fast distinction between the two forms—the story and the novel—which will settle matters once and for all. But always I myself go back to what I once heard Robert Penn Warren say in differentiating between the two: a short story, he said, is simply a story that's shorter than some other story and, though he didn't add it, perhaps amounts mainly to a difference in length but not necessarily in depth. That's all the distinction I need. But there remains, for many readers, some sort of implicit prejudice that, in the arts, anything that's short can't be very serious and the more clearheaded of us will just have to learn to live with such a misapprehension.

Well, I decline to take that option as my only choice, and I'll come out loud and bold and say, for all the world to hear—if it really cares—that I write short stories not because I can't write novels (though in dealing with some impertinent inquisitors I often say it's because I have a short attention span) but because I don't feel compelled to: they are not the right forms for the narratives, the "material" I have to tell. (Can you imagine Chekhov trying to turn "The Darling" or "The Kiss" into any other form or Saki writing anything much but the "short, short" masterpieces starring Reginald or Clovis that are almost anecdotal in their form? But look where they first appeared—in newspapers, the stories of both these authors. And nobody seems to have thought less of them for doing so.) But can you imagine such a venue today for writers of such distinction? Perhaps *The New Yorker*, itself a kind of newspaper—and one not always without spot or wrinkle—might serve as an analogy here, especially with the pieces its founder, Harold Ross, used to call "casuals." But I wouldn't want to push it too far. So are we left with the chicken-versus-egg dilemma or shall we just say who cares which of the two considerations—theme or form—comes first; they just have to go together and that's that? And to require anything else of them would be plain stupid—and just as idiotic as trying to dispense with first-person narration for some other point of view in, say, *Huckleberry Finn* or, yea, verily, even *Moby Dick*. *Theme* and *form* are equally important. And there's an end on it, as far as I am concerned.

But back now to my own case—my own "little stories." To start, I should say what many people already know—that I never dreamed of writing such things: I was trained to be a scholar and critic, a teacher, a professor in a university. But about the time I started out in the profession I began—at the suggestion of an older colleague—to try my hand at writing fiction. But look what it was, the sort it was and the attitude it embodied, and above all, the world it came out of, which was all Southern and nearly altogether oral. As long as I could remember, I had been listening to my father and his four brothers, especially, telling tales from the family past, their own and their father's too. (And since their father was a Confederate veteran who had been at

Appomattox, one didn't have to be urged to hear anything he had to tell.)

Some of these family stories were funny, the rest not necessarily so, indeed often grim or even grotesque. And I know now they grew out of the same atmosphere, the same climate as Sut Lovingood's or, for that matter, Mark Twain's. Not that they were conscious of any such *influences* or any other *literary* considerations. It simply—their style, their attitude—came inevitably out of their way of life, their way of looking at the world. And it would never have occurred to them that it was consciously chosen because of any ulterior considerations. It was a larger than life world they saw and told about, sometimes a violent and dangerous one and, for that matter, not so far removed, whether in time or in place, from the frontier. A great deal of it, I think, was based on laughing to keep from crying.

And behind it all—the rock, the foundation of both the humor and the conviction—was the human voice, always talking, whether on front porches on hot summer nights, or in Drake Brothers hardware store, which my father and his younger brother owned—very much a "community center" in our town—or perhaps even on occasion in the smoking cars then reserved for "gentlemen" on the trains of the day and, though the Drakes themselves were abstemious, always of course in the barrooms in every hamlet or town where liquor was "legal"—and also where it was not.

And more and more I'm convinced that underneath it all lay a firm, but not necessarily articulated, belief in the doctrine of Original Sin as embodied in their professed belief in orthodox Christianity. (They would never have had any trouble agreeing with Willie Stark's bold assertion that man is conceived in sin and born in corruption, and he passeth from the stink of the didie to the stench of the shroud.) And I think, by and large, this is what differentiates Southern from Northern humor to this day.

Remember that I took my doctorate at Yale and began my teaching career first at the University of Michigan, then continued it at Northwestern. And I can't speak for the present time, but in my day I felt pretty much a member of the American Resistance Movement at all three institutions, where despite their great distinction in the arts and sciences, there still seemed to be a vast number of people, both faculty and students, who devoutly believed that if you just had enough "facilities"—libraries, laboratories, and of course always *money*—you would probably in due course be able to raise the dead. And of course remember that, unlike Southerners, they had never been on the losing side of anything: they had never heard the word "no."

I've often wondered in recent years what changes the Viet Nam War brought to those campuses. I gather from brief visits back there that it was not without some enlightening consequences: historian C. Vann Woodward has suggested as much. But I do know that the two regions still laugh at different things, still perhaps are shocked by different things, the North still more easily shocked than the South. But then what else can you expect from people who still, many of them, believe in the perfectibility of man?

But back to the Southern "voice," the voices of my narrators. The concept of voice of course implies a *performer*, and there were many such in that world, my uncles' and my own—folks who knew how to tell a good tale, who weren't above spicing it up, making it more dramatic, and of course funnier—or sadder—than it began. And they all of them knew what constituted a good tale, indeed who were the best tale-tellers in their own communities. All such knowledge, such criteria went unstated of course—probably not even capable, at least for them, of being put into words. But they knew it when they heard it. And they learned from each other—from the community itself—by means of what some critics have called *the communal discipline of taste.*

And one wonders whether such a possibility even exists today, within a culture so diverse as ours and so devoid of common assumptions about man and his world and where talk is mostly not an art but a time-killer.

In the rare instances where these exceptions do exist, they are often found in the town, the village, places some would consider "backward" or even illiterate, certainly in no way sophisticated or cosmopolitan. *Community* is a word they hardly seem to understand; yet it never seems to occur to them that nothing in the world of entertainment today is predicated on the concept of community more than the movies of Woody Allen—and a very limited one it is too. (I must confess that I do enjoy them but usually against my will!) And I recall that Joan Baez once observed that there was no such thing as a Republican folk song, which reveals an ignorance of what the very idea of "the folk" is all about.

Yet good things still come out of Nazareth; and you don't necessarily have to have "been there, done that," in the parlance of these times, to speak—or write—with authority about them. (Think of Stephen Crane or Jane Austen, for that matter.) What you do need, what you must have is a good sense of drama, as I once reminded a very famous football coach when he said that though he wasn't at that time an Episcopalian, he enjoyed going with his wife to their services because of all their "parading around" and such like. And I told him he obviously liked *drama* and ought to remember that he himself was presiding over one of the biggest of all dramas every Saturday during the fall. But that's where it all begins—with real life and three-dimensional human beings, who are *frum* somewhere, as Flannery O'Connor once stipulated, at a certain time, a certain place; and also of course with every writer's inevitable subject—what William Faulkner called the human heart in conflict with itself. (Why do sports reporters—Ring Lardner, for one—often turn into first-class writers of fiction? Well, for one thing, they're born and bred to have a sharp eye for conflict.)

Well, that's the world I come out of, the background against which I write. And as I've said elsewhere, nothing much *happens* in my stories; and indeed they *are* short—sometimes no more than two or three thousand words. But some sort of completed action, some sort of meaningful change, which is the essence of fiction, doesn't depend on length or sensation but whether there is progressive development between beginning and end. And that's all you need.

Surely, because of the oral nature of what interests me, even obsesses me in what I have to tell, my stories are almost bound to be fairly short, indeed couldn't really be otherwise; and I make no apology for that. And I'm especially on guard against all those who don't read them carefully enough to see that, as with Huck Finn, there is often more than one narrative there—one, the surface one, the narrator knows he's telling and another, what you might call the subterranean one, he often doesn't realize he's telling (sometimes not altogether complimentary to himself either). But the story as such is neither one nor the other but both, in a sort of counterpoint, where they complement each other in a seamless combination that constitutes the whole. (Remember that Agatha Christie's Hercule Poirot says that if you just let a murderer talk long enough, no matter what the subject, he will sooner or later give himself away. And Jesus himself says, "Out of thine own mouth will I judge thee.")

I think you'll find that most tale-tellers and tale-writers of the kind I've suggested here are themselves great—and gifted—listeners too. That's how they perfect and refine their own art; they don't necessarily hog the floor. And like all artists, of whatever persuasion, they take from what they hear what may be suitable for their own tales. The word, *tale*, by the way, is one that comes naturally to me in talking about my work, not necessarily in the sense of country stores and cracker barrels—what one of my friends has referred to as the "*aw shucks* school." But it does suggest to me the oral and perhaps intimate nature of its existence and something of the limited things it attempts. But as in folk tales and ballads, those very limitations can suggest or imply a very great deal—often literally matters of life and love and death. And to those who object that they often can't *see* the characters I write about, I say, well, just listen to them *talk* and then you'll know how they look!

Sometimes also they observe that I often don't take Henry James' advice seriously enough about *showing*, not *telling* in what I write, indeed that I quite often use indirect discourse more than "the real thing" and thus "report" more than I dramatize. And to them I reply that the sort of thing I do is what it is and doesn't necessarily have to be shown. (Perhaps "reporters" always tell more than they show.) In any case, what I do to some extent operates on different assumptions from James' fiction; and it's perfectly capable of being seen through my particular point of view, which is often that of the first-person narrator who speaks at some remove from the immediate action and not always with what may seem scrupulous attention to chronology or even unity of plot, and who, often by seemingly irrelevant digressions in anecdotes and asides, tells us more than he knows not only about the participants in the story but also about himself and the whole community—hearsay testimony, you might say, which one discounts at his peril because the scope of the narrative may be much wider than he has assumed.

Look briefly at what that mistress of the technique, Eudora Welty, can do here. In "Why I Live at the P. O.," Sister, the postmistress-narrator, in dramatizing Mama's adamant defense of the younger sister's, Stella-Rondo, leaving her husband, Mr. Whitaker, and arriving back in China Grove, Mississippi, with an "adopted" child whose existence she has never revealed to the family, says:

> "Just like Cousin Annie Flo. Went to her grave denying the facts of life," I remind Mama.
>
> "I told you if you ever mentioned Annie Flo's name I'd slap your face," says Mama, and slaps my face.
>
> "All right, you wait and see," I says.
>
> "I," says Mama, "I prefer to take my children's word for anything when it's humanly possible."
>
> *You ought to see Mama, she weighs two hundred pounds and has real tiny feet.* [italics mine]

And again, in The Ponder Heart, Edna Earle, the narrator, discovers Uncle Daniel, the sweet but none too bright relative for whom she is part-niece and part-keeper, "loose" on the midway at the Fair, after belting her into the Ferris Wheel.

> [There he was] up on the platform of the Escapades side-show, right in the middle of those ostrich plumes...passing down the line of those girls doing their come-on dance out front, and handing them out ice cream cones, right while they were shaking their heels to the music, not in very good time. *He'd got the cream from the Baptist ladies' tent—banana, and melting fast.* [italics mine]

Thus our "seeing" is often filtered through the ear as much as the eye; and the comic, "irrelevant" asides jolt us back into the real, down-to-earth world, which, in our momentary departure from sense, we run the risk of leaving behind. Again, Shakespeare says it best: "by indirections find directions out." Different strokes for different folks indeed...

Finally, it's not how much you write—how topical, how timely, sensational or otherwise—that gives you distinguished fiction; rather, it's how valid your story is—how true, an option, says Conrad, you may have forgotten to choose. And it requires no less skill, no less talent, even genius than the "big one," as some cut-rate critics refer to the novel. All right, so the world seems to value the longer work: it's more ambitious and often more celebrated in our culture. And yes, we'd all like to have a big, fat bestseller and make lots of money. Who wouldn't? Surely, we all want to live well, and perhaps the house needs a new roof and the baby needs new shoes. But should that be our first object here? I think, finally, we must write what we must and as we must, in the form that it alone compels us to. Anything else involves misrepresentation, even falsification. And neither art nor truth will have anything to do with that.

The Writer as Hunger Artist

"...I HAVE TO FAST, I CAN'T HELP IT," SAYS THE hunger artist to the overseer as he lies dying at the end of Kafka's story. And he goes on to explain: "Because I couldn't find the food I liked. If I had found it, believe me, I should have made no fuss and stuffed myself like you or anyone else." These anguished last words might well be applicable to any number of situations where the individual thinks he has no choice but to go it alone; but I have sometimes thought them singularly appropriate for describing the writer's state of mind on occasion—if he's really honest with himself and honest with what he thinks of as his audience, his public. And believe me, I think I know something about the matter.

For nearly forty years I have been trying to write fiction—I, who was trained as a prospective college professor, through the rigors of the doctoral program and all the rest. I love teaching and always have (you couldn't stand it five minutes if you didn't) and can't really imagine myself doing anything else; and incidentally, I give thanks every day that I make my living by teaching school and not from writing fiction. Teaching is what I was prepared for, but fiction was something I just more or less blundered into. And yes, it really all started with the suggestion of a senior colleague that I might *try* writing fiction and see what happened. And I did, and I've so far published four books of stories—mostly set in my home country of West Tennessee, which, for what it's worth, is really northern Mississippi in its geography and history, its politics and economics. And I continue to work on still more stories now.

But I often think there's less and less request today for the sort of thing I write, and that conviction of course can get very depressing. In the first place, I've never been interested in trying to write a novel. When people ask me why, I say, well, I have a short attention span. And this may not be so frivolous as it sounds. The community I grew up in was one that thrived on the oral tale, the brief anecdote; and I had the very good fortune to grow up around some really gifted talkers—particularly, in my father's family, with its five brothers who all lived right there in that one county and saw one another constantly, with each one taking enormous pleasure in the company of all the rest. Furthermore, I was born late in the day: my parents were both middle-aged when I was born, and I was their only child. And I had a real live Confederate veteran for a grandfather, and he was a Virginian who had been at Appomattox. I was also fat, wore braces on my teeth, and took piano lessons. So it will probably come as no surprise to you that I spent a lot of time, when perhaps I should have been outdoors playing with my contemporaries, indoors listening to a lot of old people talk.

Now this sort of background, as a sort of wellspring if not a downright cause of Southern literary vitality, has been discussed often enough. And I think it's a valid enough account, if not explanation, which has usually been given. But why didn't it all lead me to write novels instead of stories? It certainly has—at least listening to all that talk, all those tales—for a lot of other folks who have turned into writers. And was I a writer manqué or something of the sort all along, just waiting for a catalytic prod from a colleague or someone else, to get me going?

I don't know that there are any answers to such questions, but I'll hazard a guess or two. You know that, in some ways, it's still easier to publish—and sometimes, I suspect, write—a novel than it is a story, certainly a collection of stories. William Faulkner suggested something like this: he said you had less room to fail in the story. And the novel—because it's longer—is often considered more "serious," certainly more ambitious, certainly more marketable. I've even heard it suggested that the story is concerned with only one thing, one aspect of a situation, one facet of a problem, or something of the sort. But I've never yet known the sort of formula that a story like James Joyce's "The Dead" or Katherine Mansfield's "The Fly" would fit into: I don't think either of them deals with *one* of anything. As far as I'm concerned, Robert Penn Warren is still right: a short story is simply a story that's shorter than some other story. I was infuriated recently to see Ring Lardner condescended to in print (and on the occasion of his centennial, too!) as a "mere" short story writer, also looked at askance because he wrote "funny" stories. I could say a great deal about that latter aspersion, about whose idiocy I have the strongest possible feelings, but I'll let that pass now, except to note that the world is still full of people who think that if you're funny, you can't be "serious." (They're of course confusing solemnity with seriousness, which it quite often isn't.) But I think there continues a very real prejudice against the story form for this very reason: it's short. And certainly in this big bold country of ours, bigger is often thought to be better.

But again, the sort of thing I do has always seemed to me to demand the shorter form. And incidentally, I don't think, in the good story, the right story—or the good or right anything else—you ever have much choice in the matter: the theme, the story dictates, really demands its inevitable form. (I've been told of at least one distinguished editor and critic—now, happily, long retired—who simply doesn't *like* first-person narration; but can you think of any other conceivable point of view for *Huckleberry Finn*—yea, verily, even for *Moby Dick*?) As for me, I'm fascinated still by the told tale, with highly oral qualities—and especially as an unconscious revealer, even betrayer of him who tells it and the world which lies behind him. Maybe even it's an expanded anecdote I'm after. And I know that can be perilous. I recall that once I sent a number of new stories to the editor of a highly respected and influential literary quarterly; and he returned them posthaste, as I had pretty well known he would, with the lofty observation that he didn't publish anecdotes or short, short stories: such little space as he had available in his pages for fiction, he said he reserved for more complex works. And I thought, well, so much for Chekhov, and went on my way.

Anyhow, it's usually the human voice that I hear, the voice that I work very hard to capture in all its uniqueness and authority, even in all its treachery (to the self and otherwise). And I work very hard at making it sound *right*—not just in the sense of being accurate and authentic, like a folklorist collecting data in the field, but as conveying how this character in this situation would simply have to sound if he were to be himself because style, I think, is still the man. And if it doesn't sound right in that sort of way, I know it's no good. And I usually try to catch the voice in a dramatic encounter, a *performance* or something of the sort, in a crucial scene—almost as in a traditional ballad. And I'm sure that you hear much more than you see in my stories. For what it's worth, I know that my memory, my imagination are much more sensitive to the auditory than to the visual. And I once told a friend who complained that he couldn't imagine how my characters looked just to listen to them and then he'd know! But then such descriptions as we get in the ballads themselves are often perfunctory if not actually formulaic. Maybe such a comparison isn't altogether out of place here either. I come from something like a ballad community, with behind me more than one generation of performers, tale-tellers, who had a highly developed sense of what makes a good story, a good tale. As Professor Gordon Hall Gerould of Princeton might have observed, they had a highly developed communal discipline of taste. And so I think I always knew instinctively what made for a good story, with usually a central scene or crisis in sharp relief and all else leading up to or going downhill after this climax. And that's the way, for good or for ill, my mind continues to work.

Often there's not a great deal that "happens" in my stories. Sometimes it's just someone's—the narrator perhaps—coming to see that things are different from what he thought. Or it's a character, whom I've tried to build up carefully over the main body of the story, expressing himself in one significant—and perhaps surprising—action. But that's all the action you *need*, and what you've been doing is not thus to be dismissed as "only" a character sketch or something of the sort. One way or another, fiction does involve change, it must *move*. But it doesn't have to move a great deal, you know.

I'm often set going, on a new story, by some fragment of conversation, some remembered scene, often recollected from many years ago. But it's usually something that's been there all along, surfacing from time to time but then disappearing until perhaps its moment has come. And I know it's time to try writing that story. I don't know that I think this sudden conviction is like a visitation or revelation on the Damascus road or elsewhere, but it has happened to me in some very strange places, far away from my office and my own desk and very far away indeed from West Tennessee. I can cite the Reading Room of the British Museum and an ocean liner out in the middle of the Atlantic as examples. But I've learned to obey when that moment comes, and I'm finally grateful for whatever catalyst has touched it off.

I've sometimes said that no Southerner has ever been very far away from the sound of the human voice; and some of them I've even thought might be *afraid* of silence: that's why they talk so much! But what I'm really suggesting, underneath the jibe, may have something to do, again, with the strong sense of community that has prevailed among most Southerners and certainly most of them who try to write. And it's a community that is much given to relaxed conversation, since after all most of its members are in substantial agreement about matters of faith and morals, perhaps even the supreme themes of art and song as they understand them. In any case, beginning as the fat little boy who had to sit in the corner while the grown folks talked, I've done a powerful lot of listening in my life. And as an adult, I've spent a good deal of my time as a guest in other people's houses; and that forces you to listen too. Perhaps one of the saddest things in our modern world is its lack of listening, even the willingness to listen. The great Sir William Osler instructed medical students to "listen to the patient; he is trying to tell you what is wrong with him." And we all need it, all require it some time or other, sick or well. Perhaps then my listening has often been the result of constraint rather than choice but not altogether. Because I don't think anything can be more interesting than listening to people talking about themselves and their concerns, if it's not unduly protracted. Even if they turn out to be first-class bores (and of course *they* don't ever listen to anybody), you learn something too. And most good talkers are good listeners, I've found: how else can they learn the trade?

In any case, I became early on a listener, and I'm still doing it right this minute. And people will, if you let them talk long enough, tell you most anything about themselves, sometimes unconsciously, sometimes not—and sometimes the more bizarre, the better, as one of my cousins, who is a very successful lawyer, has observed. I should add here that I haven't taught English composition thirty years for nothing either! And in the beginning I was fortunate to have the home community around me and behind me too. And do you know we still need it and want something like it today, though many of us can't seem to wait to slough it off and head for greater and greater "freedom," in the lonely crowd or elsewhere? I also note, with some irony, in the large university where I teach, the frequent use of the word "family" to describe our group, whether departmental or institutional. And in one way I find this engaging, and another way I find it sad. It looks as though even with all this freedom and blessed anonymity, people still want something to *belong* to, and man is still something of a social animal. He still needs to be *defined*—and by something other and larger than himself.

And so I write quite often in the first person, with the speaker sometimes at the center of the action or else—what can be even more challenging—with the tale-teller on the periphery, either of them telling us a great deal about himself and his community, often without realizing it. And the story is usually focused on one dramatic moment, one moment of truth, you might say; and frankly, I can't imagine telling it in any other form than the short story, and a pretty short one at that. And ten or twelve pages is long for me. *That's* what I want to do, what's eating on me (and all writers should be eaten on by *something*); and I can't imagine doing it any other way—not if I intend to write that story. Of course you could get all the narrative facts down otherwise, but you wouldn't have the same *story*. And the very word comprehends both theme and form, in my book. For what it's worth, I've never felt compelled to write a play, as friends have sometimes suggested I should. Yes, I'm fascinated by the spoken word and its dramatic possibilities; but my interest has usually led me to try realizing the drama inherent in the single moment, the brief encounter rather than in something longer sustained. The dramatic monologue, not the full-scale theater has seemed the right place for me.

And so I don't know what else in the world I can do but write the way I do, the way I must. Like the hunger artist, I might do lots of other things if I were so moved, but I'm not. Or is it something like the voice of Hopkins's sonnet, which proclaims, "*What I do is me: for that I came*"? In any case, I've wondered sometimes if I ever had another choice: perhaps it's not such a matter of "independence" and "integrity" and so on as I used to think. The hunger artist himself suggests as much. Of course I think you should always be willing to take St. John's advice and try the spirits and see whether they come from God or somewhere else. But that's only if the spirits speak to you first. (And yes, the spirits may even tell you to try a novel or a play.) But I don't think my stand here is just explaining away sloth: it's the result of something I've been forced to come to terms with, forced to accept, I think, as time has passed.

There's nothing about either me or my work that is *news* either: I don't write about social commotion, and I don't write about minorities or public issues. Furthermore, I'm not championing any causes or protesting any injustices. Indeed, I can't think of anybody whose work is less topical or "timely"—or perhaps more "limited"—than mine. If that's what you want, I say go read the newspaper, maybe even go to church. I do write about people and groups and the tensions that arise between them. Sometimes the people are very much inside the group and wanting to get out, sometimes just the reverse. But I think the individual and the group are of equal importance in my work, and I don't much take sides either when they come into conflict. I just try to show the way things are—maybe the way they were—in the world where I grew up and maybe in what's left of that world still. And that's all you really have to do when you tell a tale—just tell the truth and shame the Devil. Because you really can't ever beat *folks* and all the devilment they can get into. Faulkner has somewhere suggested something of the sort, I believe. And of course he's said the last word for everybody on what the only real subject for the writer ever is: the human heart in conflict with itself. And if you have to write my kind of stories, well, then, that's the way it is for you, I think. And you don't need to apologize to anybody either. Finally, unlike the hunger artist, maybe you don't even need to explain.

The Writer as Observer, the Writer as Outsider

Vanderbilt University May 24, 1997

MY OLD FRIEND, JOHN NOBLE WILFORD, DISTINGUISHED science writer for the *New York Times* and winner of two Pulitzer Prizes, once told me that being the son of a Methodist preacher had had a great deal to do with his becoming a writer and, in particular, a journalist.

In those days the annual conference, when the Bishop announced the "appointments" for the next year, was held in the fall, usually in November, I believe. (I think this all had something to do with the agrarian economy of those times: you couldn't get your budget in order until the crops came in and the parishioners had paid their pledges for that year.) And so, if his father, who was our preacher (according to my father, the most beloved pastor in the parsonage since "Brother Brooks," father of the distinguished literary critic), got moved to another church for the coming year, John would have to pull up stakes and enter a new school somewhere else in the Memphis Conference, where of course everybody had paired off and already made his friends for that year and there often seemed no place for him. And he began to think of himself as always something of an outsider or, as he put it, an *observer*. And thus the seeds of his future career may have been sown accordingly.

Well, my own story is not unlike that. I, too, was always something of a loner, an only child born into my parents' middle age; and I am older now than three of my grandparents were when they died. But the fourth, very much still alive then, was a Confederate veteran, a Virginian who had served in Hardaway's battery in the Army of Northern Virginia and had been at Spottsylvania Court House and Appomattox. (I still have his "parole" papers, signed at Appomattox, framed and hanging on my living room wall today.) So there was history quite literally in the house, and I never had to learn to respect it then or later.

I also was fat, wore braces on my teeth, and took piano lessons, which my grandfather began by paying for out of the meager Confederate pension granted him by the state of Tennessee. So you may imagine that I sometimes didn't really know where I belonged—or in what century; but I did feel as a rule very much alone.

My father was one of five brothers, all living there in that one West Tennessee county, all extremely fond of one another; so at Christmas we didn't have just one big family Christmas dinner, we had five. But fortunately, they were an *inclusive* family, not an *exclusive* one, and seemed always to want to share their happiness with others, never excluding them from their own blessings and joys. (My oldest uncle, a Methodist preacher and also a very fine photographer, who left us a family archive of 60 years' accumulation, naturally insisted on taking a "group picture" of the family on any and all occasions; and if there weren't enough of us on hand, he would call the neighbors to come join us because, perhaps like the biblical host, he wanted his picture, like his house, to be full.)

And that's the kind of people they were, never "excluders," but always "includers." But perhaps the most valuable thing they gave me was an appreciation of narrative. They all were excellent tale-tellers and, I now know, had a splendid sense of what *makes* a good story, usually of course taken from the family memories. Professor Gordon Hall Gerould of Princeton would have called it a very highly developed "communal discipline of taste," a set of criteria they had imbibed without thought all their lives that made them recognize a good narrative and excel in the performance thereof—though of course they could never have explained such knowledge.

And I now know that the perennial repetition of these narratives at all the family get-togethers, all of them thoroughly familiar to all the group, was not motivated by any desire to tell the *news* (everybody there had already learned them by heart, but of course at that stage, they often bored me to death) but a delight in the performance itself. It was their native art, undergirding their culture and their lives; and in giving voice to it they shared a common celebration, a common joy.

And all those years, I was unconsciously listening, never dreaming that I would someday try to write such things down for other people to read. For early in the day, I had somehow blessedly come to believe that I had been *called* to teach: no other profession had ever entered my mind. Also, I somehow knew that I wanted to teach English, and I wanted to teach it in a college or university. And thus my decisions about a career were all made before I left high school.

And so I came to Vanderbilt, then went on to Yale for my doctorate, and began my teaching career at the University of Michigan. But never in all those years did I consider writing as a profession: I thought it was fine if you had the talent, but it never occurred to me that I might have any.

And for what it's worth, I had read little of what we now think of as Southern literature. Faulkner I had heard discredited as the author of a "dirty" book, *Sanctuary*; so I did read that but found it dull. Robert Penn Warren I had heard of as "the man who wrote the book about Huey Long." Also, that he was one of the members of the group of poets calling themselves Fugitives—I never knew why—who flourished at Vanderbilt "before my time."

And I knew that most of them were very much concerned with history and its significance, especially for Southerners. But then that was no particular news to me: I had grown up, as I've said, with history literally in the house. And it was more or less like your skin: you were born with it and couldn't get rid of it so there was no use to try. And I still feel pretty much that way today; I certainly never had the feeling, like some people of my time and place, that it was some sort of private property on which I had a stranglehold. In fact, just the reverse: somehow, I thought, history didn't like to be used, whether for individual or social aggrandizement. As in Henry James' fiction, it didn't like to be meddled with. So you ended up with a respect for it but no idolatry.

But as for the then less celebrated Southern writers—Eudora Welty, Katherine Anne Porter, and, later on, Flannery O'Connor and, much later, Peter Taylor and Walker Percy come immediately to mind—I simply knew *of* them. (Yes, I had read *Gone with the Wind* and thought highly of it as both narrative and novel, indeed would later publish the first essay on it—now reprinted three times—ever to appear in an academic journal; but I've told all about that elsewhere.) What mattered then, I thought, was that I *had* done a bold, perhaps even brazen doctoral dissertation on Keats, under the supervision of Frederick Pottle at Yale, and I had also taken a wonderful course there on the poetry of the Renaissance taught by Louis Martz. (And for the record, I should like to add here that it was Professor Martz who taught me how to read *Paradise Lost*—no mean achievement then or now.)

Surely, it must be something like that I proposed to do with my life—writing the usual academic books and essays, always of course, in conjunction with my teaching. And yes, you *could* do both at the same time, with each discipline complementing and enriching the other—a belief I've held fast to all my career. But I never wanted to become a specialist, a "period" man: I preferred to be what you might call, in medicine, a "general practitioner." Some of this was simply inherent in the way I felt about all the arts (why did you have to *choose*?); some of it I got of course from my "role models," as we now call them: Donald Davidson, Cleanth Brooks, and Austin Warren. Those latter two didn't practice the "creative" arts, but they ranged widely over most of the fields in English and American literature. And they were all of them first-rate teachers. Yes, that was what I wanted to do with my life.

And then, out of the blue, something happened. One day, near the end of my first year of teaching, at the University of Michigan, I was standing outside the English office examining the contents of my afternoon mail I had just taken from the mail boxes beside the door, when my chairman, Professor Warner G. Rice, greeted me and, among other things, asked what I intended doing with my summer vacation. I replied that I was planning to go back to New Haven and work in the Yale Library on several small critical projects that had begun to interest me during my teaching. But then—and I've never been more startled—he said, "Have you never thought of trying your hand at fiction? You're full of fine tales about your family and your hometown and such things. Think about it." And that's the way it all began. (Professor Rice, I'm sorry to report, only recently passed on—though in his 98th year; but I never let him forget that it was he who "started all this.")

So later, when I was in New Haven, I found myself, day after day, sitting at one of the tables in the English Graduate Study on the second floor of the Sterling Library (from where you could always on Monday nights hear the Whiffenpoofs singing at

Mory's just across the street) setting down just the bald memories of my childhood and adolescence in West Tennessee with no attempt of course at shaping them into fictional form. Like Sergeant Friday on *Dragnet*, I just, at that point, wanted the facts.

And thus began my first book of stories, *Amazing Grace*, published nearly ten years later in 1965, then issued again, in paperback in 1980, and finally reprinted in a splendid 25th anniversary edition in 1990, with a Foreword by Professor James Justus of Indiana University and a Preface by myself, along with some of my uncle's fine photographs. And my cup did indeed run over. (It was simply one of the few things *ever* in my life in which I could find no fault!)

And now I have published six books of short stories and also what I call a "cultural memoir" of my father's family. And all this along with something close to 200 essays and reviews in the appropriate academic journals. And no one could be more surprised than I have been: as Juliet responds when her nurse asks what she thinks of getting married, it has all been an honor I dreamed not of!

It's been a lonely road in many ways. I haven't done any of the "right" things either, which is to say I've never written—or thought of writing—a novel; I've never had a book reviewed in the *New York Times*; and, though I've appeared in many of the respectable periodicals, I've hardly ever appeared in any of the first-rate *literary* magazines. For example, from the very beginning, substantial parts of all my books have first appeared in the *Christian Century* and *Modern Age* before being collected, which I sometimes think my father would have viewed as he did ordering soup in a restaurant: he said he would never do it because none of it was actually *made* on the premises, just *accumulated* there!

Whatever the case, the *Christian Century* was usually regarded as simply a "religious" magazine—and somewhat far to the left too; on the other hand, *Modern Age*, a quarterly founded by Russell Kirk and originally subtitled "A Conservative Review," was probably too far to the right for some readers. (Well, I used to think, at least I was betraying no partisan bias in the company I kept!) But of course neither of these periodicals was considered primarily "literary." Nevertheless, I was still glad to appear whenever and wherever I could, for the most part, and hoped my readers would have the good sense to sort out my stories from some of the *ideas* with which, unfortunately, they sometimes kept company. (For the record, I should like to note here that the only instance when I've ever appeared in a first-rate *literary* journal occurred in the *Southern Review* some years ago during the editorship of Fred Hobson and Lewis Simpson, who published four of my stories and, for what it's worth, never changed a single word in any of them.)

And as for my writing a novel, I tell all the demurrers (not altogether in jest either) that I have a short attention span but mainly write what I *have* to, not what they think I ought. Yes, my stories are all pretty short, and most of them are told in the first person: obviously, like the tales told by my father and his brothers, they owe something to the *tale* of folk tradition. But as for what one very exalted editor—not unknown in these hallowed halls right here—told me (in returning some of my work, which, as usual, he never let get cold on his desk) he didn't have space for "anecdotes" and "short short" stories, only for fiction of greater length and complexity than mine. I replied that, well, he was giving mighty short shrift to Chekhov! And of course I quickly went on to place them elsewhere. (Like the Wife of Bath, I hold a mouse's heart not worth a leek/ That has but one hole to start to!)

To conclude this list of anomalies, I may as well say here, to the scandal of my audience and everybody else, I don't think of myself as a "literary" person at all; I don't really *like* writers and, like Donald Davidson, don't even think much of "writing programs," which every school of higher education in the country now believes essential, but which, speaking only for myself, I often find very sad and very "American" because of course we think there's nothing in this world you can't master by taking a course in it. But Shelley himself observed, in "A Defense of Poetry," that a man cannot say, "I will compose poetry"; and Keats in one of his memorable letters a few years earlier had already noted that if poetry comes not as naturally as leaves to the tree, it had better not come at all. When you come right down to it, I've found that what you usually get from the literary crowd is mostly all *talk*; and as Hemingway observed in quite another context, if you talk about it, you'll lose it. And usually, I've found, the more talk, the less talent.

Well, you see my liabilities; I'm sure some people would say I'm only an imposter. But then, as Robert Penn Warren once wrote me, I don't write "at the height of fashion," which I took, as I believed it was intended, as a compliment. And just for the record let me tell you that that same gentleman once paid me what is perhaps the greatest compliment I've ever had about my work. And as with Professor Rice and his initial suggestion, it came completely out of the blue. About six or seven years after the publication of *Amazing Grace*, he wrote me that he had happened to pick it up again, almost by accident, and had begun to read it again and like it again, even, he said, "to like it very much" and concluded that it was "a very veracious recreation of a world." And I've sometimes wondered why I didn't die right then: it was bound to be downhill all the way after that.

As for the kind of stories I write, they're all pretty much the same thing—what an English doctor, in telling you to continue taking a prescription he has already given you, would call the "mixture as before." But I see no harm in that. Many writers never have: obsession is no bad thing in the arts, you know. Ernest Hemingway and Thomas Hardy perhaps never really wrote but one story; but every time they did, it was good—sometimes told this way, sometimes that.

Flannery O'Connor herself was perhaps even more limited. Indeed, the one time I met her—on the day which was, ironically, exactly a year before she died—she expressed a feeling of frustration at what seemed her inability to do anything else but "one thing." But I asked her what it mattered as long as she kept doing it well, and I would say the same thing now—not only about her own work but also my own. And it was she, as some of you know, who gave me my first real encouragement from a writer of distinction, even recommending me to her agent as somebody whose stories might make, as she observed to the delight of all my students, a "book of limited popular appeal."

Then of course there's Eudora Welty, who told me, from the beginning, that nobody could teach me the things I could teach myself and from whom I learned what my world had given me all along and was giving me still—an ear to listen with, to the talk that was going on all around me and had been doing so all my life, leading to my continual fascination with the spoken word and how, more often than not, it can tell you things the speakers don't realize they're telling—things not always to their own credit either. And the "whole" story is thus created by a sort of counterpoint established between the "surface" story and the subterranean one. And in what I regard as her most distinguished work Miss Welty took it and made it work dramatically, not in the sense of picturesque regionalism or local color but in the province of high art—to make us see the greatness in the little things, the truth in the remotest parts of life, to make us finally understand that it's all of it every bit outside our own doorsteps—maybe the greatest gift of all, if we but have the ears and eyes to catch it. And thus "the whole wide world," as Miss Welty might say herself, becomes ours.

As a footnote, let me add that, because of my very time and, in due course, my place, I have always been doing—and still do—a lot of listening—first as the lonely little boy sitting in the corner, with no other contemporaries to play with at the family gatherings, then later on with no permanent home of my own, spending a great deal of time as a guest under other people's roofs—always on the edge of the group but not in it.

All these people—the noted writers I've mentioned, the others, relatives and friends—all of them have taught me much, and often they have taught me things I already knew but didn't realize that I did, perhaps somewhat like the old snob in Molière who was delighted to discover that all his life, without knowing it, he had been speaking in prose! And some of what I've learned has been a wonderful discovery, that I, my own life, my own country and all its "furniture," all its inhabitants were not inconsequential and in no way ineligible for being made the very substance of art—universally true now and always.

And then there have been the blessed "encouragers," as we might call them—the friends who always stood behind me, urging me on but never blind to my faults. (The "discouragers," whose name of course is Legion, are always with us too: that goes without saying. And one's only defense against them is to develop a very thick skin and a very hard head.) But among my own supporters one of the staunchest of all was Austin Warren, my senior colleague at Michigan, who out of nothing but the kindness of his great heart, told me he wanted me to bring him a new story to read every Monday. What an act of grace that was, and what a catalyst he himself was! In all my experience, whether as scholar or teacher or writer, I've never seen his equal.

There was Donald Davidson, who wrote the best prose of any of the Fugitives and who was the first to praise my critical essays. And always of course beside me stood Cleanth Brooks, the beloved son of a beloved father, full of wisdom and grace yet always quick to assess a difficult situation for what it was, for all that he could see more sides to any conflict than almost anyone I've ever known. And surely one of the sanest men on earth and one who *loved* literature, not as a substitute for something else but for *what it really was*, and passed this love on to generations of students. (Is there one such still alive and at large today? Certainly not in many of our graduate English departments or even that exalted body, the Modern Language Association.)

And now it's finally all come to this. It's been almost 50 years since I graduated from Vanderbilt—years when I was teaching all over the country—after Michigan then Northwestern and the University of Texas before coming to rest in Tennessee. But only rarely did I return to this campus here—usually it was only for some social function or a happy reunion with my dear friend and former teacher, Ed Duncan, whom I would take to lunch before proceeding on to Knoxville or else, if going the other way, my old home in West Tennessee. But since his death in 1980 I've hardly even done anything like that, mainly just *looked* at Kirkland Tower as I drove past to have lunch somewhere else, adjusted my watch by the time on the tower clock, then nodded my head as if in recognition—of what I wasn't quite sure—and quietly said, under my breath, "Well, there it is."

And I must tell you frankly that for a good many years it all held few attractions for me. They had taken no notice of me since I left the campus after getting my M. A. degree in 1953. I had never been invited back to speak or in any other official academic capacity. And of course the old ones were dying off—in some cases, I thought, providing some fresh air up and down the halls. There wasn't even anybody left to have lunch with, and the only time I ever heard from the University came toward the end of the year when I got their annual solicitation for whatever worthy cause was being touted at the moment. I did, for reasons known only to God, come back for my thirtieth reunion, which I concluded was a dreadful mistake until I discovered that all the people I had formerly disliked were still disagreeable, and, *mirabile dictu,* I was now the youngest and thinnest looking one there! And *that* was a kind of vindication, maybe even revenge!

But then, you see, I had never really felt I *belonged* at Vanderbilt. I had never belonged to a fraternity and, in consequence, belonged to very little else. My friends were mostly a faithful band of Nashvillians, all of them bright and amusing; but they were not "members" of anything much either. And somehow I felt I was missing out on what I might have learned from a wider, more cosmopolitan acquaintance that one expects at a *university.* All this, of course, I was later to find at Yale, but I couldn't know that then.

And so I continued feeling like the observer, the outsider, pretty much as I have felt all my life. Being alone—yes, I was used to that. And I can think of no lonelier profession than that of the writer's. But this was something that went deeper; it wasn't just a question of lacking somebody to talk with about what Yeats called the supreme theme of art and song. Always I came back, like Keats, to my sole self and wondered what other choices there were before me, and I came to the conclusion that there were none. If I were to get what I had always felt my appointed work in the world done, I had to live the way I did. That was the bargain I had made years ago. And I could not go back on it now. Nor did I really want to.

But the years have been drawing nigh, as it says in Ecclesiastes, and more and more I have longed for something like a home—not as a place to live but as a place to feel I belonged. And I had been many places in my time—New England, the

Midwest, the Southwest, and always of course Europe, then finally back to my own home state. But I need hardly remind you that we've always said Tennessee was "three states in one." And I had never felt the least bit at home in East Tennessee. It was the place where I *worked*, not the place where I *lived*. And though it had many scenic wonders to offer, there was little else, I felt, in the way of the "inclusiveness" I've already cited and certainly little in the way of civility. But it had given me a job when I needed one, and I believed I had given them their money's worth. I had no real grievance there.

But I do appreciate your kindness now in asking me to turn over my "literary remains" to your library. It does make me feel that, after all this wandering, there is finally some sort of place where both they and, in a sense, the observer and the outsider may also come to rest. Not, in Robert Frost's sense, of your having to take me in when there was nowhere else for me to go, but in giving me hospitality and house-room back among something like my own kind, some place where I can once more feel I *belong*, someplace where I can still hear, from time to time, the voices of kinsmen and the laughter of friends.

What I Write About: Death and Old Women

SINCE I HAVE BEEN DRAWN MORE AND MORE INTO the writing of fiction—the last thing I, who was trained to be an English professor, ever expected or planned to do—I find myself examining my work with an eye increasingly self-critical, if not at time downright jaundiced. Certainly, since I've been trying to write, I've had occasion to learn more about the problems that confront anyone who tries to write creatively. And one of the things I've realized increasingly is just how limited most writers of fiction are. Most of them really don't have but one or two stories to tell or, as we might put it in the jazzy parlance of the times, more than one or two things in their respective bags.

For example, it could seriously be argued that Ernest Hemingway, as technically proficient as he was, wrote but one story in his life; and that was the story of the Good Sport and how he learns to face the Great Nada with courage and resolution. Sometimes, as in *A Farewell to Arms*, Hemingway focused on the initiation process itself; at other, as in *The Sun Also Rises*, it was the wisdom acquired during the process and subsequently recollected in tranquillity he seemed most interested in. But from whatever angle he told his story, it always remained substantially the same. James Joyce is, of course, regarded as one of the greatest of all innovators in modern fiction, and certainly the short story in English has never been the same since *Dubliners* any more than the novel has remained unchanged since *Ulysses.* Technically, Joyce's contributions were enormous. It is hard to imagine stories more economically written than those in *Dubliners*: he never wastes a thing, and he gets his money's worth out of every single character, action, and setting, though one can't help feeling that on occasion he chooses subjects that are extremely distasteful for the exercise of his formidable talents. ("The Dead," which I believe ends on a note of reconciliation and peace, would be the cardinal exception here.) However, I believe this question remains essentially one of taste; and there is really no occasion or justification for critical adjudication in such matters. *Ulysses*, it hardly needs saying, showed the enormous possibilities in fiction for the stream of consciousness technique; but it should be borne in mind that this seeming free-flow of thought and association is anything but that and is subjected to the most rigorous and selective of controls by the distinctive shaping spirit of Joyce's particular imagination.

But what about Joyce's subjects? Really, they seem relatively few. All his life he kept writing, in one way or another, about Ireland and the Roman Catholic Church and the individual's relationship to those formidable entities. And whether or not Joyce loved them or loathed them really doesn't seem to apply. One wonders what else he *could* have written about, no matter where he lived in later years or what pyrotechnical method he brought to dazzling perfection.

One could, of course, extend this examination indefinitely to prove that the most effective and most original writers have often been extremely circumscribed in subject and in locale, often even in technique. One thinks of Jane Austen, the daughter of an eighteenth-century English country parson, with what D. W. Harding has called her one Cinderella story to tell again and again; and yet I fancy that neither Norman Mailer nor Philip Roth in all his hairiness could have told that maiden lady much that would have been new to her about either the human condition or any of its permutations and combinations. Emily Dickinson has confounded the self-styled sages for decades, largely because of their preoccupation with artistically irrelevant biographical considerations and their reluctance to concede much to talent, to say nothing of genius. Yet she manages to roll most of the universe—or at least certain aspects of it—up into one ball, but always in terms of rural western Massachusetts, as she herself admitted when she wrote that she saw "New Englandly." A final, more modern instance might be found in the late Flannery O'Connor, who herself acknowledged her own limitations: she said she had been writing one story over and over for eighteen years. And a careful reading of her work more or less confirms this self-diagnosis: her one story concerned man's crucial and inescapable encounter with Jesus Christ, and it was always laid deep in the interior of darkest Georgia. Yet she somehow convinced many of her readers that she wrote about, as well as for, people in other climes, other places.

But I have strayed pretty far from my original purpose here, which was to examine and assess what my own fictional subjects are or seem to be and how I came by them and where they seem to be taking me. First, I should say that my interest, where my own work is concerned, lies entirely in the short story. Certainly, I don't think of myself right now as ever writing a novel. Why, it would be difficult to say. But, for good or for ill, my mind seems to conceive of dramatic situations that can be handled in eight, ten, twelve, sometimes, at the outside, fifteen pages; and then it almost inevitably shuts off. Does this mean that I am lazy or that I simply have not the staying power, the endurance necessary for the longer task? I don't know, but I should not think such a surmise necessarily followed. Perhaps my mind works somewhat along the lines of the traditional ballad, with its technique of leaping and lingering, its spotlighting briefly but intensely one particular moment of drama that may imply far more than it actually says or shows. In any case, I so far have simply not been moved to try anything longer than the fairly short story. Please note that I have said "longer" but not "more ambitious," because I am convinced that the difference between the short story and the novel is almost entirely a quantitative one. I don't believe that I would ever concede that it was qualitative.

Yet another technical question concerns my almost unfailing use of first-person method of narration. And I shall be perfectly frank and perhaps quicker on the trigger than I should be, to say that I know most of the arguments that have been urged against the use of this point of view. Henry James, surely one of the most mannered talkers and "dictators" who ever lived, said, I believe, that it was a barbarous point of view. And less exalted spirits have joined him in condemning it as the cowardly way out or the method least challenging to the professional writer. All such pronouncements leave me quite cold, I fear: as far as I am concerned, point of view is and always must be inevitable for the particular story one wants to tell. The author really has very little choice in the matter. Surely, to take one notable example, every single narrative fact in Ring Lardner's "Haircut" could have been related to us in some other way than through the narrator (the barber) who is on the periphery of the action but not at its center. But what would have been the result? We certainly would not have had "Haircut"; and Lardner, though he might have approved his own *narrative*, would certainly not have told the *story* he intended. And what of *Huckleberry Finn*? Was any other point of view really open to Mark Twain? Frankly, I think it inconceivable that the novel could have been written any other way.

Yes, my concern is with the spoken word—and for many reasons. Not the least of them lies in my own biography and geography. All my life, first as a boy and then as a man in the rural or small-town South, I have been listening to people talking—sometimes aimlessly but, when I've been lucky, telling tales, usually about themselves or their kinfolks and friends. Everything about me seems oriented toward the oral and the auditory; really, I'm not very good at describing the way people and places *look*. But, without any conscious effort on my part, nearly every word of nearly every conversation sticks with me, sometimes almost to the point of tedium if not downright obsession. Furthermore, I have had the great good fortune to grow in the midst of very gifted *raconteurs* and *raconteuses*, most of whom talked and told better than they consciously knew. Indeed, one might apply to them Gordon Gerould's principle, deduced from his studies of the traditional ballad, of the communal discipline of taste. These were all talkers who talked in and for a community that set some value on such gifts; and, without having a conscious aesthetic, these storytellers instinctively knew how to shape and form a tale until it was a good one. Embroiderers, even sometimes liars, they were called by more detached spirits in the community. But whatever view one took, he had to concede they knew how to tell a tale to make it good and make it stick. And I think a good deal of this ability rubbed off on me simply because I was there to receive it and because somehow I sensed its dramatic effectiveness.

I know one thing in particular that has always fascinated me about oral narrative is the discrepancy—or counterpoint, if we want to use a highfalutin word—between the accounts people often *think* they are giving of themselves and the events in which they or others close to them have been involved and what I see—or hear—emerging between the lines—or the sentences—as another and perhaps altogether different interpretation of the same actions. Such narrators are always, one way or another, self-revealers; sometimes they are even self-betrayers. And the Bible, we may recall, takes note of such: "Out of thine own mouth will

I judge thee." One, of course, doesn't have to adduce such authority as this to support an artistic techniques; one is altogether within reason, however, in inferring that the technique is an age-old, established one that has been made use of by storytellers since they first began practicing their art in the murky mists of pre-history.

But to return to my own case. As the only child of older parents (my grandfather fought under General Lee in the War Between the States), I spent much of my childhood not out playing baseball with my peers, as they now call them, but listening, sometimes with pleasure but often with considerable boredom, to the accounts of loves long lost and battles long ago (not necessarily the shooting kind), related by aging members of both sides of my family. The hours spent in tacking down relationships, yea, unto the third and fourth generations, with diverting side-glimpses into the muddied waters of double cousinships, were not such as to charm the mind and win the heart of a small boy, or later a teenager, any more than were the same old tales told over and over not because they were new but simply because they were good. Yet somehow I believe I realized though dimly what I was in the midst of hearing. I was hearing about people, not statistics, who had been or were right then living in a definite time and place and, most important of all, were *kin* to me. I had yet to hear of the mystique of blood, to say nothing of racist propaganda, Nazi or otherwise. Yet somehow I realized that blood really was thicker than water, that, as a wonderful old lady of our acquaintance put it, though you might choose your friends, the Lord gave you your kinfolks, and there wasn't a damned thing you could do about it. Therefore it behooved you to try to find them terrible or funny or anything in the world but dull. That indeed would have been unforgivable because it would have denied them—and by implication myself—meaning and significance. So, without knowing it, I was inhaling the very air that storytellers have always breathed—a sense of time, a sense of place, and a feeling of the dramatic in the realities of character and action—a sense of pattern, design, plot. All my youth these wells of creativity—if that doesn't sound too pretentious—were slowly and silently filling up so that, when I came to try writing fiction, no one could have been more surprised than I to find them there. I was somewhat like the Molière character who was delighted to find that, without knowing it, he had been speaking prose all his life!

It would be misleading as well as presumptuous to suggest that I grew up in some sort of community of what Francis Gummere, in his ballad studies, called the singing, dancing throng; yet the comparison is not altogether wide of the mark. There was a community of spirit and interest shared by author and audience: there was certainly not the widening disjunction between them we have come increasingly to discern, even expect ever since the Renaissance. The communal discipline of taste might not have been so exigent here as it has been in the traditional folk community, but it was unquestionably there in the community's respect and affection for both the storyteller and the tale that is told. Small wonder then that, when I came to write, my predilections were for first-person narrative and for the elemental subjects that traditionally constitute the principal concerns of the type of community I come out of.

When I use the word "elemental," someone may too quickly assume that I write strong earthy stories, redolent of both bedroom and outhouse; but such an inference does not necessarily follow. In the main, sex as a subject for fiction, though I concede its unquestioned importance in the world about me, simply does not interest me. No more does race, though I should hasten to add that I ponder our racial troubles in both the South and elsewhere as much as the average person. But neither of these concerns is particularly pressing in on me—eating on me, really—as matter for fiction. And I don't think I could ever will myself to write about either one of them. I might be concerned—very much so—about both these subjects with my head, my heart, or not to blink matters, my glands. But I believe it's only when all these aspects of the writer's personality or sensibility are working together in some sort of harmonious conjunction that he can approach anything like success as an artist, whatever may be the verdict about him as a thinker or as a teacher.

But what have I been interested in as subjects for fiction? One of them is certainly death—the second, along with birth, of what Gerould, in speaking of subjects dear to the hearts of ballad makers, calls the twin mysteries. I recall how surprised I was at first when one reviewer said of my first collection of stories that its principal character was really death: all the characters, he said, had to die or else come to terms with death in some way. On further reflection, however, I decided that this might be a rather astute assessment. Death has always preoccupied me, not, I hope, in an altogether morbid way. But I did grow up around older people, and many of them did and have died, and I've known death at fairly close range all my life. I've always had some sense of drama: indeed, I used often to wish so much of life didn't seem to be so shapeless and without significance. And there's certainly no doubt that death is dramatic and significant, no matter how or when it comes. Birth I have known less about, again because of the older community and family into which I was born. But also I should add that birth, by its very nature, doesn't seem so inherently dramatic as death: after all, the new born babe is innocent, guileless, neuter in some ways. On the other hand, death sets some sort of seal to life, and it always *means* in that it provides the occasion for some sort of summing up, to say nothing of Judgment. And we all do make such judgments, despite injunctions against doing so both in Holy Writ and in the Ancients.

But what about the old women of my title? Again, without arguing whether Southern society is essentially a matriarchy, I shall just say that I grew up in the company of many elderly female relatives and friends, all of them talkers of some, even formidable, ability. And when they talked, I listened; almost like Coleridge's Wedding Guest, I could hardly choose but hear, not always, I fear, because of the sheer dramatic fascination of their narratives. More often it was a case of being trapped with them in the same room but always remembering my raising and my manners. Nevertheless, many of these old women did seem to preside over their lives and the lives of those around them somewhat like the Fates, sometimes like weird sisters in *Macbeth*—interpreting and predicting if not shaping and forming. And when one listened to them, even because of social constraint, he found that he always heard *something*. I believe it would have been impossible for such women, given their age and place in society, to be utterly trivial and inconsequential. One doesn't have to turn farther than his television set today to learn that it *is* possible to be thus.

One might say that the old women I listened to were the midwives of drama as well as the keepers of flames: it was they who assisted into being the stories of memorable events as well as keeping such memories fresh and green. To them did one turn for the verification of dates and events, relationships and associations; and one was rarely disappointed. If old enough and wise enough, these narrators had the detachment as necessary to the writer in the practice of his craft as the passion that presumably drives him on: birth, love, life, death to them were all part of the same tapestry whose fibers were interwoven in the most complex and baffling of designs. And they rarely sought to unravel such fabrics, merely to expound on them if not explain them. Their memories were long, their perceptions were often deep, and they sometimes spoke more wisely or amusingly than they knew. They often seemed larger than life; at times they seemed to be life itself. In any case, their voices have take fierce hold of me as a writer though not to the exclusion of all others. And if these voices talk more often of death than of life, perhaps it is because they discern, in death, the greatest of all the facts of life, surely the most inescapable, and they feel that one cannot properly know anything of life until he has seen something of death.

Whatever the reason—perhaps simply because I am what I am—these are the characters, the subjects, the voices that have most tenaciously seized upon my imagination and forced themselves upon me as subjects and methods for fiction. And I feel sure that I would ignore them at my peril as a writer; indeed, sometimes I have wondered whether any other possibilities have been open to me. In any case, I believe any honest writer, who I believe is also almost bound to be a good writer, must be true to whatever voices he hears, whatever visions he sees—certainly, for the time being. Other voices, other visions may come to him in time; and then it will be to them that he must be faithful. But in doing so he will not contradict or supersede whatever truth he has told before because all his voices, all his visions, assuming that he is a truth-teller, will be part of the same seamless garment.

I have no choice at present, therefore, but to stick by death and the old women. Occasionally baffling or disconcerting but more often amusing, they have hardly ever been tedious, never really dull. As subjects and modes for fiction, they have been—and remain—perennially *relevant*—that modish word now used as a criterion (though hardly a *literary* one) to justify the most meretricious of fictional excesses and abuses, whether of race, rape, or riot. But their relevance has little to do with such fashions of the hour, news of the day, or signs of the times. Its concern is, rather, with that truth which in fiction is admittedly approached through the specific and limited but is nevertheless valid and pertinent both now and always. Such relevance is perpetual rather than transitory because its truth is ultimate rather than immediate; its significance, final rather than topical. Who can say, then, that my old women and the subject dearest to their hearts are irrelevant or impertinent today, whether for my readers or myself? They both may be realer, truer than you know; it *may* be later than you think!

Selected Bibliography of Robert Drake

by Genevieve Nicholson-Butts

A Robert Drake Bibliography
(1953–2000)

(*Editors' note: The following list was prepared by Genevieve Nicholson-Butts. It is based on a bibliography originally published in the* Mississippi Quarterly *in 1994.*)

Books and Pamphlets

Amazing Grace. Philadelphia: Chilton, 1965. Paperback Edition, Grand Rapids: William B. Eerdmans, 1980. Twenty-fifth anniversary edition, Macon GA: Mercer University Press, 1990.

Flannery O'Connor. Contemporary Writers in Christian Perspective Series. Grand Rapids: William B. Eerdmans, 1966.

The Writer and His Tradition. Knoxville: University of Tennessee Publications Service Bureau, 1969. (Proceedings of the 1969 Southern Literary Festival)

The Single Heart. Nashville: Aurora, 1971.

The Burning Bush. Nashville: Aurora, 1975.

Christmas Journey. Ripley TN: Enterprise Books, 1976.

The Home Place: A Memory and a Celebration. Memphis: Memphis State University Press, 1980. Restored Version, Macon GA: Mercer University Press, 1998.

Survivors and Others. Macon GA: Mercer University Press, 1987.

My Sweetheart's House: Memories, Fictions. Macon GA: Mercer University Press, 1993.

What Will You Do for an Encore? and Other Stories. Macon GA: Mercer University Press, 1996.

The Picture Frame and Other Stories. Macon GA: Mercer University Press, 2000.

Short Stories

"The Nine-Year-Old Evangelist." *Michigan Alumnus Quarterly Review* (December 1957): 13. Reprinted as "Brother Haynes and the Nine-Year-Old Evangelist" in *Amazing Grace.*

“The Devil Waits for Old Chester.” *Arizona Quarterly* 14 (1958): 125–32.

“Daddy and the Bull Named Herbert.” *Arizona Quarterly* 16 (1960): 39–45. Reprinted in *Amazing Grace.*

“Easy Steps for Little Feet.” *The Christian Century* (13 July 1960): 828–29. Reprinted in *Church School Worker* (January 1961): 20–22. Reprinted in *Amazing Grace.*

“Amazing Grace.” *The Christian Century* (12 July 1961): 851–52. Reprinted in *Amazing Grace.* Reprinted in *Interpreting Literature,* 4th edition. Edited by K. L. Knickerbocker and H. W. Reninger. New York: Harcourt Brace College Publishers, 1969. Reprinted in *Interpreting Literature,* 5th edition, 1974. Reprinted in *Interpreting Literature,* 6th edition, 1978. Reprinted in *Interpreting Literature,* 7th edition. Edited by K. L. Knickerbocker, H. W. Reninger, Edward H. Bratton, and B. J. Leggett, 1985. Reprinted in *Stories from Tennessee.* Edited by Linda Burton. Knoxville: University of Tennessee Press, 1983.

“Uncle John and the Trail of the Years.” *Arizona Quarterly* 17 (1961): 130–35. Reprinted in *Amazing Grace.*

“The Fountain Filled with Blood.” *The Christian Century* (3 April 1963): 432–36. Reprinted in *Amazing Grace.* Reprinted in the *Reformed Journal* 31(1981): 17–21.

“By Thy Good Pleasure.” *The Christian Herald* (March 1964): 33ff. Reprinted in *Amazing Grace.* Reprinted in *Classmate* (April 1966): 16–19. Reprinted in *The Young Soldier* (13 April 1968): 2–4, 6. Reprinted in *The Mennonite* (9 April 1968): 250–52.

“The Stark Naked Baptist.” *The Christian Century* (9 November 1966): 1382, 1384, 1386–88. Reprinted in *The Single Heart.*

“The Loner.” *Texas Quarterly* 9 (Winter 1966): 61–63.

“The Bride Groom Cometh.” *Classmate* (September 1967): 18–21. Reprinted from *Amazing Grace.*

“The Tower and the Pear Tree.” *Georgia Review* 21 (Fall 1967): 381–85. Reprinted in *The Single Heart.*

“The Pressure Cooker.” *The Knoxvillian* (May 1968): 19, 21, 24. Reprinted in *The Single Heart.*

"St. Peter Right in the Eye." *The Delta Review* 6 (April 1969): 40–43. Reprinted in *The Single Heart.*

"The Single Heart." *Face-to-Face* (August 1969): 20–24. Reprinted in *The Single Heart.*

"Will the Merchant Prince's Son Come Down the Sawdust Trail?" *The Delta Review* 6 (November/December 1969): 52, 54, 113–14. Reprinted in *The Single Heart.*

"She Was Strangely Affected." *The Delta Review* 6 (November/December 1969): 55, 114–15, 117–18. Reprinted in *The Single Heart.*

"Don't They Look Natural?" *The Christian Century* (25 November 1970): 1416, 1421–22. Reprinted in *The Single Heart.*

"Deep in the Interior and Everything and All." *The Christian Century* (3 February 1971): 159–61. Reprinted in *The Single Heart.*

"They Cut Her Open and Then Just Sewed Her Back Up." *The Christian Century* (3 March 1971): 288–89. Reprinted in *The Single Heart.*

"Wake Up So I Can Tell You Who's Dead." *The South Carolina Review* 4 (June 1972): 37–44. Reprinted in *The Burning Bush.*

"The Dream House." *Georgia Review* 26 (Summer 1972): 210–16. Reprinted in *The Burning Bush.*

"The Burning Bush," *The Christian Century* (29 November 1972): 1215–16. Reprinted in *The Burning Bush.*

"Christmas Sorrows, Christmas Joys." *The Christian Century* (20 December 1972): 1301–1303. Reprinted in *The Burning Bush.*

"A Peacock on a Sparrow's Back." *Modern Age* 17 (Spring 1973): 195–98. Reprinted in *The Burning Bush.*

"The Outsider." *Modern Age* 17 (Fall 1973): 408–11.

"Mrs. English." *Modern Age* 19 (Winter 1975): 76–81. Reprinted in *Survivors and Others.*

"The Voices in the Night." *The Reformed Journal* 31 (January 1981): 14–16.

"I Am Counting with You All the Way." *The Christian Century* (23 December 1981): 1343–45. Reprinted in *Survivors and Others.*

"Now, Baby, Do You Know One Thing?" *The Reformed Journal* 31(February 1982): 25–28. Reprinted in *Survivors and Others.*

“Remember the Errol-Mo!” *The Southern Partisan* 2 (Fall 1982): 25–28. Reprinted in *Survivors and Others.*

“The Birthday Picture.” *Motif* 2/1 (1983): 20–22. Reprinted in *Survivors and Others.*

“The First Year.” *The Southern Review* 20 (Autumn 1984): 928–33. Reprinted in *Survivors and Others.*

“On the Side Porch.” *Modern Age* 28 (Fall 1984): 372–76. Reprinted in *Survivors and Others.*

“Brutally Massacred by Indians.” *The Southern Partisan* 5 (Winter 1985): 46–48.

“Mrs. Picture Show Green.” *Arizona Quarterly* 41 (Winter 1985): 362–69. Reprinted in *Survivors and Others.*

“Miss Effie, the Peabody, and Father Time.” *The Southern Review* 22 (Summer 1986): 651–57. Reprinted in *Survivors and Others.*

“Were You There?” *The Christian Century* (15 October 1986): 901–902. Reprinted in *Survivors and Others.*

“My Sweetheart’s House.” *The Southern Review* 22 (Winter 1986): 174–78.

“Football Queen.” *The Southern Partisan* 7 (Summer 1987): 44–48. Reprinted from *Survivors and Others.*

“What Were You Doing When You Heard the News?” *Modern Age* 34 (Summer/Fall 1987): 301–304. Reprinted in *My Sweetheart’s House.*

“Memphis for the Day.” *The Southern Partisan* 8 (Spring 1988): 30–31, 41. Reprinted in *My Sweetheart’s House.*

“I Don’t Know What He’s Doing Now.” *The Christian Century* (6–13 July 1988): 641–42. Reprinted in *My Sweetheart’s House.*

“Auntee’s Message: ‘Go Ahead On.’” *The Christian Century* (26 October 1988): 943–44.

“Ella Biggs.” *The Southern Review 24* (Winter 1988): 215–21. Reprinted in *My Sweetheart’s House.* Reprinted in *Homewords.* Edited by Phyllis Tickly and Alice Swanson. Knoxville: University of Tennessee Press, 1996. 54–59.

“The Legacy.” *Modern Age* 33 (Spring 1990): 53–57. Reprinted in *What Will You Do for an Encore?*

"No More Use Than a Billy Goat, No More Time Than the Man in the Moon." *The Christian Century* (24–31 July 1991): 723–26. Reprinted in *My Sweetheart's House.*

"Deep Purple." *Modern Age* 35 (Spring 1993): 265–71. Reprinted in *My Sweetheart's House.*

"Do You Know Ben Webster? Have You Seen Him?" *The Antigonish Review,* 93–94 (Spring-Summer 1993). Reprinted in *My Sweetheart's House.*

"The Little Jewish Lady." *Modern Age* 36 (Winter 1994): 173–77. Reprinted in *My Sweetheart's House.*

"A Woman That Age." *Voices from the Valley.* Edited by Jeanne McDonald. Knoxville: University of Tennessee Press, 1994. Reprinted from *My Sweetheart's House.*

"The Living Room." *Image* 8 (Winter 1994–1995): 100–105. Reprinted in *What Will You Do for an Encore?*

"Louella and Mr. Kelly." *The Chattahoochee Review* 15 (Spring 1995): 55–60. Reprinted in *What Will You Do for an Encore?*

"The Clothesline." *Modern Age* 38 (Fall 1995): 69–74. Reprinted in *What Will You Do for an Encore?*

"The Time the Bank Failed." *The Chattahoochee Review* 16 (Fall 1995): 54–60. Reprinted in *What Will You Do for an Encore?*

"New Year's Eve." *Crossroads* 3 (Fall/Winter 1995–1996): 3–10. Reprinted in *What Will You Do for an Encore?*

Essays

"Casey Jones: The Man and the Song." *Tennessee Folklore Society Bulletin* 19 (December 1953): 95–101.

"The Reasons of the Heart." Critical essay on Eudora Welty's *The Ponder Heart. Georgia Review* (December 1957): 420–26.

"Tara Twenty Years After." Critical reappraisal of *Gone With the Wind. Georgia Review* 12 (Summer 1958): 142–50. Reprinted in *Best Articles and Stories* (May 1959): 19–20. Reprinted in Gone with the Wind *as Book and Film.* Edited by Richard Harwell. Columbia: University of South Carolina Press, 1983.

“What It Means To Be a Southerner.” Part of a symposium on the modern South. *Modern Age* (Fall 1958): 346–51.

“Manderly Revisited.” Critical reappraisal of *Rebecca. Mississippi Quarterly* 12 (Spring 1959): 86–91.

“Miss Minerva and Other Scandalized Virgins.” Critical reappraisal of Frances Boyd Calhoun’s *Miss Minerva and William Green Hill. Georgia Review* (December 1959): 443–49.

“Two Little Heroes.” Critical reappraisal of *Two Little Confederates. Georgia Review* (December 1959): 449–53.

“It’s All Because They Love You.” Critical essay on Eudora Welty’s “Lily Daw and the Three Ladies.” *Mississippi Quarterly* 13 (Summer 1960): 123–26.

“A Cater-Cornered Epic.” Critical essay on Eudora Welty’s “Why I Live at the P.O.” *Mississippi Quarterly* 13 (Summer 1960): 126–31.

“Huck among the Doctors.” Critical reappraisal of *Huckleberry Finn. National Review* (19 November 1960): 320–22.

“*The Woodlanders* as Traditional Pastoral.” *Modern Fiction Studies* (Fall 1960): 251–57. This essay appeared in a special Hardy number of *MFS.*

“Frances Newman: Fabulist of Decadence.” *Georgia Review* (December 1960): 389–98.

“The Sauce for the Asparagus: Saki’s Humorous Stories.” *The Saturday Book 20.* Edited by John Hadfield. London: Hutchinson, 1960. 61–73.

“The Last of the Innocents.” Critical reappraisal of Booth Tarkington’s *Seventeen. National Review* (29 July 1961): 58–60.

“*A Laodicean*: A Note on a Minor Novel.” *Philological Quarterly* (October 1961): 602–606.

“Saki: Some Problems and a Bibliography.” Bibliographical essay on Saki, with critical bibliography of works on him. *English Fiction in Transition* 5.1 (1962): 6–26.

“Gentlemen, Blondes, and Brunettes.” Critical reappraisal of Anita Loos’s *Gentlemen Prefer Blondes But Gentlemen Marry Brunettes. National Review* (26 March 1963): 245–46.

“Saki’s Ironic Stories.” *Texas Studies in Literature and Language* 5 (Autumn 1963): 374–88.

"Flannery O'Connor." Brief tribute to Miss O'Connor at the time of her death. *Sunday Times* (London), 9 August 1964, 26.

"The Harrowing Evangel of Flannery O'Connor." *The Christian Century* (20 September 1964): 1200–1202.

"Manners, Anyone? or Who Killed the Butler?" Critical survey of the comedy of manners genre, with special emphasis on its present state. *South Atlantic Quarterly* 73 (Winter 1964): 75–84.

"'The Bleeding, Stinking, Mad Shadow of Jesus' in the Fiction of Flannery O'Connor." *Comparative Literature Studies* 3 (Summer 1966): 183–96.

"The Lonely Heart of Carson McCullers." *The Christian Century* (10 January 1968): 50–51.

"That Dragon: Freshman English." *Classmate* 75 (August 1968): 10–13.

"Signs of the Times or Signs for All Times?: Two Literary Exempla." *The Christian Century* (25 September 1968): 1204, 1206. William Styron's *The Confessions of Nat Turner* and Bernard Malamad's *The Fixer.*

"The Paradigm of Flannery O'Connor's True Country." *Studies in Short Fiction* 6 (Summer 1969): 433–42.

"The Pieties of the Fiction Writer I: The Writer and His Past." *The CEA Critic* 32 (October 1969): 3–4.

"The Pieties of the Fiction Writer II: The Writer and His Region." *The CEA Critic* 32 (November 1969) 8–9.

"The Pieties of the Fiction Writer III: Writing the Truth." *The CEA Critic* 32 (December 1969): 8–9.

"What's Relevant about the Literary News?" *The Round Table* (May 1970): 1–3.

"The Legitimate Pleasures of Literature." *The Christian Century* (21 October 1970): 1253–55.

"A Writer's Compulsions: The Tears in the Heart, The Fire in the Head." *The CEA Critic* 32 (November 1970): 5–8.

"Thoreau as Critic: Writers and the Cats in Zanzibar." *The Round Table* (October 1971): 3–5.

"A Tumor as Big as a Grapefruit." *The CEA Forum* 2 (December 1971): 4–5.

“Bring on the Trolls! Or Where Do You Want the Little Fairies to Go?” *Folklore Forum* 5 (January 1972): 21–24.

“I Don't Know What's Good But I Know What I Like.” *The Round Table* March (1972): 1–2, 5–6.

“Hemingway: Greatness through Limitation.” *Carson-Newman College Bulletin: Faculty Studies* 5 (May 1972): 3–7.

“Cultivating My Antique Garden.” *Modern Age* 16 (Spring 1972): 189–92.

“Life Is a Terminal Illness, or, What Have *You* Lived to Tell?” *The Christian Century* (5–12 July 1972): 744–45.

“What I Write about: Death and Old Women.” *The CEA Critic* 35 (November 1972): 10–15.

“Survey Courses and the English Major.” *The CEA Forum* 3 (December 1972): 8.

“The Writer and the Corridors of Memory: My Own Case.” *U-T Daily Beacon* (2 April 1973): 1, 6.

“The Blue Remembered Hills of Lauderdale County, Tennessee: Some Part of My History as a Writer.” *Georgia Review* 37 (Fall 1973): 340–55.

“The Trains in My Life.” *Phoenix* (University of Tennessee) (Fall 1973): 23–24.

“Writers and History: My Own Case.” *The Christian Century* (26 December 1973): 1275–76.

“A Seething Confrontation and the Story's Told.” *U-T Daily Beacon* (7 February 1974): 6.

“Writing Is What You Can't Worry About.” *The Round Table* (March 1974): 1, 3–4.

“Dreams: The Artist's License.” *U-T Daily Beacon* (25 April 1974): 6.

“Teaching Fiction Writing.” *The CEA Forum* 4 (April 1974): 13–14.

“Flannery O'Connor and American Literature.” *The Flannery O'Connor Bulletin* 3 (Autumn 1974): 1–22.

“The Traveler to Himself.” *Modern Age* 18 (Winter 1974): 82–85.

“Tell Him To Wait until I Get My Shoes On.” Excerpts from *Flannery O'Connor*, 1966. *Modern Age* 19 (Fall 1975): 412–14.

"Flannery O'Connor." *Religion and Modern Literature.* Edited by G. B. Tennyson and Edward E. Ericson, Jr. Grand Rapids: William B. Eerdmans, 1975.

"Ear Mightier Than Mouth." *The Round Table* (October 1976): 1, 3, 6, 7.

Introduction to the New Edition of *Miss Minerva and William Green Hill* by Frances Boyd Calhoun. Knoxville: University of Tennessee Press, 1976.

"The Writer's Authority." *The Round Table* (March 1978): 1, 3, 4, 6, 8.

"Writing Short Stories: Table d'Hôte or à la Carte?" *The CEA Forum* 8 (April 1978): 15–16.

"Writing and Listening: A Note." *Studies in Short Fiction* 15 (Summer 1978): iii–iv.

"Hemingway and Faulkner: Tracing Their Resemblances." *The Christian Century* (15 November 1978): 1104–1106.

"Long, Long Thoughts." *The Round Table* (Spring 1979): 1, 3, 4, 7.

"The Legacy of Allen Tate." *Modern Age* 23 (Summer 1979): 272–75.

"Eudora Welty's Country—and My Own." *Modern Age* 23 (Fall 1979): 403–409.

"The Writer as Listener." *The Round Table* (Summer 1980): 1, 4–6.

"A Dutch Genre Painter." *Christianity and Literature* 29 (Winter 1980): 29–33.

"Three Southern Ladies." *The Flannery O'Connor Bulletin* 9 (1980): 41–48.

"The Scapel and the Pen." *The Reformed Journal* 31 (June 1981): 5–6.

"Southern Women." *The Round Table* (Fall 1981): 1–3.

"Regionalism in American Fiction: Defect or Necessity?" *Modern Age* 25 (Winter 1981): 68–71.

"The Perils of Authorship." *The Round Table* (Spring 1982): 1–3.

"Tell Me a Story." *The Southern Partisan* 2 (Spring 1982): 30–32.

"I Can Tell You All about It." *The Reformed Journal* (June 1982): 19–20.

"A Joyful Noise." *The Christian Century* (8 December 1982): 1269–70.

"The Writer: Behind the Scenes." *Motif* 2.1 (1983): 18–19.

"My Literary Equipment: Time, Place, and Home." *The Southern Partisan* 3 (Spring 1983): 30–34.

“Survivors.” *Modern Age* 28 (Winter 1984): 68–72. Reprinted in *New York City Tribune,* 19 October 1984, 4B. Reprinted in *Survivors and Others.*

“*Absalom, Absalom!* or Why Southerners Tell Stories.” *The Southern Partisan* 5 (Summer 1985): 50–53.

“The Lady *Frum* Somewhere: Flannery O’Connor Then and Now.” *Modern Age* 29 (Summer 1985): 212–23. Reprinted in *Realist of Distances: Flannery O’Connor Revisited.* Edited by Karl-Heinz Westarp and Jan Nordby. Aarhus, Denmark: Aarhus University Press, 1987.

“No Foolishness or I Don’t Want You to Ever Call Again!” *The Southern Partisan* 8 (Fall 1988): 38–39.

“The Rain Is Falling on the Ground, I Have No Husband Now.” *The Southern Partisan* 9 (Third Quarter 1989): 36–38. Reprinted in *My Sweetheart’s House.*

“Robert Penn Warren’s Enormous Spider Web.” *The Christian Century* (22 November 1989): 1089–91. Reprinted in the *Mississippi Quarterly* 48 (Winter 1994–1995): 11–16.

“Chosen.” *The Southern Partisan* 10 (Third Quarter 1990): 41.

“A Dead Cat on the Line.” *Mississippi Folklore Register* 24 (1990): 42–47.

“The Three States of Tennessee.” Foreword to *Tennessee: A Photographic Celebration* Helena MT: American Geographic, 1990.

“The Book, the Movie, the Dream.” *Mississippi Quarterly* 44 (Spring 1991): 183–92. (essay on *Gone with the Wind*)

“B From Bull’s Foot.” *Mississippi Folklore Register* 25, 26 (1991/1992): 86–90. Reprinted in *My Sweetheart’s House.*

“My Own House of Fiction.” *Mississippi Quarterly* 45 (Spring 1992): 127–31. This essay constituted an introduction to the papers delivered at the 1991 meeting of the South Atlantic Modern Language Association—during a special session titled “Robert Drake: A Retrospective”—as later published in *Mississippi Quarterly.* Reprinted in *My Sweetheart’s House.*

“The Writer as Hunger Artist.” *Modern Age* 34 (Spring 1992): 235–39.

“Ceremonies.” *The Southern Partisan* 12 (Second Quarter 1992): 33–37. Reprinted in *My Sweetheart’s House.*

"A West Tennessee Landholder." *The Chattahoochee Review* 12 (Summer 1992): 60–66.

"The Writer's Word." *The Antigonish Review* 91 (Fall 1992): 21–26.

"Daddy." Excerpt from *The Home Place. Sons on Fathers: A Book of Men's Writing.* Edited by Ralph Keyes. New York: HarperCollins, 1992. 4–5.

"A Back Bedroom, an Open Fire, and the Art of Fiction." *The Chattahoochee Review* 13 (Spring 1993): 85–89. Reprinted in *My Sweetheart's House.*

"The Square." *Soundings* 79 (Spring/Summer 1996): 33–39. Reprinted from *What Will You Do for an Encore?*

"Flannery O'Connor: Some Afterthoughts." *Christianity and Literature* 46 (Autumn 1996): 111–18. Read at the annual meeting of the Conference on Christianity and Literature, held in conjunction with the Modern Language Association.

Reviews

"The Novel Hart That Harbours Vertuous Thought." Review of *Still Rebels, Still Yankees and Other Essays* by Donald Davidson. *Modern Age* (January 1958): 94–96

"The Faith as It Was Given Them by the Fathers." Review of *Southern Writers in the Modern World* by Donald Davidson. *Modern Age* (Spring 1959): 203–206.

"Fierce Faith Undying." Review of *Fugitives' Reunion,* edited by R. R. Purdy. *National Review* (4 July 1959): 186-87.

"Bridging the Gap." Review of *Modern Literary Criticism,* edited by Irving Howe. *The Christian Century* (5 August 1959): 901–902.

"The Myth of the Cave." Review of *The Cave* by Robert Penn Warren. *National Review* (12 September 1959): 334–35.

"American Writers: Heretics and Saints." Review of *American Literature and Christian Doctrine* by Randall Stewart. *Shenandoah* (Fall 1959): 29–35.

"Felicitous Form." Review of *The Poems of Edward Taylor,* edited by Donald E. Stanford. *The Christian Century* (13 September 1960): 1060.

"Dante's Imagery," Review of *The Ladder of Vision* by Irma Brandeis. *The Christian Century* (1 March 1961): 270–71.

"Flat Champagne." Review of *A Victorian in Orbit* by Sir Cedric Hardwicke. *The Christian Century* (19 April 1961): 490.

"Dear, Dead Hollywood." Review of *No Mother to Guide Her* by Anita Loos. *National Review* (16 June 1961): 391–92.

"Miss O'Connor and the Scandal of Redemption." Review of *The Violent Bear It Away* by Flannery O'Connor. *Modern Age* (Fall 1960): 428–30.

"The Kingdom of God in Marigold, Mississippi." Review of *The Morning and the Evening* by Joan Williams. *Modern Age* (Fall 1961): 428–30.

"A Vatic Poet." Review of *The Long Street* by Donald Davidson. *The Christian Century* (27 December 1961): 1561.

"Befuddled Escapade." Review of *The End of the Battle* by Evelyn Waugh. *American Statesman* (Austin), 14 January 1962, E-5.

"A Modern Inferno." Review of *Ship of Fools* by Katherine Anne Porter. *National Review* (24 April 1962): 290–91.

"Howells on James." Review of *William Dean Howells and Henry James*, edited by Albert Mordell. *The Christian Century* (2 May 1962): 574.

"Yoknapatawpha Innocence Lost." Review of *The Reivers* by William Faulkner. *National Review* (31 July 1962): 70–72.

"As Old As Man Himself." Review of *The Yoknapatawpha Country* by Cleanth Brooks. *National Review* (21 April 1964): 324–25.

"Integration Comes to Georgia." Review of *An Education in Georgia* by Calvin Trillin. *Sunday Times* (London), 16 August 1964, 27

"Early-Day Waugh." Review of *A Little Learning* by Evelyn Waugh. *Austin American-Statesman Show World* (29 November 1964): 19.

"The Warder at the Gate." Review of *Concise American Composition and Rhetoric* and *Twenty Lessons in Reading and Writing Prose* by Donald Davidson. *The University Bookman* (Autumn 1964): 15–18.

"Hair-Curling Gospel." Review of *Everything that Rises Must Converge* by Flannery O'Connor. *The Christian Century* (19 May 1965): 656.

"A Tract on the Klan." Review of *The Ku Klux Klan* by William Pierce Randell. *Sunday Times* (London) (6 August 1965): 31.

"Reading for Writing." Review of *Reading, Writing, and Rewriting* by William T. Moynihan, Donald W. Lee, and Herbert Weil, Jr. *The University Bookman* (Summer 1965): 87–89.

"An Athelete Dying Young...." Review of *The Magnificent Myth* by Jonathan Root. *Southern Observer* (December 1965): 273.

Review of *Wycherly's Drama: A Link in the Development of English Satire* by Rose A Zimbardo. *Renaissance News* 18 (Winter 1965): 349–51.

"For us, the long remembering...." Review of *Donald Davidson: An Essay and a Bibliography* by Thomas Daniel Young and M. Thomas Inge. *Southern Observer* (January 1966): 11, 13.

"Miss Welty the Dreamer." Review of *"A Season of Dreams": The Fiction of Eudora Welty* by Alfred Appel, Jr. *Southern Observer* (April 1966): 88–90.

"'That Is What Fiction Means.'" Review of *The Sense of Fiction* by Robert Welker and Herschell Gower. *The University Bookman* 6 (Spring 1966): 63–64.

"The *Nada* and the Glory." Review of *Ernest Hemingway* by Nathan A. Scott, Jr. *The Christian Century* (14 December 1966): 1539–40.

"From the Nub." Review of *Effective English Prose* by Robert Cluett and Lee Ahlborn. *The University Bookman* 6 (Winter 1966): 33.

Review of *The Hero with the Private Parts* by Andrew Lytle. *Mississippi Quarterly* 20 (Winter 1966–1967): 59–61.

"Coming of Age in North Carolina." Review of *A Generous Man* by Reynolds Price. *Southern Review* 3 (Winter 1967): 248–50.

Review of *Something of Great Constancy: The Art of "A Midsummer Nights Dream"* by David P. Young. *Renaissance Quarterly* 21 (Spring 1968): 82–83.

Review of *The Far Family* by Wilma Dykeman. *Georgia Review* 23 (Spring 1969): 114–15.

Review of *The Edwardian Turn of Mind* by Samuel Hynes. *South Atlantic Quarterly* 68 (Spring 1969): 277–78.

"Miss O'Connor: The Shadow and the Substance." Review of *Mystery and Manners* by Flannery O'Connor, edited by Sally and Robert

Fitzgerald and *The True Country: Themes in the Fiction of Flannery O'Connor* by Carter W. Martin. *The CEA Critic* 32 (April 1970): 13.

"Miss Welty's Wide World." Review of *Losing Battles* by Eudora Welty. *The Christian Century* (17 June 1970): 766–67.

"Rubin on Fiction and Other Matters." Review of *The Curious Death of the Novel: Essays in American Literature* and *The Teller in the Tale* by Louis Rubin. *Southern Review* 6 (Summer 1970): 857–62.

"Her Sacred Office." Review of *The Complete Stories* by Flannery O'Connor. *Modern Age* (Summer 1972): 322–24.

Review of *Donald Davidson* by Thomas Daniel Young and M. Thomas Inge. *Tennessee Historical Quarterly* 21 (Summer 1972): 200–203.

Review of *Flannery O'Connor: Voice of the Peacock* by Kathleen Feeley, S.S.D.D. *Christian Scholar's Review* 2.3 (1972): 245–47.

Review of *The Christian Humanism of Flannery O'Connor* by Gilbert H. Muller and *Nightmares and Visions: Flannery O'Connor and the Catholic Grotesque* by David Eggenschwiler. *Christian Scholar's Review* 3.2 (1973): 205–208.

"Not Proven." Review of *The Optimist's Daughter* by Eudora Welty. *Modern Age* 17 (Winter 1973): 107–109.

"Old Lady Power." Review of *The Banishment* by Alma Stone. *Modern Age* 18 (Spring 1974): 221–23.

Review of *Margaret Mitchell's "Gone with the Wind" Letters, 1936–1949*, edited by Richard Harwell. *Resources for American Literary Study* 7 (Spring 1977): 98–101.

Review of *In Time and Place: Some Origins of American Fiction* by Floyd Watkins. *South Atlantic Bulletin* 43 (November 1978): 184–85.

"In and Out of Yoknapatawpha." Review of *William Faulkner: Toward Yoknapatawpha and Beyond* by Cleanth Brooks. *Modern Age* 22 (Fall 1978): 418–20.

Review of *A Requiem for the Renascence: The State of Fiction in the Modern South* by Walter Sullivan. *Christian Scholar's Review* 7.4 (1978): 366–67.

"Unsearchable Riches." Review of *The Habit of Being*, edited and introduced by Sally Fitzgerald. *The Christian Century* (16 May 1979): 557–58.

"Pietas Medici." Review of *Confessions of a Knife* by Richard Selzer. *The Christian Century* (14 November 1979): 1137–38.

Review of *Son of the Morning* by Joyce Carol Oates. *Orientation*, edited by Charles E. Cole. Nashville: Board of Higher Education and Ministry, the United Methodist Church, 1979.

Review of *The Interpretation of Otherness: Literature, Religion, and the American Imagination* by Giles Gunn. *Christianity and Literature* 29 (Spring 1980): 74–77.

Review of *Violence and Culture in the Antebellum South* by Dickson D. Bruce. *South Atlantic Bulletin* 45 (September 1980): 78–80.

"Home Truths, Heart Truths." Review of *A Childhood: The Biography of a Place* by Harry Crews. *Modern Age* 24 (Winter 1980): 95–96.

Review of *The Tennesseeans: A People and Their Land* by Lamar Alexander, Robin Hood, and Barry Parker. *Knoxville Lifestyle* (December 1981): 54.

Review of *Flannery O'Connor's South* by Robert Coles. *Tennessee Studies in Literature* 26 (1981): 173–75.

Review of *Why Flannery O'Connor Stayed Home* by Marion Montgomery. *Christianity and Literature* 31 (Spring 1982): 87–89.

"The Loving Vision." Review of *The Collected Stories of Eudora Welty. Modern Age* 27 (Winter 1983): 96–98.

"One Writer's Pieties." Review of *One Writer's Beginnings* by Eudora Welty. *Modern Age* 28 (Spring/Summer 1984): 276–78.

Review of *Flannery O'Connor's Vision of History* by John F. Desmond. *Christianity and Literature* 37 (Spring 1988): 60–61.

"Flannery O'Connor: A Proper Scaring." Review of *Flannery O'Connor: A Proper Scaring* by Jill P. Baumgartner. *The Christian Century* (17–24 August 1988): 742–43.

Review of *The Art and Vision of Flannery O'Connor* by Robert H. Brinkmeyer. *Christianity and Literature* 40 (Winter 1991): 191–93.

"Becoming What One Is." Review of *Becoming What One Is* by Austin Warren. *The Christian Century* (8 November 1995): 1057.

"Continuity, Coherence, and Completion." Review of *In Continuity: The Last Essays of Austin Warren*, edited and introduced by George Panichas. *Mississippi Quarterly* 49 (Fall 1996): 851–54.

"Good and Faithful Servant." Review of *Cleanth Brooks and the Rise of Modern Criticism* by Mark Royden Winchell. *Mississippi Quarterly* 50 (Winter 1996–1997): 138–40.

"Red Warren: His Heart, His Home." Review of *Robert Penn Warren: A Biography* by Joseph Blotner. *Modern Age* 39 (Summer 1997): 276–78.

Memoirs

"Donald Davidson and the Ancient Mariner." Memoir of Donald Davidson, Professor of English, Vanderbilt University, on the occasion of his retirement. *Vanderbilt Alumnus* (January–February 1964): 18–22.

"Daddy the Talker, Daddy the Lover." *The Christian Century* (6–13 August 1975): 709–11. Reprinted in *The Home Place.*

"The Old Tales, the Old Times." *Modern Age* 20 (Summer 1976): 315–19. Reprinted in *The Home Place.*

"A Christmas Visit." *The Christian Century* (22 December 1976): 1152–53. Reprinted in *The Home Place.* Reprinted in *Homewords.* Edited by Douglas Paschall and Alice Swanson. Knoxville: University of Tennessee Press, 1986.

"The Home Place." *Modern Age* 21 (Summer 1977): 308–10. Reprinted in *The Home Place.*

"The Picture Frame." *Modern Age* 21 (Fall 1977): 414–17. Reprinted in *The Home Place.*

"The Forty-Two Game." *The Christian Century* (28 December 1977): 1224–26. Reprinted in *The Home Place.*

"The Grace of God at Maple Grove Methodist." *Modern Age* 21 (Winter 1977): 87–90. Reprinted as "The Grace of God at the Maple Grove Methodist Church" in *The Home Place.*

"King Lear at Maple Grove." *Modern Age* 22 (Fall 1978): 403–407. Reprinted in *The Home Place.*

"Eashel." *Modern Age* 20 (Winter 1978): 83–87. Reprinted in *The Home Place.*

"Portrait in Black and White." *The Christian Century* (24 October 1979): 1038–40. Reprinted in *The Home Place.*

"Grandma." *Modern Age* 24 (Summer 1980): 290–94. Reprinted in *The Home Place.*
"The Big Room." *Lauderdale County Enterprise* (30 October 1980): 1.
"Celebratory Statement." Remarks on the Silver Jubilee of *Modern Age. Modern Age* 26 (Summer/Fall 1982): 386–87.
"She *Won't* Cook." *The Southern Partisan* 3 (Fall 1983): 47–48. Reprinted in *My Sweetheart's House.*
"Morning Song." *The Southern Partisan* 4 (Spring 1984): 51–54. Reprinted in *My Sweetheart's House.*
"In Memoriam: Austin Warren (1899–1986)." *Modern Age* 30 (Summer/Fall 1986): 197–99.
"For the Prestige." *The Southern Partisan* (4th Quarter 1993): 40–42. Reprinted in *What Will You Do for an Encore? and Other Stories.*
"The Methodist Church, the Democratic Party, and the St. Louis Cardinals." *The Christian Century* (24–31 August 1994): 787–90. Reprinted in *What Will You Do for an Encore? and Other Stories.*
"Cleanth Brooks (1906–1994)." *Modern Age* 37 (Winter 1995): 166–68.
"Douglass Paschall." *Tennessee Philological Bulletin 32* (1995): 112–14.
"A Letter to Cleanth Brooks from Robert Drake." An "open" letter. *Mississippi Quarterly* 50 (Winter 1996–1997): 125–28.
"My Friend Jesse Ford." *The Chattahoochee Review* 17 (Winter 1997): 75–79.

Interviews

"Robert Drake." The first in a series of televised interviews with Tennessee writers. *Talking Leaves.* Memphis Public Library. (1980).
"An Interview with Robert Drake." Interview by Jeffrey J. Folks. *Mississippi Quarterly* 43 (Spring 1990): 221–33.
"Robert Drake." *Writing in the Southern Tradition: Interviews With Five Contemporary Authors.* Edited by A. B. Crowder. Amsterdam (1990): 119–51.
"A Conversation with Robert Drake." Interview by Alan Jackson. *The Chattahoochee Review* 16 (Fall 1995): 3–53.

Selected Writings about Robert Drake

Drake, Robert and James A. Perkins. "A Robert Drake Bibliography." *Mississippi Quarterly* 45.2 (Spring 1992): 167–87.

Folks, Jeffrey J. "A Southern Realist: The Short Stories of Robert Drake." *Mississippi Quarterly* 45.2 (Spring 1992): 159–65.

Justus, James. "Raising Ebeneezers." Foreword to the Twenty-fifth Anniversary Edition of *Amazing Grace*. Macon GA: Mercer University Press, 1990.

Lawson, Lewis A. "The Whig Ethos in Robert Drake's Fiction." *Mississippi Quarterly* 45.2 (Spring 1992): 133–40.

Paschal, Douglas. "Telling and Reckoning: A Recuperation of the Drake Stories." *Mississippi Quarterly* 45.2 (Spring 1992): 151–57.

Perkins, James A. "A Sort of Central Fact about Woodville: The Railroad as Metaphor in the Works of Robert Drake." *Mississippi Quarterly* 45.2 (Spring 1992): 141–49.